BLOOD
TIES

BLOOD TIES

A BISHOP/SPECIAL CRIMES UNIT NOVEL

KAY HOOPER

BANTAM BOOKS
NEW YORK

Published in the United States by Bantam Books,
an imprint of The Random House Publishing Group,
a division of Random House, Inc., New York.

BANTAM BOOKS is a registered trademark of Random House, Inc.,
and the colophon is a trademark of Random House, Inc.

Library of Congress Cataloging-in-Publication Data
Hooper, Kay.
Blood ties : a Bishop/Special Crimes Unit novel / Kay Hooper. — 1st ed.
p. cm.
ISBN 978-0-553-80486-7
1. Bishop, Noah (Fictitious character)—Fiction. 2. Government investigators—
Fiction. 3. Murder—Investigation—Fiction. I. Title.
PS3558.O587B6 2010
813'. 54—dc22
2009037219

Printed in the United States of America on acid-free paper

www.bantamdell.com

2 4 6 8 9 7 5 3 1

First Edition

BLOOD
TIES

Prologue

Six months previously
October

ISTEN.

"No."

Listen.

"I don't want to hear." She kept her eyes down, staring at her bare feet. Her toenails were painted pink. Only not here. Here, they were gray, like everything else.

Everything except the blood. The blood was always red.

She had forgotten that.

You have to listen to us.

"No, I don't. Not anymore."

We can help you.

"No one can help me. Not to do that, what you're asking me to do. It's impossible." At the edge of her vision, she saw the blood creeping toward her and immediately took a step backward. Then another. "I can't go back now. I can never go back."

Yes. You can. You have to.

"I was at peace. Why didn't you leave me there?" She felt something solid and hard against her back and pressed herself against it, her gaze still on her toes, so much of her awareness on the blood inching ever closer.

Because it isn't finished.

"It was finished a long time ago."

Not for you. Not for her.

One

Present day
April 8
Tennessee

CASE EDGERTON RAN along the narrow trail, aware of his burning legs but concentrating on his breathing. The last mile was always the hardest, especially on his weekly trail run. Easier to just zone out and run when he was on the track or in his neighborhood park; this kind of running, with its uneven terrain and various hazards, required real concentration.

That was why he liked it.

He jumped over a rotted fallen log and almost immediately had to duck a low-hanging branch. After that, it was all downhill—which wasn't as easy as it sounded, since the trail snaked back and forth in hairpin curves all along the middle quarter of this last mile. Good training for his upcoming race. He planned to win that one, as he had won so many his entire senior year.

And then Kayla Vassey, who had a thing for runners and who was remarkably flexible, would happily reward him. Maybe for the whole summer. But there'd be no clinging to him afterward; she'd be too busy sizing up next year's crop of runners to do more than wave goodbye when he left in the fall for college.

Sex without strings. The kind he preferred.

Case nearly tripped over a root exposed by recent spring rains and swore at his wandering thoughts.

Concentrate, idiot. Do you want to lose that race?

He really didn't.

His legs were on fire now and his lungs felt raw, but he kept pushing himself, as he always did, even picking up a little speed as he rounded the last of the wicked hairpin curves.

This time, when he tripped, he went sprawling.

He tried to land on his shoulder and roll, to do as little damage as possible, but the trail was so uneven that instead of rolling he slammed into the hard ground with a grunt, the wind knocked out of him, and a jolt of pain told him he'd probably jammed or torn something.

It took him a few minutes of panting and holding his shoulder gingerly before he felt able to sit up. And it was only then that he saw what had tripped him.

An arm.

Incredulous, he stared at a hand that appeared to belong to a man, a hand that was surprisingly clean and unmarked, long fingers seemingly relaxed. His gaze tracked across a forearm that was likewise uninjured, and then—

And then Case Edgerton began to scream like a little girl.

"You can see why I called you in." Sheriff Desmond Duncan's voice was not—quite—defensive. "We're on the outskirts of Serenade, but it still falls into my jurisdiction. And I'm not ashamed to admit it's beyond anything the Pageant County Sheriff's Department has ever handled." He paused, then repeated, "*Ever*."

"I'm not surprised," she replied somewhat absently.

His training and experience told Des Duncan to shut up and let her concentrate on the scene, but his curiosity was stronger. He hadn't known what to expect when he contacted the FBI, never having done so before, so maybe any agent would have surprised him. This one definitely did.

She was drop-dead gorgeous, for one thing, with a centerfold body and the face of an exotic angel. And she possessed the most vivid blue eyes Duncan had seen in his life. With all that, she appeared remarkably casual and unaware of the effect she was having on just about every man within eyesight of her. She was in faded jeans and a loose pullover sweater, and her boots were both serviceable and worn. Her long gleaming black hair was pulled back into a low ponytail at the nape of her neck. No makeup, at least as far as he could tell.

She had done everything short of taking a mud bath to downplay her looks, and Des still had to fight a tendency to stutter a bit when speaking to her. He wasn't even sure she had shown him a badge.

And he was nearly sixty, for Christ's sake.

Wary of asking the wrong question or asking one the wrong way, he said tentatively, "I'm grateful to turn this over to more experienced hands, believe me. I naturally called the State Bureau of Investigation first, but... Well, once they heard me out, they suggested I call in your office. Yours specifically, not just the FBI. Sort of surprised me, to be honest. That they suggested right off the bat I should call you folks. But it sounded like a good idea to me, so I did. Didn't really expect so many feds to respond, and I sure as hell didn't expect it to be so fast. I sent in the request less than five hours ago."

"We were in the area," she said. "Near enough. Just over the mountains in North Carolina."

"Another case?"

"Ongoing. But not really going anywhere, so coming over to check this out made sense."

Duncan nodded, even though she wasn't looking at him. She was on one knee a couple of feet from the body—what was left of the body—her gaze fixed unwaveringly on that.

He wondered what she saw. Because, word had it, the agents of the FBI's elite Special Crimes Unit saw a lot more than most cops, even if the what and how of that was rather vaguely defined.

What Duncan saw was plain enough, if incredibly bizarre, and he had to force himself to look again.

The body lay sprawled beside what was, among the high school track team and some of the hardier souls in town, a popular hiking and running trail. It was a wickedly difficult path to walk at a brisk pace, let alone run, which made it an excellent training course if you knew what you were doing—and potentially deadly if you didn't.

There were numerous cases of sprains, strains, and broken bones in this area year-round, but especially after the spring rains.

Still, Duncan didn't have to be an M.E. or even a doctor to know that a fall while running or walking hadn't done this. Not this.

The dense undergrowth of this part of the forest had done a fair job for the killer of concealing most of the body; Duncan's deputies had been forced hours before to carefully clear away bushes and vines just to have good access to the remains.

Which made it a damn good thing that this was obviously a dump site rather than a murder scene; Duncan might not have been familiar with grisly murders, but he certainly knew enough to be sure the feds would not have been happy to find their evidence disturbed.

Evidence. He wondered if there was any to speak of. His own people certainly hadn't found much. Prints were being run through IAFIS now, and if that avenue of identification turned up no name, Duncan supposed the next step would be dental records.

Because there wasn't a whole lot else to identify the poor bastard.

His left arm lay across part of the trail, and it was eerily undamaged, unmarked by so much as a bruise. Eerily because, from the elbow on, the damage was...extreme. Most of the flesh and muscle had been somehow stripped from the bones, leaving behind only bloody tags of sinew attached here and there. Most if not all of the internal organs were gone, including the eyes; the scalp had been ripped from the skull.

Ripped. Jesus, what could have ripped it? What could have done this?

"Any ideas what could have done this?" Duncan asked.

"No sane ones," she replied in a matter-of-fact tone.

"So I'm not the only one imagining nightmare impossibilities?" He could hear the relief in his own voice.

She turned her head and looked at him, then rose easily from her kneeling position and stepped away from the remains to join him. "We learned a long time ago not to throw around words like *impossible.*"

"And *nightmare*?"

"That one too. 'There are stranger things in heaven and earth, Horatio....'" Special Agent Miranda Bishop shrugged. "The SCU was created to deal with those stranger things. We've seen a lot of them."

"So I've heard, Agent Bishop."

She smiled, and he was aware yet again of an entirely unprofessional and entirely masculine response to truly breathtaking beauty.

"Miranda, please. Otherwise it'll get confusing."

"Oh? Why is that?"

"Because," a new voice chimed in, "you're likely to hear all of us referring to Bishop, and when we do we're talking about Noah Bishop, the chief of the Special Crimes Unit."

"My husband," Miranda Bishop clarified. "Everybody calls him Bishop. So please do call me Miranda." She waited for his nod, then turned her electric-blue-eyed gaze to the other agent. "Quentin, anything?"

"Not so you'd notice." Special Agent Quentin Hayes shook his head, then frowned and pulled a twig from his rather shaggy blond hair. "Though I've seldom searched an area with undergrowth this dense, so I can't say I couldn't have missed something."

Duncan spoke up to say, "Our county medical examiner hasn't

had to deal with any but accidental deaths since he got the job, but he said he was sure this man wasn't killed here."

Miranda Bishop nodded. "Your M.E. is right. If the victim had been killed here, the ground would be soaked with blood—at the very least. This man was probably alive twenty-four hours ago and dumped here sometime around dawn today."

Duncan didn't ask how she'd arrived at that conclusion; his M.E. had made the same guesstimate.

"No signs of a struggle," Quentin added. "And unless this guy was drugged or otherwise unconscious or dead, I would imagine he struggled."

With a grimace, Duncan said, "Personally, I'm hoping he was already dead when . . . that . . . was done to him."

"We're all hoping the same thing," Quentin assured him. "In the meantime, knowing who the victim was would at least give us a place to start. Any word on the prints your people took?"

"When I checked in an hour ago, no. I'll go back to my Jeep and check again; like I told you, cell service is lousy up here, and our portable radios next to useless. We have to use a specially designed booster antenna on our police vehicles to get any kind of signal at all, and even that tends to be spotty."

"Appreciate it, Sheriff." Quentin watched the older man cautiously make his way down the steep trail toward the road and their cars, then turned his head and looked at Miranda with lifted brows.

"I don't know," she said.

Quentin lowered his voice even though the nearest sheriff's deputies—Duncan's chief deputy, Neil Scanlon, and his partner, Nadine Twain—were yards away, crouched over a map of the area spread out on the ground. "The M.O. is close. Torture on the inhuman side of brutal."

She slid her hands into the front pockets of her jeans and frowned. "Yeah, but this . . . this is beyond anything we've seen so far."

"From this killer, at least," Quentin muttered.

Miranda nodded. "Maybe it's simply a case of escalation, the usual he-gets-worse-as-he-gets-better-at-it, but...I'm not seeing a purpose for what was done here. Whether he was dead at the beginning is still arguable, but this man was most definitely dead a long time before his killer was finished with him, and that hasn't been the case with the other victims we've linked together. If this was torture, why keep going after the vic was dead?"

"For the fun of it?"

"Christ, I hope not."

"You and me both. Am I the only one having a very bad feeling about this one?"

"I wish you were. But I think we've all picked up on something unnatural here and at the other dump sites. For one thing, I have no idea what means this killer used to strip the body literally to the bone."

Quentin glanced toward the remains. "I didn't spot any obvious tool marks on the bones. Or claw or tooth marks, for that matter. You?"

"No. Or any visible signs that chemicals were used, though forensics will tell us that for certain."

"We ship the body—or what's left of it—to the state medical examiner?"

"We do. Duncan already okayed it; he's been very frank about the state of technology in this area."

"As in the fact that there *is* no technology? I mean, we've been to some pretty out-of-the-way places, but this is what I'd call seriously remote. How many people you figure the town of Serenade can boast? A few hundred at best?"

"Nearly three thousand, if you count those living outside the town limits but still using Serenade as their mailing address." She saw Quentin's brows go up again and explained, "I checked when we were flying in."

"Uh-huh. And did you happen to notice that the one motel we passed looks an awful lot like the sort that would have Norman Bates behind the desk?"

"I noticed. Though I thought of it as your typical small-town no-tell motel." Miranda shrugged. "And we both know it may not matter. If this victim fits the pattern, then where he was found is only a small piece of the puzzle. In which case we won't be staying here long."

"I wouldn't be too sure about that."

She looked at him, her own brows rising.

"Hunch," he explained. "We're only about thirty miles away from The Lodge, as the crow flies, and there were a lot of unnatural goings-on there for a very long time."

"You and Diana put that to rest," Miranda reminded him.*

"Well, we—she, mostly—put part of it to rest. Hopefully the worst part. But that doesn't mean we got it all."

"It's been a year," she reminded him.

"Yeah, to the month. Hell, almost to the day. Which I'm finding more than a bit unsettling."

Miranda Bishop was not in the habit of discounting either a hunch or an uneasy feeling expressed by someone around her, especially by a fellow team member, and she didn't start now. "Okay. But, so far, nothing leads us in the direction of The Lodge. No connection to the place or to anyone there, not that we've found."

"I know. Wish I could say that reassured me, but it doesn't."

"Do you want to drive over to The Lodge, take a look around?"

"If anybody goes, it should be someone with a fresh eye and no baggage," Quentin answered, so promptly that she knew the question had been on his mind for a while. "And probably a medium, given the age and . . . nature of the place."

"You know very well we have only two available. Diana shouldn't go because of all the baggage, and I'd rather keep Hollis close."

---

*Chill of Fear

Quentin eyed her. "Why?"

Miranda's frown had returned, but this time she appeared to be gazing into the distance at nothing. Or at something only she could see. And it was a long moment before she replied. "Because her abilities are . . . evolving. Because every case seems to bring a new ability and ramp up the power on an existing one. And that's faster than we've *ever* known psychic abilities to evolve. It's unprecedented."

"She's been in some unusually intense situations these last months," Quentin said slowly. "From the beginning, really. Hell, the trigger that made her go active was about as extreme and intense as anything *I've* ever heard of."

"Yes, she's clearly a survivor," Miranda said.*

"But?"

"I don't know that there is a but. Except that the tolerances of the human brain are likely to be higher than those of the human mind."

Quentin worked that out. "You mean she may not be adjusting to all this quite as easily and completely as she appears to be. Emotionally. Psychologically."

"That's exactly what I mean. So I'd rather keep her close for now. So far, every one of these dump sites has been just that, with no evidence that the killer remained behind in the area. At every site so far, we've collected evidence, asked a few questions, and explored what turned out to be a few dead ends, then moved on."

"So . . . less intensity to trigger something new in Hollis?"

"That," Miranda said, "would be the theory, yes. It isn't something we can keep up indefinitely, for obvious reasons, and you and I both know any given situation can change in a heartbeat. And usually does in our investigations. But short of ordering her to take a sabbatical, which would not go over well at all and could do more harm than good, it's the best temporary solution we've been able to come up with."

Touching Evil

13

"You and Bishop?"

Miranda nodded. "It doesn't fix the problem—assuming the pace of Hollis's development as a psychic *is* a problem rather than her own natural evolution—but we're hoping it will at least offer her a little breathing space to really come to terms with how much her life has changed. More time to adjust to what's been happening to her, to work on her investigative skills as well as her psychic ones. Hell, just time to move through her life without feeling there's a target painted on her forehead."

"Which she pretty much had during the whole complicated investigation of Samuel and his church."

"Yeah."

"Okay." Quentin looked around, suddenly and obviously uneasy. "Great theory, and I really hope it works out. For her sake and for ours. But I'm beginning to think this creepy but calm investigation might be turning into something else. Like one of the more intense ones. Because they should be back by now, shouldn't they?"

"**N**obody said there'd be *bears*," Special Agent Hollis Templeton whispered somewhat fiercely.

Special Investigator Diana Brisco kept her gaze fixed on the rather large specimen of black bear foraging in the brush not twenty yards from their present location and whispered back, "It's the right time of year for them. I think. Spring. They come out of hibernation and start looking for food."

"Oh, lovely."

"They usually run from people."

"You think or you know?"

"I've been reading a lot the last year. Catching up. I remember reading that. Also that they *can* climb trees, and if they do attack it's useless to fake being dead the way you can with a grizzly bear."

"I wouldn't have to fake being dead if a grizzly attacked. Hell, I won't have to fake being dead if this bear attacks." Hollis smothered a sigh. "Okay, so what do we do? Wait him out?"

"Might be a while. Looks like he's found something to eat."

Hollis watched the bear's movements for a few moments, then squinted her eyes in an effort to see more clearly through the thicket they were crouched behind and whispered, "Oh, shit."

Diana had seen it as well. Her weapon, like Hollis's, was at the ready, and though her experience with the Glock was limited to training and practice, she was somewhat surprised to realize it felt comfortable in her hand. Or, at the very least, familiar. "I say we both aim at that tree about three feet to his left. If that doesn't spook him into running..."

"It better. Because I don't want to shoot a bear, Diana."

"Neither do I. Got a better idea?"

"No. Dammit." Hollis leveled her own weapon and aimed carefully through the tangle of newly greening brush that was all the cover they had. "On three. One...two...three."

The two gunshots were virtually simultaneous, sharp and loud in the relative stillness of the forest, and both bullets struck the tree near the bear with dull thuds, sending splinters of bark flying.

The bear, either no stranger to guns or wary enough to take no chances, ran, thankfully away from them, taking the easiest path to lumber with bulky grace down the mountainside.

The two women got to their feet slowly, weapons still held ready, tense until they could no longer see the bear or hear its crashing progress through the underbrush.

Diana finally relaxed and slid her gun into the holster she wore on her hip. With no need to whisper now, she said, "First time I fire my weapon in the field and it's because of a damn bear. Quentin will never let me hear the end of it."

"Probably not," Hollis agreed, holstering her own gun. "Think they heard the shots? Or the echoes?" There had been many of the latter.

"In this kind of terrain? God knows, especially since all of us searching went in different directions. But even if it does feel like we've hiked miles, we can't be more than a few hundred yards from the original site. The others have probably gotten back there by now."

Hollis checked her cell phone for a signal, even though they had previously discovered no joy in that. Still no joy. She sighed and replaced the cell in the special case worn on the opposite side of her hip from her weapon. "Well, even if some of the others heard the shots, we have no way of verifying that they did, so one of us is going to have to trek back there."

"While the other stays here and makes sure the bear doesn't come back and remove . . . evidence?"

"That would be the correct procedure, under the circumstances."

"Great."

Hollis noticed that neither of them had taken a step in the necessary direction to verify that the bear had indeed discovered what they thought it had. Reminding herself that she was a more experienced agent than Diana and therefore the de facto lead investigator between the two of them, she moved around the brush that had sheltered them and made her way carefully to the spot yards away.

Diana silently accompanied her, both of them wary, both keeping one hand on their weapon until they had to pull aside a tangle of brown vines in order to see what they suspected.

The bear had discovered human remains.

The women took a step back and looked at each other. Hollis had no idea whether her own face was as pale as Diana's but thought it very likely. No matter how many times she'd been forced to view human remains after a violent end, it didn't get any easier.

Probably a good thing, that.

And she didn't know which was worse—finding fresh remains or those that had lain out in the elements long enough to have gone through several stages of decomposition, as this one had.

The smell made her stomach churn.

Diana said, "That was some hunch you had. To leave the trail and head in this direction. To come this far. Because otherwise..."

"Otherwise," Hollis finished, "I doubt anybody would have stumbled onto this body. Recognize the vines?"

"Kudzu. This patch starts farther down the slope. The stuff covers and smothers everything in its path."

Hollis nodded. "It dries up in winter but comes back stronger than ever in spring and summer. The vines can grow several feet in a single day." She paused, forcing herself to look down at what was left of, she believed, a woman's body. "It sure as hell would have hidden her from everything except some predators and small animals."

"Which raises the question: Is she here by accident or design?"

"Yeah. If she wound up here accidentally, it probably won't tell us much. But if she was left here deliberately..."

"Then this body, unlike the one by that popular hiking trail, was never meant to be found."

"That would be my guess. Whether the same killer is responsible is another question entirely."

Brows raised, Diana said, "I know I'm still pretty new to all this investigative stuff, but isn't it stretching things a bit to assume there's a second killer operating at the same time in such a remote area?"

"It's stretching things a lot. But besides not knowing if both these victims were killed by the same person, we don't even know if this victim was murdered at all. Natural deaths do occur in terrain like this on a regular basis."

"Yeah. But you don't believe there was anything natural about this." It wasn't a question.

Hollis shrugged. "I think we're usually not that lucky. So we assume murder until evidence says otherwise."

"Gotcha."

Hollis looked around them with a slight frown and, thinking aloud, said, "The killer we've been tracking for more than two months has used dumping sites all over the Southeast, so there's no way for us to be sure just where his home base is. Maybe near here, maybe not. According to the profile, he may not even have a base and could be completely transient."

"Giving us precious little info to work with."

"To say the least. But if both these people are his victims, it's certainly a new wrinkle. He's spread out his dumping sites before now over hundreds of miles—not hundreds of yards. And this is the first time we've found two victims who, I'm guessing, were killed within a week of each other. The guy on the trail was very recent, and this woman at least a few days and probably a week ago."

Diana drew a short breath—through her mouth—and let it out slowly. "I'll take your word for it, especially since I'm barely half-way through the crime-scene-investigation manual." She was one of the newest members of the SCU team, having joined less than a year before. "And, I repeat, that was some hunch to draw you way out here. Except it wasn't a hunch, was it?"

"No."

"You saw her?"

"I caught a glimpse." Hollis frowned again. "It was odd, though. They usually stick around long enough to at least try to communicate. She barely let me see her at all, and she wasn't close."

"But she led us here. Probably realized her body would never be found otherwise."

Hollis looked at Diana. "You didn't see anything? Anyone?"

"No. But I don't often just *see* them here on our side, at least not without the help of a storm or some other external energy. For me, it's usually a far more deliberate thing, you know that. I have to concentrate, pretty much go into a trancelike state. Or else it happens when I'm asleep."

She hated that, more now than she had in years past, when she had been consciously unaware of her psychic forays due to the many medications her father and various doctors had used to control her "illness." Neither Elliot Brisco nor any of those doctors had considered for even a moment that she might not, in fact, be ill but merely . . . gifted. Diana hadn't considered it either. She had been utterly convinced she was mentally unstable at best and out of her mind at worst.

Until she met Quentin Hayes. And had been both educated and wholeheartedly accepted by him and the members of the SCU.

For the first time in her life, she didn't feel like a freak.

"Diana?"

She yanked her attention back to the present, saying parenthetically, "I hate it happening while I'm asleep. Very disconcerting."

"I can imagine. Very well, in fact."

"Yeah, you never really told me after our little experiment what you thought about that visit to the gray time." It was the name she used for a place or time that seemed to be a sort of limbo between the spirit world and the world of the living.

"It was creepy as hell. I don't envy you the ability to go there." Despite being a medium herself, Hollis had been completely unfamiliar with that gray and lifeless limbo, which was just one more affirmation of Bishop's belief that every psychic was unique.

"You never told Bishop or Miranda about it either, did you?"

Hollis offered her a twisted smile. "I don't have to be telepathic to know they're both . . . concerned about me. Seems I'm a bit of a freak as psychics go, and they aren't quite sure what's going to happen to me as time goes on. Neither one has said it in so many words, but I gather the most recent tests showed that the amount of electrical activity in my brain is excessive even for psychics. Whether that turns out to be a good thing or a bad one is apparently very much in question."

"I wish you'd told me that before I took you into the gray time."

"Don't *you* start worrying. I'm fine. Just . . . exploring my abilities, that's all. I'd rather have some idea of what I can do *before* yet another deadly situation opens up, without warning, yet another door in my psychic world. Less disconcerting that way."

"If you say so." Diana didn't look especially convinced, but another glance down at the remains distracted her. "Do we flip a coin to decide who stays here with her?"

"No need; I'll stay. She might pay me another visit if I'm alone. Besides, you seem to have a better feeling for direction in this kind of terrain, so you're a hell of a lot less likely to get lost. Plus, there's Quentin. You two are connected and you usually sense him, right?"

Diana's expression went a bit guarded, but she said readily enough, "Usually. As a matter of fact, I'm reasonably sure he either heard the shots or felt something, because I think he's heading this way."

"Well, go meet him, then, will you, please? The less time I have to spend here waiting for a spirit or a bear, the better."

"I hear that." Diana turned away, adding, "Sit tight. I'll be back with the others ASAP."

"I'll be here." Hollis was left staring down at the remains of a woman who had, assuming that spirit was hers, died far too young.

There wasn't a lot left of the body. Hollis knew enough to recognize that both maggots and small scavengers had consumed most of the soft tissue. There was some skin left, and quite a bit of long blond hair clung to a small patch of scalp that was still attached to the skull.

She had beautiful teeth, straight and gleaming white.

Must have cost a fortune at the orthodontist.

Hollis knelt gingerly, telling herself the smell wasn't at all overpowering as she did her best to look for evidence, for clues to how this woman died. To study the scene as she had been taught.

The first clue surprised her, both because she had missed it until now and because it struck her as unexpectedly sloppy that the killer had left it behind: A loop of plastic bound fragile wrists together behind the victim's back. It was the sort of binding that law-enforcement units often used these days in a big operation or when they otherwise ran out of metal handcuffs.

It was also quite possibly the sort of plastic tie found commonly in boxes of garbage bags and in the gardening and home-improvement sections of most DIY stores.

Hollis pushed aside that wry realization and continued to study the remains. The bear, she decided, had...pawed...a bit, so it was difficult to even guess in what position she had been when she'd been dumped here. Right now she was more or less faceup, forearms, wrists, and hands mostly beneath her and legs twisted, splayed apart at the thigh area but tangled together around the ankles and feet.

There was no sign of another plastic tie, but Hollis wondered if the ankles had been bound as the wrists were. Possibly.

There was also, she realized suddenly, absolutely no sign of any clothing whatsoever. It made her throat tighten to think of a young woman, perhaps already dead or perhaps still alive, in agony and terrified, dumped here in a wilderness of dirt and vines, bound and naked. So unspeakably vulnerable. So very alone.

It stirred memories Hollis would have given much to forget.

"Hey."

Hollis nearly jumped out of her skin. She looked up and was angrily aware of the crack in her voice when she demanded, "Where the hell did you come from?"

Two

WEST," REESE DEMARCO REPLIED matter-of-factly. "I'd finished searching my grid and was heading back when I heard the shots."

Of course it would have to be him. Hollis abruptly remembered that DeMarco was, among other things, telepathic, and she made rather a production of rising to her feet and brushing off the knee of her jeans.

"There was a bear," she explained briefly. "We scared it off. Diana went to report while I waited here."

"Ah." He looked down at the remains, his coldly handsome face as usual utterly without expression. He was dressed as casually as the rest of the SCU team was today, in jeans and a white shirt underneath a lightweight windbreaker, but the informal attire did nothing to soften the almost military crispness of his stance and movements, that truly visible sense of considerable strength and the training and ability to know how best to use it.

Hollis had seen that in other ex-military types, but in DeMarco there was something just a little bit...excessive...in his straight posture and almost hypersensitivity to his surroundings. He seemed to her too alert, too ready to explode into action. He made her think of a cocked gun, and she had no idea whether a dangerous hair trigger lurked inside him.

She couldn't see his aura unless he allowed her to.

He wasn't allowing her to.

"I gather the bear discovered these remains?"

She shoved the oddly disjointed thoughts aside. *He's a telepath, remember? Don't let him into your head.* Not that she had any kind of a shield she could use to keep him out if he wanted in. Dammit. "Yeah."

"Is that what brought you two so far off the trails?"

"Not exactly."

His gaze shifted, pale blue eyes fixed intently on her face. "You know, we *are* on the same side, Hollis. You don't have to be so guarded with me. I'm not trying to read you."

She wondered if that meant he wasn't reading her—or simply didn't have to try in *order* to read her. She didn't have the nerve to ask. "Was I being evasive? Sorry. Diana and I weren't following the bear, we were following a spirit who led us to this area. *Then* we found the bear. Which had just found what was left of this body."

"That must have been an interesting encounter."

"You could say."

DeMarco returned his dispassionate attention to the remains. "Probably female, probably on the young side. Blond. Great teeth. Her hands were bound behind her back and there's no sign of clothing, so highly unlikely this was an accidental death. Most likely a sexual assault, though whether that was the intent from the beginning is impossible to say. That's as far as my crime-scene and forensic knowledge can take me."

"About the same for me. Except that it seems obvious she's been out here longer than the male victim."

"Yes. The bear wasn't the first scavenger to find her."

Hollis didn't like the silence that fell between them, so she filled it with what amounted to thinking aloud. It was becoming something of a habit with her during investigations. *Because, after all, with telepaths always underfoot, what the hell…*

Besides, she wondered if he'd agree with her conclusion.

"This body was left—what—a good fifty yards off the nearest trail?"

"About that."

"Place like this, nobody's likely to be riding or hiking. The trees and underbrush would hide anything left here from the air even now, without full summer foliage."

"Once it greens up, the kudzu would just about ensure anything left here would be hidden from two feet away. In any direction."

Hollis nodded. "This is a fairly level spot, but the slope is steep above and below it. Not all that easy to get to. Between the terrain and the wildlife, the chances of discovery are virtually nil. Or would have been, if we hadn't been led so far off the beaten paths. So…"

"So, unlike the other body, this one was not intended to be found." DeMarco considered for a moment. "I wonder which is the most significant—that he was meant to be found or that she wasn't."

That angle hadn't occurred to Hollis. Still thinking out loud, she said, "The killer—assuming it was the same killer, of course— couldn't have assumed we'd search this far out after finding the other body." She frowned. "I don't like two assumptions in one sentence."

"One's a negative," DeMarco pointed out.

"Does that matter?"

"Maybe. It's not a wrong assumption, I'd say. In fact, the location of the other body should have guaranteed police focus would have been *away* from this area. And even with our expanded search, it's well outside the grid. There'd be no reason to imagine any of us would have found this body."

"If the killer knows police procedure, sure. If it's the same killer." She paused, then said, "Are you suggesting the guy on the trail could have been intended as a distraction, to prevent anybody from finding her? Because it seems to me she was a lot less likely to be found if we hadn't been here in the first place, combing the area looking for evidence in another crime."

"Maybe our killer is very paranoid. Or maybe he couldn't risk even the chance that we might find this body."

"Because he has a connection to her? Because she wasn't a random stranger to him?"

"Could be."

"Then why not just do a better job of disposing of the body? He could have buried her." Hollis didn't know why she was arguing with DeMarco; his possibilities made as much sense as her own did.

"Not out here. Too much granite to end up with anything but a uselessly shallow grave. And where there isn't granite, the roots of these trees would make digging by hand difficult and time-consuming if not impossible."

"There are easier places to dig."

"Granted. But maybe he was short on time. Maybe he had to get rid of the body in a hurry."

"Okay. But—" Hollis felt it before she saw any sign of it. Tension, so sudden and powerful that it was like a live current in the air. Then DeMarco turned his head, looking at her, almost looking *through* her, and she saw his eyes change in a heartbeat, his pupils dilating as if he had been thrust without warning into pitch-black darkness.

For the first time in months, she was able to see his aura radiating outward at least eight or ten inches from his body, and it was unlike any she'd ever seen before, distinctly unlike his normal reddish-orange high-energy aura: In this moment his aura was a deep indigo shot through with violet and silvery streaks.

She barely had time to grasp all that before she realized he was lunging toward her. Even as he knocked her off her feet and carried her to the ground, she felt something tug at the shoulder of her jacket and heard the distinct, weirdly hollow *craa-aack* of a rifle.

Diana did have an almost uncanny sense of direction, a talent she had discovered only in the last year or so, but her physical conditioning and endurance, unlike that of most of the other team members, were still considerably under par.

She hated that.

No matter how many times Quentin or Miranda reminded her that she was playing serious catch-up after spending almost her entire adult life in a senses-dulling haze of various medications, she couldn't escape the feeling that she should have been... further along by now. Physically stronger, at the very least.

"You're stronger than you know," Bishop had said, only a couple of weeks before.

Yeah, right.

The truth was that she had drifted through her life, completely detached, uninvolved in... anything. Diana honestly wished she could believe that all the doctors who had tried one medicine or therapy or treatment after the other had done it only because they'd had her best interests at heart and sincerely thought she suffered from some unnamed mental illness. But what she believed was that her father was a wealthy, powerful man, and what Elliot Brisco wanted, he got.

He'd wanted his only daughter's life under his control. And though he still claimed his actions stemmed from love and concern, Diana had come to the conclusion that he had been driven as much by that need to control what was "his" as by a deeply rooted fear of anything he didn't understand.

Such as psychic abilities.

Diana tried to shove the painful musing aside, wishing her father hadn't intensified his efforts in the last couple of months to try to convince her one more time that she'd made a mistake in joining the FBI. And, especially, the SCU.

It was no accident, she thought, that he had been applying more pressure just when she was becoming involved in her first field assignment.

Consciously or not, he knew exactly how to undermine her confidence in herself.

Never mind him. Concentrate on the job at hand, dammit.

Leaning against a handy maple tree to catch her breath, she decided that the shortcut that had seemed such a good idea really wasn't. The trade-off of avoiding the greater distance of twists and turns for a more direct route meant she was forced to do a hell of a lot of pretty rugged climbing to get over a ridge.

"Suck it up," she muttered to herself. "You're surrounded by people who don't even get the *concept* of quit."

That reminder did little for her self-confidence, but at least it caused her to push herself away from the support of the tree and press onward.

And upward.

No more than twenty or so yards farther, near the crest of the ridge, she stopped to lean against another tree, but this time not only because of her burning legs and thudding heart.

Quentin was near.

It was weird, that... sensation. More than knowledge or awareness, it was a tangible connection she couldn't really explain—and had so far refused to examine closely. Even after all these months, she invariably caught herself resisting, pulling away from that powerful inner tugging, not allowing herself to be drawn toward Quentin as every other instinct insisted she must be.

Bishop said it was because she had lived so much of her life under someone else's control and that, once all the medications were out of her system and her father's authority over her had been legally and practically severed, she was bound to instinctively fight for her independence—even against a connection that posed no threat to that independence.

He had said this out of the blue one day while he was teaching

27

her a few basic martial arts moves, and Diana had somewhat indignantly believed he did it only to distract her so he could maintain the upper hand in the match—until she thought about it later. First she recognized that he had hardly needed any sort of distraction, given his skills. And she recognized second that not only was he right in what he'd told her but also that she never would have brought up the subject herself, and what he'd told her was something she really needed to know.

Which figured. Bishop, she had discovered, was like that. He picked up on the things one didn't want to discuss and matter-of-factly made one discuss them.

Or at least consider them. She hadn't been willing to discuss that particular subject, her prickly defenses going up immediately. She just wasn't ready to talk about her father and all the baggage he'd left her with. Not with Bishop.

And only very rarely and briefly with Quentin.

That made her feel guilty as hell, even though she was reasonably certain he knew exactly what was going on in her head. Because Quentin, with highly uncharacteristic patience, had not demanded or even asked for any kind of commitment from her, giving her all the time she needed to come to terms with both her new life and startling abilities and with a tie to him that had nothing to do with domination.

At least she thought that was why he hadn't—

"Diana?"

Thank God he's not a telepath.

"Hi." She was relieved to note that she'd had time to catch her breath and didn't sound as out of shape as she was.

"We heard shots." He hadn't drawn his weapon but was visibly tense, his gaze scanning their surroundings warily.

"Hollis and I ran into a bear." When he quickly focused on her face, she added, "Not literally. But we needed to scare it away. It found something, Quentin. Another body. Or what's left of one."

"Shit. Murder victim?"

"We think so."

He let out a short little breath. "Okay. Miranda's on her way with a couple of Duncan's deputies. She said Reese would be there with Hollis before we get back to them."

"How does she know—" Diana broke off as she realized.

Quentin was nodding. "I've never quite figured out how she and Bishop do it, but they always seem to know where each of us is at any given moment, in relation to them and to each other."

"That's a little . . . unsettling," Diana admitted.

"You'll get used to it." He paused, reflecting, then added, "Or not. Come on, let's go."

"You're assuming I can find my way back there."

"I know you can find your way back there." His voice was matter-of-fact. "You're as good as a compass."

"My one skill," she muttered.

"One of many. Your father called again last night, didn't he?"

"He calls nearly every night," she said, trying to make her voice careless. "He's stubborn as hell. So?"

"So stop letting him damage your confidence. Diana, you're a valued member of this team because you have abilities and skills. In case you haven't noticed, the SCU isn't exactly the easiest team to join, and nobody gets in unless Bishop knows they can contribute to an investigation."

"Yeah, but—"

"No buts. You earned this. Okay?"

After a moment, she nodded. "Okay." She turned to begin to re-trace her steps, thankful that the way back, at least, was mostly downhill. "Do you think we have two killers?" she asked over her shoulder.

"I think it's unlikely. Stranger things have happened—certainly when we're around—but the odds are against it."

"That's what we—" The *craa-aack* of a shot cut her off, and Diana jerked to a stop, half-turning to look at Quentin. "What the hell?"

"That was a rifle. And none of us is carrying a rifle."

"Where did the shot come from? With all the echoes, I couldn't tell."

"I think it came from the other side of the valley."

"A hunter?"

"I don't think so."

Diana didn't have to be urged to continue on. Or to hurry.

"**S**tay down."

DeMarco's heavy weight lay on her for only an instant before he was rolling away, weapon in hand, eyes narrowed as he peered through the underbrush to scan the mountain slopes surrounding the valley below them. One of his hands lay only inches from the murdered woman's skull.

"Sorry," he added briefly.

Without moving otherwise, Hollis fingered the neat hole in the shoulder of her jacket and managed a shaky laugh. "Sorry? Because you probably saved my life?"

"As fast as you heal, that's debatable. No, I'm sorry I had to knock you down like that without warning."

"There wasn't really time for a warning. I get that, believe me." Hollis was a bit proud of the fact that her voice was—almost—as calm as his. She rolled onto her belly but continued to hug the cold ground as she drew her weapon. "I don't suppose that shot could have been accidental." It wasn't a question.

He answered anyway. "Probably not. That was a high-powered rifle, and I doubt it's the sort of weapon used by hunters in these parts."

"Then somebody was shooting at me?"

"At one of us. Or intending to shake us up."

Hollis wondered if anything had ever shaken up DeMarco. Somehow she doubted it.

"I don't see anything," she said after a moment, scanning the area as he was—or at least as much as she could make out through the underbrush. Not that she was all that sure what she was looking for. "Speaking of which, how the hell did you know that shot was coming?"

He didn't reply immediately, and when he did his tone was almost indifferent. "I caught a glimpse of something from the corner of my eye. Probably sunlight glinting off the barrel of the gun."

Hollis glanced up at what had become, hours before, a heavily overcast sky and said, "Uh-huh. Okay, keep the mysterious military secrets to yourself. I don't mind being told it's none of my business." Despite the words, her voice was, to say the least, sarcastic.

"It's not a military secret, Hollis."

Something she couldn't identify had crept into that indifferent tone, and for some obscure reason it pleased her. "No?"

"No." He glanced at her, then away, as he added, "I can feel it when a gun is pointed at me or anywhere close to me."

"Always?"

"So far as I know."

"Is that a psychic ability?"

Again, he hesitated briefly before replying. "Bishop calls it a primal ability. Guns pose lethal threats: I sense a threat. It's a survival mechanism."

"Sounds like a handy one, especially in our line of work."

"It has been, yes."

"You still sensing a threat?"

"Not an imminent one."

"Meaning the gun isn't pointed this way anymore, but the shooter might still be . . . wherever he or she was?"

"Something like that."

"Then maybe we can get up off the ground now?"

He sent her another glance. "I could be wrong, you know."

"Are you?"

He didn't answer immediately, which surprised her. From the first time they'd met, she had sized up DeMarco as a man full of self-confidence. Possibly to a fault. She figured he was the sort who would view any hesitation as weakness.

That was one reason she always felt slightly on the defensive with him, because she was prone to hesitate. A lot.

Deciding this wasn't one of those times, she gathered herself to get up off the ground. Instantly, DeMarco's free hand shot out and grabbed her wrist, holding her still just long enough.

The bullet hit the tree nearest them with a dull thud, bark went flying, and the *craa-aack* of the shot echoed as the first one had.

If Hollis had gotten up as planned, she likely would have taken that shot just about dead center in her chest.

DeMarco released her wrist. "Now we can get up." He did.

Hollis remained where she was for a moment, studying the reddening marks of his grip on her arm. Then she accepted his outstretched hand and got to her feet. It struck her as she did that she was completely confident in DeMarco's certainty that the gunman would not shoot again, and she wondered about that.

She really did.

"So it *was* intended for me," she said, holding her voice steady despite her pounding heart. "I was the target."

A rare frown drew his brows together as he continued to scan the mountain slopes facing them. "Maybe. Depending on his position, we could have been at least partially visible even when we were on the ground. Or maybe he couldn't see you about to get up, and that was just a final shot aimed where we were a few minutes ago, intended to keep us pinned down here and give him more time to get out of the area. Either way is possible. We should be able to determine a rough trajectory using the bullet that struck that tree, and the first one if we can find it."

"And if the trajectory confirms what you suspect?" she asked, knowing he had a point to make.

"Then the shooter was on the other side of the valley."

Hollis looked, then frowned as she slowly holstered her gun. "I'm not all that good at estimating distance, but . . . that's not close."

"No. But for a trained sharpshooter with a good scope, not an impossible distance."

"You're thinking he missed on purpose?"

"I'm thinking with the sort of gun and scope I suspect he's using, he was more likely to hit what he was aiming at than to miss with the only two shots he fired."

"He might have missed with the first shot only because you were quicker. Have I said thank you, by the way?"

"You're welcome." But DeMarco was staring toward the other side of the valley, his eyes narrowed again. "Why draw attention to his presence? Dumb idea. We wouldn't suspect he was there otherwise. He could have watched every move we made here."

"Why would he want to?"

"That's the question. Possible answers: Because he wants to see us in action. Because he wants to observe our reaction to this victim, this dump site. Because we've been here only a couple of hours, new players he wants to get to know. Or . . . because he likes to watch. Likes to see how people—law enforcement or otherwise—react to what he's left for us."

"But we've agreed this body wasn't meant to be found."

DeMarco nodded. "So . . . he wouldn't expect to see us here. Any of us. Any*one*, for that matter. He had every reason to expect no one would be at this location."

"Which means neither of us was a target?"

"Not a target he would have expected or planned for. A target of opportunity maybe. We were here, one or both of us are on his hit list, so he took his shot. But if he didn't expect anyone to find this victim, what's he doing on the other side of the valley with a high-powered rifle? And why was it more important to him to shoot at one or both of us, giving away his presence, rather than simply waiting and watching in order to gather intel?"

Hollis wasn't sure what she would have replied to that, so it was a good thing that Quentin and Diana arrived then. Both had guns drawn and were visibly alert and wary.

"We heard the shots," Quentin said.

DeMarco explained, with a minimum of words, what had happened.

Hollis silently poked one finger through the bullet hole in her jacket.

Characteristically, Quentin's comment to her was somewhat flippant. "You just can't stay out of trouble, can you?"

"Apparently not."

Diana was scanning the mountain slopes ringing the valley. "Jesus, it's a wilderness. Whoever fired those shots could be anywhere. Even if we knew exactly where he was, it'd take us forever to get to that spot." She paused, then added, "And aren't we awfully exposed standing here?"

"The shooter's done for now," DeMarco said, holstering his weapon.

Diana eyed him. "You read his mind across a valley?"

"No. But he's done. For now."

Noting that Quentin was also holstering his gun, Diana followed suit. *I'm learning to trust all of them. Or maybe I just trust Quentin.* It wasn't an easy thing for her, trust. It still caught her by surprise when she became aware of feeling it.

Pushing that aside, Diana forced herself to look down once again at the remains of the second victim. *Poor thing. What happened to you? Who did this to you?*

Unlike Hollis, Diana tended not to see the recently dead. The spirits she saw—most of them what she called guides—were usually messengers of a sort, connecting with her so she could pass on information, so they could show her something she needed to see or in some other way help an uneasy spirit find rest and peace in whatever lay beyond this life.

So she wasn't worried about being confronted by the spirit of this poor woman. And she was glad about that.

The physical remains were bad enough. Horrible. Her stomach lurched a bit, but the queasy sensation remained a low-grade awareness that she could, if not suppress, at least cope with. For the moment. That, she supposed, was professional progress of a sort. At least she hadn't disgraced herself by losing her lunch.

Attempting to keep up the professional façade as long as possible, she returned her attention to Hollis and said, "So the shooter was aiming at you? Why were you a target?"

"Beats the hell out of me. But Reese says it could have been either of us."

"Okay. Why would either of you be a target? I mean, did this guy shoot at two SCU agents specifically? Or one of you specifically?"

"Could be either," Quentin said. "We've made enemies over the years, individually and as a unit. We do try, and mostly succeed, to keep our pictures out of the news, so if you two were recognized as SCU agents I'd be surprised. None of us is wearing an FBI jacket, so that isn't obvious. We are carrying weapons, though—handguns, and they mark us as likely cops."

"Yeah," Hollis said, "but right before you guys got here, we'd pretty much established that the shooter probably wasn't expecting *anybody* to be here, because he wouldn't have expected this victim to be found."

"You're assuming the shooter was the murderer," Diana said.

"I don't want to assume anything else," Hollis confessed. "Because we really don't need some random maniac with a high-powered rifle running around in this mountain wilderness shooting at us while we're trying to investigate—" She broke off, frowning.

"A less random maniac?" DeMarco murmured.

"You know what I mean. One killer in an area this remote I can just about buy. But not two of them."

"Unless it's a tag team," Quentin offered. "I still say it's unlikely, but the possibility has to be considered."

"It's a possibility I'd rather not think about," Hollis told him. "Besides, from all I've read and heard, that would be *seriously* unlikely."

"True. So, what would the killer gain by shooting?"

Diana said, "Maybe he wanted us to know he's been watching."

Hollis frowned at her. "But he couldn't have known we'd *be* here, that's the point."

"Not only here," Diana told her. She realized she was being stared at and raised her eyebrows at DeMarco. "You think he is—or was—somewhere across the valley, right? And higher up than we are now?"

"Probably. I'm guessing at the trajectory of the shots, but it seems more likely than not."

"Well, then."

Quentin shook his head. "Sorry, Diana, but whatever's so obvious to you, the rest of us seem to be missing."

"Don't you guys know where we are?"

"In relation to what? Other than being on the side of one of these mountains, I don't really—" Quentin frowned suddenly.

Diana was nodding. "If he was across the valley and higher up, then he had a bird's-eye view of the dump site where the *other* victim was discovered. We're not that far away, and the other site faces south, just like this one does. With the shooter across the valley, facing north, he could easily cover both sites. He's probably been watching all day."

New York City

FBI Director Micah Hughes stared rather sourly at a famous painting of nymphs frolicking, barely conscious of other visitors to the museum wandering in and out of this room. He was more aware of the uniformed guard who strolled through in seemingly casual but exquisitely precise intervals of eight and a half minutes and even more aware of strategically placed cameras.

The museum knew all the tricks required to guard its treasures.

"Relax, Micah. Anyone would think you were planning to rob the place."

Hughes didn't relax. He also didn't turn his head, and he kept his voice low. "You usually pick less-public meeting spots. And I don't like the idea of turning up on a security tape talking to you. No offense."

"None taken. You don't have to worry about any type of recording. That part of the system is undergoing routine maintenance for the next half hour."

"And I'm supposed to...trust that information is accurate?" He'd nearly said "take your word for it," but had managed to stop himself just in time.

"I would, if I were you." The very distinctive voice was pleasant.

But when Hughes stole a quick glance at his companion, he noted that the half smile on that handsome face was more dangerous than it was reassuring and that those regular features gave nothing else away. The man was tall, slender but broad-shouldered and athletic, and could have been any age between fifty and sixty-five. Whatever his age, his vitality was obvious, and there clung to him an ineffable air of power.

One of the movers and shakers of the world, Hughes knew. He also knew that few people would have recognized the man's name, and fewer still his face. He had been very successful at keeping a low public profile for a very long time.

Hughes concentrated on what he needed to say. "Look, I've done everything you asked of me."

"Yes, you have. Thank you."

"And I've done everything you asked of me because I believed it was in the best interests of the Bureau and this country to rein in Noah Bishop and his unit of mavericks and misfits." It was a clear and concise statement, and Hughes was proud of it. He'd been practicing it in his head for weeks.

He had not acted out of malice. He had not acted out of jealousy or resentment. He had not acted out of greed. And he most certainly had not acted out of fear. That was what he wanted to make absolutely clear to the other man.

"Nothing has changed, Micah. Bishop is still a danger. His unit is still a danger."

"I'm not so sure of that. Not anymore."

"Why? Because they managed to stop Samuel, killing him in the process?"

"They didn't kill him."

"Someone else may have held the knife, but they most certainly destroyed him. And you know it."

"I don't know what happened in the Compound, and neither do you. I have Bishop's report, backed up by his team and by the local chief of police, that Samuel was stabbed to death by one of his followers.* No other witness has stepped forward to dispute what happened. I also have boxes of evidence that Samuel was responsible for more murders than I want to think about, including that of the daughter of a United States senator."

"Micah—"

"Whatever you want to say about it, however you choose to view it, Bishop and his team stopped a serial killer. One of many they've stopped. That is beyond dispute."

The other man was silent for a moment, then said, "So he's finally won you over, I see."

Hughes paused as the guard strolled through the room several feet away from the two men, then said evenly, "I don't like Bishop. I believe he's arrogant and ruthless, that he has a tendency to play by his own rules rather than the rule of law, and I profoundly distrust these . . . paranormal abilities claimed by him and by his agents."

"But he's successful. And that's enough for you."

"He gets results. Positive results. He catches, cages, or otherwise destroys killers who are, without any doubt, a menace to public

---

*Blood Sins

38

safety. He does it without fanfare, keeping himself and his people out of the media as much as possible, and he does it without making the Bureau look bad, to the public or to other law enforcement agencies. If anything, the work of his unit has improved the image of the FBI in recent years. And we needed it."

"I see," the other man repeated. "You've taken the time to read all the files in more detail."

Hughes could feel himself beginning to sweat. "I didn't want to let my dislike color my judgment. So, yes, I've gone back over the entire history of the SCU. Studied Bishop's record and those of the agents in his unit."

"You were impressed."

"They're an impressive group of people. Mavericks, yes. Misfits, certainly. Most if not all of them have seriously traumatic events in their pasts that should, at the very least, have rendered them unsuitable and even unfit for law-enforcement work."

"That alone should tell you—"

"All passed the standard Bureau psychological evaluation and have passed all follow-up evaluations. Whatever happened to them, they've coped extraordinarily well with the trauma. In addition to that, Bishop has set as a requirement for his team regular physical evaluations, from medical to strength and endurance. Those people are tested at every level, far beyond Bureau standards or requirements. As a group they're some of the most healthy and fit agents in the Bureau." Hughes hesitated, then added, "They're even assessed by a group of researchers I had no idea worked within the Bureau. Paranormal researchers."

The other man let out a short, derisive laugh.

Hughes refused to allow himself to sound defensive when he said, "I'm told that particular group has been a part of the Bureau since the middle of the last century, during the Cold War, when it seems every major power was conducting legitimate research into the paranormal."

"Governments fund *crackpot* research all the time, Micah, and we both know it. But ours didn't get far with its remote-viewing experiments, did it?"

Hughes was more than a little surprised at that, though wondered why he was. In a know-your-enemies sense, his companion had quite probably looked into the history of paranormal research. He was, after all, a careful, thorough man.

"The remote-viewing experiments were less than successful," Hughes admitted. "But other experiments have shown more promise. And I'm told that Bishop's unit has produced a staggering amount of raw data from the field as well as in the lab, enough to keep the researchers busy for decades."

"My tax dollars at work."

Hughes ignored the scorn. "I don't pretend to understand any of it and, as I said, I profoundly mistrust the very concept of psychic abilities, much less psychic abilities used as investigative tools. But Bishop has indisputably made it work; his success rate is in the ninetieth percentile. And his unit functions as a team better than any other unit in the Bureau."

"Which is enough for you."

"I'm the Director of the FBI. The successes and failures of my agents reflect well—or badly—on my judgment. And in my judgment, the Special Crimes Unit *must* be considered an unqualified success."

"Micah—"

"All these months, and I've got nothing—absolutely nothing—I can use even to reprimand Bishop, let alone bust him."

The other man took a step so that he faced Hughes more squarely and said, "You're taking heat, aren't you? You've been warned to back off."

Shit.

"Senator LeMott." It clearly was not a guess.

"I told you he was a powerful man. But it isn't only him. From all I can gather, Bishop made a deliberate effort even before he formed his unit to cultivate the sort of connections he could call on for support. People inside *and* outside the Bureau, in the government and in the private sector. Very important, very influential people. And they appear to support him without reservation."

After a pause, the other man said, "I could ruin you, Micah."

Hughes refused to flinch or look away. "Yes, you could. But it wouldn't change anything, not for you. Because I can virtually guarantee you that any successor of mine would also support Bishop and the SCU. Unless and until he does something unacceptable to the FBI, he will not be interfered with. Not by us."

For a long, long moment, Hughes wasn't sure what would break the stalemate. And then, completely expressionless, the other man turned and walked away.

Hughes watched him go. Watched the guard stroll through the room, casual and anything but. Then he turned in a different direction and made his way out of the museum, keeping his expression neutral, slightly preoccupied. When he was outside, he walked half a block to where his car and driver waited and got in.

Only then did he relax. Just a bit. The driver, without asking, started the car and pulled out of the space.

Hughes drew in a breath and let it out slowly, wondering, not for the first time, if he had chosen the wrong line of work. He reached for his cell phone and punched in a number from memory. It was answered on the first ring.

"Bishop."

"We need to talk," Micah Hughes said. "Now."

Three

DOGS," SHERIFF DUNCAN OFFERED. "Not 'til to-morrow, of course, but at first light. With people getting lost in these mountains as often as they do, we have nearly a dozen canine search-and-rescue teams in the area, and they have a very high success rate. They can track just about anything or any-one. The SOB *must* have left a trail from those bodies to wherever he was perched out there today. And since the rain's holding off, dogs should be able to pick up on it."

Chief Deputy Scanlon added, "Three of the teams have handlers trained by law enforcement and they're licensed to carry, so they wouldn't be going out there unarmed."

"He won't be hanging around," Quentin pointed out, "so what would be the use? I'm betting he policed the area and gathered up his spent shells, as well as any other evidence that showed he was there. This guy is a pro, and a pro isn't going to leave evidence for us to find."

"Defeatist." Shaking his head, DeMarco added, "Not that I don't agree with you. Waste of manpower. He's long gone, at least from that spot."

Quentin nodded. "I'm also betting that if we wanted to waste

42

manpower and go looking, we'd find an old deer blind or something of the sort, a place he could have spent the day in relative comfort."

Probably almost as comfortable as they were now, Quentin reflected. Because they weren't all that comfortable. The "conference room" of the Pageant County Sheriff's Department was barely large enough to house a table that just about seated the six of them—if you didn't mind keeping your elbows tucked in and could bear office chairs so old that with the slightest movement of their occupants they shrieked instead of creaked.

Scanlon leaned against the doorjamb; the room couldn't fit another deputy.

There was one small and lonely window, its dusty blinds closing out the night that had come with the suddenness typical for springtime in the mountains. There were two tall filing cabinets crammed into one corner. Two shorter ones near the door provided a reasonably clear surface for a chuckling coffeemaker, a motley collection of mugs—most imprinted with high school or college team emblems or rude or arguably witty slogans—and the disposable conveniences of paper sugar packets, powdered "creamer," and plastic stirrers.

Not that anyone at the table had moved toward coffee that would likely, Quentin thought, taste like something drained off an engine.

Shoved up against the walls in another corner was an old slate-topped desk, which took up way too much space and was used, apparently, only to provide a surface for an ancient printer, a tall and leaning stack of yellowed file folders, two disconnected keyboards, and a shiny new multiline office phone.

The phone wasn't plugged in.

Quentin was sure he had worked in more depressing rooms, but he could not at the moment call any of them to mind.

Sheriff Duncan had already apologized for the deficiencies of the old building and this cramped room, even suggesting that they could probably commandeer the dining room of the bed-and-breakfast he had recommended for the duration of their stay.

"Please," he had said, "don't stay at the motel. The roaches tend to carry away your shoes in the night."

Miranda had gravely accepted the advice, allowing one of Duncan's part-time deputies to call and book the necessary rooms for her team and another to transport the agents' overnight/weekender luggage to the B&B. But she insisted that for this first real meeting of the group, the sheriff's conference room was fine.

"It's been a long day and we're all tired anyway. We can start fresh in the morning, maybe at the B&B if the management doesn't mind."

"I'll call Jewel—Jewel Lawson, the owner and housekeeper. I'm sure she won't mind. Your group will all but fill the place up anyway, and there won't be any other guests to disturb."

"Thanks, Sheriff."

"Call me Des, please. All of you. We're pretty damn informal here, as you've seen. Hell, I have only six full-time deputies, plus a handful of part-timers I don't even allow to carry guns." He shook his head. "We're so in over our heads with this one it's pathetic."

"That's the truth," Scanlon murmured.

"Don't beat yourself up about it," Quentin advised them. "Nobody's really prepared when monsters come to visit. You just hope they're passing through and go away soon."

"Leaving as few bodies as possible behind them?" Duncan said.

"That's the idea. With a little luck, we won't need to stay more than a night or two in this B&B of yours."

But restless as cops tended to be with a job at hand—wanting to get at the thing even though there wasn't, as yet, much to work with—they weren't in any hurry to get out to the B&B and settle in.

DeMarco said, "With the remains on their way to the state medical examiner and no hit yet on either set of prints, all we've got is speculation. And way too many questions."

Quentin nodded. "The biggest one in my mind—at the moment, at least—being why Reese and Hollis were shot at. If that was our killer, it was a boneheaded move, drawing attention to his presence."

"Maybe he panicked," Diana suggested.

"Maybe. But if we're right about the distances involved out there, this guy really is a pro, a trained sniper. And they aren't generally given to panic."

DeMarco, an experienced sniper in his previous military life, said, "It does take discipline. And discipline tends to breed patience."

"Or a reasonable facsimile of it," Miranda, a certified sharpshooter, agreed. "What bothers me is that the profile is wrong."

DeMarco was nodding. "If a sniper that good is going to kill, chances are it'll be with his rifle and scope, and from a maximum distance. Hands off, cold and clean, as per his training. Not up close and personal."

Miranda said, "Those people were all but butchered, and that's definitely up close and personal."

Diana said, "Maybe killing from a distance stopped being satisfying somewhere along the way. Maybe he decided to get his hands bloody."

"Serial killers do evolve," Miranda agreed.

Duncan stared at her. "Serial killers? Don't there have to be at least three killings with very similar M.O.s before anybody can declare there's a serial killer at work?"

Miranda looked steadily back at him. "That ongoing case I mentioned?"

"The one that had you over in North Carolina this morning, before I called? What about it?"

"It may turn out to be the same case, Des."

Duncan looked around the table at the other agents, one at a time, then focused on her face. "There've been more bodies, more victims? Found like these two people were?"

"Found in similar ways, at dump sites in three states. Victims who were tortured before death."

The sheriff was scowling. He leaned back a bit, swore beneath his breath when his chair groaned loudly, and said, "I admit I don't know much about torture, but we've all heard more than we'd like to about it in recent years. I gather this isn't the sort of torture done to get information?"

Miranda shook her head. "As far as we've been able to determine, the victims possessed no valuable information on any subject of interest, no connections or ties to organized crime or the military or any paramilitary or terrorist organization. They were average, ordinary, everyday citizens, innocent of anything except whatever it was about them that drew the attention of a killer. A killer who apparently likes to watch his victims suffer."

"Jesus Christ." Duncan looked more than a little queasy. "You hear about that kind of thing, see it in the news, but you never expect it to turn up in your own backyard."

"We don't know that it has, especially given this new wrinkle of a pro with sniper training. There's been no sign of those particular skills up to now. But it's a possibility, especially if these two victims have no connection to each other and no discernible enemies."

"So what you're telling me is that either your serial killer has wandered into—or through—my little town or else I have a home-grown killer on the wrong side of sanity with a pretty vicious grudge against this man and woman." Duncan frowned suddenly. "A man and woman who, so far, haven't turned up on any missing persons reports in the area; I have one of my deputies sifting, for at least the third time, through reports going back a month."

"The male victim was probably alive and well yesterday," Miranda reminded him, "so may not have been missed yet, especially if he lived alone or took regular business trips. The woman, on the other hand..."

"Dead at least a few days," DeMarco contributed. "Maybe as long as a week. Even if she lived alone and had no family, she most likely had a job and should have been missed by now."

Hollis leaned forward, winced as her chair protested loudly, and said, "Maybe we haven't cast out a large enough net. These were clearly dump sites, and we have no way of knowing where the vics were actually killed; there's nothing to say they're even local."

"True," Miranda agreed. "It was certainly true of at least three of the previous victims, assuming the same killer. Until we get positive I.D.s, we have no way of knowing where they belonged. We should check missing persons reports in a radius of at least a hundred miles."

"For starters," Quentin murmured.

"I have my people on that already," the sheriff said. "We'll expand the search, though."

Several chairs squawked as their occupants moved restlessly, and Miranda rose with a rueful smile. "In the meantime, I think we've done all we can for today. The B&B is just up the street, isn't it?"

"Yeah, three blocks up the hill, an easy walk. And you've got two good restaurants between here and there, both serving decent food and both keeping reasonable hours."

"We may decide to take your suggestion and set up a kind of command center at the B&B, assuming it's okay with the management, and the technical specs allow us to use our laptops and other electronics. I'll call you in the morning and let you know."

As the others rose to the accompaniment of creaks and groans, Duncan sighed and said, "I think that's your best bet. We have some fairly undependable high-speed Internet access here, but Jewel's place was renovated a couple years back and she installed all the latest tech stuff, including wireless."

"Sounds good. You know where we are if anything new turns up overnight; otherwise, we'll see you in the morning."

Duncan escorted the agents as far as his small bullpen, where one of his part-time deputies, without the sense to even try to look professional, was leaned back in his chair, feet up on his desk, reading a magazine. A second part-timer was staring intently at her computer monitor.

The two full-time deputies for this shift were out on patrol.

Without bothering to remove his feet or put down his magazine, Dale McMurry said, "Somebody delivered rental SUVs for the agents, Sheriff. I was told to say they're parked out front, keys under the mats."

Before Duncan could think too much about "rental" vehicles in a town that didn't boast a rental company or ask any questions about who had delivered said vehicles, Miranda said pleasantly, "We'll just leave them out front tonight, if they won't be a bother parked there."

"No, no bother. Lock 'em up, but they shouldn't be disturbed here overnight. See you folks in the morning."

As the doors closed behind the agents, McMurry said plaintively, "I thought feds always wore them jackets with *FBI* written in huge letters on the back."

Bobbie Silvers said, "You watch too much TV. This is a small town, and they don't want to stand out any more than they have to."

I'm going to lose her to some outfit in a much larger town. Duncan sighed and said to her, "Any luck?"

"No, sorry, Sheriff. I've been through all the calls we've gotten in the last month—four times now, just to be sure I didn't miss anything—and not a single still-missing person is in here."

"Okay. Reach out to the surrounding counties, at least a hundred-mile-radius. Sheriff's departments, police departments, highway patrol. And the state bureau too. Find out who's on their missing-persons list and whether any of the names might even possibly match up with our victims."

"Will do, Sheriff."

"Neil, you go on home and get some rest," Duncan told his chief deputy. "I'll need you back here first thing tomorrow."

"Right."

McMurry said, "What about me?"

Duncan stared at him. "You get your feet off the desk, Dale. And then I want you to find some WD-40 and go into the conference room and oil every one of those goddamn chairs."

BJ watched.

The building was old, its bricks musty and, on this northern side that would be shadowed even in daylight, smelling faintly of damp. But in the little-used alleyway between it and the building beside it, he was surrounded by darkness and felt sheltered.

Protected.

He watched them as he'd learned long ago to watch a dog whose temperament he was uncertain of, almost from the corner of his eye rather than directly. He glanced at them and then away, allowed his gaze to roam among them without lingering, avoiding a stare that one or more of them would likely sense.

They were special, and he had to be careful; he had learned that much today.

But it was surprising how much one could see only in glances.

Five of them, wearing casual clothing designed to help them blend in or, at the very least, not stand out as feds. Two men, three women. Mostly, he judged, in their thirties, people who moved with the ease of those comfortable inside their trained and active bodies. Strolling along the sidewalk, moving slowly up the hill toward the B&B where he knew they would be staying, at least for tonight.

They had stopped at one of the two restaurants along the way from the sheriff's department, sitting at one table near the front window as they ate and talked among themselves. He had seen a few smiles but judged that they had not engaged in a great deal of meaningless social conversation.

He wondered if, in another place or time, they would be friends.

Still, there was a look about them he recognized. Like soldiers in the same battle unit or cops walking the same beat, they were all focused on the same things, the same tasks and information. And they carried that air about them no matter how relaxed they might appear, that inner wariness and tension, that alertness to their surroundings.

To danger.

The slightly taller of the two men was the least successful at hiding the coiled spring of readiness inside him. Every move he made—even simply walking with a cat-footed lightness—gave it away. He had good instincts, very good instincts. And quite probably more than mere instincts.

Otherwise he never would have been able to save the Templeton woman's life.

"Take her out if you get the chance."

More than one chance had come and gone. But there would doubtless be another.

He watched them walking away from him. It was a short street, all things considered, with short small-town blocks that city blocks would have sneered at, and he was able to watch the group, without leaving the shelter of his alley, all the way to the B&B.

An easy building to get inside. He had, the previous night, and had taken the time to look around, so he was completely familiar with the layout. Just in case.

He watched them go up the steps to the wide front porch and linger momentarily in the welcoming light at the door before being invited inside. The door closed behind them, and they passed from his view.

Just about to turn and go on to other chores scheduled for tonight, he was halted by a glimpse of movement in the shadows of the sidewalk near the B&B. He had to narrow his gaze and concentrate intensely, but within seconds he made out the shape of another watcher flitting along in the dark and quiet wake of the feds.

He wasn't sure if the other watcher was a man or a woman; whoever it was clung to the shadows as though a part of them, giving away little of any other substance or shape. And when that moving shadow settled down at last, it was in one corner of the small front yard the B&B boasted, among tall shrubbery and inside the wrought-iron fence that was more decorative than protective.

A car drove quietly past, and the watcher noted that the other one was so completely hidden by the shrubbery or by skill that even the passing headlights failed to expose him—or her.

He hesitated a moment longer than he should have, then withdrew slowly back through the alley to where he had parked his own car, mentally adding another player to the game. An unknown player, with unknown motives.

Interesting...

It was nearly ten o'clock that evening when Miranda stepped from her room out onto the second-floor balcony that wrapped three sides of the Victorian-era building. She wasn't yet dressed for bed, which was a good thing since the temperature hovered just a few degrees above freezing. Comfortable in her sweater and jeans, she leaned against the high railing and looked up and down the very quiet, softly lit Main Street of Serenade.

"Like a postcard, isn't it?" The low voice came from behind her, near the corner of the building where the balcony turned along its side. "The perfect come-and-visit-us view the chamber of commerce wants the outside world to see."

Miranda didn't look around but replied quietly, "They so often do, these sweet little towns—look picture-postcard perfect and so inviting. Maybe that's why the monsters hunt in them." It was a truth she had learned several years before.*

"Yeah. Isolated geographically and technologically. Where, even if people lock their doors, the locks are easy to pick or break and the only other security consists of the family dog sleeping at the foot of the bed. A town small enough that most know their neighbors but not so small that strangers are seen as a threat—especially

---

Out of the Shadows

since they bring tourist dollars when they come to visit the Blue Ridge."

"Not many visit here, I'd say. Only a couple more B&Bs in the area, both smaller than this one."

"And one fleabag motel. Yeah, I saw that."

"Figured you would. What else did you see?"

"You guys were being watched. All the way from the sheriff's department. While you were in the restaurant too."

"The alley on the other side of the street?"

"Yeah, he's not as bright as he thinks. Which does not, of course, make him any less dangerous. More so, probably. I let him catch a glimpse of me just to give him pause. Not enough to I.D. me, of course. Anyway, he's at that fleabag motel. Paid cash, used an alias to check in. John Smith, if you can believe that. I'm figuring he's down for the night."

"Was he today's shooter?"

"Pretty sure."

"You found his vantage point?"

"Gabe did." Gabriel Wolf was a Haven operative. As was his twin sister, Roxanne. And they formed a unique team.

"Was Quentin right?"

"Yeah. An old hunter's blind. No real evidence to be found, including foot-, tire-, or hoofprints. Nothing in the blind worth taking to court except one little smudge Gabe believes could have been made by binoculars."

"So we were watched all day."

"Seems likely. The guy must have hiked in and out, sticking to all the granite outcroppings and ridges to avoid leaving prints. And judging by how good he was at that, and how twisty and difficult his path must have been, our guess is he's determined and disciplined as hell and he knows his way around these parts."

"This area specifically?"

"Yeah."

"Then he probably isn't the killer we've been tracking."

"Unless you find something that more strongly ties the bodies here to those we've been following, our guess is not. The one thing our killer's previous dump sites have in common is that they were handy to roads. The two vics today, not so much. But that isn't really good news. Given the distance between his position and the second dump site, this guy today is a pro sniper, and I mean a well-trained and well-equipped one. Probably military at some point, maybe recently. And soldiers with his type of skills tend not to stop the work just because they take off the uniform."

"A private contractor."

"The war created a lot of them. And with the current lousy economy, legit jobs are getting harder to come by."

"Paid assassin?"

"That's our take. DeMarco is a better person to ask about that sort of thing, but it makes sense given the skill necessary to even attempt that shot today. If we're right, Hollis may have a price on her head. It's the simplest explanation. Thing is—"

"The simplest explanation," Miranda finished, "is seldom the right one in our world. For one thing, why single out Hollis? She's taken the brunt of things more often than any other agent, but not usually because she was on the offensive. She's stayed out of the spotlight. She's made enemies the unit has made, but not on her own behalf. She's never been a primary agent on any investigation, not so far, and we haven't sent her in undercover. Under wraps for all the good that did, but not undercover."

"There's that. All that. What we can't get past is that he watched all day. Hollis was visible a lot of that time, close to motionless long enough and often enough to give him a clear shot—if that was his only goal, his only reason for waiting out there all day. But he did wait. Until late in the day and after the second victim was found. Almost as if that was what he was waiting for."

"Maybe hoping we wouldn't find that victim. Or maybe what Diana suggested. Mind games."

"Could be. Especially if he recognized any of you as belonging to the SCU." There was a pause, and then, wryly, "It's getting a bit like the Old West these days, only in your case the hotshot young gunslinger riding into town to challenge the famous veteran is a twisted serial killer eager to pit his smarts and skills up against the SCU."

"I really hope that isn't the case."

"Yeah."

Miranda was silent for long minutes, her gaze roaming absently up and down the quiet, peaceful scene of Main Street, Small Town, USA. Finally she said, "If Hollis was the target, she's become a threat to someone. A very specific threat to a very specific someone. And I'm finding it difficult to believe that would be wholly unconnected to our investigation these last weeks."

"It doesn't seem likely."

"No. It doesn't."

"If nothing else, the shooter could have been following you two as you pursued the investigation. Under orders not to do anything until..."

"That is the question, isn't it? Until what? Maybe...somewhere along the way, through some action or simply by her presence, Hollis became too much of a liability to the killer. And yet she has some of the least-invasive, least-threatening abilities. She's a medium and a self-healer, and she sees auras. Where's the threat in any of that?"

"Something we can't know until we find out who—or what—she threatens."

Miranda drew a deep breath and then allowed it to escape, misting in front of her face. "Yeah. And in the meantime, we have these murders to investigate."

"That we do."

"While we keep Hollis safe."

"Might be easier just to take the shooter out."

"Easier, but probably not the right call. Take him out and chances are somebody else will be sent to do the job. Somebody we might not see until too late. At least this guy is an enemy we've spotted, one we can keep an eye on."

"True. So we watch him? Stick close?"

"Like white on rice. And, Roxanne—be careful. Be very careful. You and Gabe both."

"Copy that. Get some rest tonight, will you? All you guys are running on fumes, and that is not a good thing."

"I know."

"You have guns. Dangerous things in sleep-deprived hands."

"And you've made your point."

"Good. We'll watch tonight. Time enough tomorrow to try to figure things out."

"I hope you're right," Miranda said.

"That you'll figure things out?"

"That we have time enough to do it."

For a long time now, Diana hadn't needed sedatives to sleep, but she still required time to wind down and something boring to occupy her mind while her body gradually relaxed and her nearly ever-present guard came down. The usual remedies, like a hot bath or shower and glass of warm milk, didn't do much for her.

For her, either a few games of solitaire—the old-fashioned way, with actual cards—or a boring documentary on TV tended to work more often than not.

On this particular night, it was "not." Weary though she was, nothing seemed to work.

Her room in the B&B, one of only three doubles with two queen-sized beds, looked out onto a pretty little courtyard at the rear of the building. It was pleasant and comfortable, and since each guest room was a suite with its own tiny sitting area and generous bathroom, and there were eight of the suites, each agent had his or her own space. That was not a little thing, they had discovered, to have some room and privacy during an investigation. It provided at least the illusion of normalcy.

Most of the time.

And it helped. Most of the time.

But Diana didn't think the problem tonight was her surroundings. She'd been on edge since she and Quentin joined this investigation a couple of weeks before, and she wasn't sure why. Maybe it was because this was the first real SCU case she'd been assigned, and she was still uncertain of her training and abilities.

Maybe it was because her relationship with Quentin was still tentative and wary.

Maybe it was the case itself, twisted and depressing as serial-murder investigations tended to be. With little evidence and few leads, she had the hollow feeling they were pretty much chasing their own tails, waiting for a break in the case that might never happen, while viciously murdered and tortured victims were being cast aside like garbage and contemptuously left for them to find.

Contemptuously?

It was an easy guess, she decided, requiring no particular skill as a profiler—which she wasn't. But she had begun reading up on the subject, as she was reading up on so many others, and what stuck in her mind was the accepted fact that most if not all serial killers developed and followed very specific, unique rituals—many involving burial or whatever means they chose to dispose of bodies. Some rituals were even weirdly respectful, with victims dressed in clean clothing and laid out in carefully dug graves.

This killer very clearly didn't see his victims as people deserving of any respect, not before death and not after.

Diana realized she was endlessly shuffling her deck of playing cards and tossed them aside with a half-conscious curse. She leaned against the pillows banked behind her and stared across the room at an old, mostly black-and-white documentary on TV about World War II.

So he feels contempt for his victims. No big surprise there. Nothing helpful there. Miranda probably had that little bit of information nailed with the first victim. If not before.

The real problem, she decided reluctantly, was that she felt pretty damn useless. Despite intensive training over the last months, she didn't feel qualified to investigate a single murder, let alone a string of them. Even as . . . just one of the team. Not only had she never been any sort of cop, but her entire adult life—right up until little more than a year ago—was more dreamlike than real in her mind.

Except for scattered instances of a psychic ability she was still coming to terms with—which had been notably absent for weeks now—she had literally sleepwalked through her life.

And Diana wasn't entirely sure she wasn't still doing that, at least some of the time. How else could she explain her very calm reactions today—to the bodies, the bear, Hollis nearly being shot?

Jesus, I didn't even ask Hollis if she was okay.

Not that Hollis had seemed all that concerned about getting shot at, but despite the other woman's casual friendliness and humor, Diana didn't think she knew any of the agents well enough to manage a decent guess at what they might be feeling at any given moment.

Except Quentin. Maybe.

But that wasn't what was really bothering her.

Am I still sleepwalking? Is that what's going on here? Why I feel so uneasy and uncertain all the time? So . . . out of place and unsure of myself? Given the opportunity to live a full life, to get into the game, did I opt out?

No matter what Quentin says, was Dad right when he said I wasn't cut out for this sort of job, right to believe I wouldn't be able to handle it? Is that why I've been so hesitant, so uncertain? Do I believe him?

Is that why I've been pushing Quentin away?

She didn't want to admit that might be true. Didn't even want to think it might be true.

Decided not to think about it at all.

Oh, yeah, that's the grown-up way to handle it. Just put your head in the sand.

She told her inner self to shut up and rummaged among the rumpled bedclothes for the TV remote. Then, determinedly keeping her mind blank, she began to channel-surf, looking for something even more boring than an old documentary about World War II.

Four

DIANA OPENED HER EYES SLOWLY, then sat up a lot faster, shoving the covers aside to sit on the edge of her bed.

Her bed—changed. Weirdly one-dimensional, a photograph without light or shadow. Like the room that was dull and without color or life or warmth. It was filled with that oddly flat, colorless twilight that was not day and not night but somewhere in between. She had always suspected that this place lay somewhere outside time, apart from what she knew and understood time to be. That it was something between the living world and whatever lay beyond it.

As far back as she could remember, she'd called it the gray time.

She turned her head and looked at the clock on her nightstand, which had boasted large red digital numbers in a readout easy to see. Now it was blank, featureless and numberless. All clocks were the same here, missing numbers or missing hands and numbers.

No time passed in the gray time. Funny, that.

Creepy.

Diana got out of bed, not bothering to find slippers or even socks, though her feet were cold; it was always cold in the gray time, and no amount of clothing or blankets had ever made a difference. Besides, she wasn't physically *here*, after all. At least—

She looked back, both relieved and, as always, unsettled to see herself still there in the undisturbed bed, sleeping, face peaceful. Her physical body breathed, its heart beat. It lived.

But everything that made her emotionally and psychologically Diana—her personality, her soul—no longer occupied that body. She couldn't see the thread connecting the two halves of herself but knew it existed. Knew how fragile it was. How easily it could be severed.

Yeah, great job scaring yourself. Stop thinking about what could happen. Just move.

"Remember all this in the morning. No matter what happens. There's no more forgetting now," she told her sleeping self, unsurprised by the hollow, almost echo of her voice. Normal, for the gray time. And so was the faint and faintly unpleasant smell.

Her own alert readiness and familiarity with this place was also normal, and she wondered as she always did why she never felt this sure of herself in the real world. It would make so many things so much easier, she thought, if she could feel this way all the time.

That rueful awareness had barely dawned when she started around the foot of the bed toward the door and was jolted to a stop by what she saw. "What the hell are you doing here?"

"Beats me," Hollis said, looking around her warily. She was standing just inside the door to the hallway. "This is your world, not mine. I was asleep in bed, minding my own business, a minute ago. I saw me there. Which was an experience I'd rather not repeat, thank you."

"I told you not to look back."

"Hey, I was curious. And at least I didn't turn into a pillar of salt, so, you know, thankful for that. Why'd you pull me in?"

"I didn't," Diana said slowly. "I've only done that once, when we tried it months ago—and I was surprised as hell that it worked."

"Then why am I here?"

"That was my question, remember?"

Hollis shivered and absently rubbed her bare arms. "Damn. If I'd known this was going to happen, I would have worn flannel pajamas instead of this nightgown."

Diana was about to explain that more clothing wouldn't have helped the chill, but then she took a second look and said, "Huh. That's an awfully...um...Not something you usually pack for a work trip, is it?"

"Can we just get on with it, please?"

"Get on with what?"

"Whatever it is I assume I'm here for."

"I don't *know* what you're here for. Or why I'm here, when I haven't been able to get here for weeks even when I tried."

"Something to do with the case, no doubt. The more deeply involved in an investigation we get, the more apt we are to find all our senses reacting—including the extra ones." Hollis shrugged. "At any rate, one thing I've learned in the SCU is that you take things as they come. We're here now, and there has to be a reason why we're here. What's your normal procedure? Just start walking and see where your guides—isn't that what you call them—take you?"

"Yeah, usually. If a guide shows up, that is."

"I don't think I'll ask what happens if no guide shows up. Just lead the way, will you? If I remember correctly, being here in your gray time is physically draining, and we were both tired to begin with."

"It's not *my* gray time." But Diana moved past Hollis and led the way from her room.

As soon as they stepped out into the hallway, it became apparent that they were no longer at the B&B.

"Oh, man, this is creepy," Hollis breathed.

Diana looked over her shoulder at the other woman. "I don't recognize this place. You do?"

"I hope not. I really, really hope not." Hollis didn't as a rule give much away in terms of her expression, but the strain in her voice was impossible to miss, and her eyes were huge.

Diana looked around them. They stood at what appeared to be an intersection of two seemingly endless corridors. Each corridor was hospital-clean and gleaming even in this dull gray twilight, and each was lined with closed doors that were all identically featureless with the exception of gleaming grayish handles.

"Looks ordinary enough to me," she said, returning her gaze to Hollis's very still face. "I mean, no weirder than other places I've visited in the gray time."

"But you've never been here before?"

"I don't think so. Why? Where is this place?"

Hollis drew a breath and let it out slowly. "The first time I saw it, I was in somebody else's dream.* Found out later it's a real place. And the real place is . . . Once upon a time, it was an asylum. Back in October, I met the monster who was caged there. He strapped me down to a table, and . . ."

"Hollis?"

"And he almost killed me."

Reese DeMarco leaned on an elbow as he studied the map spread across his bed, his gaze moving intently from one highlighted spot to the next. Two of the highlights were close together and repre-sented the two bodies found in Pageant County today. Or, rather, the previous day, since it was after midnight now. The other six were spread farther apart, over three southeastern states.

He was looking for a pattern.

He wasn't finding one.

Not that it surprised him. The SCU was made up of serious and experienced monster hunters with the added edge of psychic abili-ties, and they were successful because they were very, very good; if a rational pattern in this madness had existed, the efforts of the rest of the team likely would have found it by now.

Blood Dreams

Eight murders committed in just over eight weeks. Five women, three men. All apparently tortured—with a singular creativity—before they were killed, and the most recent two further mangled and defiled after they were dead. No connection between the victims. No real enemies in any of their backgrounds individually, and virtually no commonalities among them as a group except for race: All had been white.

And all, with the exception of the most recent two, had been dumped like garbage by the side of various roads.

DeMarco frowned as he thought about that one more time. Until Serenade, the victims had been, as far as they could tell, shoved out of a car, possibly even a moving car.

Which, as Miranda had noted, pointed to the possibility of a second murderer, or at least an accomplice, since shoving a body out of a moving car was not an easy thing to do, and shoving one out of a stationary car required at least a few moments and some strength—or help.

That, more than anything else, had made this case, this investigation, unusual even for the SCU. One serial killer rampaging through their towns or counties was virtually always more than the local or state police could handle; they simply weren't set up, with the procedures, the equipment, or the personnel and experience, to track down a killer of that sort, especially if he was only passing through and had no connection to the area.

Two serial killers, or one with an accomplice, put them into a smaller category than the relatively small one of serial killer: A conspiracy to commit murder was rare, and a serial killer with a partner or a sidekick was even more so. Only a handful of such cases had ever been documented by law enforcement.

"We're keeping the possibility to ourselves for now," Miranda had told DeMarco earlier in the evening, just as she had told the other agents on the case. "As well as we can, anyway. No leaks to the media. Nothing written in our reports. We don't even discuss it among ourselves unless we're absolutely sure we're alone. And that includes not telling local police—unless and until we know the killers are in the area and we have a shot at finding them."

"You know there are two of them, don't you?" DeMarco had asked.

"We believe there's a good chance." *We* meaning she and Bishop. "But we're not certain, Reese. Until we are, we investigate this case according to procedure and the evidence, not speculation."

DeMarco had been about to remind her that they speculated all the time, when something she'd said before began to nag at him. "Nothing in our written reports? We don't let the Bureau in on what's going on?"

"We don't speculate in our reports about something we have little or no evidence to support."

He eyed her. "Oh, they are really not going to be happy with us about that."

"When we stop these killers, that'll be the only thing anybody who counts remembers about the investigation. That the killing was stopped."

"I doubt the Director will be one of those people."

"That's okay. There are others. Noah's spent a great deal of time and effort building a network of support, and that network will hold. No matter what the Director thinks."

"And what about Bishop's enemy? Whoever's been reporting SCU movements back to the Director since—what—last summer? If we don't know who that was—or is—we can hardly stop the leaks. And if we mean to withhold info from the Bureau, we damn sure need to make sure they don't catch us doing it."

Miranda hesitated, then said, "Noah's working to resolve that situation. It's one reason he's not here. Until he does, we're doing what we can to keep a low profile and not draw undue attention to the SCU."

"On a serial-murder case with six certain and two possible victims already? Good luck with that."

"We've managed so far. The local police have been willing to work with us, willing to not…overreact…to a body dumped in their jurisdictions, especially since none of the victims have turned out to be local citizens. Since the victims have been dumped over so large an area, *and* since no single police department or sheriff's department has had to cope with more than one, media attention has been minimal and brief."

"But we've got two possible victims in the same area this time."

"Yes."

"Somebody's going to connect the dots soon enough, Miranda. You know that. There's a story here."

"Yes. And an even bigger story if word breaks that we suspect a pair of killers. Which is why we keep that quiet as long as we possibly can."

DeMarco shook off the memory of that conversation and frowned once again down at the map, this time not really looking at it. He felt oddly…cold…all of a sudden, tense and alert in a way he recognized, every sense flaring, expanding beyond himself to seek out and pinpoint a threat of some kind. He looked up, scanned the room warily. But nothing seemed out of place or otherwise amiss.

Pleasant bedroom, neat and attractive without being overly fussy, which suited him. The TV was on and tuned to MSNBC but muted.

He had removed his shoulder holster, of course, when he at least nominally turned in for the night, but his weapon lay within easy reach. Reaching out slowly, he put his hand on it but didn't draw it from the holster.

Because everything he felt told him the threat he sensed was not anything a bullet could stop.

DeMarco didn't particularly like to think about many of his experiences in the military, but they had certainly left him with sharpened instincts in addition to his psychic ones. In those days, it had meant the difference between dying—and coming out alive to not talk about it.

These days it meant a sense that was not quite psychic telling him something was off-kilter around him.

Shit. With my luck, this place is haunted.

But he didn't think that was it. He wasn't particularly sensitive to spirits, for one thing, and for another this didn't feel like a threat to himself but to someone or something else.

DeMarco's unique double shield made him hypersensitive to the various energies associated with paranormal abilities, but only when he allowed the outer, protective shield to drop and concentrated on using what made the inner shield so remarkable: If his focus was good enough, he could either make that second shield vastly stronger and more impenetrable or else turn it into a kind of magnet that drew in and interpreted—so to speak—psychic energies.

He couldn't steal anyone else's ability, but he could hamper their power to project anything forceful outward, and he could tune in to whatever frequency was being used.

"Like a radio," Quentin had once noted helpfully. "And every other psychic is on a different channel."

Which simplified an ability that was incredibly complex but defined it well for all of that.

DeMarco was pretty sure somebody in the house was experiencing psychic phenomena. What he wasn't sure of was whether that person was a threat—or was being threatened.

Either way, it didn't bode well.

Swearing under his breath, DeMarco sat on the edge of the bed, then closed his eyes and began to concentrate, dropping his outer shield completely and attempting to tune in to whatever was happening.

Almost immediately, he was hit with a wave of stark terror.

Frowning, Diana said, "October? That was when you guys were tracking the killer of all those women in Boston, including Senator LeMott's daughter, right?"

"Yeah. The monster in this place—or a place identical to this—was the killer."

"Who was taken out of circulation. Locked up."

"Oh, yeah."

"Then why are we here?"

Hollis drew another of those get-a-grip breaths and said, "The end of that case turned out not to be. It was connected to what happened later, in January, in Grace."

"In North Carolina. The church, Samuel. Yeah, that was the party I didn't get invited to."

"Be glad. We lost some good people there, and very nearly lost a lot more."

Diana didn't like to think of Quentin—of the *team*—in danger, but she had read the reports and knew what had happened. She knew how terribly high a price had been demanded of them in order to stop that killer.

"Samuel is dead. The church now is made up of a group of mostly bewildered people who aren't even sure they want to be a church anymore, none of them a killer and none claiming apocalyptic visions. It's over."

"Maybe not," Hollis said, staring down each of the endless, featureless hallways in turn. "Maybe we only thought it was over."

"Hollis—"

"Shouldn't there be a guide by now?"

"Maybe. Sometimes I have to walk a bit on my own before I find them. Or they find me."

"I really don't want to explore these hallways, Diana."

"Hollis, this isn't real. I mean, it's like a dream; we aren't here in the flesh. Nothing can hurt us here."

"Nice try, but I know enough about your gray time to know that if our spirits—our consciousness—get trapped here, somehow cut off from our bodies, then we don't come back."

It was another reminder of something Diana didn't like to think about, but she nodded reluctantly. "Yeah, but I'm pretty sure that's rare. Besides, I can handle it. I've been doing this nearly all my life, and I've never *not* found my way back out."

"First time for everything."

"You had to say it."

"Sorry. Diana, I find your gray time unnerving enough in concept, but to be here in *this* place is . . . Let's just say I've been in some majorly scary situations, and this one is right up there with the worst of them."

"Okay, then, we leave. Now." Diana gripped her fellow agent's wrist and said, "Close your eyes and concentrate on the place you want to get back to. Your room in the B&B."

Hollis wavered visibly. "We might learn something here—"

"Fear is weakness, and neither one of us wants to be weak here, trust me on that. We're going back."

Hollis closed her eyes and kept them closed as long as she could. Did her best to concentrate, to focus. But the stillness of the place, the faint odd smell that made her think of rotten eggs and maybe a place too close to hell, the cold that seeped into her very bones, all of it worked on her nerves so that she finally opened her eyes. "Diana?"

"Concentrate."

"We're still here."

Diana opened her eyes and looked around. Steadily, she said, "Okay, then it looks like we have to stay long enough to see what we were brought here to see."

"Great. That's just great."

Still seemingly utterly calm and comfortable in this unnatural place, Diana said, "I'm not going to let you go. We're going to start walking until we find whatever it is we're meant to find here." She waited for Hollis's nod, then chose a hallway, apparently at random, and began to walk.

Hollis didn't question the choice. She was totally out of her element here and had to trust that Diana's experience would lead them—and lead them safely.

Diana tried the doors one by one as they reached them, but each one was locked. The hallway continued to stretch before them, seemingly infinite, with door after door locked and impenetrable.

After a while Hollis began to be more conscious of her weariness than of her fear. Every step required more effort, a heaviness dragging at her. Her breathing grew more labored, and she felt a bit light-headed.

Diana, who appeared to be unaffected, looked back at her with a frown as she paused in the middle of the corridor. "I've got to get you out of here."

"You won't get an argument." Hollis tried not to huff and puff as she said it.

Down the corridor a bit, one of the doors swung inward with a faint but audible creak.

"Oh, that can't be good," Hollis said.

"Maybe it's the way out."

"Yeah, right. They always make that mistake in horror movies. Let's not, okay?"

Diana hesitated, then said, "My instincts are telling me to go that way, Hollis. To step through that doorway. All my experience is telling me the same thing. I've got to get you out, and right now that looks like the only viable option."

Hollis allowed herself to be pulled along as Diana headed for the door, but said, "You should talk to Dorothy. Ruby slippers. Click your heels, there's no place like home. All that jazz."

"Yeah, I need a reliable shortcut out. I get it," Diana said. "So far, though, I've been at the mercy of the guides pretty much. And when I've *had* to get out, I've gotten out."

"Wasn't Quentin your lifeline a couple of times?"

"Yes. But I survived on my own doing this for twenty-some-odd years before he came along."

"No need to bristle. I was just asking." Hollis was staring at the partially open door they were approaching, most of her attention on that.

The way out?

Or a doorway leading to something infinitely worse?

Hollis did her best to tamp down a rising, unreasoning panic. Not that there was no reason to be afraid in this otherworldly place, this gray time, where everything was outside her experience. But the degree of fear was something she had never felt before. And considering everything she had experienced since a horrifically violent event had changed her life forever, that was an unsettling realization.

Why was that partially open door scaring the shit out of her? What were her own instincts or senses trying to tell her?

Diana said, not quite defensively, "I was not bristling. I just . . . I don't want to have to depend on Quentin like that."

"Okay, I get that, I do. Now, are you absolutely sure we need to walk through that door? Because I've got an awful feeling that whatever is waiting for us in there is not a good thing." She intended to add a few stronger sentiments but stopped, frowning.

"Hollis?"

"That's odd. Really odd. It feels almost like something is pulling at me." She looked down at Diana's hand on her arm, then shook her head. "Not you. Something . . . I'm sorry, Diana, I—" Hollis vanished, there one instant and gone the next, like a soap bubble.

Her first realization was that she was so tired, moving hardly seemed worth the effort. *Breathing* hardly seemed worth the effort. But Hollis did breathe and, eventually, did move. She fought to open her eyes. And fought to say something, if only in a whisper.

"Damn, that was—"

She was in her bed, that much she realized, if sluggishly. Strong arms were holding her, and against her cheek she could feel the steady beating of a heart.

Wait, that's not right.

It felt right, or at least it felt good, felt safe and maybe even something better than safe, but it was unfamiliar.

"Hollis?"

She caught her breath, then concentrated all the strength she could muster into the effort required to push herself away, to sit up in the bed on her own and stare at him.

"Reese? What the hell?"

"I think that's my question. Want to tell me where you were just now? Because a major part of you wasn't here." His hands remained on her shoulders for support.

She was sure it was for support.

"I was—wait. How did you get into my room?"

"I picked the lock."

Hollis blinked at him, trying mightily to get her sluggish mind moving with some semblance of normalcy. That struggle was complicated by the fact that she could see his aura, and it was so unusual in color and full of what she took to be sparks of flickering power that all she wanted to do was stare at it. "Why?" she managed to ask finally.

"It was the fastest way to get in here."

"That's not what I meant. Why did you have to get in here?"

"You were in trouble," he said, calm and matter-of-fact. His face was expressionless as always, though his pale blue eyes seemed to be darker than normal.

She blinked again. "I was?"

"You were afraid. Terrified. And weakening fast."

"Wait," she said again. "You were in my head?"

"Not exactly."

"Then what? Exactly?" She was feeling stronger. And she was feeling defensive.

DeMarco didn't seem disturbed by that.

"I could sense that something was wrong in the house, that the energy here had changed. It felt like a threat."

"And you're hypersensitive to threats," she remembered.

He nodded. "So I focused on that and realized the threat was directed at you. I knew you were in a bad place. I also knew you couldn't get out of there alone. So I came to help."

Hollis was trying to concentrate and finding it very difficult. "How did you know you could? I mean, where I was . . . That isn't a place you just walk into, not unless you're a medium. Hell, not unless you're Diana."

"Hollis—"

She felt a chill go through her and stared at him. "Diana couldn't find her way out. She tried—and couldn't. And where she is, that awful place . . . Oh, my God. What if he's dead? What if he's dead and back there torturing people all over again? Torturing souls this time? What if he has Diana strapped to that table now?"

Diana had no idea what had happened, but she didn't have a good feeling about it. At all. She hesitated there where Hollis had vanished, trying to decide whether she should continue on through that invitingly half-open door or turn back and make a concerted effort to get herself out of here.

"Diana."

She frowned at the grave young girl who had appeared as abruptly as Hollis had vanished. A guide she didn't recognize, though that wasn't at all unusual; she seldom encountered the same guide twice.

"Who're you?"

"I'm Brooke." The girl, who couldn't have been more than twelve or thirteen when she was alive, said reprovingly, "Diana, you aren't supposed to bring living people into the gray time. It's dangerous for them. And for you too."

"Is she okay?"

"Yes. This time."

"Look, I didn't intend to bring Hollis in."

"No. But you did once before. You brought her in deliberately. And that opened a channel."

Diana didn't like where this was heading. "You mean Hollis can turn up here whenever she likes?"

"No. I mean she can come here when you do. That she'll be drawn here when you open the door. Because it's her nature. She's a medium. The last person you should have brought in here."

"Shit."

"It's taken you a lifetime of experience to be able to come here and move around without losing all your strength. Without the constant danger of becoming trapped here. Hollis hasn't had that. She could get lost here. She could die here."

"I'll make sure that doesn't happen."

"Diana—"

With a gesture that swept aside the subject for the moment, Diana said, "Brooke, why am I here? Hollis said this place was where a killer was . . . kept. On the living side. But that's over. He isn't here now and he can't hurt anyone anymore."

Brooke shook her head and took a step back, then turned toward the partially opened door. "Everything's connected, Diana."

A typically guidelike response.

Diana followed but said, "Nothing like this has ever happened here in the gray time, not to me. What is it you need me to do for you?"

"I need you to find the truth."

"What truth? How you died?"

"No. It started long before I died. That's what you have to find. The truth buried underneath it all."

"Brooke, I don't understand what you mean."

"You will." The young guide walked through the open door.

Diana paused, drew a deep breath, and then followed.

To her surprise, she found she was back at the B&B, though it took her a moment to recognize the hallway in which she stood. She looked around, frowning, but finally oriented herself.

It was the hallway outside her room.

Brooke was gone.

Still, Diana was all too aware that her "trip" into the gray time was not over. Because she was still there. The hallway was gray and cold, everything still and peculiarly one-dimensional. The little side table between her door and the one to Quentin's room looked as if it was a part of the dull gray wall, and the prints hanging on the walls might have been grayish crayon smudges for all the depth they displayed.

She looked at Quentin's door for a moment, tempted, then told herself she had already been here too long. Her legs had that heavy sensation she recognized, and it was a bit harder to breathe than it should have been. She might not tire easily in the gray time but she did tire eventually, and when she did, the progression toward exhaustion was rapid.

She needed to leave.

With still little idea of why she had been brought into the gray time and feeling very frustrated about it, she went to her own bedroom door, opened it, and went inside.

Except it wasn't her room. It was Quentin's.

He was sitting on the edge of the bed and rose to smile at her. "Diana. I've been waiting for you."

She stared at him, aware of the niggling sense of something not right, something . . . off. "Have you?"

"Yes, of course."

"Why?"

"You know why. We belong together. I've been waiting for you to realize that. To accept it."

Diana was straining to listen, and with more than her ears, but it was difficult because she was growing colder and colder. And her strength felt as though it was draining away. As though someone had pulled a plug.

"You have to accept it," he said in a reasonable tone as he came toward her. "It's the way things have to be, Diana. I know what's best for you. You can trust me."

"No." She fumbled behind her, trying desperately to find the door handle. "No, I can't trust you."

"Diana—"

"You're not Quentin," she said.

Five

EVEN AS SHE SAID IT, his face began to change, to distort into something she instinctively recognized as evil, and the only thing Diana knew for certain was that she did not want to see what it would ultimately become.

Who it would become.

She scrabbled frantically behind her for the door handle, and her mind reached as well, everything inside her reached, for the way back, a way out, for safety.

Warm, strong fingers closed over hers.

Diana opened her eyes with a gasp to find herself sitting up in her bed, in her room.

She was staring at Quentin's face. Not gray and colorless, not a façade over something unspeakably evil, but warm and alive and *Quentin*.

He was sitting on the edge of the bed facing her, both his hands holding both of hers, watching her with that steady, rock-solid intentness that made her feel so safe and yet, on some deep and nameless level, so terribly uneasy.

"What happened?" she asked, unsurprised by the drained sound of her own voice.

"You tell us."

Diana looked quickly around to find that Hollis was sitting on the foot of the other bed in the room, wearing the somewhat sexy nightgown she had worn in the gray time. Except now she was also wearing one of the B&B's thick terry-cloth courtesy robes over it. She was paler than normal, and the skin around her blue eyes bore a shadowy, bruised appearance that made her look very fragile and very tired.

DeMarco leaned almost negligently back against the dresser a couple of feet behind her, dressed as he had been that day, in jeans and a white shirt. He looked wide awake and not in the least tired.

It was Hollis who had spoken.

"We were in the gray time," she said. "You and me."

Quentin said, "Something we'll talk about later."

Diana knew he was bothered and knew why, so she kept her gaze on Hollis. "I remember," she said slowly.

Hollis nodded. "We were in a . . . a very bad place."

"The hallways. All the doors. You said it had been an asylum."

"Yeah. What happened after I was pulled out?"

"How were you pulled out?"

Hollis sent a somewhat rueful glance over her shoulder at De-Marco. "Reese thought I was in trouble."

"I didn't think you were, I knew you were," he said imperturbably.

Diana looked at him. "And so you just . . . pulled her out?"

"It seemed the thing to do."

Diana studied that coldly handsome, impassive face, then returned her gaze to Quentin's much warmer and more expressive one. "That's . . . interesting."

"I thought so," Quentin said. But he was clearly unwilling to follow that interesting tangent, since he immediately added, "But what I want to know is how you two ended up at that old asylum. Especially since it's been razed to the ground."

Startled, Diana said, "It has? It doesn't exist anymore?"

"After what happened there, the property owners barely waited until all the evidence had been collected and it was declared no longer a viable crime scene before they sent in the bulldozers. The buildings were destroyed, and everything that could be burned was. The rest was buried, and buried deep. Last I heard, the plan was to haul tons of topsoil to the spot and plant trees for the forestry service. Nobody wants to build any other structure there. Ever."

She frowned. "I don't know if I've ever been taken in the gray time to a place that doesn't exist."

DeMarco pointed out, "You do call it the gray *time*—not the gray *place*. Must be a reason for that. It could be out of sync with our time, even be another dimension. There are plenty of theories about that sort of thing—that time isn't as linear as we think it is, that other dimensions exist."

Diana gently pulled one hand from Quentin's grasp to rub the nape of her neck. She felt stiff and very tired, and there was a fuzziness to her thoughts that made it difficult for her to think straight. "Okay, sure, it's possible. Maybe even probable; it's certainly something I've considered before. But why that place—in any time or dimension—if what happened there is over and done with?"

"Maybe it was my fault," Hollis said. "What happened there . . ." Her eyes slid to the side, as if she would have looked back at DeMarco, but she didn't turn her head. "It wasn't all that long ago, and with back-to-back cases since, I haven't had a lot of time to . . . process . . . everything. I suppose it's possible the place was so much on my mind that we were both pulled there. I still have nightmares about it."

It was Quentin's turn to frown. "I don't blame you. But what I know about Diana's abilities tells me that if you two found yourselves in that place, it's not because of old memories but because there's some connection to what we're doing now. This investigation. This killer."

Hollis kept her gaze on Diana and repeated, "What happened after I was pulled out?"

"Nothing unusual—at first. A guide appeared. A young girl, maybe thirteen or so. Said her name was Brooke."

DeMarco said, very evenly, "Brooke." His face didn't change, but his weight shifted slightly and he crossed his arms over his chest. As if he needed to move.

Quentin sent a quick glance back at DeMarco and then said, "Assuming it's the same girl, Brooke was one of Samuel's . . . sacrifices. Though we never found a body, there was an eyewitness to her death. From what that witness said, it was a horrible way to die."

The reminder jogged Diana's memory. In addition to reading all the reports, she had talked to Quentin about the case and knew that DeMarco had spent more than two years undercover inside that "church." She couldn't imagine how much strength that must have taken, to pretend for so long to be someone else without losing who you really were. Even more, to be forced by the role to be unable to act to protect innocent victims. Victims you might well have known. Might have been close to.

Like Brooke.

"I'm sorry," Diana said to him.

DeMarco nodded slightly but didn't say anything.

"What did Brooke say—or do?" Quentin asked.

Diana concentrated on remembering. "Typically cryptic, like most guides. I asked her why I was there, in that place, because Hollis had been so—had reacted so strongly to it. So I asked why there, if everything was over and that place was no longer important, no longer mattered. Brooke said everything was connected."

DeMarco said, "But didn't say how."

"No. Before I could ask, she said she needed me to find the truth. I asked if she meant the truth of how she died and she said no, that it had started long before she died. 'The truth buried underneath it all,' she said."

Quentin frowned again. "Yeah, I'd call that cryptic."

"No kidding. I told her I didn't understand, and she said I would. Then she walked through a door—" Diana looked at Hollis, interrupting herself to clarify, "That open door."

Hollis nodded. "I'm guessing you followed her through it?"

"Yeah."

"And?"

She really didn't want to answer, but finally Diana said, "And I was back here, outside in the hallway, but still in the gray time. Brooke was gone, and I was alone. I opened what I was sure was my door, the door to this room. Only when I came in, it was Quentin's room instead." She wished suddenly that he wasn't holding her hand, and yet she couldn't seem to draw away.

He was looking at her intently, waiting, and Diana did her best to meet his gaze and sound as matter-of-fact as possible. "You were there, waiting for me, expecting me. Except it wasn't you. You—it—looked like you and sounded like you. But I knew it wasn't you."

"What was it?"

"I don't know. It...was coming toward me, smiling, saying—" Diana broke off, wishing she wasn't so damn *tired*, because if she'd had her wits about her she could probably think of a dozen reasons why the others in this room didn't need to hear any of this. And then she could keep it to herself, as she wanted. But she *was* tired, her thoughts were fuzzy, and they were telling her that maybe this was important for the case, maybe it wasn't as intensely personal as it felt.

"Diana?" Quentin's voice was steady. "Whatever happened in the gray time, whatever was said or done, you know that wasn't me, know I wasn't there. Right?"

"Right." She nodded. "Right."

"We can leave," DeMarco offered, matter-of-fact, and Hollis nodded grave agreement.

Diana got a grip on herself. *Be a professional about this, dammit. If you're going to be any help at all...* "No, of course not. Because it has to mean something to the case. It has to be connected some-how. Brooke said it is, and the guides don't lie. And maybe one of you can work it out, because I can't seem to."

Hollis said, "Okay, then. Tell us what the fake Quentin said."

"He said...that we belonged together and that he'd been wait-ing for me to realize it. That I had to accept it because it was the way things had to be. That he knew what was best for me and I could trust him." Avoiding everyone's gaze, she hurried on, "Here's the thing. The gray time is an almost-empty place, between worlds or times, whatever. That's why there's no substance, no color or light or shadow, no depth or dimension. It's a place to...travel. Like a road through a cold desert. Not a place where you want to pause any longer than necessary, let alone a place to live in."

"Okay," Hollis said. "I would certainly agree it isn't a place to live in. And so?"

Fumbling for the right words, Diana said, "It's also a place of truth, or always has been. Absolute truth. Like everything else has been stripped away, with only the truth left. I see the guides there, and once before I felt some...thing...truly evil there. But I don't see deception, and none of the guides has ever lied to me. As far as I know, anyway. They never tell me everything, and as I said they're more often than not damn cryptic, but there's never been any at-tempt to deceive. Not like this."

DeMarco said, "You're sure you have no idea what it means? The deception?"

"No."

"How many times have you had company in the gray time? From this side, I mean."

Trust DeMarco to home in on that. "Once before," Diana said reluctantly. And before anyone else could comment, she looked steadily at Hollis, adding, "I'm sorry, Hollis. I should never have done that."

"It was my idea."

"I know. But it was wrong, and I should have known why."

"Why?"

"Because you're a medium too. The last person I should have taken there. And now you're sort of . . . connected to the gray time, almost like I am. At least according to Brooke."

Hollis blinked. "Which means?"

"If Brooke was right, if she wasn't trying to deceive me, it means that whenever I visit the gray time, whenever I open that door, you'll be drawn there too."

"Whether she wants to be or not," DeMarco said, and it wasn't really a question.

Diana nodded. "She's a medium, and we're hardwired to communicate with the spirit world, one way or another. Most of us open doors, the way Hollis opens doors. But those doors are almost always meant to work only one way, allowing the spirits to come here, to this plane of existence. According to Bishop, I'm the only medium he's ever encountered who . . . walks with the spirits on the other side of the door, in that place or time in between. And I've spent my whole life—even if it was mostly subconsciously—learning how to do that, learning how to exist over there, as safely as possible. Hollis, I thought I could protect you too, but . . . now I'm not so sure."

Hollis began to chew on a thumbnail and without moving her thumb managed to say clearly, "This is the whole pillar-of-salt thing, right? The consequences?"

"Bishop's Second Rule," Quentin murmured. "There are always consequences."

Momentarily distracted, Diana said, "What's his First Rule?"

"Some things have to happen just the way they happen."

"Oh, right. He mentioned that. You mentioned that."

DeMarco said, "It's something we've all learned. The hard way." He paused, adding dryly, "Though I hadn't realized we were numbering Bishop's rules."

"Quentin is," Hollis said. "Of course Quentin is. And can we get back to my own pillar-of-salt consequences? Sorry to sound selfish, but I really would like to know what the worst outcome might be.

What to be on guard against if—when—I find myself in the gray time again."

"You already know, Hollis. The worst outcome is that you could be trapped on that side of the door when it closes." Diana drew a breath and let it out slowly, fighting to hold her voice steady as the reminder brought back an old but still-aching memory. "Lost, with no way of getting back to your body. And a body cut off from its spirit, deprived of its soul...can't exist very long without medical intervention."

"Medical intervention? You mean—"

"I mean machines. To keep the body breathing, the heart beating. Under those conditions, the body can last years. Decades. But you wouldn't be there. You wouldn't be there ever again."

Bobbie Silvers was proud to be a deputy. Of course, she wasn't a *real* deputy, not yet; she was only partway through the training manual, and the sheriff refused to let her even begin weapons training.

Still, she was young, energetic, and determined, so she knew it was only a matter of time until she made it to full deputy status.

In the meantime, she worked as hard as she could to prove to Sheriff Duncan that she was deputy material. If he asked her to do something, no matter how seemingly routine or unimportant, she went above and beyond to make sure she did a thorough job of it.

Which was why she was, in the middle of the evening and the middle of her shift, still at her computer terminal, poring through missing-persons reports—covering a radius of five hundred miles.

"Give it up," Dale McMurry advised. "Sheriff's gone home for the night, and, besides, there isn't much anybody can do 'til morning."

"The only thing I *can't* do until morning," she told him without looking at him, "is talk to a first-shift deputy or other officer. Law enforcement is 24/7, Dale, or didn't you know that?"

He grunted. "It took you ten minutes to find the right state bureau guy and get their list, and twenty to get the one from the cops two counties over. At this rate, you'll be at it until midnight and still not get done."

"The county doesn't pay me to sit with my feet up and read magazines," she told him. "If I'm still working on this when the next shift shows up and it's time to clock out, so what? As long as I'm making progress—trying to make progress—then I'm doing my job."

"I'm doing my job," he said, mildly defensive. "I'm waiting to answer the phone. So far, it hasn't been ringing much." He got out of his chair and went to change the channel of the TV resting on a nearby filing cabinet, grumbling underneath his breath at the lack of a remote.

"Don't turn on wrestling, please," she said, still without looking at him.

"What do you care? You haven't taken your eyes off that screen since you talked to the SBI guy."

"I care because you get too caught up in the so-called action and end up yelling and throwing things at the screen. Find a nice cheerleader or beauty competition instead. You drool quietly."

He threw a balled-up piece of paper at her.

Bobbie ducked, sent him a smile to indicate she was only kidding, and went back to her work. Not that she had a whole lot to work *with*. From the remains of both victims, only the barest of preliminary descriptions could be listed with any certainty—and height, weight, eye color, and probable hair color in the case of the female left things pretty damn vague.

The list Bobbie had painstakingly compiled from five hundred miles around Serenade now contained more than a hundred names of people reported missing and not yet found.

With so few specifics about their victims, Bobbie wasn't about to try to narrow that list on her own. But what she could and did do was to include a brief profile on each of the missing men and women. Most of the details were in the reports she'd gathered from other law-enforcement agencies, so it was an easy—if tedious—matter to condense the information under simple categories: *Height; Age; Weight; Coloring; Missing From; Missing Since; Reported Missing By; Criminal Record* (it was almost always *no* under that category); *Financial Problems; Unexplained Financial Transactions; Beneficiaries of Death.*

That last one creeped Bobbie out, but it had to be noted, because at least half a dozen of the missing people carried hefty life-insurance policies left to spouses. Not so unusual, of course, but worth noting, in her opinion.

So Bobbie noted it. And noted all the other bits of information she had gathered. And then she put it all on a somewhat crude spreadsheet, hoping that something would help the far-more-experienced FBI agents identify the two poor souls whose remains had been found so horribly tortured and mangled.

And it wasn't until just before midnight and the end of her shift, while barely aware of Dale yawning over a less-than-involving seventies-era sitcom, that Bobbie saw something unexpected. Very unexpected.

She rechecked all the information she had, bit her lip for a moment in indecision, then reached for the phone, hoping to find another second-shift cop in another quiet law-enforcement agency with time on his or her hands and the will to stay past this shift and dig just a little deeper.

"So nobody comes back from being lost in the gray time?" Hollis held her voice steady.

Diana shook her head. "Nobody, as far as I know. Because even if the body is kept alive on this side, the gray time really is a corridor between two realities. Nothing belonging to either side can exist in there indefinitely; the guides have told me that much. For us, from this side, the exhaustion becomes overwhelming, all our energy is drained away, and..."

"And?"

"And our spirits apparently pass on to whatever lies beyond the gray time. I'm told there's peace to be found there. But I'm also told peace isn't necessarily the destination for every soul."

"So there is a hell," DeMarco said, sounding thoughtful. "I've always wondered."

Diana nodded a bit hesitantly. "I think so. At least it sounds that way, that something...unpleasant...is waiting for at least some spirits. Calling it hell is probably as good as anything else."

Hollis said, "Let's not get sidetracked by a philosophical—or theological—discussion, if you don't mind. Not tonight, anyway. Diana, you're basically telling me that if I got trapped in the gray time and couldn't find my way out before the door closed, I'd be dead."

"Afraid so."

"And the door closes—how?"

Diana blinked. "You know, I haven't really thought about it that way. Because there are doors in the gray time that seem literal, and they open or close without seeming to affect me."

"Guess," Hollis suggested.

"Okay." She thought about it for a moment. "My guess is that if anyone of this world stays in the gray time too long or ...somehow...wanders too deeply into the gray time, gets too far away from their physical self, then the door would close. The door we open as mediums. I suppose, thinking about it, that it's less a door than a connection that gets severed—the connection between the body and the spirit. Cut that tie or have something cause it to snap, and...and it doesn't get repaired. The spirit can't return to the body."

"Well, that doesn't sound fun." Hollis's voice remained calm, even somewhat sardonic. But her eyes were wide and dark, and she continued to chew on her thumbnail—until DeMarco stepped away from the dresser, reached around to grasp her wrist, and with seeming gentleness pulled her hand down and away from her mouth.

Very interesting indeed, Diana thought, distracted again.

Hollis turned her head briefly toward him and said, "Leave me my vices, will you?" But her voice was still calm, and her hand remained in her lap where he had put it.

"That's not a vice, it's just a bad habit," he said. "If you're interested in vices, I'll go find some booze. Don't know about the rest of you, but I could use a drink."

Diana shook her head. "Not me. After spending most of a lifetime medicated to the gills, I don't drink." As personal as the first part of that information was, she was completely aware that most if not all the other SCU agents knew at least some of her history. As Quentin had pointed out with a shrug, even stuff never said out loud was known when there were so many telepaths around.

Hollis laced her fingers together in her lap and said, "I'm so tired one drink would knock me on my ass. Diana, I hope you have a few tricks you can teach me to protect myself over there. But even if you don't, stop blaming yourself, okay? It *was* my idea to go the first time. I can deal with the consequences. I'm a survivor."

"She is that," Quentin agreed. "More lives than a barrelful of cats, if you ask me."

Diana wished that made her feel better. It didn't.

Either seeing that or else pursuing a thought of his own, Quentin added, "And then there's Reese. After tonight, I'm betting he could be Hollis's lifeline and pull her out before she gets lost."

"Happy to oblige," DeMarco said.

"Let's hope it isn't necessary," Hollis said without looking at him, her tone rather careless. "Anyway, at the moment I'm more interested in what happened after I was pulled out tonight. Why something in the gray time—presumably a spirit—tried to trick you, Diana. And what it was trying to trick you into doing. Or believing."

"I don't know."

"Can you speculate? Guess again?"

Diana shook her head, trying to throw off the last tendrils of that weird fuzziness in her mind. "I can't even imagine what it might be."

"Sure you can," DeMarco said.

She stared at him, frowning. "Oh? And how is that?"

He didn't appear to be the least bit bothered by her stiff tone. "First, stop assuming it was a spirit. Just because we haven't encountered another medium who can walk in the gray time doesn't mean one doesn't exist. In fact, it's almost certain one does, since psychic abilities aren't unique. Certain aspects, sure; I have a double shield and, so far as we know, that's unique. But most psychics have a shield of some kind, and without knowing every single one of them I could hardly be sure there isn't another double shield out there."

"He has a point," Quentin noted thoughtfully.

DeMarco nodded and said to Diana, "You can walk in the gray time, and you're exceptionally strong there because of most of a lifetime's experience. But on two separate occasions, Hollis has been able to function there as well."

"If you can call it functioning," Hollis muttered.

"I can," DeMarco told her, then added before she could comment, "She may not be able to open the door to the gray time, but only one previous visit enabled her to form a connection to that place, to be drawn back into it when Diana opened the door. Which could mean it's a lot more accessible to mediums than we've assumed and that others have been drawn there as well. And that, somewhere, another medium exists who was drawn to cross through that doorway rather than just open it for spirits. Curiosity alone would surely drive at least some to wonder what it would be like. And it's a small step from wondering to attempting."

Hollis said, "It would better explain the deception. I mean, if the guides have never attempted to deceive you, why start now? But if it's another psychic trying to do that..."

DeMarco finished: "...what better way to attempt a deception than to show you a face you trust?"

"It makes sense," Diana allowed. "At least as much as any other possibility does."

Quentin said, "It also opens up the probability that this particular enemy knows you well enough to *know* who you trust. Or has been watching long enough to . . . draw certain conclusions."

Diana wasn't sure which possibility made her more uneasy. But both of them did. She was about to comment on that when the sudden ringing of a cell phone made all of them—except DeMarco—jump. He reached back to pick up Diana's cell phone from the dresser, looked rather automatically at the caller I.D., and then tossed the phone to land within Diana's reach.

"Elliot Brisco. Your father, I gather."

Diana reached her free hand to pick up the phone—and turned it off midway through its ring tone. "Yeah. He's been out on the West Coast—and never considers time differences when he's calling me. Or anyone else, for that matter."

"Could be an emergency," Hollis suggested.

"Trust me, it isn't. Just him ready to argue one more time that joining the FBI was the worst idea of my life." She drew a breath and let it out slowly, then ruthlessly got them back on topic. "Okay, so let's assume for the moment another medium *was* there in the gray time. And either knows me well enough to be sure of who I trust or else has been able to read me. I don't have much of a shield, right?"

It was DeMarco who answered. "Not much of one, no. But you don't broadcast like Hollis does, so it would probably take a fairly strong telepath to read you." Before Hollis could make an indignant comment, which she seemed about to do, he added, "But there's nothing to say another medium with a lesser telepathic sense might not be able to read you far more clearly in the gray time than on this side of the door. Or even another medium who isn't telepathic at all. A lot of the *rules* we've come to accept in this world, this reality, may not be true in that one. In fact, the chances are pretty good that there are a lot of differences over there."

Diana wished she could dispute that, but the more she thought about the possibility, the colder she felt. "So another medium could be reading me in the gray time. And maybe...influencing me?"

DeMarco was utterly matter-of-fact. "Maybe. We're generally more vulnerable in an unconscious state—which is what your dreams and trances amount to."

"You're strong in the gray time," Quentin reminded her.

"Am I? What if I only think I am? There's...something I've never been able to explain about the gray time. It hasn't happened often, but throughout my life I've awakened from trips there to find my physical self somewhere other than bed. Somewhere dangerous."

Quentin nodded, clearly remembering. "Up to your waist in a lake. Driving your father's sports car at high speed when you were too young to drive at all."

"Yeah. And there were other things, awakenings I haven't told you about. Finding myself in other dangerous places or just baffling ones. Sometimes miles and miles from home. With no memory or understanding about what I was doing there. Or what I was meant to do. At the time I thought those things were more symptoms I was losing my mind—or had already lost it. Once all the meds were gone and I could think clearly, once I knew I was a medium and understood what that meant, I guess I thought I'd been trying to help a guide get a message to someone but that my body and spirit were still so out of sync, things got confused and I tried to act before knowing what it was I was supposed to be doing, before I was even awake."

"That sounds possible," Quentin said. "Maybe even likely."

"I guess. Looking back now...I don't know what to think."

In his usual neutral, pleasant tone, DeMarco said, "But it's equally possible that someone could have been trying to influence you. Make you behave in ways you wouldn't have consciously done."

"Even when I was a child?"

"Maybe especially then. When it was still new to you, still something you were trying to learn to control."

The possibility that someone could have been following her around in the gray time all these years, without her knowledge or even awareness, made Diana feel cold to the bone. It felt like a violation, a rape of her mind, of herself. She forced herself to speak calmly. "I suppose it's possible. But—"

Still in that impassive tone, DeMarco said, "Psychic abilities often run in families."

Understanding, Diana said, "My mother was psychic, I believe. Probably my sister, Missy, as well. But they've both been dead for years."

"Is it possible your father—"

Diana laughed, hearing how brittle it sounded. "No. My father isn't psychic. At all. My father doesn't believe in psychics. He was convinced my mother was mentally ill. He chose to believe I was mentally ill rather than accept the possibility I might be a medium. How's that for not believing in psychic abilities?"

DeMarco's expression didn't change, but his voice softened somewhat when he said, "I'm sorry. I didn't intend to open up old wounds."

"Oh, no need to be sorry. You didn't reopen anything. He more or less said that about a week ago. So, still a fresh wound, I'm afraid."

Quentin said, "Diana, I told you it takes some people a lot longer to come to terms with this. My father still refuses to accept I'm a seer, and he's known it for years."

"Yeah, well, your father didn't threaten to have you committed when you first told him, right?"

Hollis said, "Your father seriously did?"

Diana nodded jerkily. "He was deadly serious, believe me. Quentin can tell you; he was there. So was Bishop. I don't know what Bishop said to my father later, but whatever it was, it at least stopped him threatening me. Now he just . . . It's like water dripping

91

on stone. I don't belong in the FBI. I'm out of my element. I'm going to get myself killed. On and on."

"I'm sorry," DeMarco repeated.

She looked at him, then at the other two, and sighed. "No, I'm sorry. That's . . . personal junk. Baggage. We all have it. Mine doesn't alter the possibility that somebody could have been there with me in the gray time, trying to influence me—for whatever reason."

"Creepy," Hollis noted.

"I'll say. Especially when I don't have a clue who it might be— and have never been aware of another presence there."

Quentin said, "Maybe because there wasn't one. Look, this is all speculation."

"But possible," DeMarco noted.

Quentin sent the other man a quick frown, then said to Diana, "Never mind that now. Let's focus on what happened tonight. How did you know it wasn't me?" His voice was calm and steady, as was his gaze when she finally looked at him. "We both know I could have said those words, most of them at least. So how did you *know* it wasn't me?"

"I just . . . knew. Almost from the first instant. It felt wrong. Like something was off. And all my strength was draining away suddenly, too suddenly. As if . . ."

"As if you were under attack?" DeMarco asked. "Because when I was pulling Hollis out, that's what it felt like to me."

He sat up and swung his feet off the bed, reaching immediately for the bottle on his nightstand.

A strong hand beat him to it, removing the bottle from his reach, and the visitor said, "Not just yet. Tell me."

"Look, this shit isn't easy, you know. Takes a lot out of me, I told you that. I'm tired and thirsty. I need—"

"You need to tell me what happened in the gray time. Now."

He studied the visitor for a moment, then sent a longing glance toward the bottle and shrugged, trying not to look as wary as he felt. Money was great, and he was as willing to use his God-given talents for hire as a gifted artist was to sell his paintings; a man had to make a living, after all. But this particular "buyer" made him nervous.

Ruthless men with scary agendas made him nervous. Especially when they looked dangerous as hell.

"Tell me," the visitor repeated.

"Okay, okay. But I'm not so sure you're going to like what I have to say, Bishop."

"You let me worry about that."

Six

DEMARCO WAITED UNTIL Hollis disappeared around the corner of the hallway toward her own room before saying to Quentin, "If someone's been influencing Diana for years, we need to know about it." He kept his voice low, since Diana's closed door was only a few feet away.

"Doctors were influencing her for years. Her father was influencing her for years. The goddamn meds they had her on to *treat* her because they didn't understand or refused to accept her abilities influenced her."

"You know what I'm talking about."

"Yeah, well, we don't need to know more about that tonight." Quentin kept his voice low as well. "Look, she's been through a lot. A hell of a lot. She's made progress in the last year, but she's a long way from feeling secure in herself and her abilities, especially with Elliot Brisco trying to undermine her confidence just about every step of the way."

"He sounds like a real prince."

"He's a very wealthy man accustomed to getting what he wants. And he wants Diana back under his control. To protect her." Quentin shook his head. "I try to be sympathetic, because he lost his wife and Diana's sister, Missy, thirty years ago, and he naturally doesn't want to let go of his only surviving child. And I've tried to stay out of it as much as I can, because it just isn't smart to interfere between a parent and child—even a grown child. And especially between a father and daughter."

"True enough."

"Yeah. Though I've wanted to deck the man more than once, I don't mind telling you." Quentin shook his head. "But that's not a situation that's going to change anytime soon. What's concerning me now is Diana's reaction to the idea that someone else, some other medium, might have been hiding in the gray time with her since she was a child, watching her and, yes, maybe even influencing her. It's bound to spook her. Hell, it spooks me."

"It should spook all of us, Quentin, and you know it. What happened with Samuel plus all the other little leaks and breaches in security we've had to deal with these last few months are clear evidence that someone inside the SCU has been passing on information, to the Director and possibly to others."

"We don't know it's one of us," Quentin protested, because he had to.

"We don't know it isn't. In fact, it more than likely is an SCU team member, considering how little specific information about the unit gets out otherwise. Given that strong possibility, we've got two alternatives: Either an SCU member is deliberately and consciously betraying the rest of us, or else a psychic outside the unit has found a way to tap into one of us—maybe more than one of us—and get information without our awareness."

Quentin didn't like hearing either possible scenario voiced aloud, mostly because he'd considered both long before now. But all he said was, "It can't be Diana, and I mean *can't*. Not only is she new to the SCU, but up until a couple of months ago, she was in training, completely uninvolved in any of our cases."

"You didn't talk to her?"

"Not details, not until we were set to join this investigation and she needed to be brought up to speed. And she didn't see any of the reports until then."

"Okay. Still, if her ability makes her vulnerable in any way to outside influences, we need to know about it."

"Not tonight," Quentin repeated.

"Personal feelings aside—"

"My personal feelings *are* aside, at least about this. Reese, so far the only remotely psychic activity we've had in this case has involved Hollis, Diana—and the gray time. I haven't seen anything, and if she's being straight with us, Miranda hasn't seen much. Unless—can you read her?"

"Miranda? No. Almost always no, but definitely no here and now. I assumed it was because she and Bishop are apart, both shielding and guarding their connection, because it's a vulnerability."

"Which it is, at least when they're separated by physical distance."

DeMarco nodded. "And with Bishop worried about a possible traitor, he'd most definitely guard his vulnerabilities."

"*Traitor.* That's . . . a strong word."

"It's a strong thing. A dangerous thing. And you know it."

"I know every team member," Quentin said. "And many of the active Haven operatives. And none of them is a traitor."

"Consciously, at least. Let's hope not."

Reluctant, Quentin said, "If it's unconscious, unknowing—if one of us is being influenced or at least tapped into—then it has to be on a level you telepaths obviously can't reach, or one of you would have picked up on it by now."

"Probably," DeMarco agreed. "And if it's that deep, chances are it *is* below the level of conscious thought."

"So it may be only through our mediums that we find answers in this one. In the gray time, where we've seen the first real sign of some kind of deception. And if it is, we can't risk shaking Diana's confidence to the point that she's unable to open that door. Because none of the rest of us can do it."

DeMarco drew a breath and let it out in a short sigh, a bit impatient but accepting. "Logical. Even practical. But . . . if it was me, I'd want to know there might be something hiding in the corner."

"She already knows that much. And I agree it's a possibility that needs to be discussed. But leave the timing of it up to me, okay?"

"All right, it's your call. Just do us all a favor and remember that somebody took a shot at us, moving this case from investigative to actively dangerous. For us. I don't know about you, but I hate wearing those goddamn vests."

"So do I. Though if you're right about the skills of that sniper, he's just as likely to go for a head shot."

"Nice thing to remind me before bedtime. Thanks."

"Speaking of, what the hell time is it anyway? I left my cell in my room."

"Quarter after two," DeMarco replied, without looking at his watch.

"You know or guessing?"

"I know. Like Diana's internal compass, I have an internal clock. Usually accurate to within five minutes."

"Then why wear a watch?"

"Because I can. They don't go dead on me the way they do on most of the rest of you; my shield apparently holds the energy in. At least until I use my abilities, and then only if I'm pushing full strength."

"Which I'm guessing you don't often do."

"Without knowing whether it'll blow a fuse in my brain one day? No, not often. I'm big on self-preservation."

"When it comes right down to it, we probably all are. Genetically hardwired for it." Quentin took a step toward his room, then paused to add, "Interesting that within the unit you and Hollis have the highest levels of electrical activity in your brains."

"I'm sure it frustrates the hell out of Bishop." When Quentin lifted a brow at him, DeMarco explained, "Another item on the growing list of paranormal inexplicables neither lab work nor fieldwork has provided answers for. Or, really, any basis to even begin comparing: My abilities and Hollis's are very, very different."

"Almost opposite," Quentin agreed. "Which raises the question—"

"I think we've had enough questions for tonight, don't you? We're supposed to meet in the dining room at eight; it would be nice to get at least a little sleep before breakfast."

"Oh, yeah, you can say that again. I'm so beat I can barely think. See you in the morning."

" 'Night." DeMarco made his way back toward his own room, pausing for only an instant outside Hollis's closed door. Her light was on.

He wondered if she'd sleep at all tonight.

His hesitation was so slight he doubted she could have heard it in his footsteps. If she could have heard his footsteps at all, which was even more doubtful. In any case, DeMarco returned to his own room.

Long habit made him check the windows, the closets, all the corners, even under the bed before he relaxed. The habit didn't strike him as extreme; he had lived with it for too long.

He sat down on the edge of his bed and pushed back the loose shirt cuff covering his left wrist. The watch was metal, with a buckle, and it took him several careful tries to pry it open.

The metal was a bit melted.

He grimaced slightly as he peeled the watch off his wrist, revealing scorched skin where the metal had touched it.

Aloud, he muttered, "Note to self: Stop wearing a fucking watch."

He tossed the ruined watch toward his open suitcase and briefly examined his wrist. Not a bad burn, just painful enough to be annoying. He carried a compact first-aid kit with him when he traveled, another long-standing habit, but didn't bother to dig it out of his bag. The burn was slight enough and would probably be all but gone by morning.

They usually were.

Not that it had happened very many times. He was a cautious man, after all, and rarely threw that caution to the winds.

But this was the second ruined watch of the day, dammit. The first one had possessed a leather strap fashioned so that no part of the metal watch touched his skin; that watch was now tucked in a side pocket of his suitcase, its metal parts all fused and melted together—an event that had occurred at about the time DeMarco knocked Hollis to the ground to avoid a sniper's bullet.

At least it didn't burn me.

He wondered rather idly if a scan of his brain right now would show even more electrical activity than its previous high, which had occurred just after the final confrontation at the Church of the Everlasting Sin. In that deadly hour, during a battle that had been charged with sheer, raw power, the energies hissing in the very air around them had undoubtedly changed all of them in ways they hadn't even begun to calculate.

Maybe in dark ways. Dangerous ways. A sobering thought, but more than possible; Samuel's energy had certainly been dark, and God knew there had been plenty of that blasting their way. It wasn't as if any of them carried around some special protection against negative energy—the opposite, if anything. Energy affected them, period.

Energy as black and negative as Samuel's...God only knew how that might affect them.

DeMarco had a hunch that was the major reason Miranda had kept Hollis with her since the investigation into the church ended; of them all, Hollis had shown the strongest—or at least most obvious—response to the attack against her, developing an entirely new ability, full-blown and extraordinarily powerful. DeMarco doubted that even she knew for sure how else she had been changed, for good or ill.

Just like he didn't know what that energy might have done to him. Maybe especially him, since he'd been close to Samuel, right there in the Compound, virtually every day for more than two years.

How can I not be changed by that? All the roles I've played over the years...That role may have cost me the most.

He hadn't dwelled on it because that wasn't in his nature, but he had to wonder how he had been affected. Changed. He had no doubt at all that he had been, because he felt...different. In some ways stronger, but in other ways just different. The certainty of that and the uncertainty of precisely how different he might be now lay uneasily in the pit of his stomach—the constant low-level dread of an unknown he couldn't control.

But he knew himself well aside from that and knew that, caution and training notwithstanding, he was a creature of instinct and always had been.

No doubt always would be.

He thought Hollis was probably going to have a hard time with that.

Hollis stifled a yawn and then took another swallow of the B&B's rather excellent coffee. She hadn't slept very well after returning to her room the night before, especially since she hadn't even closed her eyes until after four, but at least the bone-deep weariness was gone.

More or less.

And breakfast, served by the B&B's cheerful owner, Jewel, and by an equally cheerful young maid named Lizzie, had been both delicious and plentiful. So Hollis felt reasonably ready to face another day.

Reasonably.

She wasn't so sure about Diana, however. The other woman was noticeably pale and hollow-eyed this morning and was definitely withdrawn. Quentin had been watching her closely, if unobtrusively, until he'd left the room just minutes before to go to Jewel's office for an expected fax.

Miranda and DeMarco were busy shifting a few tables around and setting up workstations, assisted by the still-cheerful Lizzie, so Hollis took the opportunity to speak quietly to Diana.

"Did you sleep at all?"

"Not really. Does it show?"

"A bit." Hollis looked around the pleasant dining room, with its big, bright windows and comfortable furnishings, then joined Diana at the small table where she sat with both hands wrapped around a coffee mug. "All this is mostly setup, you know. Just getting ready to work. Nobody'd mind if you went back to your room and took a nap."

"I'd mind. Besides, I don't really want to sleep."

Hollis didn't have to ask why. Instead, she said, "So I guess in all these years you haven't figured out a way to keep yourself out of the gray time when you don't want to visit."

"I might have." A touch of bitterness entered Diana's voice. "If I hadn't spent so many of those years medicated, with virtually no control over what I consciously thought or did. My subconscious wasn't looking for control, it was busy learning to function separately in order to provide an outlet for the mediumistic abilities. Or at least that's what Bishop says."

"And he has an annoying habit of being right."

"Yeah, well, he also believes it may take a while—months, maybe even years—before my conscious and subconscious minds become . . . integrated normally. Or what passes for normal with psychics."

Slowly, Hollis said, "Did Bishop seem to consider the separation a strength or a weakness?"

Diana frowned. "I'm not quite sure. He said he could envision situations in which there could be some benefit to having an independent subconscious. To be honest, the very idea sounded so unnerving that I didn't ask him anything more about it."

"Can't say that I blame you."

Keeping her gaze fixed on her coffee cup, Diana said, "Yeah, it sounded way too much as if my own subconscious is...an alien thing. Something not under my control. Listen, do you think Reese might also be right? That another medium could have been in the gray time with me all these years? Some of the time? Every time?"

"I don't know about that, but I have to admit, when he pulled me out, all I could think was that maybe Samuel's pet monster had died and that his spirit was in the gray time—all ready to torture spirits the way he had bodies. Because that's where we were, in the asylum where he did that."

"There's a creepy thought."

"No kidding. But Reese said the killer is still very much alive. And he's right; I looked it up later, just to be sure. He is still alive, still imprisoned. In a padded cell, actually."

"He...isn't a medium, right? That pet monster?"

"Far as we've been able to tell, he has zero psychic ability. And several of our psychics were able to read him, so we're as sure as we can be."

"So it couldn't be him in the gray time. But Reese's theory still makes sense, doesn't it? That somebody, another medium, *could* be in there, watching me?"

Hollis kept her tone deliberate. "I think it's easy to theorize— when you haven't been there." She waited until Diana looked at her, then added, "You're comfortable and confident in the gray time. Strong. I think if another medium had been there, you would have known it, the same way you instantly knew that the fake Quentin was just that."

Diana drew a deep breath and let it out slowly. "That's what I've been telling myself."

"Believe it. Trust your instincts."

"I guess that's all any of us can do."

"True enough." Hollis lifted her own cup in a slight salute. "So here's to trusting our instincts. And to me finding an anchor on this side so I'm not yanked into the gray time against my will.

Or, if I am yanked in, that an anchor here means I can pull myself back out."

Diana lifted her own cup, but said dryly, "Yeah, well, thing is . . . you have an anchor on this side."

Hollis felt suddenly uneasy. "I do?"

"Uh-huh. Reese."

Now Hollis knew why she'd felt unease instead of relief. Because something inside her had known Diana would say that. She kept her voice low. "Look, just because he was able to pull me out—"

Diana was nodding and kept her own voice low when she said, "Yeah, just because. Hollis, Reese isn't a medium and wasn't able to open a door to the gray time, but he was able to pull you out of there nevertheless. *Find* you and pull you out, neither of which is an easy or simple thing to do. We may not know a whole lot about how my connection to the gray time works, but one thing Quentin and I found out is that a nonmedium on this side can act as a lifeline— and an anchor. But that's only if there already exists some kind of connection or tie between you and that person, and only then if he can touch you physically on this side."

Hollis could feel herself beginning to frown. "So that's why you and Quentin had such an odd reaction when Reese said he pulled me out."

"That's why. It was a bit . . . unexpected."

Shaking her head, Hollis said, "No, there has to be another reason. Because there's no connection between us. I barely know the man."

"Well, there's knowing . . . and then there's *knowing*."

"I don't know him like that either."

A little laugh escaped Diana. "I didn't mean knowing in the biblical sense."

"Oh." Hollis tried not to look too self-conscious. "Well, knowing how, then?"

"You'll have to tell me that. All I know is that a psychic's strength has nothing to do with it. We experimented in the lab, and Bishop and Miranda *together* couldn't connect with me in the gray time. None of the telepaths could. One seer—You know Beau Rafferty, right?"

"Maggie Garrett's brother? Yeah, a bit."

"Well, he's the only nonmedium I've ever physically encountered in the gray time. There in spirit, I mean, but visible to me. And not dead." She frowned. "Anyway, that was an extreme case, extreme circumstances, and he's scarily powerful, so that probably explains how he was able to get in. And out. But Quentin . . . Quentin can connect with me there. I don't see him or even hear him, but I know if I reach for him, he'll be there. And he'll pull me out."

"Oh." Hollis hoped she didn't look as unnerved as she felt. "Which means?"

"What I said. There has to be a connection, a tie. Bishop believes a close blood relation, even a nonpsychic, could possibly do it given a strong enough motivation, though that's a theory we haven't tested."

"Because of your father's attitude?"

"Yeah, asking him to participate in a lab experiment exploring his daughter's psychic gifts would not go over well at all. In fact, I suspect he'd go back to trying to buy a judge and have me committed."

Hollis blinked. "Buy a judge?"

"He's never let morals or ethics get in the way when there was something he wanted." Diana shook her head. "Never mind him. The point is, failing a blood relation, and given what we know, the connection has to be something emotional or psychological. Or psychic, of course."

Hollis seized on the latter. "Must be psychic. Somehow." Then she remembered. "Back in Samuel's Compound that last day, there were weird energies all over the place; we were all affected by them, probably even changed. I know damn well *I* was changed. So maybe it happened then. Maybe while Reese was reaching out to try to dampen Samuel's energies and I was trying to do my thing, some of our energies got . . . tangled."

Solemn, Diana said, "That sounds as likely as anything else. Maybe Reese, at a critical moment for each of you, tuned in to your frequency, as Quentin would say. Only it happened during a time when both of you were being exposed to unusual energies, and that made a fleeting contact something a bit more . . . substantial."

Hollis felt herself frowning again. "Yeah, I'd bet that was it. Something like that, anyway. Still, I'd . . . I'd rather not have to depend on him to drag me out of the gray time if I get in trouble there."

Diana smiled ruefully. "Believe me, I really don't want to depend on Quentin either, not like that. But I don't know if either of us has a choice, at least for now."

Hollis wasn't at all happy about that and wasn't sure she wanted to even begin to examine her mixed emotions on the subject. So she was relieved when Quentin returned to their becoming-a-makeshift command center then, fax in hand.

"Things just got very interesting," he announced, after a quick look around to make sure the agents were alone in the dining room.

"Don't you mean more interesting?" Diana shook her head. "Because I haven't been bored yet."

"More interesting, then. Since we're not completely up and running in the command center here, the sheriff faxed this through as soon as his office was notified. It looks like we're being—you should excuse the word—haunted by Samuel. So to speak."

Miranda looked up from the laptop she was in the process of setting up and frowned. "He does seem to be a part of this, at least in spirit, doesn't he? What now?"

"If everybody recalls, we had one supposed church member AWOL and unaccounted for there at the end: Brian Seymour. Part of the security team."

"In his own mind, maybe," DeMarco muttered.

"Yeah, well, as we all know, he vanished without a trace. And we never found out for sure who, besides Samuel, he was working for."

"Senator LeMott denied it was him," Hollis noted.

"And since LeMott was straight about everything else—finally, when it was all over with—we pretty much have to believe him. So Seymour has been a very large question mark in a supposedly closed case."

"Until now," Diana prompted.

"Until now. Well, sort of. He's still a question mark, only of a different kind. We finally got a hit on the prints from the male victim." Quentin waved the fax he was holding. "Got his rap sheet right here. He is—or was—Brian Seymour, aka David Vaughan, the name he was born with. Nothing serious on the sheet, just some petty theft, B&E, minor assault. Dropped off the grid about five years ago, when the church records indicate that he went to work for Samuel."

DeMarco leaned back in his chair with a lightly exhaled breath, eyes suddenly narrow in his usually expressionless face. Methodically, he said, "Somebody reported it to the Director when Galen was shot, and there were only three of us who witnessed that. Carl is still involved with the church—such as it is—so highly doubtful it was him. It wasn't me. Brian's disappearance marked him as the likely snitch. But there was no sign whatsoever that he was linked to the Bureau. No sign he ever acted as a police or other law-enforcement informant. In fact, despite his seemingly easygoing personality, the man was all but a ghost and too careful for me even to get a clear set of his prints."

"Yeah," Quentin said, "and we all know you took it personally that you were never able to track him down after that whole manufactured history of his fell apart."

Ignoring that, DeMarco said, "And now, months later, he turns up as a victim in a serial-killer case we're investigating? Unless there's a connection we don't yet know about, I'm guessing the odds against that have to be astronomical."

Hollis said, "And it's just plain weird. Very weird. It can't be co-incidental. Can it?"

"I don't believe in coincidence," DeMarco said.

Quentin shook his head. "Neither do I. Not this kind, at any rate. So... two very different cases, one of them apparently solved months ago, just linked up. And what do we do with that?"

Speaking up finally, Miranda said, "We find out a hell of a lot more about the common denominator. David Vaughan: aka Brian Seymour."

Hey, what'd you do, pull a double shift?" Duncan asked, pausing in front of Bobbie Silvers's desk.

"You said we could sign up for overtime if we wanted. I signed up." Before he could protest further, Bobbie hurried to add, "I think maybe I found something interesting, Sheriff."

"You mean about these murders?" He was honestly surprised, not because he doubted her investigative instincts but because she'd had so damn little to work with.

"Yes. At least—maybe."

Duncan rested a hip on the edge of her desk. "Okay. What?"

Bobbie didn't have to gather her thoughts; she'd been rehearsing what to say for more than two hours as she waited for him to arrive. "First, I reached out to all the other law-enforcement agencies, as ordered, and asked for any missing persons who might possibly fit our victims. Only I went five hundred miles out rather than a hundred."

Duncan winced. "Given how little specific information we have, that must be some list."

"More than a hundred names," she admitted.

"That's a hell of a long list, Bobbie," he pointed out.

"Yeah. I didn't want to try to eliminate any on my own, for obvious reasons. I don't know enough about the victims. But every missing-persons report had snippets of additional information, some of it not listed in the computer databases but written in by the investigating officers. Years ago I had a really experienced cop tell me that there are always things in the paper file that don't fit into any of the forms—some hunches by the investigating officer, naturally, but also bits of hard data. So I went looking for that kind of information."

Duncan cocked his head as he studied her. "You got cops to dig out and read through files for you in the middle of the night?"

"I owe a deputy in the next county over a drink," she said somewhat sheepishly. "The rest were mostly bored and willing to help out."

Suddenly uneasy, Duncan said, "We're not ready to go public with any of our speculation, Bobbie."

She nodded. "I told them I was updating our missing-persons database and, because of spotty Internet out here, I had to do most of it manually. Boring second-shift work. They were sympathetic."

"First spot comes open on the day shift is yours," Duncan promised.

Bobbie grinned, then tried her best to recapture her professional air. "Well, I'm nowhere near done yet, but I did cover about two dozen of the reports so far, closest first. So within a fifty-mile radius, I've probably got detailed reports on two-thirds of the missing persons."

"You're not working three straight shifts," Duncan warned her.

"Don't worry, Sheriff; I'm so tired I wouldn't even try. But I've got a start, and if you and the agents think it's necessary, or even worthwhile, I'll pick it back up when I come in this afternoon. That's assuming the agents don't take up where I left off and get it all finished by then."

"Okay. So what in that two dozen reports so far struck you as interesting?"

"Just one report, actually. You know how things stick in your mind? Well, about a year ago, there was all that excitement over at The Lodge. Remember?"*

"When that kind of thing happens practically in your backyard, you remember. It was a real mess. They found old bones on the grounds—and in some cave nobody knew about. Human bones. And they had a murder at the time. Somebody went nuts and killed one of the maids." He frowned. "I seem to recall the feds were in on that one too."

Bobbie was nodding. "One fed in particular—Quentin Hayes. The local investigating officer, Captain Nathan McDaniel, noted in the file that Agent Hayes had visited The Lodge several times over the years and that he had a childhood connection to the place. I . . . uh . . . read about it at the time. I was curious."

"At the time" had been just after she got her job with the Pageant County Sheriff's Department.

Duncan frowned but said mildly, "Don't do that again, Bobbie. Use your position here to satisfy personal curiosity."

Sheepish again, she said, "Yes, sir. I know better now, honest."

He was satisfied she did. "So Quentin spent some time at a pretty reclusive resort thirty miles from here. Don't see as how that would have anything to do with the murders here."

"Neither did I. Until I found another connection." She opened the topmost file of the stack on her blotter and turned the page so he could read it if he so chose, even though she was relaying the information. "Reported missing ten days ago, Taryn Holder, age twenty-eight. Blond hair, brown eyes, five foot seven, a hundred and twenty pounds. Single. Her boyfriend in Knoxville reported her missing when she failed to return from the latest spa break she was in the habit of taking at least twice a year."

Duncan got it quickly. "At The Lodge?"

"Yeah. She was last seen checking out and driving away. She never made it home."

---

*Chill of Fear

Miranda said, "You should give that deputy a raise. Whether this pans out or not, she showed real initiative."

Duncan nodded. "Yeah, I'm bound to lose her to some big-town police department. Or to you lot. Look, I sent her home to get some rest, but if you need any of my people to help out later on—with anything that doesn't involve carrying or using a weapon—I'd recommend Bobbie."

Miranda smiled. "She's one of your part-timers."

"Yeah. She grew up in a hunting family and probably knows how to handle a gun better than I do, but she hasn't gone through the training yet, so I'm not about to issue her one. That aside, she's smart, she learns fast, and as you can see she's ambitious and resourceful. Plus, she just plain enjoys the work."

"We may well need her." Miranda looked at the stack of files with a rueful sigh. "Unless another murder victim turns up far outside your jurisdiction, we might be staying in Serenade awhile longer than I'd anticipated."

"Because of what Bobbie found?"

"That. Also the fact that this location is fairly central in relation to the other murders, so it's a good base for us geographically, especially given the helicopter we have at our disposal. And . . . this is a small town, quiet. No TV station, and the one newspaper is a weekly. Working here, we have a better shot at avoiding the media spotlight, at least a little longer."

It was Duncan's turn to sigh. "I know it's a judgment call as to when to go public with this kind of information, but if this is a serial killer with eight notches already on his belt . . ."

DeMarco spoke up then to say, "No commonalities, Sheriff. We don't have a clue how he's choosing his victims, how he's hunting them, or how often he needs to kill. Warning people that a killer is on the loose when you can't also tell them how to protect themselves is only going to lead to panic." He shrugged. "Chances are, your people here are already doing what they can. Locking their doors, bringing outside dogs in at night, sleeping with shotguns within reach. They would have started taking steps yesterday morning, when word of the first victim got around. By last night, after we had a second victim, I'm betting the whole town was on alert."

"True enough." Duncan looked at him curiously. "You're from a small town?"

"No. But people are pretty much the same all over."

Duncan nodded, then said, "Well, since I'm sure I'd only cramp your style by hanging around, I'll head back to the office." He held up a hand when Miranda would have spoken, and said with a rueful smile, "No need to be polite about it; we both know it's the truth. Since the ID on the male victim marks him as an out-of-towner, I'll have my people ask around, show his mug shot, see if we turn up anybody who saw him. But I'm guessing all we'll turn up is zip. His body was dumped here, like you figured. Chances are he never walked here on his own two feet.

"As for the female victim, if she turns out to be this Taryn Holder from Knoxville, it would seem like she was dumped here as well. Why here I don't know, and what that shooter yesterday has to do with either I also don't know. Honestly, I'm hoping he was just passing through, happened to see what was going on, and got crazy stupid enough to take a couple of shots at cops."

Quentin murmured, "Could be."

"Yeah, well. We all know that isn't likely. But if it turns out that neither of the victims is local, that sniper is pretty much your problem—unless he decides to keep on shooting at people. Especially if he's your serial killer. We aren't equipped to even start to hunt for a serial killer, like I told you. But if there's anything me or my deputies *can* do for you, let us know. If you need another warm body or two, for research or knocking on doors or filing paperwork, whatever, say the word. Until then, we'll go about our usual business and try to stay out of your way."

"Thanks, Des," Miranda said, matter-of-fact. "We'll keep you informed of any progress we might make."

"If it concerns my county and this town, I expect you to," he said, an unexpected trace of steel entering his drawl. Then he smiled again. "Otherwise, I'm not all that nosy. You don't have to send these files back; Bobbie made copies for you. Good hunting."

Quentin gazed after the sheriff for a moment, then said rather absently, "I like him."

"You like anybody who gets out of your way," Miranda noted.

"It's a lot less trouble when they do." Quentin drew a breath. "Okay, if nobody else will say it, I will. If the sheriff's industrious young deputy is right about the I.D. of our female victim, we could have another connection to another prior case."

"You're stretching, don't you think?" DeMarco said, but not as if he really believed that.

"Am I? What's the good of being psychic if we can't take an unexpected fact and make an intuitive leap or two?"

"Especially," Miranda said, "when we haven't caught a single break in this case so far."

"I'm not arguing," DeMarco said. "Speculation tends to consist mostly of intuitive leaps, anyway, and we do plenty of speculating."

Hollis said, "You noticed that, huh?"

"It sort of sticks out."

When Hollis looked at Miranda with lifted brows, she smiled faintly and said, "It's his military background. Every ex-military agent we have is the same. Just a little bit uncomfortable with speculation."

"I didn't say I was uncomfortable," DeMarco retorted. "But defining a thing is important, that's all. And, so far, what we have here is speculation."

Quentin said, "Okay, then let's speculate. We know David Vaughan, aka Brian Seymour—look, I'm just going to hyphenate the names for convenience, okay? We know Vaughan–Seymour was involved with the church in North Carolina, definitely on Samuel's payroll and maybe someone else's. On our side, of those of us here,

Reese, Hollis, and I were active in the investigation. Now we may have a connection between the second victim here and The Lodge, where, a year ago, Diana and I were involved in what became an official investigation of a new murder and a lot of old ones."

Slowly, Diana said, "That makes you the common denominator, Quentin."

"So far." He was looking steadily at Miranda. "But we haven't tried to tie any of the six previous victims to old cases of ours, have we?"

"No," she replied. "There was nothing in the profile, no hint we should have been looking for a connection to us or to past cases. So we had no reason at all to go in that direction."

"I'd say we have a reason now."

Hollis nodded and said, "Let's suppose for a minute. Suppose we *do* find that the other victims can be tied, however tenuously, to previous cases. Not only cases Quentin worked on, but others too. Is that the key here, or at least something we can use to break open this case? Are we looking at a serial killer who just found a nifty new way of choosing his victims? A more than usually twisted version of a copycat?"

"No copycat as far as the actual murders go. The M.O. is different," DeMarco pointed out. "No victims tied to Samuel's church showed signs of the sort of torture and mangling found on Vaughan–Seymour's body."

Half under her breath, Hollis said, "No, they showed signs of an even creepier sort of torture."

"The point," DeMarco said, "is that the victims in this case were killed and tortured in ways completely unlike any previous SCU investigation I'm aware of."

Quentin said, "Yeah, there was no victim at The Lodge killed or left the way the female victim here was. So Reese is right: no copycat, at least as far as killing the same way, leaving the bodies the same way."

Hollis said, "But if we find out that every one of the victims *does* have some kind of tie to a past case, that has to be the way he's selecting his targets. Right?"

"I'd say so. Which takes us to a whole new level of serial killer." Miranda was shaking her head. "Because someone able to go to all the trouble of researching the SCU—in itself not an easy thing to do—is not your typical serial killer. To then kill people who can be tied in some way to cases or places where we investigated, choosing them for that reason only . . . That's not about fulfilling his need to kill, the motive that drives virtually all serial killers. That's personal. That's a message. It's about us."

Grim, Quentin said, "We're back to this enemy of Bishop's?"

"Maybe. An enemy of the SCU." Miranda shook her head again. "We're getting way ahead of ourselves. These two victims make for a hell of a coincidence, I'll grant you—but they could be just that. Until we check out the other six victims and see if there are any ties to past SCU investigations, we're wasting our time speculating."

"So," Quentin said, "we go back into all the files."

She nodded. "There are five of us; we'll each take a victim's file and start digging, and we'll hand off the files until each of us has the chance to study every one of them. All the information we have so far is in our own secure database; after we go through that, we start reaching out to the individual law-enforcement agencies and cops who worked on each of the murders. Maybe they know something that didn't get shared at the time. Maybe there are other seemingly unimportant notes jotted down in every one of the files."

Hollis had to ask. "And if that's what we find?"

"Then," Miranda said, "we have a completely different investigation on our hands."

Seven

Haven

THE BOY WAS JUST BEGINNING to toss and turn in his bed, muffled little sobs escaping him, when Maggie Garrett got her hands on him. Almost at once, he stilled, quieted.

Sitting on the side of his bed, Maggie kept her hands on him. Her head was bowed, eyes closed.

Ruby Campbell watched silently from the doorway, her tiny poodle, Lexie, in her arms. It was a scene Ruby had witnessed many times since she and Cody had come here weeks before, but it still fascinated her to watch the shadows of emotions flit across Maggie's face, the pain and fear and grief.

Because they weren't Maggie's emotions but Cody's. She absorbed them, took into herself all the horrible memories and fears that tormented the little boy, and gave of her own healing energy to make him whole again. So he could sleep for the rest of tonight and maybe smile tomorrow.

Ruby knew this was helping Cody, because it was helping her. Helping her to accept that her father was gone and that her mother, back in Grace, at the church, was only the physical shell of the person she had once been.* A smiling, pleasant shell with no memory, as far as anyone could tell, that she had once loved a daughter named Ruby.

It was still very hard, accepting that. But Maggie helped. And Ruby was more grateful than she had words to express. Because it didn't hurt quite so much now. Because she was with people who accepted and understood what she could do, people who cared about her. And because she felt safe here, safe in a way she hadn't felt in a long, long time.

Maggie took away Cody's nightmare and soothed him back into a peaceful sleep as Ruby watched. And then she tucked the covers around him gently and got to her feet.

"Ruby, honey, what are you doing up?" Maggie spoke quietly as she came away from the bed.

"I knew Cody was having nightmares," Ruby answered simply. "Even with the lamp on, he still has them."

"I see." With a gentle hand, Maggie guided Ruby back out into the hallway; with her other, she pulled Cody's bedroom door almost closed. "Well, he'll sleep now. And he won't have another nightmare tonight."

"I know. Because you took his nightmare away, let it scare you instead of him." Ruby looked up into what she thought of as the sweetest face she'd ever seen, a pretty face surrounded by a cloud of dark red hair. Gentle golden eyes smiled down at her.

A real face, with nothing different underneath. Nothing bad. Nothing ever bad.

"Something like that." Maggie turned her toward the bedroom just across the hall and added, "The sun's not even up yet; go back to bed, honey. Does Lexie need to go out?"

"No, I took her out when she woke me up hours ago."

"Okay, then. You two get some sleep, and we'll see you at breakfast."

"Good night, Maggie."

---

*Blood Sins

"Good night, Ruby." Maggie didn't move from in front of the children's bedroom doors for some time but stood there with her eyes closed, all her senses focused, until she was satisfied that neither of them was frightened or even uneasy. That Cody was sleeping peacefully and Ruby beginning to drift off as well.

Then she opened her eyes and, rubbing the back of her neck somewhat wearily, walked down the long corridor. She passed several closed bedroom doors before turning a corner into a shorter hallway that led to the lamplit master suite.

"Did he wake up this time?" John asked.

"No, I got to him before he could." Maggie shrugged off her robe, then climbed into the big bed beside her husband. "Ruby was awake, though. Again. Said she knew Cody was having a nightmare. Those two definitely share a connection. If the genetic tests Bishop ordered hadn't proven otherwise, I'd think they were siblings."

John Garrett pulled her into his arms, her back against his front, so that they spooned, so that he could help warm her slightly chilled body—a physical consequence of the energy she drew on in order to connect empathically with someone else. He drew the covers up around her and then held her as he felt her begin to relax. He wasn't the least bit psychic, but he knew how tired she was. He also knew from experience that it would require some time for her to relax enough to be able to sleep again and that talking quietly helped more than silence.

"This is taking a lot out of you," he said.

"I'll be fine. Besides, what's the point of all this if I can't help them? They're just kids, John. They shouldn't even have to remember everything they've been through, much less have to relive the pain and horror of it over and over again."

"Except that our tragedies shape who we are every bit as much as our triumphs do," he said. It was an old debate. "They need to remember, babe. They don't need to hurt, I agree with you there. They don't need to have nightmares. But they should remember what they've lost. What they've been through. It's important."

"Yeah, well, since I don't have the ability to take away their memories, they'll remember."

"Would you, if you could? Really?"

She was silent for a moment, then sighed. "No, I suppose not. But it's . . . hard. Feeling what they feel. Samuel was a monster, that cult he created incredibly destructive, and the damage both did is going to linger on for years, maybe for lifetimes. These kids will carry the scars of what he did to them all the way to their graves."

His arms tightened around her. "I know. But *you* have to know that you make things better for them. Dull the pain, help them conquer the fear. Without you, it'd take years of therapy for them to get past what's happened to them. If they even could. Bishop made that plain enough."

"Well, he was there. He saw. And I'm pretty sure both the kids talked to him; he has a way with kids."

"I noticed. But am I wrong in believing his interest in them isn't entirely based on compassion?"

"I think you know him well enough to trust your own instincts on that one."

"Okay. So what is it? Does he believe one of them is this 'absolute psychic' he's convinced is out there somewhere?"

"I don't think so. Bishop's absolute psychic, theoretically, has absolute control over his or her abilities. That's not the case here. But these kids . . . They have a lot of power, John. We don't have to put them in a lab and hook them up to machines to know that. A lot of power they've spent their young lifetimes struggling with."

"Is that why it's still taking so much out of you to help them, even after weeks?"

"I think so. For so long they've had to protect themselves, to hide inside their own minds. But . . . that's where the pain is. And the fear. It's where I have to go to help them." Her voice was finally beginning to grow sleepy. "The thing is . . . that's where the power is too. . . ."

John could feel his wife relax totally, in that boneless way that told him she was asleep. He listened to her breathe for a while, his cheek against the soft thickness of her hair as he held her securely.

Sometimes he could almost convince himself that he could keep her safe always. Sometimes.

But it never lasted, that certainty. Because Maggie never hesitated to go willingly into the dark horrors of pain and terror that were other people's traumas, absorbing those destructive emotions into herself in order to heal the sufferers.

It was what she did. It was who she was.

John had only recently nerved himself to ask Bishop if there might be a limit to what Maggie could ultimately endure.

"I wish I could answer that, John, but I can't. The theory is, Maggie's innate sense of self-preservation would stop her from absorbing more than she can handle. Stop her from expending too much of her own energy to heal others. But we don't know that's true."

"And if it isn't? You're telling me this could kill her?"

"I'm telling you we don't know. That's why we work as hard as we can to learn as much as we can about these abilities. For answers to questions like yours. In the meantime, we're all feeling our way, if not blindly then certainly in the dark." Bishop paused. "I know none of this is what you bargained for. But you know as well as anyone that we give hostages to fortune. That we can't always protect those hostages, hard as we try. Not with all our strength. Not with all our determination. Not with all the knowledge and abilities we can command."

John knew the mantra. "Because some things have to happen just the way they happen."

"Some things. Not everything. I'm a bad loser, John. You're a bad loser. So we'll hold on to what's ours with all our might."

"And beat fortune?"

"Bend it at least. When we can. As much as we can."

John tightened his arms gently around his sleeping wife, then turned his head slightly toward the bedroom window, watching the rising sun pierce the blood-red horizon.

If I was a superstitious man, I'd call that a bad omen.

Good thing he wasn't at all superstitious.

"John?"

He looked at the doorway to see Ruby standing there, her eyes huge in her very pale face. Even the tiny poodle in her arms looked fearful.

"Ruby, what—"

"Something bad's going to happen. Something really bad."

Serenade

It was nearly ten that morning, and Hollis had just begun reading through her second file of the day when she saw it. "Shit."

All around the room, her fellow team members looked up from their laptops, but it was Miranda who said, "What is it?"

"Victim number five, Wesley Davidson." Hollis kept her voice even. "He was born in Hastings, South Carolina. I worked my first case there almost two years ago. A serial killer who went after blondes."*

Miranda said, "You were teamed with Isabel."

"Yeah."

"And used up one of your nine lives there, if I remember correctly," Quentin contributed.

"At the time, I thought I'd used up the only life I had." Hollis frowned at the screen of her laptop. "I'm barely into the file, so there may be more—but isn't that enough? A connection, however tenuous, to a past case?"

"Well," Quentin said, "given that Taryn Holder—assuming our female victim here is identified as her—just stayed at The Lodge and was last seen leaving there, with no further connection I've been able to find, and Vaughan–Seymour was peripheral to the investigation

---

*Sense of Evil

of Samuel's cult, I'd say mark that one as connected and move on to another file. But I'm not the boss."

Miranda smiled faintly. "The boss agrees—more or less. Read all the way through the file if you don't mind, Hollis. Something else may jump out at you."

DeMarco said, "Three victims out of eight establishes a pattern, at least to my mind."

"Yes," Miranda agreed. "But is there any kind of meaning in the pattern, other than some vague connection to the SCU? If this *is* about us—about the unit or Noah—I'd expect there to be more to the pattern than what we've seen so far. A killer smart enough and driven enough to have chosen his victims like this is the sort who'd want to show off. And show up those of us investigating his crimes."

"Catch me if you can," Diana murmured. "If you're smart enough to put together the puzzle pieces I've left for you."

"Exactly."

Hollis nodded. "So we keep reading."

"We keep reading. And I think it's time we set up a couple of whiteboards and begin charting all this—now that we have something to chart. The rest of the supplies should be in the SUVs we locked up at the sheriff's department last night."

DeMarco got to his feet. "I'll go. Since I've been undercover and off the grid for the past two years and more, I'm the least likely to recognize one of the connections to past SCU investigations."

Miranda tossed him the keys. "I'm not sure what's packed where, but you should be able to leave one of the vehicles where it is for now."

"Copy that."

As he left the dining room, Hollis rubbed the back of her neck, already feeling the strain of sitting for too long in one position at her laptop. She shifted a bit in her chair, thinking she was stiffening up, and only then realized that she was cold.

Very cold. As if someone had suddenly opened a window into winter.

The physical reaction was always the same. All the fine hairs on her body stood out as though electrical energy filled the room, and goose bumps rose on her flesh as the chill spread through her.

And there was still a jolt of fear—less now, but still that uncomfortable sense that some doors were never intended to be opened by the living. Not, at least, without some dreadful cost.

Slowly, Hollis forced herself to look up.

At first, the room appeared just as it had been, with her fellow agents intent on their workstations and oblivious to her sudden tension.

"Hollis."

She caught her breath and turned her gaze to the doorway that DeMarco had passed through only moments before.

Not quite in the dining room but a couple of steps out in the foyer stood a familiar figure. Appearing entirely solid and hardly ghostlike, she had long fair hair and an anxious expression.

"Hollis, go after him." Her voice was clear and strong.

"What?" Hollis was barely aware that Diana was gazing at her in puzzlement, that Miranda and Quentin exchanged looks before beginning to rise from their chairs.

"Go after him. Stop him. *Now.*"

"Why? Andrea, what're you—"

"If you don't stop him, he'll die. Do you understand? He'll *die.* There's a bomb in one of the cars."

Quentin said, "Hey, is she—"

Hollis didn't hear the rest. She jumped up so abruptly that her chair fell over behind her with a crash, and she raced from the room. Andrea had already vanished by the time she reached the foyer, but Hollis hardly noticed.

She flung open the front door, banged through the screen door, and was across the wide porch and jumping over the steps down to the walkway before she could even begin to look for DeMarco. She drew in a deep breath to yell his name.

And was yanked off her feet and into the shadows of the big magnolia tree that shaded half the front yard.

Dale McMurry hadn't stayed past his shift as Bobbie had. He wasn't the ambitious sort, really. The gig as a part-time deputy offered decent pay and good benefits, and more often than not he served as a less-than-glorified file clerk.

Which suited him just fine.

He didn't mind at all living rent-free in his parents' basement, where his mama still cooked for him and did his laundry. It gave him a handy excuse for why all his "relationships" ended by the third date: Girls figured out quickly that he wasn't a great prospect for their future.

Of course, some might also have figured out that he was gay, but since they hadn't asked and he hadn't told, he allowed himself to believe they just thought he was a loser.

His dad might sneer at a loser, but at least he wouldn't beat the shit out of one.

So far, anyway.

His second-shift job allowed Dale to let himself into the house after midnight, when the old man was usually asleep in front of the TV, and his mama never woke him for breakfast until his dad was at his own job as a mechanic for one of the car dealerships in Serenade.

The arrangement worked for Dale.

However, he wasn't such a mama's boy that he wanted to spend all his free time at home. So on that sunny Wednesday morning, he drove his car downtown and parked in the back lot at the sheriff's department, then walked the block or so to one of the few recreational spots the town could boast, at least for locals: a game room with pool tables, arcade games of various eras, and the latest thing in video poker machines.

Dale didn't have a gambling problem. What he had was a crush on the assistant manager of the local bank, who often spent his lunch hour at the game room.

Since it wasn't quite lunchtime, Dale got himself a soda from the snack area, then sat down at one of the arcade machines near the front window, where he could both watch the door and see the sheriff's department.

Sheriff Duncan hadn't expressly forbidden it, but he disliked any of his deputies, even the part-time ones, hanging out in the game room, *especially* in the middle of the day.

The street was quiet. Dale noted idly that the two SUVs left for the feds were still parked out front of the station. He fed a few quarters into the machine and began zapping aliens.

Gabriel Wolf was not what anyone would have called a patient man—except in his work. In his work, he had all the patience of his namesake when hunting, with the skills, reflexes, and cunning to match. He could track just about anything over just about any kind of terrain. He also possessed a kind of sixth sense that wasn't quite psychic, which often told him where his quarry would be—even if that quarry was more predator than prey. And he preferred to flit among the shadows whenever he got the chance.

He considered it an irony of the universe that his twin sister, Roxanne, was the night hunter of the pair.*

Don't blame me for that.

"I'm just saying, maybe splitting the duty the way we have may not always be the best way to go about things, that's all." He spoke aloud out of habit but kept his voice low so nobody would think he was talking to himself and maybe come after him with a net. "Why not shake things up a bit? I could try a nap in the daytime; you could try a nap at night. These abilities of ours are supposed to be trainable. Right?"

Blood Dreams

Trainable up to a point, but you know the limits as well as I do. Look, if you want to try again, we will. But not in the middle of a case, all right? Pay attention to what you're doing.

"How hard is it to walk, for Christ's sake? I haven't needed to pay a lot of attention to that for more than thirty years. I'm roaming around in a Christmas store, Rox, just innocent as hell, like any tourist, looking at a lot of sparkly shit I don't want to buy. And how come so many of these little towns *have* Christmas stores, anyway?"

Because they're popular. Because tourists come from miles around for a good one.

"Yeah, yeah. Want a snow globe? There's one here with Santa and his sleigh inside."

I think I have—

When his sister's thoughts broke off abruptly, Gabriel could feel the familiar crawling sensation of unease; if he *had* been his namesake, the fur would have been standing up stiffly all along his spine. After a lifetime of sharing thoughts, sometimes the absence of them was far more important. "Rox?"

Let's not play innocent tourist anymore, Gabe. You need to get out of here and to high ground. Something is happening.

"What is it?" He was already moving toward the exit, but casually so as not to draw the attention of the few other browsers or the store clerks with their slightly comical elf hats.

Not sure. Something closer to the center of town. Wait. Lemme concentrate.

There was a pause in his mind as Gabriel smiled automatically at the clerk nearest the front door, waved a friendly hand, and exited the Christmas store.

Got it. Our sniper is back.

Gabriel slid behind the wheel of their rental and started the car. "What, in town? In broad daylight? That doesn't sound like a pro. Are you sure it's him?"

Pretty sure. He isn't shooting. Watching. He's watching. . . . Oh, shit, Gabe. I think maybe we should have taken him more seriously, kept eyes on him no matter what.

"We kept eyes on him—until he headed out of town and hit the highway hours ago. You put a bug in his car; we'd know if he came back. I checked just before I went into the store, and there was nothing." Gabriel dug into the backpack in the passenger seat until he found the GPS tracker. He turned it on and checked the small screen. "Still nothing in the area. That car isn't within fifty miles of Serenade."

Maybe he switched cars. Maybe he did a sweep and found the bug. All I know is that he's back—and he has toys I didn't find in his room or his car. Very dangerous toys. The kind that go boom.

"Shit. Has he—"

He's planted one of them in an SUV that's parked in front of the sheriff's department. Goddammit, it's one of ours. One of the two vehicles supposedly left locked up last night. It hasn't gone off. Yet. And I think...our people have been warned. But he doesn't know that. Dunno if he has a remote or the bomb's on a timer, but he wants a seat near the show.

Gabriel didn't wait to hear more. He put the car in gear and headed toward the downtown area, where he could leave the car and proceed on foot wherever he needed to go. Which was—

He's up high, but the only unobstructed view of those vehicles is close in because of the little cluster of the taller buildings right there in the center of town; you should be able to find a rooftop a couple of blocks from the sheriff's department without him seeing you. I don't know if you'll be able to get up higher than he is. And I'm not sure exactly where he is. There's something...weird about it. Weird about him.

"What do you mean?"

I don't know. Something I wasn't feeling last night. Something cold. Something off. I don't know, Gabe. But I don't like it.

Gabriel pulled out his cell phone, keeping his eyes on the road as he hit a number on his speed dial.

You're calling Miranda.

"Damn straight. If this lunatic is capable of building a bomb and willing to set one off, tagging along behind while he has his fun is not my idea of protecting or serving."

We aren't cops.

"No, but we're here to hunt a killer. And if this one is perched on top of a building with his finger on the trigger of a bomb, I want permission to take his ass out."

"It's okay," DeMarco said.

Hollis was conscious of nothing but her pounding heart for a moment or two, then realized that Reese was holding her against his side quite easily with one arm, his gaze scanning the seemingly peaceful Main Street of Serenade. The two black SUVs parked in front of the sheriff's department several blocks down the sloping road were visible from where they stood.

She wondered if he was even aware of holding her, then wondered why on earth she was thinking about unimportant things when there was a *bomb,* for Christ's sake.

"What do you mean, it's okay?" she demanded, out of breath from her wild dash out of the building. She was almost sure that was why she couldn't seem to breathe evenly. "You knew?"

"You broadcast," he reminded her. He glanced down at her, one brow lifting as he added, "And loudly under moments of . . . stress. I have a hunch I'm going to have a headache for the next hour or so."

"I know I will," Miranda said as she and the others joined them. "And I had my shield up. Jesus, Hollis."

"Sorry."

"Keep in the shadows of this tree," DeMarco warned. "Once my ears stopped ringing—so to speak—I could feel him out there. It's hard to get a fix on him, but I'm sure we have a return visit from yesterday's sniper. He's watching."

Hollis was about to demand that DeMarco let go of her when he did.

Damn telepaths.

Quentin said, "Why is he still hanging around?"

"Hollis was told there's a bomb in one of the cars," Miranda said, "so presumably he's hanging around to kill one or more of us." She sounded very calm about it.

"Told by whom?"

"Andrea."

He frowned. "Andrea? Spirit Andrea, from Grace?"

"And from Venture." Miranda frowned slightly too. "She seems to be connected to you, Hollis."

Hollis found that more than a little unnerving. "I don't know why, especially since I've yet to figure out who she is. Or who she was." She paused, then added slowly, "You know, she might have been the spirit that led us to the female victim's remains yesterday. I didn't get a really good look, and what I saw was a lot less distinct than I'm used to, but ... it could have been her."

"Instead of the victim?"

"Could have been."

"She seems determined to help us. Or help you."

"I wish I knew why. As far as I can tell, she hasn't been connected in any way to our cases. I mean, she warned me about Ruby, gave us a clue that helped Tessa save her, but ..."

Miranda said, "She's connected somehow; otherwise she wouldn't keep showing up. We just haven't found the connection. Yet."

Diana interrupted the speculation to say wryly, "Guys? Sniper? Possible bomb? I mean, I know I'm new at this sort of thing, but doesn't a bad guy in the flesh take precedence over a helpful spirit? If we're speculating?"

"I'd say so," Quentin agreed.

"My question," DeMarco said, "is whether he has one of the cars rigged to blow when a door's opened or an engine starts, or whether he's sitting out there with a remote and a pair of binoculars, able to detonate whenever he likes."

"Either way," Quentin said, "we didn't come prepared for bombs. And I have a hunch the Pageant County Sheriff's Department doesn't have a bomb squad."

Miranda stepped away from them—toward the B&B, still protected by the shadow of the big tree—and pulled her cell from the case clipped to her belt.

As she called the sheriff, the others continued to watch Main Street uneasily.

"I don't get this guy," Quentin said. "He's not acting like any serial I've investigated or even heard about."

"Maybe he isn't one," Diana said. When all eyes turned her way, she added, "I don't mean he isn't killing multiple victims; I mean he isn't *literally* a serial killer. But if he's targeted the SCU, if that's what this is all about, then like Miranda said earlier, we have an entirely different kind of investigation on our hands."

Hollis said, "Especially if it's still a possibility that there are two of them involved in all this. One could be the cool-headed sniper with a methodical agenda, and the other could be the sadist with blood literally all over his hands."

Eight

"**A**NOTHER PET MONSTER?**"** Quentin speculated, then shook his head before any of the others could offer an argument for or against. "No, if we've got two involved here, it feels more like a partnership to me. Maybe it's just a hunch, but that's the way it feels to me. Two individuals with a plan. Working together."

"But what's the plan?" DeMarco asked. "To destroy the SCU? Because that sounds a bit ambitious to me, especially if the idea is to pick us off one by one."

"It does make a kind of sense, though," Hollis said, still thinking about the possibility of two enemies working together. "Using this . . . method. The murders are quite effective at drawing us out, making us visible. And they couldn't be—you should forgive the phrase—normal murders, because then we wouldn't be involved. So, serial murders spread out over multiple states, particularly gruesome in nature, with bodies dumped where they're quickly and easily found, the killings so bizarre and seemingly random that local and state cops or even most FBI units can't effectively investigate."

"Enter the SCU," Diana continued. "Because gruesome and bizarre is pretty much our bailiwick. First two investigators, Miranda and Hollis, with Reese coming and going. Maybe that wasn't enough for them. Maybe they wanted more of us involved, for whatever reason. To test us, or their skill. So the killings continued, the torture and mangling of the victims' bodies escalating. Quentin and I join the team a couple of weeks ago, so a larger SCU presence."

Quentin frowned. "You know, maybe those shots yesterday really weren't about killing either of you guys. Maybe they were about making us sit up and take notice. Maybe one or both of these bastards decided it was time we knew we were being watched. More fun for them, if we knew about it. More of a challenge."

"That's a lot of maybes," DeMarco complained. He was still scanning Main Street, still keeping an eye on the so-far undisturbed and unexploded SUVs parked in front of the sheriff's department. "And it all hinges on the premise that this rampage is about us, about the SCU. If we're wrong about that basic supposition, then we could allow others to die while we're looking in the wrong direction."

"That's just as true the other way," Quentin said. "If we ignore signs pointing to a motive behind this simply because we find the motive hard to swallow, then we're no closer to stopping the killer— or killers—and the rampage continues."

"True."

Diana shook her head and said, "It still all boils down to guesswork, so far, at least. I thought psychic abilities would make this sort of thing easier."

"Sometimes I think they make it harder," Quentin told her. "In fact, I think that a lot."

To Hollis, Diana said, "Not that I'm doubting you, but considering what happened last night in the gray time, do you think this Andrea might have been deceiving you? Lying about there being a bomb?"

"I don't think so. She was awfully convincing. Awfully upset, now that I think about it. But I'm still relatively new to this stuff, so I can't be a hundred percent sure about it."

"So there may not be a bomb?"

"Rationally . . . yes. There may not be a bomb."

Quentin said, "But you aren't sure, and we can't take the chance there *isn't* a bomb."

DeMarco looked at Hollis, his brows rising slightly. "What does your gut tell you? Was Andrea lying? Trying to trick you?"

Slowly, Hollis shook her head. "No. No, I really don't think she was trying to trick me. I think she wanted—needed—to warn me. Because there's a bomb in one of those cars."

"That's all I need to hear," DeMarco said, returning his gaze to the quiet, peaceful street. "So now the question becomes, how do we get out of this with as few casualties as possible?"

"**G**abe, I've got the sheriff getting ready to send the few people he has out to try and clear as much space as possible around the vehicles. Where are you?" Miranda asked.

"About two blocks from the station." He parked the car as he spoke, getting out with his cell and his keys and without the backpack. "I'm armed. And I think I can find this bastard." He locked the car and dropped the keys into one of his jacket pockets.

"What does Roxanne think?" The question was curiously literal.

Tell her I think he's on top of that old theater building half a block down from the station. There's no fire escape, no outside stairs, so you'll have to go up from inside the building.

Gabriel relayed the information, adding, "The building's for rent, Miranda. Empty. There's a rear entrance." When she seemed to hesitate, he added, "Look, I know you wanted to just watch this guy, but if he's willing to blow up a nice little town, I say the time for watching is over."

"Yeah." She sighed. "You won't get an argument about that. But I don't like you going up there alone, Gabe."

"I don't think we have time to argue about it." He was nearly at the rear of the old theater building, where he'd been heading since he stepped out of the car. He could see that the old door was barred by an equally old padlock. "You guys are blocks away, and for all we know one or both of those SUVs are packed with explosives. Maybe even nails and other kinds of shrapnel. An explosion could destroy a lot more than those vehicles, and we both know it. I can take the bastard out."

"All right." Whatever hesitation Miranda might have felt was clearly past. "But don't kill him unless you have to. We need to be able to talk to him if at all possible."

"Copy that."

"Leave the cell on; with a little luck we won't lose the signal."

"Copy that," he repeated. "Talk to you on the other side." He slid the cell, still on, into the other pocket of his jacket and then drew his weapon from the shoulder holster he wore underneath it. "Rox? The lock?"

Working on it. Tougher than I expected. The lock hasn't been opened in a while, I'd say.

"So he used the front entrance to gain access. Wonder whether he had a key or broke in."

In full view of anybody on Main Street, I'm guessing he had a key. He had to look and act normally enough not to attract any undue attention. Just a minute more...

There was a brief pause, and then Gabriel heard a click, and the old padlock swung free. He got rid of it and used muscle to force the door open, not at all happy when the ancient hinges creaked loudly.

Stairs. Just to your right. There's no electricity, Gabe.

"And it's dark as pitch." He barely whispered it, pausing for only a moment inside the door to allow his eyes to adjust a bit to the dark.

These stairs go up to the projection room, I think. From there, we'll have to find the door that leads to the roof.

"When was it ever easy?" With fumbling fingers, he found a rough old handrail and began to climb the dangerously creaky stairs as swiftly as he dared.

"**W**ait—" DeMarco gestured toward the street. "A couple of Duncan's deputies are coming out. Damn, looks like the part-timers. I guess the rest of the first shift is out on patrol."

Hollis said, "They aren't very good at acting casual, are they? Their body language is tense as hell. There's the sheriff. He's a lot better at seeming nonchalant, I have to say."

Miranda rejoined the group near the walkway in time to hear that and said, "As expected, the sheriff has no bomb squad, but he has a call in to Knoxville for the nearest one. Only a couple of his part-timers are at the station. He's sent them out with orders to stay far away from the vehicles and keep the area around them clear. He's going to try to get to the restaurants and stores in the immediate area, alert them to clear themselves and their customers out—or, at least, get away from windows facing the street. We're going to give them five minutes to do as much as they can."

"You're thinking we have to detonate the bomb?" DeMarco said, after a quick glance at her.

"I'm thinking we need to be ready if we have to," Miranda replied. "The nearest bomb squad is more than an hour away—and the lunch crowd, such as it is, is about to head to the downtown restaurants. We don't have the equipment to safely inspect those vehicles, or even to effectively barricade the area, and we don't have the luxury of time."

"If he has a remote, one of us will have to approach before he's likely to trigger it," DeMarco said.

"I'm hoping we're the ones with the remote." She nodded to the keys in his hand. "We can unlock, raise the cargo doors, and start the engines from here. Maybe that'll set off the bomb. If not..."

"The sort of body armor we have isn't going to protect us, Miranda. Not from a bomb."

"Tell me something I don't know. Still, it's all we've got. Before any of us approach those vehicles, we get the vests on."

"Copy that."

But neither DeMarco nor any of the others moved, all their attention fixed on the vehicles a few short blocks away.

Quentin, after gauging the distance between the vehicles and the buildings around them, said, "There is not a whole lot of room down there. And way too many glass windows. I gather you're also hoping for a small bomb or bombs with a small blast radius."

"That would be my preference," Miranda said. "Since explosives have never been part of the M.O. so far, I have to believe whatever he brought with him or got his hands on in the last twelve hours or so isn't likely to be very large or very complicated."

"Which," DeMarco said, "means a remote detonation is a bit more likely. Wiring explosives into a vehicle's electrical system or using some kind of timer is more difficult and time-consuming, even if he knows what he's doing. And since those vehicles have been right out in the open since last night, I'm guessing he didn't want to risk spending any more time than necessary near them."

Diana shook her head and said, "You're all so calm about this." She sounded decidedly tense.

Hollis murmured, "You'd think so, wouldn't you?"

DeMarco looked down at her, a very slight frown pulling at his brows. "Hollis, what are you trying to do? I can feel the effort."

"Yeah, it's . . . hard. But electrical energy is electrical energy, right?" The strain in her voice was evident. "And explosives are . . . inherently unstable. Probably giving off waves of energy just being themselves. I'm trying to see if there's an aura of some kind around . . . Huh. What do you know? I see a funny sort of shimmer above the second SUV. A kind of red haze. Nothing above the one in front."

Miranda said, "Reese, do you still sense him out there?"

"Oh, yeah, he's watching. I still can't pinpoint a location, but I think he's up high. Maybe a rooftop."

"You think he's using his scope or binoculars?"

"Binoculars. I don't feel a gun. Not yet, anyway. But I am having a little more trouble than usual tuning him in." He reached into a pocket and pulled out a handkerchief, handing it to Hollis. "Here."

"What—" She felt the tickle underneath her nose and pressed the cloth there, adding a muttered, "Damn."

"I told you I could feel the effort," DeMarco said.

"It's just a little nosebleed, that's all."

"Yeah, right."

Miranda checked her cell, frowned, and muttered, "Damn, lost the signal."

"What signal?" Quentin asked.

As if she hadn't heard him, Miranda said, "A minute left. Hollis, when this is over, I want you to—"

That was when one of the SUVs exploded.

Dale McMurry both heard and saw the explosion. In fact, he was damn near knocked out of his chair—though that may have been more of a rather drastic flinch on his part than the force of the actual blast.

Like everybody else, he went running outside and toward the station, so shocked by the very notion of something exploding in this normally very peaceful place that he didn't think it through.

Or consider possible consequences.

Gabriel had just reached the old theater's projection room when he heard the explosion. And felt the vibration shudder through the old building.

Shit.

"Goddammit, Rox, where the hell are the stairs to the roof?" Even though his eyes had adjusted and there was—inexplicably— what appeared to be a dirty skylight far above, he could see no sign of a door or another set of stairs upward.

Wait...Over there, behind those shelves sticking out into the room.

A couple of rusted and ancient film cans on one of the shelves mutely proclaimed the reason for its existence in the room, but Gabriel didn't pause to think very much about it. He found the door right where Roxanne had indicated. It was unlocked, opened easily, and gave access to steep stairs leading up.

Climbing them swiftly and silently, he breathed, "Can you give me a sense of where he is?"

I'm still not sure. It feels...weird. Cold. Distant. I should understand what that means, I know I should, but I don't.

At the top of the stairs was another door, and it, too, opened easily under his careful hand. No creaking hinges betrayed him, but he was too wary a hunter not to move with exquisite caution. He opened the door just a few inches at first, to give his eyes time to adjust to the late-morning brightness of the rooftop, then eased it farther open.

Be careful, Gabe.

"Copy that." The whisper was automatic; all his attention was focused on the roof.

It was, for the most part, a flat, tarred roof, various exhaust vents and other pipes sticking up here and there. The stairs had ended on the roof in a kind of dormer, and in the heartbeats it took him to orient himself, Gabriel realized that the front part of the building was behind him.

And behind the dormer.

There's nowhere else he can be, assuming he's still up here. And he has to still be up here. Unless he's a damn bird.

Gabriel would have copied that, but he was concentrating on every careful movement as he eased around the dormer to find the sniper's vantage point. But the caution proved to be unnecessary.

"He's not a bird," Gabriel said out loud, relaxing and slowly holstering his weapon.

What the hell?

Yesterday's sniper—if the very expensive rifle lying beside him was any indication—half-sat with his back against the four-foot parapet wall, where he had apparently crouched to watch the street below. His legs were splayed apart, his hands limp on either side of his hips. He looked rather like a hunter, wearing faded jeans, much-used hiking boots, and a camo jacket, with a backpack nearby.

In one limply open hand was a small black box with a simple toggle switch, apparently the detonator he had used to set off his bomb.

In the other hand was a silenced automatic.

The hole in his right temple hadn't bled much, probably because of the gaping exit wound on the left side of his skull—which had. Blood and tissue were spattered all over the sand-colored bricks.

He was an ordinary-looking man, clean-shaven, with brown hair, and brown eyes that stared sightlessly into eternity.

Gabe, this doesn't make sense.

"You're telling me." He kicked the pistol away from that limp hand just to be sure, then hunkered down and reached to check the pulse. As soon as his fingers touched the dead man's skin, he had to fight not to jerk his hand away in an instinctive reaction.

"Christ."

Gabe?

"He's cold, Rox. And I mean really cold. There's no way he detonated that bomb and then killed himself. This guy's been dead for hours. Hell, maybe for days."

But, what—

That was when they heard the *craa-aack* of a rifle.

From somewhere in the street below.

They didn't decide to abandon the cover of the B&B's shaded yard when the SUV blew, they simply ran toward the sheriff's department, training and instinct guiding them. Because the explosion was bigger than it should have been, blowing out windows on both sides of the street for more than a block and sending hot chunks of metal and melted plastic in all directions.

It was impossible to even guess whether anyone had been hurt but easy to see that the damage to surrounding buildings was substantial. Still, human nature being what it was, the SCU team was only about halfway down the hill when townspeople began pouring out of buildings both damaged and whole.

Hollis heard both Miranda and DeMarco swear, presumably about the curious putting themselves in harm's way, but she was focused on the flaming hulk that had been a gleaming black SUV.

The bomb had been of considerable size, if she was any judge. The SUV only vaguely resembled a vehicle, and pieces of it—or of whatever had been inside it, or of the bomb itself—were still raining down, on the streets and on the curious townsfolk who had rushed out to see what happened.

Hollis turned her attention from the fiery wreck, fighting to ignore the skip in her heartbeat when she saw that DeMarco had gone immediately to the SUV in front, the one that hadn't exploded, and was moving it away from the burning one. So it wouldn't blow up from the heat of the other one, she assumed.

Idiot's going to get himself killed. Dammit, what if I'd been wrong about only one having a bomb?

She shoved that thought away and hurried to help the others try to move the people back and out of danger.

Dale McMurry stopped short yards away from the burning vehicle, staring at it in fascination. He was aware of other people around, of bewildered shouting and curses, of a few folks calling the names of others frantically, but all he could think was, *Damn, what a show!*

Like something in the movies. It was incredibly bright and incredibly loud, with bits of still-burning debris showering the street and the sound of glass tinkling almost musically as shards of it fell.

Entirely forgetting that he was a deputy—even if only a

part-time one—he stood there in the middle of the street and watched the show. Watched the sheriff appear from somewhere and begin trying to shepherd people back toward the buildings. Watched the feds arrive, not even out of breath despite running several blocks, and while one of them moved the undamaged—or at least unexploded—SUV away from the burning one, the others joined in the efforts to get people off the street.

It occurred to Dale only then that the danger might not be over, and he found himself pondering that with a curious detachment. Nothing had hit the SUV; he had been watching, after all. It had just . . . blown sky-high.

Which meant it must have had explosives in it.

A bomb. And that meant that somebody had deliberately set explosives in order to destroy the SUV. And maybe a healthy chunk of Main Street.

Maybe even a few people.

That was when Dale wondered, for the first time, if maybe the show wasn't quite over yet.

He didn't even have time to really get scared about that before feeling a tremendous punch to his back, as though a two-by-four had slammed into him. He saw his sweatshirt sort of balloon out from his chest, the pale gray material turning scarlet, and a strange-tasting hot liquid bubbled up in his mouth.

He didn't actually see the bullet. But as the world tilted crazily and the pavement reared up to meet him, Deputy Dale McMurry realized he had been shot.

And it wasn't anything at all like the movies.

Diana wasn't quite sure where she was at first. Oh, she knew she was in the gray time; that was unmistakable. Everything was gray and still and cold and silent. And there was the unsettling odor, faint though it was, of rotten eggs.

But where was she within—or outside—the gray time?

She looked around herself with a frown and finally recognized the place as, oddly, the cramped conference room at the sheriff's department, where they had sat the evening before, speculating about the case.

And that was odd because she almost always began a visit to the gray time in the room in which she had been sleeping or had otherwise managed to put herself into a trancelike state.

Almost always.

Still frowning, she left that cramped room and moved through the building toward the front door. The empty desks, the round clock—handless and numberless—high on the wall, the silent TV and telephones she passed, all held the eerie qualities of the gray time: the lack of depth or dimension, the lack of color or light or shadow.

She wondered if she would ever truly get used to it.

Probably not.

Probably not supposed to.

Because even without putting it to the test, Diana believed what she had told the others, that the gray time was not a place or time for the living and that no living thing would be able to exist there except temporarily.

She walked out the front door of the building and paused, surprised but not sure why. Main Street, town of Serenade. The street looked like streets in the gray time always looked. Like every place in the gray time looked. Eerie. There were vehicles parked here and there, including the two SUVs left for them the night before.

No people, of course.

The gray twilight surrounded her. She felt cold and absently rubbed her arms, even though she knew it wouldn't help. The presence of the two vehicles bugged her, though she wasn't sure why.

"Okay, so where's my guide?" she asked aloud. "I don't want to wander around in here—out here—with no idea where I'm supposed to go or what I'm supposed to see. Come on, a little help here."

As usual, her voice sounded oddly flat, almost hollow.

After what felt like a long minute or so, she shrugged and

continued down the walkway toward the street. She walked around the nearest SUV, sparing it no more than a glance as she passed.

She paused in the street, wondering where the hell she was supposed to go with no guide—

"Diana."

Finally. She turned to find the same guide who had greeted her the previous night.

"Brooke. Okay, why am I here? I don't remember falling asleep and, besides, isn't it the middle of the day?"

"Is it?"

"Please, let's not do the cryptic guide thing, okay?"

The little girl nodded gravely. "Okay. You came here because you had to, Diana."

"And why is that?"

"I need you to concentrate."

"On what? And why?"

"On Quentin. Reach for him, Diana."

"Before I've done whatever it is I've come here to do?"

"This is what you've come here to do."

Diana frowned. "That doesn't make sense."

"It will. Reach for Quentin. Hold on to the connection the two of you share."

Deciding to humor the guide, Diana thought about Quentin, thought about reaching for him. But even as she did, she knew the effort wasn't a complete one, because she was wary of that connection and used it only when she had to.

There was a sudden flash, as if lightning brightened the twilight for an instant. And for that instant, Diana had the sense of color and noise and life. Of people around her, and movement.

Just for an instant.

Something very similar had happened nearly a year before, when she first met Quentin. When the connection between them began to form, or they both recognized that it had been there for a long time. She still wasn't quite sure which it was.

When she began to consciously remember the gray time for the first time in her adult life.

"Brooke, I don't—"

"Diana, you have to try harder."

Diana was beginning to feel cold, and not because of the normal chill of the gray time. She concentrated, this time reaching for Quentin with more focus, more will.

A lightning flash, this one lasting several seconds. The noise was almost deafening, a roar, the sound of thudding feet and loud voices, a curiously musical tinkling, like wind chimes. Or maybe it was glass breaking and falling to strike some solid surface like concrete or asphalt. A wave of heat swept over her, yet she still felt cold.

Almost at her feet, a young man she vaguely recognized lay on the street. A woman and a man knelt on either side of the young man, and they were pressing what looked like somebody's yellow shirt against his chest. The yellow material was turning scarlet, and the young man, more blood trickling from the corner of his mouth, stared up into the sky with a look she recognized.

He was already dead.

The lightning flash was gone, and she was in the gray time again with only Brooke.

"That poor kid," she said. "He's one of the deputies, I think. What happened?"

"You don't remember?"

"Am I supposed to?" A nameless unease crawled over her, cold and slithering.

"Reach for Quentin, Diana. You have to."

She was even more reluctant now, but not for the same reasons. Now she wasn't afraid of the connection. She was afraid of what the connection would show her.

"You have to," Brooke insisted.

Diana braced herself inwardly and then concentrated, reached for Quentin again.

The bright daylight almost hurt her eyes for a moment or two, and the noise was still deafening, with people running about and shouting, and the SUV burning, and—

She turned her head a little, more in response to the noise and brightness than out of conscious intent, and that was when she saw. She took a step, and then another. And felt her legs go weak.

. Yards away from where the young man had fallen lay another bleeding body, surrounded by other frantic people trying to stop the bleeding, trying by sheer force of will to hold life in a vessel even her layman's eye recognized as too damaged to sustain life on its own.

"Diana! Listen to me—hold on to me. Do you hear? Diana, don't let go of me. Goddammit, do not let go of me!"

Quentin's voice was a hoarse shout, his bloody hands holding one of hers tightly, so tightly, while others on the team worked over her still body.

She wished she could see his face, but the angle was wrong.

The bright daylight flickered, dimmed, flickered—and she was back in the gray time, facing Brooke.

"I'm sorry, Diana."

The cold that swept over Diana then was horribly familiar, a chill terror from her childhood, from seeing a beloved mother lying still and silent in a hospital bed and knowing there was no soul inside.

"Oh, shit," she whispered.

Nine

SHERIFF DUNCAN PAUSED in the doorway of the waiting room and then entered hesitantly. "Any word?"

From her position gazing out one of the big windows that boasted a panoramic view of the mountains in daylight but offered a nighttime view only of the lights of the city below, Miranda said, "She's still in surgery. They haven't told us anything yet, good or bad."

Duncan wanted to say something about no news being good news, but a check of his watch told him that Diana Brisco had been in surgery way too long for there to be any hope of good news. Nearly twelve hours now; it was well after midnight. She had been airlifted directly from the scene to this major medical center more than fifty miles from Serenade, where one of the best trauma units in the Southeast was, in all probability, her only chance for survival.

If she had any chance at all, which the EMTs called first to the scene had very clearly doubted.

He looked at the other two people in the room, noting that Hollis had at least washed the blood off her hands—though a fair amount remained to stain her light-colored sweater—and that

145

DeMarco watched her with an almost imperceptible frown between his brows.

Realizing who was missing, the sheriff asked, "Where's Quentin?"

Hollis replied, "With Diana."

"In surgery?"

She nodded, staring into space rather than meeting his gaze.

Again, Duncan found himself groping for words. "I've never heard of *any* hospital or surgeon allowing something like that. Surgeons, especially, are pretty much God in an operating room."

DeMarco said, "You didn't see his face. Even God would have thought twice before trying to separate him from Diana."

Miranda turned from the window to say, "Nobody in there is happy about it, but they did the best they could, wrapping Quentin in sterile sheets and dousing whatever they couldn't cover with antiseptic. There was no time to lose and no sense wasting any of it arguing with him. Especially when it was obvious to everyone what the outcome would be."

"I'm surprised they didn't try to knock him out," Duncan murmured.

"You didn't see his face," DeMarco repeated.

Duncan really wished he had. "I hope somebody disarmed him" was all he could think of to say.

"I did." DeMarco didn't offer details.

"How's the situation in Serenade?" Miranda asked, clearly not all business but making a good show of it.

"Hell," the sheriff replied frankly. "Though a bit quieter now than it was all afternoon and most of the evening. Thank God more of your people showed up to lend a hand. We have multiple injuries, damaged buildings with glass and other material still falling into the street if the breeze picks up, state cops and feds and firefighters crawling all over the place, the media crawling all over the place— and a whole lot of terrified people. But of the townsfolk, only the one fatality, so far."

"I'm sorry about Dale," she said.

"So am I. He was just a kid marking time in a uniform, with nothing special planned for his future. But he should have had more time to find something special for himself."

"Yes." She drew a breath and let it out slowly. "I'm sorry we brought such tragedy to your town, Des."

"You didn't bring it." He kept his voice stoic. "That maniac you've been tracking brought it. I just hope you get the son of a bitch."

"We will."

Though her voice wasn't especially emphatic, somehow he believed her. Maybe *because* her voice wasn't especially emphatic.

Miranda said, "Dr. Edwards is in Serenade?"

"Yeah, she arrived with the first group of your people. In one of the choppers. I hope you don't mind that I hitched a ride on one heading back up this way. The pilot said his orders were to fly up here and stand by to ferry some of you back to Serenade."

"It's a lot quicker than driving," Miranda said. "And you're welcome to the ride. As soon as we get some word about Diana..."

Duncan assumed that Miranda, at least, would need to get back to Serenade fairly soon; another SCU agent had arrived with the first group of them and had stepped in to fill her role as lead investigator, something the sheriff gathered was very much a temporary thing. But from the sound of it, Quentin was here for the duration, whatever that might be. Duncan wasn't sure about the other two.

Before the silence could stretch too far, he said, "Your doctor seems to believe our clinic has enough of the basics for her and her assistant to work with, and the rest she brought with her." He paused. "Never seen a doctor travel with so many boxes of equipment."

"She's a top-notch forensic pathologist," Miranda said. "I should have called her in yesterday—or, rather, Tuesday—instead of sending the two murder victims to the state M.E."

"From what I saw, calling in her and her mobile lab is a major production, so not something to order up if you aren't even sure how long you'll be staying. The first chopper couldn't even hold her assistant, just her and the equipment." He paused, then added, "Anyway, she's going to do the autopsy on Dale. And she's been working on the guy your people found on the roof of the old theater. Said right off the bat he'd been dead at least twelve hours when he was found."

Slowly, DeMarco said, "So, not yesterday's sniper but at least possibly Tuesday's."

Hollis said, "That doesn't make sense. Two snipers? What, has somebody sicced an army on us?"

"If so, it's not a very efficient one," DeMarco said without emotion. "Two misses on Tuesday, and only one shot fired yesterday. I have to believe he didn't just get . . . lucky . . . yesterday. If the deputy wasn't the target—and I think we all believe he wasn't—then either it was sheer bad luck that he stepped in front of the bullet aimed at Diana, or else the sniper was showing off and meant to get both of them with a single shot."

"Why Diana?" Hollis was staring down at her clasped hands. "That doesn't make sense either. She's not even a full agent yet; she hasn't had *time* to make any enemies."

"The way we were running around out there this morning, it could have been any of us," DeMarco pointed out. "He probably marked all of us as agents on Tuesday, while he was watching from that deer blind. We have no way of being sure Diana was the specific target yesterday. He could have intended to just get an SCU agent, period."

"Especially since the shots on Tuesday were fired at you and Reese," Miranda reminded Hollis.

"Okay, but two snipers?"

Miranda said, "I have a hunch we'll find that the man killed on the roof of the old theater was . . . pure theater. Staged, posed, for us to find. Another victim."

DeMarco nodded. "It makes more sense that way. If nothing

else, it had our people focused on the wrong building, the wrong place, which gave the real sniper more time to do what he intended to do and get safely away. Plus, finding a body arranged that way is bound to be a distraction for us, another . . . red herring."

"Maybe because we were getting too close?" Hollis said, a hopeful note in her voice.

"I wish I thought so," DeMarco said.

Nodding, Miranda said, "I wish I did too. But it feels to me more like him just being clever. Playing games. Staging a 'sniper' for us to find, and on the roof of an old theater, is pretty dramatic."

Before anyone could respond to that, a doctor came in to the room. Wearing scrubs and exhaustion, he looked around with eyes too old for his youngish face and settled immediately on Miranda as the one to speak to.

"She's made it through surgery," he said, in the flattened voice of someone who had been fighting a long battle he was afraid he might have lost. "We've done as much as we could to repair the damage. Her heart stopped twice on the table, and we've got her on a ventilator. Honestly, I'm surprised she made it this far. But she's strong—and he's not letting go. If she makes it through the next forty-eight hours, she has a chance."

"A chance for full recovery?" Miranda's voice was steady.

"I don't know," he said bluntly. "There are some . . . variables here I don't really understand, including an unusual amount of electrical activity going on in her brain."

"Going on now?"

"We've done three scans, initially to check for damage to the spine because the bullet passed so close. On the first scan, her brain lit up like a Christmas tree. Very unusual. So we scanned again, after we got her a bit more stabilized, and again after surgery. A hell of a lot of activity in the first and third scans, much less in the second. As if she's in and out. Or maybe using energy in a peaks-and-valleys kind of rhythm. But the peaks are very high, very intense.

Too intense. If they occur too often or last too long . . . I frankly don't know how long that can go on before it damages her brain, just the way a high fever would."

Hollis said steadily, "You can't be sure of that."

He looked at her briefly. "No. But it's what my training and experience are telling me."

Miranda said, "The brain activity is in an area you wouldn't expect it to be?"

"In several areas I wouldn't expect. And all I feel certain of is that she's a long way from being brain-dead. Whether that will have any positive effect on her physically or will do the opposite is a question I just can't answer."

He sighed. "The bullet missed her spine, but there was a lot of damage and she lost a lot of blood. I've seen people come back from worse. Not many, but some. Look, there's nothing any of you can do for her now. She's being settled in the ICU and will be there for days yet." *Assuming she survives.* "No additional visitors for at least a few hours, not until morning preferably, and even then I'm asking you to make it one at a time and brief. It's difficult enough for the doctors and nursing staff to work around Agent Hayes.

"Go get cleaned up, get some sleep. I have your number, and I'll call you if there's any change." His mouth twisted slightly. "Or he will."

"We appreciate you allowing Quentin to stay with her, Doctor."

"There wasn't any allowing about it, and you know that, Agent Bishop." He shrugged. "I've seen something like that only once before, and I believe it made all the difference that they were able to stay together. I'm not too proud to accept all the help I can get. So. The staff has instructions not to interfere with Agent Hayes."

"Thank you."

"If she has family, I think it would be best to call them in. As soon as possible."

"Thank you," Miranda repeated. Then, as he began to turn away, she said, "Doctor? When her heart stopped, you had to shock her."

He nodded, then said simply, "Agent Hayes never let go of her hand, and he never even flinched. One day I'd like very much to talk to you about that. Because I've never seen anything like it in my life."

"It might be best," Brooke said, "if you went to the hospital on this side. To be near..."

"My body?" Diana heard a slightly brittle laugh escape her, a sound given an eerie cadence by the hollow almost-echo of the gray time. "What's the point, when I can't get back to it?" She was sitting on a cold bench on a hauntingly silent and empty gray time Main Street in Serenade, where she had been since her second attempt to connect with Quentin had shown her something she very much wished she had never seen.

She had no idea how much time had passed in the living world.

Was she already dead? If she was able to bring herself at least partway back so she could see something of the living world, even if only for a split second, would she see her terribly wounded body laid out on a slab in some cold and sterile morgue?

Or had she been sitting, frozen, on this bench for long enough that she would see her own funeral?

Jesus.

"You're still holding on to the connection with Quentin," Brooke observed serenely.

"It's more like he's holding on to it. On to me."

"Well, he's a stubborn man."

"Yes," Diana murmured.

"And he had a...jolt or two of power that helped him hold on. Helped make the connection stronger. He's determined to hold you, no matter what. Even to pull you back."

Diana could feel that, faintly, a steady pull with an occasional more-urgent tug she was powerless to obey. "For all the good it'll do. I've tried to reach out for him, but...I can't. Not this time."

And she had tried. Desperately.

Why didn't I reach when I had the chance? Really reach, really connect with Quentin the way he wanted.

The way I wanted.

Too late. Dammit, too late now.

The anguish of that was more painful than anything she had ever known.

"Don't give up, Diana."

"Yeah, right." She shivered, unable to stop the memories that washed over her. Herself as only a toddler, being led by her father down a long hospital corridor lined with rooms filled with people even her baffled, frightened child's mind had known were more dead than living. People who lay silent and still in their beds, machines beeping and hushing as they recorded heartbeats and "assisted" the bodies to draw air into their lungs.

And, finally, being led into one of the rooms. Held up by her father so she could see . . . her mother. Or what was left of her. A still body, its heartbeats recorded by a beeping machine, another machine forcing it to breathe.

Just a body.

Diana had known beyond a shadow of a doubt that her mother was no longer there. And that she was never coming back.

What she knew now was that her mother, in a desperate attempt to locate her lost daughter, had pushed her psychic gifts beyond limits she could control, severing the tie that bound her spirit to her physical self. It had been only a matter of time before her body, kept alive by machines, finally ceased to function.

Diana had blocked those memories for a long, long time, because terror and grief had threatened to overwhelm her and because, barely a year ago, she discovered that she shared her mother's gifts—and the risks involved in using them.

Only it hadn't been a case of her pushing her gifts, as her mother had, but a sniper's bullet that had fatally wounded her body and severed her spirit's connection to it.

"Not severed. Not completely, at least. It doesn't have to end that way, Diana."

"Doesn't it? Hasn't it already?" Hard as she tried, Diana couldn't hold her voice steady.

Matter-of-fact, Brooke said, "You would have moved on by now. Mediums almost never linger here."

"Almost never."

"Because they understand death far better than most people. They understand it's a change but not an ending. So they tend to be ready to move on, to take the next step in their journey. But you haven't. You're still here. Which means there might be something you can do to change things for yourself."

"Or it might just mean I'm stubborn too. Holding on to life even when there's no real hope."

"We shape our own fate."

"Do we?"

"Some of it. Maybe most of it. If you have a stronger reason to live than to die, perhaps you can make that happen."

For the first time she could remember, Diana heard the words of a guide and was afraid she was being deceived. Could she trust Brooke to tell her the truth? About anything?

So far, she had not felt that sense of wrongness that had alerted her to the false Quentin. Brooke looked exactly as she had looked before, spoke in the same way, and nothing about her seemed false or off. But Diana didn't trust herself to sense anything in particular, not now, because the probability of her own death was a black cloud of terror and regret wrapping around her, smothering her.

Accepting this fate was no easier because she knew something of herself would survive death, that there was some existence afterward. She didn't want to die. Didn't want to leave the living world.

She didn't want to leave Quentin.

She wasn't ready. Not now. Not yet.

Trying her best to push all that aside, she heard herself responding to the guide, attributing her casual, almost offhand tone to sheer instinct. "Make that happen? Do something to change my own fate? What, here? I don't *do* anything in the gray time, Brooke, except talk to guides."

"This time maybe you can."

"Yeah, like what? Figure out who shot me? I doubt he's on this side." She paused, then added quickly, "He isn't, is he?"

"No."

Diana wondered if she could believe that. If she should.

What if he's here? Could he find me here? Could he hurt me even more on this side? Hollis was afraid Samuel's pet monster could have, if he was dead. How do I know the sniper isn't capable of that, whether he's alive or dead?

Do I even understand this place, this time, as well as I always believed I did?

Could there be someone else here, another psychic, watching her? Watching and perhaps exerting some kind of control or at least influence over her? And, if so, how could that person, that being, hide in a place where there was no darkness or light, where there were no shadows?

"You have to look for the truth."

"The truth underneath it all, yeah, I remember. I don't have a clue what you meant by that, but I remember."

"It's all about ties. About connections."

Diana sighed. "Between what? People? Places? Events?"

"All that."

"Thanks. That was a lot of help."

Brooke turned and walked away.

Diana looked after her for a moment, then got up from the bench and quickly followed. She didn't know where she was being led and had the awful fear that she could end up someplace a lot worse than an eerie Serenade Main Street, but one thing she was absolutely sure of was that she didn't want to be alone in the gray time.

"Hey, wait up."

"Keep up," Brooke said, without turning.

"You've got a mouth on you for a kid."

"You of all people should know I'm not a kid," Brooke said as Diana caught up with her. "None of us is a child in the gray time, even if we died as children. I've lived and grown up and died more than once, and I remember every life when I'm here. We all remember it here."

That did startle Diana, even though it explained a lot; she had been communicating with unnervingly mature "child" guides all her life. But it also raised the question... "Wait. I don't remember another life. Just the one. What does that mean?"

"It could be another sign that you don't belong here."

Diana began to feel more hopeful even as she wondered, again, if she could believe what any guide said.

"Then again," Brooke continued, "it could just mean you're a new soul."

Resisting the impulse to swear out loud as she was swearing inwardly, Diana instead struggled to keep her voice steady when she said, "So people who believe in reincarnation are right?"

"Let's say they're on the right track."

"Karma?"

Brooke didn't need the question clarified. "There are far worse hells than a pit of fire and torment. And better heavens than pretty clouds and harp music."

"And we reap what we sow?"

"We're called to account for our actions in one way or another, never doubt that. It's all a question of balance. The universe likes things to even out. Sooner or later."

Diana wanted to think about that but became aware that they were no longer walking along Serenade's Main Street. Everything around her seemed to blur for an instant, and then she realized that she was, once again, in the gleaming, featureless halls of that one-time asylum.

"Brooke, why are we here?"

"Because we have to be. You have to be."

"I thought you wanted me to go to the hospital where my—where I am. This can't be that place, because this place doesn't exist in the living world. Not anymore."

"You have to be here," Brooke repeated.

"She's lying to you," a new voice said calmly.

Diana stopped, turned very slowly, and wasn't at all relieved or happy to see Quentin standing in an open doorway just behind them, smiling at her.

"I know I should go back with you, Miranda," Hollis said. "I know the doctor said there was nothing we could do for Diana here. But..."

"But you think otherwise?" Miranda showed no signs of impatience, even though the sheriff had gone ahead to tell their pilot that they were ready for the trip back to Serenade.

Hollis hesitated, then moved her shoulders in a gesture not quite a shrug. "I don't know what I think. But what I *feel* is that I need to stay close, at least for now."

"You realize that staying here will be difficult for you."

"Yeah. Yeah, I figured that out a few hours ago." Hollis didn't look at DeMarco, even though she could feel him watching her.

Miranda nodded and said, "I thought you'd seen at least a few spirits since we got here."

"It was worse downstairs in the trauma unit. A little better up here." Hollis avoided looking toward the hallway visible from this waiting area. "But they're still...awfully vivid. And I can't seem to close the door."

"Probably not one you opened." Miranda offered her a twisted smile. "I know from experiences with my sister that there are some places where spirits walk, and hospitals are at the top of that list. Mediums really can't help seeing them."

"I can handle it," Hollis said, hoping she could.

"I don't doubt you can. It just won't be easy. Look, Hollis, we don't know how the gray time works, but we do know Diana has always been convinced there are souls who end up there, discon-nected from their bodies. Trapped, at least for a while, before they can move on."

"Or come back. Yes." Hollis was praying DeMarco would keep his mouth shut; they hadn't gotten the chance that morning to re-port the events of the night to Miranda, especially the part about Hollis now being drawn to the gray time whenever Diana opened the door. And Hollis wanted it to stay that way, at least for now. Be-cause she had no doubt that Miranda would not approve of the risky plan taking shape in her mind.

"You believe she's there?"

"The doc said her heart stopped twice. We know it stopped once back in Serenade. If the gray time really is a corridor between this world and the next, I think it's likely that's where Diana's spirit would go. It's a place she's comfortable in, confident, almost at home. It could be a refuge for her in a situation like this one."

"A place to hide?"

"Maybe. With all that trauma to her body...maybe. She told me Bishop believes her conscious and subconscious minds haven't fully integrated yet after all the years of being medicated, and one thing her subconscious had gotten very good at was protecting it-self. What her subconscious, her spirit, knows best is the gray time. I really think retreating there would be almost automatic. If so, she's still halfway in this world, this reality. At least half alive. She might try to contact one of us. Maybe Quentin. Or maybe me."

"I agree she may have gone there. But we don't know if her con-nection with Quentin is strong enough to keep her anchored on this side. Not if she truly died." Miranda's voice was on the edge of emo-tionless but didn't quite make it.

"All the more reason for me to stay close. Even if she's lost that anchor, another medium might be able to see her. Speak to her. Maybe even help her."

DeMarco spoke up for the first time to say, "You don't see the spirits of people you know, coworkers. Right?"

"I haven't. That doesn't mean I can't. And since Diana's a medium, it might make it easier for me to see her. Maybe. I just... believe I should stay, Miranda."

"Then you'll stay."

"So will I," DeMarco said.

Without looking at him, Hollis said, "You don't have to."

"I'll stay," he said to Miranda. "If Diana was the target and not just one of us chosen at random, our insane sniper might decide to come here and finish the job."

"The thought had occurred."

"So I'll stay. Even without being at her bedside or outside her door, I should be able to sense a threat to her."

"Without a connection to her?"

"I still have her blood on me," he replied, his voice remote. "That's enough of a connection."

Miranda didn't question that. "Okay."

"Galen's on-site now?"

"He flew one of the choppers."

"Then you've got the best watchdog on the team." DeMarco nodded. "And if you tell him I said that, I'll deny it."

Miranda smiled faintly. "Gotcha."

"What about the twins?"

Unsurprised that he knew, she replied, "Hopefully still in the background, unless the sniper spotted Gabe. But even if he was spotted, Roxanne certainly wasn't. We also have a few more team members on-site now, as the sheriff noted."

"Might be playing into the sniper's hands," DeMarco pointed out. "With so many of us here, he could be setting us up for a turkey shoot."

"Don't worry, we won't make it that easy for him." Without waiting for a response, she added, "I'll speak to the doctor again before I leave and make sure you're both cleared to stay near Diana—for her own protection."

Hollis said, "Thanks. And keep us posted on what's happening in Serenade, will you?"

"I will." Miranda turned her head just as Sheriff Duncan appeared in the doorway. He was carrying two overnight bags and looked somewhat bemused.

"Your pilot asked me to bring these in," he told Miranda, as he set the bags in a couple of the waiting-room chairs. "He seemed to be sure that Hollis and Reese would be staying."

"Thanks, Des." Without explaining a thing, Miranda merely said to DeMarco, "There's also a change of clothes for Quentin in your bag. Assuming either of you can persuade him to leave Diana long enough for a hot shower and a meal, that is."

"We'll do our best."

Miranda nodded. "One last thing. I need to contact Diana's father and let him know what happened."

With a slight frown, Hollis said, "I . . . don't think she'd want that."

"Neither do I. But she hadn't decided absolutely to completely cut that tie, and absent written instructions to the contrary, I have to follow procedure. If you don't already, you should both know that Elliot Brisco is an extremely powerful man, and he's not been at all happy about Diana's involvement with the FBI."

"Understatement," Hollis murmured.

"Yeah, he's likely to be spewing fire and brimstone."

DeMarco smiled, though only someone who knew him well would have seen wry amusement in the expression. Anybody else probably would have felt the need to find a warm corner somewhere. "If I could handle Samuel's brand of fire and brimstone, I imagine I can handle Brisco's."

"True enough. Just wanted to warn you. And to tell you that one thing Diana *did* put in writing, as per procedure before coming on her first assignment, was that Quentin holds her medical power of attorney. Which means that in addition to being worried about

Diana's condition and pissed about the direction she chose for her life, Brisco is also going to be powerless to make medical decisions for her. Men like him really don't like to be powerless."

"Oh, boy," Hollis said with a sigh. "Aren't we going to have fun."

"Well, you should have at least a brief respite before you have to deal with him; he's likely to be at one of his companies on the West Coast or in New York, possibly in London or even Hong Kong."

"I'll hope for the latter. And find a way to make peace with my conscience if he gets here too late."

"And we'll all hope that's not even an issue," Miranda told her.

"Amen."

"See you two later." She briskly gathered up the sheriff as she left the waiting room, allowing him no chance to do anything but wave at the two remaining behind.

"It's not a risky plan," DeMarco said as soon as they were alone in the room, "it's an insane plan."

"Maybe, but thanks for not giving it away." Hollis frowned at him as several thoughts occurred. "Or do you think Miranda got it too? Because I was broadcasting?"

"You weren't. And after what's happened in the last two days, Miranda's shield is about as solid as I've ever known it to be. And a lot more solid now than it was when you got through before the bomb went off. My guess is that she and Bishop close every possible chink in that shield when they're under attack or expect to be. It's a trade-off: a diminished ability to use the extra senses but also a lot more protection."

Hollis nodded but said, "I wasn't broadcasting?"

"Not so much. Either you're learning to shield or else an insane plan makes you secretive on every level."

Then how could you read me? She didn't ask aloud but stared at him, still frowning.

He returned her suspicious gaze with a completely unreadable one of his own.

Hollis decided not to ask out loud. "Anyway, I don't know if I'll even have the chance. I'm way too wound up to sleep."

"I won't stand by and let you sedate yourself, Hollis."

"Will you quit doing that?"

"Just making an educated guess."

She wished she believed that.

"The point," DeMarco said, "is that even if you managed to get to the gray time and find Diana there—what then? What is it you believe you can do to help?"

"I don't know."

"You nearly didn't make it out the last time."

Hollis opened her mouth to respond, then closed it.

DeMarco was nodding. "Maybe because the two of you were under a kind of attack from someone else in the gray time. An attack—and an attempt to deceive Diana."

"We don't know what any of that meant."

"We know Diana was shot yesterday. When the shooter could have aimed at any of us, he picked her. I don't believe it was random in any sense of the word. He aimed for Diana, and he hit her. Put that together with the gray time visit the other night and I'd call it a pretty goddamn good indication *somebody* is out to hurt her, at the very least."

"That's not what you said earlier."

"Well, it wasn't exactly something I could be so definite about to Miranda without going into what happened Tuesday night. Which you very clearly didn't want me to do."

Damn telepaths.

Hollis drew a breath and let it out slowly. "Okay. Granted. There's a better than even chance someone has targeted Diana. A chance that person can attack her spirit as well as her body, and maybe even more violently. But... Look, when you pulled me out of the gray time, you weren't actually in there with us, right?"

He nodded again. "Right. It was more like I reached in an arm to pull you out. I had the sense of coldness, of something...unpleasantly nightmarish. But I wasn't there. Didn't see or hear anything."

"*Nightmarish*. That's a good word for a very creepy place."

"A place Diana is very, very familiar with," DeMarco reminded her.

"Yes. A place she's visited most of her life. But you weren't there. You don't understand how strange and...lonely...that place really is. How absolutely desolate."

"Hollis—"

"She's always gone there with a purpose, to help someone else. I think that's one reason she's been strong there, how she's been able to move through that place or time or whatever it is without being the least bit afraid. But...what if, this time, she knows, Reese? What if she's in there, *stuck* in there all alone, and she knows what happened to her?"

"Then I'm sorry for her. But I still don't know what it is you believe you can do to help her."

The hell of it was, Hollis didn't know either. But she also knew she couldn't just stand by without trying something.

Anything.

Ten

ROXANNE WOLF CHECKED the perimeter of Serenade for the fourth time, moving slowly and being very, very thorough. She also had to be extremely cautious—because it was quite dark all around the outskirts of downtown due to the power outage, and because the small town was still playing reluctant host to more cops, more FBI agents, and way too much media, not to mention electric-company crews still working to restore power.

Which meant there were a hell of a lot of unfamiliar faces wandering around, strangers roaming not only the scene of the bomb blast but the entire town, even this late.

Flashlights jabbed through the darkness here and there, several times narrowly missing Roxanne as she slipped through the night.

"I could trip over him and not know it," she muttered softly.

He could be right in the middle of everything, Gabriel agreed as his twin returned to the roof of a building very near the edge of town, where she had one of the best vantage points possible—and three separate ways down.

"Normally I'd say there was a slim chance," Roxanne told him. "But not this time. This bastard has balls enough for anything. Hell, he could be carrying a badge of some kind, or be tech support or

EMS or one of the media; in all the chaos, who's going to think about screening I.D.s to make damn sure everybody is who they claim to be?"

Miranda will.

"When she gets back here, sure. But it'll take way more time than I like to check everybody." Roxanne raised her binoculars and studied the brightly lit center of downtown. Dozens of cops in various uniforms and nearly as many FBI agents, wearing windbreakers sporting the acronym prominently, were still moving about with clipboards and notebooks and the tools necessary to interview witnesses and collect and tag the evidence literally scattered over two blocks.

The media people remaining this late had been herded into one area at the north end of Main Street, held back from the cops and technicians working the scene by yellow crime-scene tape and several watchful deputies.

The part-time deputies, Roxanne had noted, looked more than a little shell-shocked, but they were clinging to training and doing their best to be professional in the face of chaos none of them could have been prepared to face working in this pleasant small town.

Picture-postcard perfect. Gabe's voice was wry in her mind. *The chamber might want to rethink the advertising.*

"Yeah."

The muted roar of several portable generators powering the big work lights was the loudest sound in the otherwise unnatural quiet of the small town. It set Roxanne's teeth on edge. She had the restless, skin-crawling uneasiness that warned her something darker than the night was prowling Serenade, and she had learned to trust that very human sense.

Yeah, he's close. But I can't quite get him. It's almost like . . . there's too much negative energy blocking me. Interference of some kind. Maybe the violence of the bomb. Or maybe something else.

"Maybe just him. Right in the middle of everything, like you said. Why do I feel like he knows us a hell of a lot better than we know him?"

If he's been watching long enough, he very well could. He must have found our tracker and ditched his car. Came back here with a different ride. And he's probably been on foot since then, moving around. We won't be finding him or his things in a motel room, not again.

"Dammit. I wish Miranda would get back here."

She'll be here soon. In the meantime, whatever the other cops and the media are doing, the SCU agents are focusing where they need to. Identifying that staged shooter on the theater's roof. Although...

"Although what?"

I'm beginning to wonder if that even matters, Rox. Five'll get you ten when they I.D. the guy they'll find he was a hunter out in the woods yesterday, maybe last night.

"Because?"

Because those were the clothes he was wearing, because the backpack held minimal rations and camping gear, and because I don't believe our guy had all that much time to get fancy.

Roxanne shifted a bit to keep her muscles from cramping up but was wary of moving very much, even though it was dark.

"So he found an easy victim and just left him up here with the gun. Makes sense. But..."

But what?

"I sensed the shooter on that roof, Gabe."

Sure you did—at first, before we got to the old theater building. But by the time we got there, you were already saying what you felt was different, odd.

"Okay, but if I was sensing him because he'd been there, how'd he get off that roof so fast—and get himself positioned at street level at the corner of the courthouse blocks away?"

They knew he'd been there because he had left them a mocking bit of proof: a shell casing, standing neatly on end right there on the concrete—with a circle of red chalk around it just to make sure the dumb-ass police couldn't possibly miss it.

Bastard.

I don't know, Rox. I still doubt he took the chance of coming out the way he must have gone in, by the front door. Too many people would have seen him leave. Maybe he had a rope and managed to rappel down the outside of the building while we were inside. He could have come down in that little alley between the theater and the next building over. I doubt anybody would have seen him.

"Maybe—though we didn't find any sign a grappling hook was used, did we?"

No. But we weren't really looking for that, were we?

"Point is, I shouldn't have felt anything at all once the real shooter was off that roof, not if the dead guy was an innocent victim."

Maybe you were picking up residual energy from the gun, Gabriel offered.

"Yeah. And maybe it was something else."

Like what?

"I don't know. But the possibilities are scaring the hell out of me."

From another vantage point not so very far from where he was perfectly aware Roxanne watched, the sniper did his own sweep of the town, gazing through infrared binoculars of a highly advanced design, his lips pursing unconsciously as he noted the continued presence of numerous law-enforcement officers.

That wouldn't make things easier.

Not that he cared. He loved a challenge. Besides, it was a not-unplanned-for development.

He changed the settings on the binoculars as he focused on the brightly lit few blocks around the heart of town, where most of the activity was centered. He spotted one individual in particular down there, tracked the methodical and professional actions with a critical eye, and waited for a moment of stillness and privacy to make contact.

Any trouble?

The response came back immediately, strong and clear.

Of course not. The I.D. is absolutely authentic and so am I. With all the new people here on the scene, nobody's going to question me. They'll never suspect a thing.

BJ wasn't so sure. *Maybe and maybe not.*

I'm telling you, they won't expect this, especially if you keep doing your job. And he keeps doing his. Where is he?

You don't know?

Don't play games with me, BJ. If you aren't keeping a leash on him, we're all fucked.

He's occupied with his latest toy, all right? He'll be perfectly happy for at least the next eight or ten hours.

And he won't be found?

Something else BJ wasn't too sure of, but he didn't allow even a tinge of doubt to creep into his response. *Not a chance in hell.*

Good. So we're ready for the next step.

We're ready. Any preference?

With so many profilers around, we don't want to go getting too predictable. I vote we take out a noncombatant.

It was a possibility they had discussed. In fact, they had discussed just about every possibility either of them had been able to dream up.

Best to be prepared, always.

That'll be easy enough. Whole town is crawling with them, even at this hour.

So pick your shot. But wait. Until she gets back. Until she can see it happen. We need to keep her rattled and off balance.

BJ considered. *Don't know that I've ever seen her rattled.*

She needs to feel threatened, under attack.

She doesn't already?

Some. But not enough, because he's not here yet.

You're sure?

Very sure. We can't finish this, once and for all, until he's here.

Copy that.

Now leave me alone for a while. I need to concentrate.

Copy that.

BJ closed the door in his mind with the ease of a lifetime's practice and used his other senses as he continued to scan the busy little town. It wouldn't be so easy this time, he knew, to take his shot and get away clean. Not even with night providing excellent cover. Because there were more people hunting him now, including the Wolf, who had already come too close too many times in the past twelve or so hours.

He really wanted to take out the Wolf. Both Wolves.

But that wasn't the plan. Not yet, at least.

He swept the town again and then occupied himself for several minutes mentally going over his escape route, until he was sure there wouldn't be a wasted motion or a wasted moment.

When he was sure the plan was solid, he went back to scanning the town, considering first this potential target and then that one, deliberately looking for something unexpected.

Something none of them would see coming.

And all the time he searched, he listened for the sounds of a returning helicopter.

Haven

Bailey dropped her shoulder bag onto a chair and sighed as she studied John and Maggie Garrett. "Do you really think this is a good idea?"

"I think it's a lousy idea," John said without hesitation.

"I'm not crazy about it myself," Maggie added. "But she's absolutely adamant about it, Bailey."

"She's twelve years old, Maggie. Do you really believe she should be the one making the decision?"

"Yes. I do."

Without showing much surprise, Bailey merely said, "And what does Bishop say?"

"You know what he said. He told you to come and get Ruby and take her to Serenade."

"Serenade. Where a bomb went off and one of our people was shot. Where a serial killer dumped two of his victims and where a sniper—possibly the same serial killer—is at large, still armed and probably still pissed. Where the media is nosing around and way too many cops are tripping over one another, and the townsfolk are scared witless. *That* Serenade?"

"That Serenade."

"Jesus, Maggie. I knew Bishop would go out on some pretty long limbs, but I never expected to see you on one of them."

"There's a lot at stake."

"I know what's at stake. And I know what Ruby is capable of. But she's just a kid." Bailey shook her head. "Look, ethics and morals aside, what about legalities? You two were appointed Ruby's temporary legal guardians, along with Bishop and Miranda, while Ruby's mother and those other weirdly passive church members are assessed by psychologists and social services. But there are rules about temporary guardianship, and I can't believe any judge would think it's a good idea to take Ruby to a town where we have an active investigation going on. Especially one that's turned as violent as this one has."

Her voice steady, Maggie said, "Ruby wants to go. One of her guardians will be there. We have legal permission."

"Jesus," Bailey repeated.

"Keep her safe," Maggie responded simply.

Without pointing out all the difficulties in that request, Bailey said instead, "While she does what? And what does any of this have to do with her, anyway?"

From the doorway of the study, a very small voice said, "I have to be there. In Serenade. It's important."

Bailey turned her head to look at Ruby. "Why?"

"I can't tell you that. I'm sorry, but I can't. It could change the wrong things if I told you. It could make it all worse."

"Did you tell Bishop?" Bailey asked directly.

"No. But...I think he knows why. Part of it anyway."

Bailey looked at Maggie with lifted brows. "And that doesn't make you curious as hell?"

"What do you think?" Maggie sighed. "But if I've learned anything in my life, it's that people have to be free to make their own choices."

"Agreed. People. Not kids. Kids need us to watch over them. We both know that."

Shaking her head slightly, Maggie said, "In case you hadn't noticed, Ruby is a very old soul."

"I am," Ruby offered gravely. "And I haven't been a kid in a long, long time, Bailey."

"Still."

"It's okay. I know what I'm doing," Ruby said.

Her frowning gaze on the serious girl, Bailey said, "Ruby, it's dangerous there. People have been killed. People have been...hurt. Badly hurt. It's not a place where you should be."

"I wish I didn't have to go there." Steady though her voice was, there was a forlorn note in it. "I wish....But I have to."

Maggie looked at Ruby for a long moment, seemed to hesitate, then said to Bailey, "The jet's standing by. Galen will meet you at the other end and take you to Serenade. You'll get there before dawn, and with all the commotion, chances are good nobody will even notice. There's a house very close to the B&B where most of the team is staying. He'll get you there safely and keep watch afterward. You're to keep Ruby inside and out of sight."

In clear protest, Ruby said, "But, Maggie—"

"That's the deal, Ruby. You stay inside and out of sight. You obey Bailey. If there's anything you need Miranda or the rest of the team to know, you tell Bailey and let her relay the information. But you do not go outside or even show your face at a window. And if

Bailey or Miranda tells you it's time to go, you don't argue. Under-stand?"

Ruby nodded slowly. "I understand."

"What about Lexie?" Maggie asked, referring to the absence of Ruby's constant companion.

"I've given—She's going to stay here with Cody, if that's okay."

"Of course it's okay. But are you sure, honey?"

"I'm sure. She hates plane rides. She loves Winston, Reiko, and Archie," Ruby added, referring to the three dogs belonging to the Garrett household. "And, besides, it'll be . . . quieter here. So she won't be afraid."

"And you won't have to hide her?"

"I don't expect I'd have to. But . . . just in case. She should stay here with Cody. He'll take care of her."

Maggie nodded. "Is your bag ready?"

"Yeah. I packed a while ago. I'll go get it." And when John took a step forward, she waved away help, adding, "It's okay, the bag is on wheels. I can get it."

When she had gone to get her bag, John shook his head and said, "That kid really is way too old for her years. Christ, I hope Bishop knows what he's doing."

"He usually does," Bailey said, her tone more wry than reas-suring.

"Okay, but since when does he use kids as soldiers?"

"She was a soldier against Samuel at that church of his," Bailey reminded him quietly. "Without her very powerful help, they never could have defeated the bastard."*

John shook his head. "That was different. She'd been left for dead and pretty much had to be there, had to help them fight—in pure self-defense if nothing else. But there was no deliberate, pre-meditated decision to put her in the line of fire."

"Well," Bailey murmured after a moment of silence, "a good

---

*Blood Sins

lawyer could probably argue it the other way. Bishop being Bishop and all. But I get your point."

Maggie said, "He seems determined to keep her out of the line of fire in this case. And as safeguarded as possible. But she wants to be in Serenade, and he agreed it was a good idea. Maybe he believes she'll see something that'll help."

"She saw what happened to Diana while she was here," John reminded his wife. "Far away from Serenade. For all the good it did. We couldn't stop it, after all."

"Because we couldn't get in touch with them in time. If something else is going to happen and she's closer to the scene, there may be time enough for a warning to make a difference."

"Miranda's a seer, and she's on the scene."

"And you know as well as anyone that seers have little if any control over what they're able to see. Miranda didn't have a premonition, not about what happened to Diana. But Ruby did."

"There's nothing to say she'll have another one."

"There's nothing to say she won't."

John gave up that argument; none knew better than he that, gentle though she was, his wife possessed a core of steel. And she was stubborn as hell when convinced she was right about something. "Look, I have no idea exactly how many agents are there by now, or even what specific psychic abilities are being focused on the investigation, but I'm willing to bet that every SCU agent and Haven operative in Serenade has a lot more experience than a twelve-year-old girl. Experience with psychic abilities *and* with defending themselves from a determined enemy."

"I'm not so sure," Bailey said. "You didn't see what Samuel did to his flock. And I mean the ones who survived."

"I saw these kids," he told her. "I've heard them cry out in the night and I've seen what it does to Maggie to take away at least some of their terror and pain. I know they went through hell, Bailey. Which is why I don't believe Ruby should be going into a war zone."

It was Maggie who said quietly, "John, you know I don't like this any better than you do. If Bishop had been the one asking, I would have said no without hesitation. But it wasn't him. It was Ruby who asked to go. Who insisted she had to. Ruby feels with every fiber of her being that she has to be there."

Bailey said slowly, "And you don't find that odd, Maggie? Odd that Ruby specifically saw what would happen to a woman she'd never met before? A woman to whom she had no connection?"

"It happens."

"To older psychics, yeah, some, though not many. But virtually never with kids. They need a connection. It can be as simple as a touch or as complex as a psychic link or a blood relationship, but they need some kind of connection. You know that."

"She met Quentin. I assumed the connection was there."

"What if it wasn't?"

"Bailey—"

"What if it wasn't, Maggie? What if Ruby's connection is to someone—or something—else entirely?"

To that question, Maggie had no answer.

It was John Garrett's habit to check the big house every night before going to bed. They had an excellent security system for both the house and grounds, and the three large mixed-breed dogs who lived with them had the run of the house and were very protective, especially of Maggie. But he nevertheless needed to check doors and windows for his own peace of mind before he could relax and sleep.

Not that there, so far, had been any trouble here. Still.

The dogs accompanied him on his nightly rounds, their relaxed attention additional proof that nothing threatened the house or its occupants, at least for now. Which was all the reassurance John ever expected.

There were several Haven operatives living and working in the house currently, but that wing of offices, common spaces, and bedroom suites boasted its own self-contained security system—plus another four dogs, at the moment—and he never felt the need to either check the locks or invade the privacy of those who, by necessity, considered this a second home.

Finally satisfied that everything was as safe and secure as possible, he returned to the bedroom floor of the private wing.

"Go to bed," he told the dogs quietly, and each obeyed at once, retreating to their individual comfortable beds tucked away in niches of the hallway near the master bedroom.

John wondered why he bothered. By morning he would, as usual, wake to find at least two of the dogs sharing his and Maggie's bed, with the third sprawled across the bedroom sofa.

Shaking his head in wry amusement, he went into the master suite, leaving the door open a bit because, if he didn't, Maggie would just slip out of bed sometime in the middle of the night to let the dogs in.

"Everything locked up tight?" She was at the window, her back to him.

He was instantly alert, bothered by a note he recognized in her voice. Pain.

"Yeah. Are you okay?" He crossed the room and put his hands on her shoulders, feeling the tension, the slight tremors. "Missing Ruby already?"

He felt a stronger tremor shake her.

"Yes," she murmured. "I miss her."

"Maggie, are you upset that she didn't tell you why she felt so strongly that she had to be in Serenade?"

"Not because she didn't tell me." She turned to face him, and he saw that she had been crying. "Because she did."

Serenade

Special Agent Tony Harte looked at the post-midnight activity still going on around Main Street and shook his head. "Has anybody been keeping track of all the law enforcement and the technical people working here? The electrical crews, FBI agents, the county sheriff's department, Tennessee Bureau of Investigation, plus fire departments and EMS units from about three counties. It's beginning to look like a First Response convention."

Special Agent Jaylene Avery glanced up from the bagged shell casing she was examining and said, "The sheriff thought of that hours ago, Tony, long before he left for the hospital. He assigned that task to his chief deputy. What's his name—Scanlon? The one over there near the courthouse, looking harassed."

Tony followed her gaze until he located the tall, well-built, middle-aged man who wore his crisp uniform with an air of definite authority. "Oh, Neil. Met him earlier. Now that I think about it, he wanted a good look at my badge and wrote down the number."

"He's the one keeping track, at least of law enforcement," Jaylene said. "Though I doubt he's had time to authenticate anybody. Just gathering names and badge or other I.D. numbers is taking hours. Nobody'll really stand still for him, poor guy."

"At least the bomb squad from the TBI has done their thing and gone away."

"They didn't have much to do," Jaylene pointed out. "Collect a few bomb fragments that aren't likely to give us much more information than we already have. We all know we aren't dealing with a bomber specifically, so there isn't likely to be an identifying characteristic about that bomb. We know he's not a terrorist. We're reasonably sure his motive isn't money. So all their expertise was fairly wasted."

"I'd just like to know where the bastard is now. It doesn't take any extra powers to feel that creepy sensation of being watched. And, speaking of, are you getting anything from that shell?"

"Wish I could say yes. Unfortunately, I can't." She frowned. "Nothing at all, no sense of the sniper's personality or motives. I might as well be holding a rock for all the vibes I'm getting."

Tony sighed. "It was worth a try."

"Are you getting anything?" she asked him.

"Other than the general sense of panic and fear all around us, no. That's pretty damn strong, though, to be coming through to even my low-degree telepathy. Almost crackly with static. It's beginning to give me a headache, and that doesn't happen often, believe me. People are very worried that the sniper-slash-bomber isn't finished."

"I don't blame them. That's worrying me too. And the media isn't helping." She nodded to an area about a block from their position near the blast site, where yellow crime-scene tape stretched across the road and, along with several deputies, held back the small but determined crowd of reporters and film crews jostling for the best angle from which to report on the bomb. And the murders.

The twenty-four-hour news cycle, the modern bane of law enforcement everywhere—at least as far as Jaylene was concerned.

Tony nodded but said hopefully, "If they stay the rest of the night and want any sleep at all, it'll have to be in that roach motel on the edge of town, so maybe they'll start clearing out anytime now."

"I don't think so. The ones who were going to leave left, before midnight. The rest are more stubborn. Or just believe they're onto a bigger story than the one Sheriff Duncan offered."

"Well, two murdered bodies and a bomb blast might spell 'probable survivalist with a grudge,' but I don't think that's as uninteresting as the sheriff obviously hoped it would be."

"Still better than 'probable serial killer with a trail of bodies in three states and a new taste for bombs,' " Jaylene pointed out.

"True enough."

"Anyway, I think the media is here for the duration. Unless something a hell of a lot more interesting happens elsewhere."

"Yeah. And I guess it'd be wrong to hope for a disaster somewhere else."

Jaylene looked at him with raised brows.

"Kidding," he explained.

"You sure?"

"I swear. Look, at least most of the locals decided they didn't much fancy being on TV and retired to their homes. Probably barricaded their doors and cleaned their guns."

"I think I would if I were them," Jaylene murmured.

"Yeah, I'm not all that happy out here under the work lights myself. When people like Galen and the twins believe our sniper is still too close for comfort, I pay attention."

"Me too."

"I hate body armor, Jay."

"Me too," she repeated. "But there's no sense making it easy for the bastard, right?"

Tony sighed. "Right. And has anyone warned all the media people that standing out here in the glare of their own bright lights without any protection at all *might* not be the best idea in the world?"

"I've warned them twice myself."

"Idiots. Sheriff Duncan has given them the only statement he means to until at least tomorrow—I mean later today—so all they can even do now is film on-the-scene bits for cable news and the morning shows. Still, far as I can see, we've got a lot more talking heads than actual investigative journalists, so maybe even those that stay won't be nosing around."

She continued to eye him. "You're a glass-half-full kind of guy, aren't you?"

Appearing seemingly out of thin air to join them near the sidewalk, Galen said, "He definitely is. Except about the weather. For some reason, the weather tends to bug him."

Tony started at the first word. "Damn, will you quit doing that? That's three times so far. You're worse than a cat, sneaking up on people."

"I didn't sneak. I walked. You just didn't hear me."

Jaylene smiled faintly but said to Galen, "Any word on Diana?"

"She made it through surgery, but the next forty-eight hours are going to be critical. I take it the doctors aren't too hopeful—but let's call them glass-half-empty sort of guys and hope for the best ourselves. Miranda's on her way back with Duncan." He glanced at his watch. "They should be touching down in another half hour or so."

"How about the others?"

"Staying, I take it. I didn't ask why."

Soberly, Jaylene said, "I know why Quentin's staying. I don't know the other two well enough to guess."

"DeMarco staying puzzles me," Galen admitted. "Unless he has a personal stake or Miranda ordered him to stay, I'd expect him to be heading back here, where all the action is. We could definitely use him, especially if the sniper isn't done."

"If Diana was a planned hit, DeMarco may be staying as guardian," Jaylene offered.

"That's not a role he favors. Watching and guarding are too tame for his tastes."

"Since when is guardian duty tame?" Tony wanted to know. "Didn't it get you shot last time?"

"Yeah, but that's an unusual outcome. Mostly it's a lot of watching and waiting for something you hope isn't going to happen."

Mildly, Jaylene said, "After more than two years undercover, maybe DeMarco's ready for a lower-key job."

With a grunt, Galen said, "Trust me, if he's low-key it's because the role calls for it. Otherwise, it isn't in his nature. Guy's wired and ready to blow pretty much all the time."

"That sounds dangerous," she said, still mild.

"It is. But he also has incredible control and self-discipline. And if you tell him I said so, I'll deny it." Galen shrugged. "Anyway, I guess we'll find out all about it when Miranda gets back. Or not."

Tony said, "I gather you didn't find anything on the last sweep?" Galen was one of several agents who had been prowling the perimeter of the town all evening, and Tony couldn't help but wonder how many times they had missed each other by a hair in the darkness. Then again, maybe ex-military types had special signals they exchanged in such situations.

Tony imagined Galen sounding some kind of birdcall in the night and hastily pushed the ridiculous image from his mind. He managed to do so without laughing out loud, which he considered something of an accomplishment.

Unaware of his fellow agent's amusement, Galen said, "I found three roaming locals with shotguns, which I confiscated after escorting the owners back home. I am not winning any popularity contests here."

"I doubt any of us are," Tony said. "Two days ago this was a peaceful town. Look at it now."

Jaylene said, "We were following a killer. It's not our fault the trail led here."

Frowning, Galen reached for the bagged shell casing she was still holding and studied it for a moment before looking at his companions. "Maybe it is our fault. I mean, granted, none of our people appeared to be targeted before those shots at Hollis and DeMarco on Tuesday. But one working theory is that this is about us—about the SCU. Right?"

"Yeah, that's what Bishop said when he gave Jaylene and me our orders," Tony agreed.

"Okay. Then if this bastard is only now taking shots at us, maybe it's because this is where he wanted us to be."

"Which," Tony said slowly, "raises the question: Why here? If we've been lured or led, why is the showdown here?"

Eleven

DIANA LOOKED at the gray Quentin in this gray time or place and knew it wasn't the real Quentin. Her Quentin.

"She's lying to you," he repeated, still smiling.

Brooke didn't argue or dispute the charge; she merely looked from him to Diana, her gaze dispassionate.

"Say something," Diana told her.

Brooke shook her head. "In this, I can't interfere. You have to decide for yourself what's truth, Diana. What's real."

"I know he—that—isn't real," Diana said, her gaze fixed on the smiling not-Quentin.

"Of course I'm real," he said.

"You're not Quentin."

"Well, there you may have an argument."

Diana blinked, then frowned. "Please don't tell me you're trying to be funny. Because I'm really not in the mood."

"Look, I only meant that this . . . form . . . was chosen in order to better communicate with you."

"Chosen? Chosen from what?"

He looked surprised, the expression confirmed when he said, "That's not the question I expected you to ask."

"Glad I could surprise you. Answer the question."

"Well, chosen from those in your life you trust. Precious few of them, actually. Your trust in Quentin is the least...shadowed."

"Who *are* you?" she demanded.

"Now, that's the question I expected."

"So answer it."

He looked at Brooke, brows lifting. "Demanding, isn't she?"

"She has reason."

"Another arguable point, I suppose."

"You're wasting time," Brooke told him.

"Time is something I have in abundance."

Brooke tilted her head to one side, as though listening to a distant sound, and said, "Not really."

The not-Quentin's face tightened, though he continued to smile. "Are you trying to get in my way, little girl?"

Brooke didn't correct his seeming assumption about her age but instead said in a musing tone, "See, the thing about the gray time, the thing Diana understands, is that nothing living can exist here for long. Actually, not even spiritual essence can exist here for long. And there's a reason for that."

Diana wasn't sure what was going on but felt compelled to say, "It's because this is a corridor, a place to travel. Not a place to live in."

"And?" Brooke prompted.

For a moment Diana was even more confused, but then she realized what it was Brooke wanted her to say. "And...there's a pull from each side of the corridor. The living side—and what lies beyond death. They both pull constantly. That's why it's gray and flat and cold here. That's why it's so tiring for me to be here. This place saps strength, energy."

"Energy," Brooke murmured. "Power." Her gaze never left the face of the not-Quentin.

He stared at her for a long moment, then turned and went back through the open door, closing it behind him.

Left with Brooke in the seemingly endless corridor lined with closed doors, Diana said, "What the hell just happened?"

"Maybe I bought you a little more time."

"Before what? And I thought you said you couldn't interfere?"

Brooke was frowning now, but her voice was almost absent when she said, "I wonder if you have any idea at all how many people want you to live, Diana."

"Listen, this isn't one of those *It's a Wonderful Life* things, is it? Because if it is—"

"No, of course not. That's Hollywood stuff."

Diana managed a shaky laugh. "As opposed to the gray time, and seeing spirits, and, oh, I don't know, having visions of the future or the past or seeing auras or making people see what you want them to—*that* sort of stuff? Because Hollywood angels make it all look a lot simpler than I've seen it in my actual life."

"You have a point."

Reluctant humor fleeing, Diana sighed and said, "Brooke, give me a clue, will you? You say I'm here because I have to be, here to do something. That . . . thing . . . dressed up to look like Quentin says you're lying. And the only thing I really know, the only thing I *feel*, is that one of you is trying to deceive me."

"You have very good instincts."

"Brooke, for God's sake!"

"I can only tell you so much, Diana. Help you so much. Most of this you have to figure out on your own."

"Why?"

"Just because. It's the rule."

"Why did I know you were going to say that." Suddenly aware that she was beginning to feel more tired, Diana fought off a chill from someplace even colder than the gray time and said, "So you can't tell me who or what that is pretending to be Quentin."

"No."

"Can you at least tell me what I'm here to do?"

"I've already told you that, Diana." Brooke turned and began to walk again down the endless corridor. "You're here to find the truth."

Diana followed. "Yeah, you said. The truth underneath it all. Underneath all of *what*, Brooke? How many layers do I have to peel back before I can find the truth?"

"Several," Brooke admitted. And then, surprising Diana, she added, "There's the truth at the heart of the investigation you're involved in. The truth of why you were shot. The truth of your relationship with Quentin. The truth of who is trying to deceive you—and why."

"And the truth underneath it all?"

"That too. Uncover the other truths, and that one will be exposed."

"How am I supposed to uncover any of them here, Brooke?"

"The best way you can. And . . . I expect you'll have help."

Hollis really hoped DeMarco had been right when he said secretiveness kept her from broadcasting her thoughts—and intentions—all over the place. But she wasn't counting on it. She was trying her best to keep her mind quiet and still, pretending to sleep.

She had never been more wide awake in her life, despite being so tired it was a bone-deep ache.

They had been moved to a smaller, more private waiting room just down the hall from the ICU, a space clearly designed for the families of intensive-care patients to spend long hours; several of the chairs were actually recliners, and fairly comfortable ones at that.

Then again, maybe a bed of rocks would have felt no different, Hollis thought.

She opened her eyes a bit to look at DeMarco, deliberately glancing and then looking away so as not to awaken that ever-vigilant primal sense of his. Not that she posed any sort of danger to him, but she had a hunch that sense could warn him about anything he wanted it to.

Such as her leaving the room to do something that was probably really stupid.

He appeared to be asleep, eyes closed and hands clasped peacefully across his lean middle, the recliner tipped nearly all the way back. His face—that unexpectedly, almost unnervingly handsome face—was relaxed in a way it never was when he was awake.

Hollis didn't trust that seeming serenity, especially since she couldn't see his aura. But according to the big clock on the wall, it was nearly five A.M., and she didn't want to wait any longer. From what she remembered of her own hospital stays—though the ICU tended to have its own rhythms and bursts of activity—the general hospital routines began early.

Her chances of getting caught and ushered away from Diana increased considerably as the time for doctors' rounds and mealtimes and visiting hours grew closer.

Almost holding her breath, she slipped from her recliner, grateful there were no creaks or squeaks to betray her, and eased her way to the door. A glance back at DeMarco showed him still sleeping. Hollis wasn't sure she believed he was asleep, but she did believe it was now or never.

She opened the door just far enough to allow herself to pass through it and within seconds stood out in the hallway, her heart pounding.

Oh, shit.

In her determination to keep her mind calm enough to deceive DeMarco, she had forgotten the other little thing guaranteed to test her nerves here in this place.

Spirits.

She could see five of them in this single stretch of hallway— three men and two women—wandering around aimlessly, their expressions mixing uncertainty and confusion with dread. All of them wore regular clothing rather than hospital gowns, and Hollis wasted a moment wondering fleetingly about that; where had she read or heard or been told that spirits wore the garments in which they'd died, at least until they completely left this world?

"You can see me?"

Hollis realized she was rubbing her hands up and down her arms, because the gooseflesh was actually painful. She felt very cold, and everything except the anxious woman standing in front of her seemed to have faded . . . or receded . . . or become less real.

Almost as though she herself had one foot in the world of the dead.

Jesus, is this how it started for Diana? Have I always been able to step toward the gray time but never realized it?

Drawing a quick breath, she whispered, "I can see you. But there's somewhere I have to go right now."

"No, please—just tell me. Am I dead?"

Before Hollis could answer, a nurse whose lively print scrubs appeared weirdly faded began to bustle past her and then stopped, her preoccupied expression turning inquisitive.

"May I help you, Agent?"

Hollis cleared her throat. "No. No, thank you. I needed to stretch my legs a bit." *And please move a little to the right, because you're half standing in this poor woman. . . .*

"Don't wander far, please." The nurse smiled and bustled on, completely unaware of having passed through the spirit of another woman.

"I am dead, aren't I?" the spirit whispered.

Hollis glanced around quickly, hoping no one else was nearby to see her apparently talking to herself. She kept her voice low. "I'm sorry. I really am. But I can't help you. A friend of mine is still alive, and I have to get to her right now."

The spirit took a step back, nodding. "Oh . . . okay. I understand. It's just . . . I don't know what to do now." She looked up and down the hallway, adding somewhat forlornly, "Isn't there supposed to be a light?"

Oh, shit.

"I'm sorry. I don't know. But I believe you can...move on...if you want to."

"I guess I should want to, shouldn't I?" The spirit nodded and wandered away, looking even more lost and alone than she had before.

Hollis felt worse than useless and made a mental note that, if she survived all this, she would devote a *lot* more time to the study of mediums in general and her own abilities in particular, so she at least would know the right thing to say to these poor souls. But for now she moved away from the waiting room and headed toward the ICU, keeping her gaze directed downward as much as possible so she wouldn't make eye contact with any of the other spirits.

There were four more wandering around the ICU.

There were also two nurses.

Guessing that asking to visit Diana at five in the morning wouldn't go over at all well, Hollis slipped into a room marked EMPLOYEES ONLY, which turned out to be a supply closet. Keeping the door open just a crack, she watched the nurse's desk.

The waiting was difficult enough, but what really unsettled Hollis was the realization that the whole place had a grayish sheen to it and a kind of remote dimness, as if she was looking at something farther away than she knew it to be. No matter how many times she rubbed her eyes or tried to shake off the sensation, it remained.

Only the wandering spirits looked colorful and close and real, their auras bright with energy.

And that was creepy as hell.

It was another long fifteen minutes before one of the nurses was called away from the desk by something clearly not an emergency and the other turned her back to Hollis to take what looked like a personal phone call.

Hollis was able to slip past the nurse's desk and into the ICU.

There were only three patients: two men and Diana. All three were on ventilators, so the haunting sound of machines breathing for people was the first thing Hollis was aware of. Then there were the other machines, beeping and clicking as they monitored and measured. Lights blinked faded red numbers. Bags hanging above the patients dripped liquids into tubing and then needles and then bodies; bags hanging lower on the beds received fluids the bodies no longer required.

Trying to ignore all that, Hollis was relieved that at least there were curtains on either side of the beds and, in Diana's case, they were drawn far enough to provide for some privacy. She stepped into the semi-private space.

"Hey, Hollis."

His voice was low and rough, still hoarse from shouting the day before and maybe from talking to Diana ever since. His fair hair looked as if fingers had been raked through it many times, even though he was holding Diana's hand tightly with both his, and on his face was a hollowed-out look of exhaustion and desperation and a terrible need.

Hollis had to look away from that, but when she did it was to see Diana in the bed, lying so still and unnaturally straight. A machine breathed for her with a *hush...thump* repeating steadily, and other machines monitored her heartbeat and blood pressure and whatever else they monitored. There were bandages and drains and...

It was even harder to look at Diana. Not because of the machines or tubes or bandages, but because she had the same gray sheen as everything else, and that scared the hell out of Hollis.

"Hey, Quentin." She tried to hold her voice steady.

"They told me she might not make it." His gaze was fixed on Diana's face. "They're wrong about that, you know. She'll make it. She has to make it."

"I know."

"Do you? I didn't know, not really. Not the way I know now. Not until I saw her go down, saw all the blood and...That's when I knew. It happened so fast, so goddamn fast, there wasn't even time to tell her. All these months I could have told her. And didn't. What kind of fucked-up sense does that make?"

Hollis was silent.

He turned his head finally and looked at her, with eyes she knew were blue but looked grayish, bloodshot, and darker than she'd ever known them to be. In a queerly conversational tone, he said, "I can't see the future. Not now, not when I need to. I've tried and I can't. But there's one thing I can see. No matter what they say about brain scans and a heartbeat, Diana isn't here. I'm holding on as hard as I can, as hard as I know how, but . . . I'm holding her body, not her soul."

"I think you're holding her soul too. Her spirit."

"She isn't here," he said.

"I mean you're holding something of her anchored here. So she can find her way back."

"Will she?"

"Yes. Because she has to."

He nodded slowly. "Yes. I'm not letting go. No matter how long it takes, I'm not letting go. Even though . . ."

"Even though?"

"This was her nightmare, you know. As a little girl, she saw her mother like this. Maybe like this. A body with a beating heart, breathing because of a machine. A body without a soul."

"She'll come back, Quentin."

He nodded again. "Because she has to."

"Yes. Because she has to."

Hollis had thought she might persuade him to leave Diana for at least a few minutes, but now she didn't even try. Instead, she said, "Why don't you put your head down and try to rest."

"I might hurt her," he said.

"You won't." Hollis found a small pillow in her hands and didn't even question where it had come from. She leaned across the bed and placed the pillow so that all he had to do was turn a bit sideways and put his head down. It wouldn't be the most comfortable position, but at least he might be able to relax.

"Rest," she told him. "You won't be any good to Diana or anyone else if you don't."

"I don't want to stop looking at her," he murmured.

"It's okay. Just close your eyes for a while."

Almost as soon as his head touched the pillow, Quentin was out. But his grip on Diana's hand didn't weaken in the slightest.

"So now what?" DeMarco asked.

Hollis turned her head and looked at him. "Did it amuse you to watch me trying to sneak out of the room?"

"It did, yes." He didn't crack a smile.

Damn telepaths.

"Now what?" he repeated.

They were both keeping their voices quiet.

Hollis didn't bother to dissemble. "I want to try something. It probably won't work, but I have to try."

"Not a visit to the gray time, I hope."

"No, something else. But . . ." She hesitated.

"But what?"

"Nothing. I'll—" She broke off when DeMarco grasped her arm and half-turned her to face him.

"But what?" he asked. "I heard what Quentin said. Things happen fast, and we can run out of time. So tell me what's worrying you now. Don't make me wonder about it later."

"I figured you'd just read my mind."

"No. Tell me, Hollis."

She drew a breath and let it out slowly, trying not to be so conscious of time ticking away. "It's . . . the spirits. The place is full of them."

"I gathered that from your conversation with Miranda before she left. What's changed?"

Hollis hesitated again, then said, "Ever since I came out of the waiting room, since I stepped through that doorway, they're the only things that look real."

"What do you mean?"

"Everything else is . . . sort of gray."

He glanced around them, then said, "It's a sort of gray place, really."

"No, that's not it. Quentin and Diana . . . you. You've all got a gray tint. Washed out. Like a TV picture with the color turned down. And the only auras I see are around the spirits."

DeMarco considered that for a moment, a slight frown between his brows. "So you think you may have opened a door to the gray time."

"If I have, it's my own screwy version, because this isn't like Diana's gray time. At all. Her gray time is empty of people and spirits—except her guides—and it's desolate, like I told you. Cold and empty. But this . . . I'm seeing the living and the dead, and the dead have more color, more—hell, more life. So I don't know exactly what I've done, Reese. Or how I can undo it."

Or if I can undo it.

He nodded toward Diana. "What were you planning to do here?"

"I can heal myself. Miranda's sister is a medium, and she can heal others. I figured it was worth a shot."

"That takes energy, right? Strength?"

"Yeah. If healing others is anything like healing myself . . . yeah. A lot of energy, especially for injuries this serious."

"I doubt you have much to spare," he noted coolly.

"I'm hoping I'll have enough. At least to help, if only a little. It might take only a little to make all the difference."

"You're going to do this no matter what I say."

Hollis nodded.

"Okay. Then we'll worry about this almost gray time later. Give it a shot."

Something about his voice made her look at him questioningly, not even sure what she was asking. But DeMarco was sure.

"Something I noticed back in Serenade," he told her. "In all the commotion, you probably missed it. The thing is, when Diana's heart stopped, it wasn't the CPR that got it going. You put your hand on her and called her name. That's when her heart started beating again."

Diana said, "Is there a point to this? Walking down this endless corridor as if we expect to find something?"

"You tell me."

"Jesus, Brooke, I thought we were done with the cryptic guide routine."

"Somebody's getting cranky."

"No, somebody's getting pissed. I've been following you guides for most of my life, doing my damnedest to help you even when I couldn't help myself, and now when I could use a little quid pro quo, all I get is more of the same old bullshit."

"Whether you believe it or not, Diana, I am helping you."

"Helping me burn off energy so I'll die faster?" Diana knew her voice was harsh, but she couldn't help it.

"No. Helping you search for the truth. Look at these doors as we pass them. Think about what may lie behind them."

"Another fake Quentin, probably."

Brooke paused in the corridor to look at her, then continued on. "All right. Then think about this place. The fact of it."

"The fact is, it doesn't exist. Not anymore."

"Why not?"

"Because it was an evil place and it was destroyed."

"Why was it evil?"

"Because it held an evil creature. Because evil things were done there. Horrible things."

"So why do you suppose we're in that evil place now?"

"We aren't. It's gone."

"In a . . . replica of it, then. A reasonable facsimile of it."

"Because you want to mess with my head, most likely."

"Diana."

She sighed. And tried to think, if only because she didn't want Brooke to get pissed and vanish, leaving Diana alone here. Not that she'd ever known a guide to get pissed, but still. Always a chance.

"Why are we here? Quentin said..." She steadied her voice with an effort. "Quentin said there has to be some connection. Between this place and the investigation. Or else why does this place keep coming up? Why do I keep visiting it in the gray time?"

"Everything is connected, Diana."

She frowned. "So this place is tied to the investigation in Serenade? How?"

"That's your truth to uncover."

"Dammit."

Quite abruptly, one of the doors opened as they came abreast of it, and the fake Quentin smiled at her. "You really want to quit listening to that child. She doesn't know what she's talking about."

Diana had stopped instinctively, and a glance showed her Brooke had stopped as well. But the guide remained silent, and it was left to Diana to respond.

"What do you want?"

"I want to help you, Diana. You know that. I only want what's best for you. I know what's best for you."

"You've said that before. But you're fake. You're a phony wearing Quentin's face, and I want to know why."

"You know why."

Do I? Or is this...thing...lying?

She went with her gut, saying, "No, I don't know why. All I know is that you're lying to me."

"Am I?"

"Yes."

His tone suddenly silky, he said, "Wouldn't you rather concern yourself with the body back in that hospital? Wouldn't you rather be worrying about whether you're going to live or die?"

She knew he was trying to manipulate her, trying to make her fearful and uncertain. But she didn't know why. To weaken her? To make her more vulnerable? Just for the hell of it?

He was good, though. Good because it worked at least a little, as her thoughts turned, however briefly, to her terribly wounded body and the terrifying uncertainty of whether she would be able to reclaim it.

For an instant she thought she could feel Quentin's hands—both of them—holding one of hers, and she looked down at that hand wonderingly.

"He won't be there, Diana. When you really need him to be. When you finally have the courage to reach for him. He won't be there."

She looked at the fake Quentin and for the first time felt only anger. "You're wrong."

"No. He won't be there. He'll disappoint you."

Diana shook her head. "You don't know him. Whatever you are, you don't know him. But I do. I might not be able to count on anything or anyone else, but I can count on Quentin."

"Now you're the one who's wrong."

Turning her gaze to the silent guide, Diana said, "You aren't going to help me, are you?"

"I'll help all I can." Brooke's gaze was fixed on the fake Quentin, with a peculiar watchfulness Diana found almost more unnerving than anything else. "But you have to find the truth here on your own, Diana."

"Because that's the rule?"

"Frustrating, I know."

"Can you at least give me a damn hint?"

Brooke looked at her finally and said matter-of-factly, "He's here because you allow him to be here. See what's underneath the mask and he'll have no power over you."

"I don't—" Diana turned her head again only to see the door closed and no fake Quentin confronting her. Slowly she said, "I don't know how to look underneath the mask."

Brooke began to walk again. "Well, perhaps you'll figure that out while you're here. Perhaps you'd better."

"Threat or warning?"

Ignoring that, Brooke said, "We're here for a reason, Diana. In this place for a reason. Think it through. Why would you come in the gray time to a place that no longer exists?"

"Because..." The flippant response in her mind vanished as a far more serious—and frightening—one occurred to her. "Because... the *evil* still exists."

Brooke turned her head and smiled at her. "Now, that wasn't so hard, was it?"

"You mean I'm right?"

"Doesn't it feel right?"

To her surprise, Diana realized that it did. Then a chill cold enough to make itself felt even in the gray time stole through her. "The evil still exists. But—they stopped him. He's in a cage."

Brooke continued walking, her face serene.

"Brooke, the evil creature that killed in this place, the creature that nearly killed Hollis—he *is* caged. No longer killing. No longer dangerous. They got him."

"If you say so, Diana."

"If I say so? You mean he's still dangerous?"

Sending her a calm glance, Brooke said, "You have to think in layers, Diana. Peel away one layer at a time."

Diana walked for a time in silence, glancing rather idly at each door they passed as she grappled with the question of how the evil that had existed in this place could still exist—and be connected to what had happened and was happening in Serenade.

Layers.

Layers...

She stopped walking, staring at one of the doors that wasn't quite as featureless as all the others, hardly aware that Brooke had also stopped and was waiting, silent. Slowly, as Diana stared, a shape was forming on the door at eye level.

It was a cross.

"My God," she whispered. "Not the puppet—the puppet master. The evil hand on an evil creature's leash. Samuel."

Nurse Ellen King came around the curtain prepared to pour wrath all over whoever had dared to invade her ICU without permission. But the sight that met her eyes stopped the words before they could even form.

On one side of Diana Brisco's bed, Agent Hayes finally slept, slumped mostly sideways with his head on a pillow near her knees, his hands still holding one of hers.

He'll have a monster crick in his neck, she thought. Her professional gaze checked the monitors, and she was both surprised and pleased to see that Diana's vital signs were stronger, steadier.

Then she saw the other two federal agents. Saw the tall, slight brunette on the other side of the bed from Agent Hayes slump as though all the strength had drained out of her. Saw the big, powerful blond man lift her as though she weighed nothing and cradle her carefully in his arms.

"Hey, is she all right?"

He turned, holding the brunette, and said, "She needs to sleep. Do you have an extra bed?"

Ellen King looked at that almost-expressionless, handsome face, and thought fleetingly, *That's twice I've seen that look. Wow. I wonder if she knows.*

Then she got a grip on herself and said, "Yes. Yes, of course. Follow me." And led the way.

Twelve

Serenade

NAOMI WELBORNE INTENDED to one day anchor a major news program, and she intended to do so before she was thirty-five. So she had ten years in which to pay her dues, on top of the three she had already spent at the small eastern Tennessee station where her blond good looks had gotten her on the air only to chirp brightly about the weather.

Naomi was better than that and she knew it. She was tired of being called in to be on air only as the weather girl in a short skirt, or for what amounted to a sixty-second filler if the real news happened to run short that day. She was tired of being assigned, instead of real news stories, story scraps the station manager cheerfully called *human-interest necessities* for the station.

"Because people'll stop watching if we feed them nothing more than depressing stuff, Naomi."

Human-interest necessities. Warm and fuzzy stories about little kids and heroic dogs and people who lived to be more than a hundred. She'd gone to so many goddamn birthday parties she suspected confetti was permanently embedded in her hair, and if she saw one more mutt awarded some medal or other for barking when he smelled smoke or learning to turn on a light switch because his owner couldn't, she was afraid she'd borrow a gun from one of her cop contacts and shoot herself.

Enough was more than enough.

Naomi had been working on the final draft of her resignation letter the day before when the radio scanners at the station suddenly went berserk with activity. Police, fire departments and EMS, emergency electrical crews—all called to Serenade. There had been an explosion of unknown origin...cop down...at least one federal agent critically wounded...one known civilian casualty...deadly sniper still at large...

Naomi looked around the almost-deserted newsroom of the station and realized happily that fate had decided to reward her for her patience by dropping into her lap what looked to be a real career-making story.

The station manager had been obviously and insultingly doubtful about it when she lobbied hard for the assignment, but since all the other reporters were out, she was all he had. Reluctant, he sent her and a cameraman to Serenade.

"Just get some footage and try to get statements from witnesses and maybe a cop if any'll talk to you. And remember, Naomi, we can't compete with the cable-news outfits, so don't try to get fancy. Just get the story and don't get in the way or step on anybody's toes doing it. Understand?"

"Sure, Keith."

"Tell me you understand that I mean what I say."

"I understand, Keith, okay? You really don't have to worry about anything at all."

Oh, she understood, all right. She understood this was her chance, and she was damn well going to take it.

Which was why she stubbornly remained, despite the complaints of her cameraman, with the shrinking group of reporters and camera crews behind the yellow tape long after most of the action—or at least most of the *filmable* action—had ended. And long after they'd heard anything more than a polite but distant "Keep back, please," from any of the grave-faced deputies on the other side of the tape.

Dawn wasn't far away, and the cleanup was all but done.

Dammit, I don't have a thing for the morning news show.

The body of the young deputy was gone, presumably to be autopsied, although Naomi was baffled as to why; everyone knew the poor kid had been shot, killed by the single bullet fired that day by the sniper. A single bullet that had also critically wounded a federal agent.

Not that any of the cops were willing to confirm that.

What remained of the wreckage of the destroyed SUV had been loaded onto a rollback and taken away, reportedly into the garage of the sheriff's department—although she had missed that while trying to get a reluctant witness to say something on camera.

Dammit.

Broken glass had been swept from Main Street, the other rubble—made up of wood and brick and concrete and twisted metal—had also been removed, and numerous men had worked through most of the night to board up the shattered windows in the blast radius. One by one, the fire engines had departed, along with several EMS crews from neighboring counties.

The black van labeled EXPLOSIVES DISPOSAL UNIT, whose technicians Naomi would have sold her best shoes and possibly her soul to interview on camera, had slipped away early on, though another larger van—some kind of mobile command center, she guessed—remained parked across the street from the sheriff's office.

Visibly alert men wearing obvious body armor and holding guns were stationed in front and back of the van, not even bothering to try to be casual about it, and both agents and deputies continued to go in and out as they had for hours, all night long. But they had positioned the big work lights in such a way that none of the news crews had been able to get a shot of the van that wasn't obscured by the glare.

No way to shoot the good stuff, and all the rest was boring as hell. Even the electric crews had calmly and methodically—and with a minimum of sparks, dammit—restored power to most of Main Street sometime after midnight and were now working on blown transformers farther out.

And not one of the numerous FBI agents coming and going throughout most of the night had spared even a glance toward the media, no matter how loudly the questions were shouted.

"Give it up," Rob, her cameraman, advised dryly. "We should go home and get some sleep. They aren't going to say a damn thing, on or off the record. The deputies might as well have tape over their mouths, and the feds just plain know better."

"They have to talk to us sooner or later," Naomi said.

"No, they don't. They let the sheriff be spokesman because it's his town, but the truth is they aren't going to tell us squat until they're damn good and ready. And if that explosion was caused by a bomb—"

"You know it was."

"I know witnesses think it was and cops aren't saying. But if it was a bomb, you can bet it'll be days—if ever—before anybody official confirms that. With all the terrorist shit going on in the world, people hear the word *bomb* and panic. Nobody wants a panic, especially in a nice little town that depends on tourists for at least some of its livelihood."

Naomi had stopped listening after the bit about it being days before anybody official would confirm what had happened. She didn't have days. She was lucky Keith hadn't already sent another reporter out here and recalled her. And if it *was* a bomb he most surely would.

Unless, of course, she managed to get something really juicy on tape.

"Whatever you're thinking," Rob said, "please put it out of your pretty blond head. I'd like to live to a ripe old age and retire with a gold watch, or some shit like that."

She smiled at him very sweetly. "You just keep the camera ready—and for Christ's sake keep the shot in focus."

"Hey, you do your job, Barbie, and I'll do mine."

"Oh, I'll do my job, all right. Shut your mouth and follow me."

Rob followed her as she began to work her way back from the crime-scene tape and closer to the buildings on one side of Main Street. But he didn't shut his mouth until he'd muttered, "If I'm staying awake all fucking night, there damn well *better* be something to film."

That wish would haunt him for a long, long time.

There was more room inside the mobile command center than one might expect, even with all the machinery and other equipment, but it was still very crowded, despite the fact that most of the agents and Sheriff Duncan remained standing.

"Unfortunately, we don't know much more than we did when you left, Miranda." Special Agent Dean Ramsey, SCU, had arrived with the first wave of agents after the bomb blast and shooting. As one of Bishop's senior primaries, it had fallen on his shoulders to make order out of the chaos in the temporary absence of Miranda, who had been and still was the lead investigator on this case.

Ramsey, who had recently retired from the military when Bishop recruited him, was older than most of the other agents at forty-five but kept himself in peak physical condition. He was above medium height and slender, an auburn redhead with level brown eyes and a tough look about him that said you'd want him on your side no matter what the fight was about.

And he had retained something of an army crispness in how he relayed or requested information, wasting few words. "But we have managed to determine at least a few facts. Tony?"

"We identified the body on the roof of the old theater," Tony reported obediently. "Not that it's going to help us much. He's a local, and the sheriff confirms he's a known hunter."

"Even out of season," Duncan said with a heavy sigh. "But he follows—followed—the rules otherwise, and he was a careful, safe hunter."

Tony nodded. "Cal Winston, forty-three. Divorced, father of two kids, who live with his ex in Gatlinburg. Neither of the guns found with him is registered to him; his own guns are still in his home here just outside town—with the exception of his hunting rifle, which is missing. All of his guns were duly and legally registered, and he kept them in a gun safe."

"His kids," Duncan murmured. "Didn't want to take any chances there. He was . . . a careful man, like I said. He was a good man."

Gravely, Miranda said to him, "I'm sorry, Des."

"Yeah, me too. Has anybody called his ex?"

"Not yet," Tony volunteered.

"I'll do it, then. I knew them as a couple before Cal had a stupid summer and ran Sheila off."

Nobody asked him to elaborate.

Tony said, "Appears he was very well liked. No enemies we've found yet, and everybody seems honestly stunned that he's dead. Apparently wasn't the type to get anybody stirred up against him, and definitely wasn't the type to commit suicide."

Miranda was silent for a moment, then frowned. "The guns found with him—anything?"

Tony shook his head. "Not much. Serial numbers filed off both guns, but the handgun's probably the gun that killed him. No gunpowder residue on his hand; plus he was a lefty but shot in the right temple, so it's a safe bet he didn't off himself. It was a close-contact wound, though, so whoever it was all but pressed the barrel against his head before pulling the trigger."

"Up close and personal," Jaylene murmured.

"Yeah. So I'm guessing either the sniper practically fell over him and had to kill him, planned to make this kill different just to mix things up, or else needed him on his feet right up until he got him on that rooftop."

"What about the rifle?" Miranda asked.

"Could be the weapon used on Tuesday and yesterday—it's the right caliber—but we won't know for sure until the ballistics report is in. Probably later today." Tony paused, then added, "Hell of an expensive gun to waste. The real killer must have known that leaving it on a roof with a fake sniper-slash-bomber wouldn't fool us for more than five minutes. That bugs me. I don't know why, though."

There was another brief silence.

"We inventoried the backpack found with him," Dean said, picking up the report in his methodical way. "Nothing unusual for a hunter expecting to spend a few days in the woods, and looks like everything belonged to him. Only his own prints were found."

Miranda looked at Jaylene with a lifted brow, and the other woman nodded, saying, "There was . . . no sign it wasn't his stuff."

Returning her gaze to Dean, Miranda waited.

"The explosives experts say there was nothing special about the bomb, certainly no signature they recognized. It was some of the newer plastic explosive, but the stuff is fairly easy to come by if you know who to ask. The remote detonator was ready-made and could have been purchased from just about any well-equipped gun or munitions dealer."

"Which we have a lot of around here," Duncan offered.

Tony nodded. "I'll say. And a few of them on the watch list, Miranda. But nothing jumps out."

"Okay. Still, we'll run the usual checks and see if we can chase down the dealer. It's an assumption but a fair one that our sniper was here Tuesday evening, left, and apparently returned by early yesterday morning with the explosives. I'd like very much to know where he got them."

Dean said, "The time span gives us a rough radius for our search, since he couldn't have gone all that far—and back—in only a few hours. We'll have some extra personnel to search: The Bureau field office in Knoxville is happy to help. They'll send out agents as early as possible this morning and start canvassing gun and munitions dealers, army surplus, weapons experts, and anybody else the sniper might have dealt with. It is, as the sheriff said, a pretty long list, and it'll probably take several days to cover all the ground, but we'll go through it as fast as we possibly can."

"Good. Did Dr. Edwards confirm time of death for Mr. Winston?"

Without the need to consult his notebook, Dean said, "Eighteen to twenty hours before he was found."

She drew a breath and let it out slowly. "So there's no way he was our shooter on Tuesday. No big surprise, I think."

Sheriff Duncan said, "What I don't get is why the shooter went to all that trouble. Maybe Cal being in his way was just happenstance; that was probably his deer blind your people found on Tuesday, and maybe he was in it when the sniper needed it. Or maybe he came along later and was a serious problem for the sniper. So killing him I get. But then to transport a sizable man a considerable distance—whether he was on his feet and protesting or literally dead weight—only to haul him to a rooftop and prop him up for window dressing? What would be the point?"

"A distraction," Miranda said. "For us. And we've been distracted. We've had to use resources to identify Mr. Winston and eliminate him as a suspect. Had to take time. Trouble."

Duncan was frowning. "So—what? The whole point was to slow you—us—down? Stall for time? Why?"

"I don't know," Miranda said.

"But you believe that was why?"

She hesitated, then said, "I believe that was part of the reason. I also believe the shooter was mocking us. Taunting us. He believes he's smarter than we are. More clever. And he wants us to know that."

BJ had waffled back and forth for the better part of an hour while trying to decide on his target. He had put the crosshairs of his scope on first one possible and then another, his finger caressing the trigger and a soft "Boom" whispering from his lips each time.

But he didn't pull the trigger.

None of them was quite right.

He noted that the activity was winding down on Main Street and knew his time to choose and execute for maximum shock value was running out, but a voice in his head kept urging him to wait.

Not yet. Keep watching. Mark them all. Remember them.

We'll get to them all in good time.

Wait. The timing has to be just right.

It was a voice he knew. A voice he listened to.

He waited.

Even when the helicopter touched down near the courthouse and she joined her team, stood talking to them for several minutes near the van housing their mobile command center, he waited. Even though it would have been so easy.

So very easy.

He put the crosshairs of the scope on her face, a face so close he felt he could reach out and touch it. The scope didn't allow him to see the electric blue of her eyes, but he'd seen them in the daylight so they were easy to imagine. Electric blue eyes in a just-about-perfect face.

He thought about how quickly he could destroy her beauty and her life, but he waited. His finger caressed the trigger, and he whispered "Boom," but he waited.

He watched her go into the mobile command center, wondering if he had missed the shot for tonight.

No. Wait.

He waited.

Naomi lurked. She didn't think she was very good at it, since her pale blond hair made her sort of neon, and with power for the streetlights back on it wasn't like it was truly *dark* out there anyway, but she did her best. She was a little surprised at first that none of the deputies or agents appeared to notice her—or didn't feel she was worth shooing away if they did notice her. She was, in fact, a bit miffed by that. But eventually she decided that everybody was probably just tired.

It had been a long night.

Besides, there really wasn't anything much to see anymore.

Still, she didn't dare go near the mobile command center. She had a hunch the guys with the visible guns were a whole lot more alert, a whole lot less tired, and a whole lot more inclined to view her and her cameraman as threats worth taking note of.

And possibly shooting.

Ignoring the way Rob grumbled under his breath, she lurked in the spot she had chosen carefully, in the shadows beneath the now-ragged awning of one of the downtown restaurants, not more than twenty yards from the command center.

"The deputy was killed right over there," Rob said suddenly, pointing to a spot only a few feet away from them.

"I know that." They hadn't cleaned the street of everything.

"And the agent was shot not far from where that command center of theirs is parked now."

"I know that too. What's your point, Rob?"

"Just that we're not very far away, that's all. And they haven't caught the guy, you know."

"He's miles from here by now," she said.

"You know that for a fact, do you?"

"What, you think he'd be stupid enough to hang around with this whole place crawling with cops and feds?"

"He was stupid enough to shoot a cop and a fed. That puts him high on the stupid list, as far as I'm concerned."

Naomi took her eyes off the command center temporarily to look at him. "You're scared."

"I'd be right up there at the top of the stupid list if I wasn't."

"For God's sake."

"What? I'm not allowed to admit this whole situation gives me the creeps? An explosion tears apart a nice town, one deputy—just a kid!—killed and a federal agent critically wounded, a nutjob sniper on the loose out there, probably watching us right now for all we know, and I'm not supposed to let it shake me up a little? Jesus, Naomi, you take the cake. Is there *anything* you can see other than that anchor chair in New York?"

She was surprised and knew it showed when he laughed.

"It's no secret, believe me. I've been with the station for fifteen years, and I've seen about a dozen like you come and go. All puffed up with their plans to sit in one of those big chairs in New York. And you know what? Not one of them made it there."

"I will," she told him flatly. "I'll make it there." She returned her gaze to the command center and saw that several of the feds were coming out of it. She immediately hurried forward, gesturing for Rob to follow her. "Turn the camera on. Now. Film everything."

"Christ, if I get arrested for this—"

As they neared them, she heard one of the men ask, "Where's Galen, anyway? He missed the big meeting."

"He had an errand," replied a tall, gorgeous brunette.

Man, she'll make great television.

"Agent? Agent, Naomi Welborne, Channel 3 News. If you could say just a few words to calm some of our nervous viewers?"

To her delight, the woman paused in response, though her expression could hardly be said to be encouraging. If anything, she seemed a bit distracted.

"Look, Ms. Welborne—"

"Just a few words, please." Naomi smiled with all the charm she could muster. "Please, we've been standing out here all night. If I go back to the station without anything at all, my boss will can me."

The brunette gave her a wry look. "Nice try, Ms. Welborne."

Don't let her walk away, dammit.

Desperate, Naomi said, "Okay, maybe he won't can me, but I'll be doing the fu—freaking weather again. Come on, give a fellow professional woman a break, won't you? I'm not asking you to spill your guts, just give me something I can run with for the morning news. Do you believe the explosion and shooting yesterday are connected with the remains found here this week of two murder victims? Do you believe locals are involved?"

"Sheriff Duncan gave the press a statement hours ago, Ms. Welborne. I really have nothing to add."

She would have moved away, but Naomi took a couple more steps and turned a bit so the other woman would see her face more clearly in the glow of the streetlight.

"Come on, at least let me confirm the report that agents of the FBI are spearheading the investigation into yesterday's bombing—"

"Nice try," the fed repeated.

She won't admit it was a bomb. Shit.

"Okay.... There was a federal agent wounded yesterday, right? That's what everybody is reporting, what the police scanners said. Shot with the same bullet that killed that young deputy. Do you think it was a freak shot, or do you believe he was that good?"

"Ms. Welborne—"

"The agent was airlifted from the scene almost eighteen hours ago, isn't that so? How is she?"

"She's . . . holding her own." The brunette glanced at Rob with a slight frown as he shifted a bit to the side to get a better angle.

Naomi hurried on. "Then she'll be okay?"

"We don't know yet. Ms. Welborne, I appreciate that you're trying to do your job, but I can't say anything more. Now, if you'll excuse me—"

Oh, shit.

"Agent—"

———

207

There. Now. You know what to do.

BJ smiled. He centered the crosshairs of his scope, and his finger caressed the trigger.

"Boom," he whispered.

And squeezed the trigger.

Thirteen

AM I RIGHT?" Diana asked her guide. "Is one of the truths I'm here to uncover the truth that Samuel wasn't destroyed at the church Compound like the report said?"

Matter-of-fact, Brooke said, "He was killed. You know that's true because your friends were there. Quentin was there."

"Yeah, but...he—Quentin said the energies there that day were really strange and everybody was affected by them. That there was lightning plus the weird energies *plus* several psychics using their abilities in ways they never had before. That was where Hollis found out she could heal herself after Samuel tried to kill her. And the little girl—Ruby. She helped the Haven operatives and SCU agents fool Samuel."

Brooke was silent, merely looking at Diana serenely.

"They did an autopsy before he was cremated," Diana said. "I read it. I looked at the damn stomach-turning photos. The doctors wanted to know if there was anything different about him physically. Bishop wanted to know the same thing."

"And what did they find?" Brooke asked.

"His brain was...They said it wasn't normal. Wasn't healthy. Not tumors or anything, not cancer, just not healthy. Something about the color of the tissue and the weight of the brain. They said they'd never seen anything like it." She hesitated. "Maybe because of all the electrical energy he channeled, his brain was . . . changed."

Again, Brooke's reaction was silent waiting.

Diana hardly noticed, thoughts and speculations tumbling through her mind almost too fast to absorb. "But they believed they destroyed his psychic abilities before he died. Burned them out, using a massive blast of pure energy he couldn't withstand. They were almost certain. He was no threat, no threat at all." She stared at the grave, seemingly young guide. "Were they wrong about that?"

Brooke countered with another question. "Were they the only ones capable of deception, do you suppose?"

Diana looked around at the grayish but gleaming corridor, endless, stretching both ways as far as she could see, all the doors featureless. Except for the single one with a cross, a shape that seemed now to be scorched into the metal. "He fooled them?"

"What do you think?"

"I think Bishop isn't easy to fool. Quentin isn't easy to fool."

"Maybe it wasn't easy. Maybe it cost Samuel—a lot."

"Like what?"

"Maybe he had to learn what everyone has to. That even the best-laid plans seldom go as we expect. Maybe he didn't have quite the mastery over his own fate that he believed he would."

Diana frowned. "So he somehow fooled them . . . but lost control there at the end."

"Maybe."

Thinking about it, a very unsettling question occurred to Diana. "Can you kill pure evil? Can you destroy it?"

"What do you think?"

Diana drew a breath and let it out slowly. "He didn't move on," she whispered, the realization an icy lump in the pit of her belly. "He was ready for them somehow, ready. . . ."

She returned her gaze to Brooke's calm face. "He had premonitions. He saw the future. Is it possible he knew what would happen? Possible he knew how they meant to destroy him?"

Brooke pursed her lips, for all the world as if discussing something casually. "Well, premonitions are tricky beasts, and interpreting them isn't always easy. You can know the fact of something without necessarily knowing how it will come about."

Diana considered that, her mind still racing. "So he might have known he'd lose. That no matter what it was they meant to do, no matter how hard he was able to fight them, in the end he'd still lose. They'd take his abilities. He might even have known that someone close to him would take his life. And knowing that, he would have planned. He would have found a way . . . for something of himself to survive."

"Energy is never destroyed," Brooke pointed out. "Only transformed."

"Bishop knows that."

"Maybe he and the others believed the energy *was* transformed. There was so much power all around them when they were fighting Samuel, even in them. Changing them. And at the end there were so many broken bodies to mend—and to bury. And Samuel was gone."

"Maybe," Diana finished, "they needed to believe that."

Brooke nodded. "Maybe they did."

Diana felt a cold so deep her bones ached with it. She had been so cold for so long she wondered if it was possible to ever be warm again.

She looked around once again at the corridor, at the representation of a place where more than one evil soul had done terrible things. "That's why I keep coming back here to this place. To this . . . representation. Because this is where he grew so powerful. Where he absorbed so much dark energy his evil creature created. This is where he meant to destroy them the first time. Bishop, the others. Where he tried."

"Tried and failed," Brooke reminded her.

"Yes. But he lived to try again. Lived to grow stronger. And that time he was in a place where he felt even more powerful. The closest thing he had to a home. So why am I not there, at the church's Compound? Why is this place more important?"

Brooke was silent.

This place. Corridors. Shiny and sterile. Endless corridors... A place to move through...

And then she got it.

"He's here, isn't he? Here in the gray time. His spirit didn't... That black and twisted spirit found a way somehow to stay in the gray time all these months. To hide here."

"Do you think it was in his nature to hide?" Brooke asked neutrally.

Diana's answer came slowly. "No. No, I read the profile on him. He was all about attention, adulation. Worship. But... it would have been in his nature to wait, maybe. If he had a plan. If he believed there was a way for him to go back."

"How could he do that? Go back? His body is ashes now, scattered on the wind."

"He'd need another one," Diana said automatically. "If he means to go all the way back, means to live again in the flesh. If he finds a way to do that, the power to do that. It's... just barely possible. I've seen it happen before.* But it wasn't permanent. The struggle of two minds for dominance, the energy of two souls in one body is—"

She broke off, and for one dizzying moment the whole gray time world seemed to spin around her. "He isn't—he won't—he doesn't want *my* body. Does he?"

Dispassionate, Brooke said, "If that was his plan, I would say two things went wrong for him. Your injuries were far more severe than he'd anticipated, and Quentin refused to let go."

---

*Chill of Fear

Diana looked at her numbly, and Brooke nodded. "Whatever his plan might have been, this is the reality. He's been trapped in this cold, desolate place for a long time, and he wants to live again."

"But—"

"He wants to live again, Diana."

Serenade

Miranda was regretting her impulse to answer the insistent questions of the young TV-journalist-wannabe even before she glanced several feet away to see Tony watching with slightly raised brows and Jaylene looking rather pointedly at her watch. Easy to read their expressions without the need for telepathy. They were all exhausted, and if they hurried they might be able to sleep an hour or three before they had to be up and at it again.

So why wasn't she hurrying?

God knew she was so tired she was responding on automatic anyway, offering nothing useful to the eager blonde with the sharp eyes of some bird of prey that most probably ate its young.

I'm too tired for this. Bound to make mistakes. Time to go.

"...Ms. Welborne, I appreciate that you're trying to do your job, but I can't say anything more. Now, if you'll excuse me—"

"Agent—"

That was when the world blew up.

Miranda was still looking at the younger woman, and even though she knew it was all happening in split seconds, time seemed to almost stop so that she saw every horrible detail.

Naomi Welborne's face just sort of...split and flopped open. Blood and bits of tissue sprayed Miranda, almost blinding her. The TV reporter jerked to one side and started to go down, still holding her microphone.

Only then did they hear the *craa-aack* of the high-powered rifle.

After that things happened fast.

Miranda's instincts and training kicked into gear, and she dove toward the nearest building, hooking an arm around the stunned cameraman to take him down as well. A quick look showed her that her people were also diving for cover, as were the other cops and feds. Even the few remaining media on the other side of the crime-scene tape had the sense to at least hit the deck.

The same glance showed her that Jaylene had been hit in the upper arm and was pretty much being dragged by Tony behind one of the big decorative trash containers on the sidewalk.

Wonder if the bastard meant to get two again . . . Where the hell is he . . . has to be using a night scope . . .

A weird silence fell.

Miranda found her weapon in her hand even though she had no memory of reaching for it. Her dive had taken both her and the cameraman into the shadows of a three-story building; a quick and rough calculation told her she was most likely out of the sniper's line of sight.

Most likely.

"Jaylene?" she called.

"I'm okay. Just a flesh wound. Tony's already got the bleeding stopped." She sounded calm.

Tony called out, "She needs a medic, Miranda." He, too, sounded a lot calmer than he had any right to be.

From closer to the mobile command center, Dean called, "Shot came from the south, definitely. Angle says he's in or on a building close by, not farther away or higher up. We've got people fanning out."

"Have them stick close to the buildings," Miranda responded, barely having to raise her voice in the eerie silence. "Every building checked, Dean, and when they're clear I want somebody posted at every entrance and exit."

"We'll run out of manpower."

"Use what we've got until reinforcements arrive. Have one deputy or agent cover more than one door whenever possible. If we can't find this bastard, we can at least flush him out and force him to move farther away. This is not going to become his goddamn shooting gallery."

"Copy that."

In an almost conversational tone, Tony said, "We have reinforcements coming?"

"We do now," Miranda replied.

"Great. What about the reporter? Any hope?"

"No. She's gone." A whimpering sound drew her attention, and Miranda looked down at the cameraman lying like a log beside her on the pavement. "Are you okay?" she asked mechanically, even as her mind registered the absurdity of the question. There were spatters of blood on one side of his face, and a small piece of what looked like brain tissue clung to the lens of his camera.

He stared at her with huge, unseeing eyes and continued to whimper like a terrified child.

Miranda couldn't really blame him. Some part of her wanted to curl up somewhere and whimper. But that wasn't a part she could give in to. She hesitated for only a moment and then reached to activate a small device hidden in her ear.

"Roxanne?"

"Here. Sorry, Miranda—I don't know how he slipped past us." The voice in her ear was quiet, but more because it was faint than because Roxanne was speaking quietly. They hadn't been sure these new coms would work in this area at all, but with the help of the tactical command center's booster antennas, the signals were at least somewhat effective within a half-mile to a mile radius here in the downtown area.

"Never mind that now. Can you sense him?"

"That's the thing. We've been trying and we can't. It's like there's some kind of interference; both of us have headaches, and we don't *get* headaches. Even now we can't tell you for sure where he was, whether he's on the move, or where he's heading. Nothing."

"Copy that." There wasn't much else Miranda could say.

"We were watching Main Street." Roxanne's voice was grim now. "Saw what happened. Gabe's guess of the trajectory is that the bastard was on the roof of that two-story building by the library at the south end of Main Street. But it's just a guess. We're headed there now."

"Watch yourself."

"Copy that."

The cameraman was whimpering louder.

Ignoring him, Miranda raised her voice to say, "Tony, can you get Jaylene to the command center?"

"Yeah, I think so. Can you move?"

"Well, since I don't intend to lie here all day, I'm damn well going to try." It had been, she realized, no more than five minutes since the sniper's bullet had killed the reporter.

The sky was lightening as night edged toward dawn; it wouldn't be long before the people who worked in the downtown restaurants showed up to begin cooking breakfast. And following soon after would be the townsfolk who normally ate breakfast at their favorite spots before beginning their own busy days.

Normal days.

I wonder if this town will ever be normal again.

"Come on," she said to the cameraman.

"I—I don't—"

"I don't either," she said grimly. "But I think a moving target will be harder to hit than a stationary one, don't you?"

He gave a choked gasp and then turned onto his belly and scurried like a crab toward the building.

He left his camera. Miranda picked it up and followed him, not scurrying but keeping low. When they were pressed up against the building, she led the way north toward the command center.

Although why I don't think he'd shoot some kind of explosive shell in there is beyond me.

Because it looked as if someone had definitely declared war in this once-peaceful little town.

The question was, who?

Hollis started awake, emerging from a nightmare filled with blood and fire and screams, her heart pounding.

DeMarco's arms tightened around her. "Go back to sleep."

Confused, she realized that they were in bed together. Well, not *in* bed together, but *on* a bed together. Not under the covers, certainly, but only their clothing separated them. She was on her side and he was behind her—close behind her, so that she could feel just about every inch of him—with his arms around her.

She was very conscious of his heart beating steadily against her back and his breath stirring her hair.

Okay, how did this happen?

"Your attempt to heal Diana wiped you out," he said.

"Will you stop that?" Despite her best efforts, her voice was a bit unsteady.

"It was logical that would be your question."

"Yeah, you always say something like that. I don't believe you." She realized they were in a tiny bare room lit only by a dim lamp on a low nightstand in one corner. And the bed was . . . not large. Still in the hospital? If so, not in a typical patient's room. Maybe a room where interns and residents napped when on call?

"How did I—how did we—get here?"

"I carried you."

Carried me?

"Oh." She couldn't think of anything else to say about that.

"Go back to sleep," he repeated. "It isn't even seven-thirty, so you barely got in a nap. And you really need to rest."

"What about Diana? Did I help her at all?"

"I think so. The nurse who ran us out said Diana's vital signs were more stable than they'd been all night."

"We were run out?"

"In a manner of speaking."

She waited a moment, then prompted, "Why were we run out?" It wasn't the only detail about which she was fuzzy. She remembered making the attempt to help Diana heal, remembered the hot pulse of energy that seemed to well up inside her own body, and then... nothing. It was as if she'd fallen into a deep black hole of silence.

DeMarco said, "Visiting an ICU patient without permission at five in the morning generally raises the ire of the nursing staff."

"Oh." She seemed to keep falling back on that useful syllable.

There was a big part of Hollis that wanted to just relax and enjoy the warmth and odd sense of security she felt lying there with him, but another part of her felt wary to the point of having to fight not to stiffen up. The battle was a rather subdued one, however, since she was so tired she could hardly think straight anyway.

"You need to rest," he repeated.

"I've been resting. Apparently."

"You've been unconscious. Big difference."

"I feel fine," she lied.

"Hollis. You need to sleep."

She hesitated and then, because it was easier when she wasn't looking at him, said, "I think I'm afraid to sleep. Afraid I might get drawn into the gray time when I'm not strong enough to pull myself back out again."

"I won't let that happen."

"No?"

"No."

"I think I had one foot in there earlier. Or... something a lot like it."

"And I think you're in a hospital holding a lot of pain, where a lot of people have died, and you're a medium. They looked more real to you because that sense was wide open, and your other ones were all but shut down from exhaustion."

Hollis thought about that and decided she liked his explanation better than her own. Because his explanation enabled her to give way to the weariness and begin to relax again. And once she began to relax... "Or it could be my eyes," she said, blinking sleepily, trying to keep the little lamp in focus.

"Your eyes?"

"Well...these eyes. They aren't mine, you know."

"Of course they're yours."

"I mean I wasn't born with them."

"I know what you mean."

"Do you? Did you read my file or my mind?"

"Go to sleep, Hollis."

She closed her eyes finally but murmured, "I see differently with them, you know. Through them."

"Do you?"

"Uh-huh. Hard to explain. Colors are different. Sometimes...my depth perception is...off. And there are...lions. I mean lines. Extra lines around things. Some things. Sometimes. Plus...the auras... around...living things. It's...weird. I think...I'm weird...."

DeMarco waited a moment longer, but her even breathing told him she was finally asleep again. He didn't relax but instead concentrated—as he had been concentrating during the last couple of hours—on keeping his shield extended just far enough to enclose Hollis as well as himself.

It was something of an experiment, since he'd never attempted to use his shield this way before, but he knew it was possible: Miranda could do it, and some of the SCU guardians, like Bailey, could too. And since he *was* able to project some of his energy outward to dampen the strength of other psychics, he figured—as Hollis had in her attempt to heal Diana—that it was worth a try.

Something he had to try, since he knew damn well that Hollis

KAY HOOPER

didn't have the energy or strength right now to wander around in
the gray time. And if that *was* where Diana's spirit had gone, if
she had opened that door, then Hollis would most certainly be
drawn there when she slept and what few guards she could claim—
virtually all of them emotional ones—came down.

She was completely defenseless when she slept. He actually had
to concentrate to avoid reading her, and even when he did so he
could still hear the distant whispers of her thoughts, her dreams.

She was not going to like that. At all.

He wasn't entirely certain he liked it himself. Not, at least, as it
stood now. Just as she had felt she had one foot in the gray time, he
felt he had only a partial connection to her, and that one very elu-
sive and uncertain. Not so surprising, considering that they had met
only a few months ago and both had been too active in investigations since to have much of a personal life. Still, he knew what he
wanted.

DeMarco was a patient man, but he had lived on the edge far too
long to have any illusions about the security of one's life. As
Quentin had discovered in a single horrifying moment, time could
run out in a heartbeat, leaving the most important words unsaid—
possibly forever.

But he also understood what had kept Quentin silent for so
many months; being a telepath, DeMarco had picked up information he undoubtedly had no right or business knowing, and the
unsought and unwanted insight told him that Diana had more emotional scars than any woman should have to carry in a lifetime.

Rather like Hollis.

One woman kept medicated by doctors and a domineering father since childhood, supposedly for her own good, forced to drift
through her own life with no say in her future; one woman brutal-
ized in a horrific attack that had left her terribly damaged, body and
soul. And both with powerful psychic gifts they continually struggled to master.

It was no wonder the men in their lives—and the men who wanted to be—faced an uphill battle.

DeMarco allowed that realization to rise in his mind, then dismissed it. He had never walked away from a fight in his life and didn't intend to start now.

He concentrated on shoring up his shield, his arms tightening around Hollis to hold her securely, even as a thread of his awareness remained focused on that room down the hall where Diana clung to life.

DeMarco was utterly convinced that both women were in deadly danger, and not only from a sniper's bullets.

Serenade

There hadn't been time for sleep after all, but at least Miranda and a couple of the others—they divided into shifts for the purpose—had been able to grab a hot shower and change before sitting down to a more than welcome breakfast at the B&B. Jewel and Lizzie, very subdued, served them and then left them alone.

"Are you sure you're all right?" Miranda asked Jaylene.

"Good to go. The medics put in a few stitches and gave me a shot to guard against infection. I don't even have to wear a sling. I'm fine, Miranda, honestly." She paused. "How are you? I mean, even with everything we see in this job, having somebody's head just about blown off right in front of you has got to be traumatic."

"I imagine it'll hit me later," Miranda replied, knowing she sounded almost as tired as she felt. She fleetingly remembered looking into the bathroom mirror before her shower and the shock she'd felt at the blood on her face, but she shoved that aside. Later. Because she didn't have time right now to sort through her own emotions.

There was so damn much to do.

Dean was still out, supervising agents and deputies in the

grimly methodical sweep of the town that had yet to discover any sign of the sniper—other than another mocking shell casing left circled for them to find. Galen was still missing, a fact Tony had to comment on.

"Where is he? Because we could sure as hell use him."

"We are using him." Miranda shook her head at his inquisitive look. "Trust me, Tony, he's where he needs to be."

Sighing, Tony said, "I guess I should have expected there to be a few things you haven't told us. God knows it's become business as usual for the SCU."

At least he doesn't sound bitter about it.

Miranda forced herself to eat a few more bites of the food she was sure tasted delicious under other circumstances, fought the surge of queasiness, and then looked at Tony and Jaylene. Longtime SCU agents. Trusted agents. Friends.

Slowly, she said, "Neither of you was involved in the investigation into Samuel and his church, so you weren't there at the end, when Noah and the others confronted him. Neither was I. But Noah and I are connected, you know that. So, to a certain extent, whatever affects him also affects me."

Jaylene asked, "How did it affect him?"

"We're still working that out. But let's just say it hasn't been a positive experience for either of us. You may have noticed he isn't here. And on a case this serious he normally would be."

Tony said, "He's been keeping tabs on the investigation, obviously. And as usual, he seems to have a pretty damn good idea where any of the rest of us are at any given moment. Voodoo, I call it."

Miranda knew he wasn't serious but said, "It's always been one of his gifts that when Noah cares, a connection gets formed."

"Voodoo," Tony insisted. Then he grinned faintly when she looked at him. "Somehow I find that thought more acceptable."

"You're weird," Jaylene told him.

"Without doubt." He sobered. "With things happening so fast, lousy technical communication, and no time for reports, I assume he's mostly keeping tabs through your link?"

Miranda shrugged. "Some. No matter how much we shut it down, things get through. Thoughts. Emotions. I know he's been worried; he knows I'm tired. Like that. But there's . . . something different I feel in him now. Something darker."

"Should we be worried?" Tony asked slowly.

"Honestly, I don't know. Whatever's going on, he seems to be handling it. For now, at least."

They absorbed that for a moment in silence. Finally Jaylene said, "I thought he was working on trying to find out who was reporting SCU information and actions back to the Director."

"He has been."

"And?"

In a deliberate tone, Miranda said, "Whatever he knows he hasn't shared."

Tony was frowning slightly. "Is that why you've both been shut down tight as a couple of drums pretty much for weeks now?"

She nodded. "It's been difficult. For him and, honestly, between us. He's changed. Everyone there at the church that day was changed by what happened. Literally changed. There was so much energy in the very air around them, and so much of it was dark, negative. Some of the changes have been . . . unpredictable."

"In what way?" Tony asked.

"Not following any pattern recognizable to us even after all the years of study and fieldwork we've accumulated. Hollis made a quantum leap forward in psychic terms, you both know that. She changed the most and is still changing, probably because she took a direct hit from Samuel and nearly died from it. But Galen also took a direct hit, and despite the fact that he isn't psychic in the traditional sense, he's been experiencing some phenomena we can't explain."

"Such as?" Jaylene was intent, patient.

"He almost reads as telepathic," Miranda said. "But not quite.

We carried out what tests and experiments we could before he lost patience, and all we were left with was the knowledge that since that confrontation at the Compound, he sometimes, faintly, hears voices."

"Normal if he's a telepath," Tony said. "But not so normal if he isn't."

"Exactly."

Jaylene said, "He seems the same as before to me. I mean, nothing appears to be bothering him."

"He's not the sort to show what he feels. But I think we can all assume he's having a difficult time with the situation."

"Then why's he here?" Tony asked bluntly.

Miranda grimaced. "Because one of the voices told him he needed to be here."

After a moment of silence, Tony said, "Please tell me you're kidding."

"Sorry."

"But . . . Miranda, if he's *not* psychic—"

"I know, believe me. If he's not psychic, he could be schizophrenic, even psychotic. Tell me, have *you* seen any signs of either?"

"No. But I'm not a doctor, shrink or medical."

"Neither am I. But I've known Galen a few years now, and I don't believe there could be such a fundamental shift in his personality without those changes leaving very obvious signs. Or at the very least detectable ones."

"So you trust he's mentally healthy?"

"As much as any of us is," she murmured.

Jaylene said, "Did the voice happen to tell him *why* he needs to be here?"

"No."

"Forgive me for sounding paranoid, but do you know that for a fact or only because he told you so?"

"Because he told me. I'm not reading much of anything from anyone right now. Closed down tight as a drum, remember? The fact that Hollis got through—loud and clear, no less—before the bomb exploded says more about her strengthening abilities than about mine."

"Is she a telepath now?" Jaylene asked.

"Not in the sense we understand. She can't receive at all, as far as we can tell. But she's gone beyond simple broadcasting because of the lack of a shield. She can send—and at full wattage, as Quentin would say."

"That could be a handy little tool," Jaylene said, thoughtful.

"Yeah, we're hoping it will be." *Assuming all this doesn't overload her brain...*

"Are *your* abilities changing?" Tony asked. "I mean, because Bishop was there at the church Compound, and through him, through your connection, whatever happened affected you as well?"

"Yes. My abilities are . . . changing. And, before you ask, I'm not entirely sure just how they're changing, only that they are." Before they could probe more into specifics, she added, "Like I said, the others there that day were changed too. Quentin isn't aware of it, but he's developing a secondary ability; Paige picked up on it during the debrief afterward."

Paige Gilbert was the unit's "Geiger counter," as Quentin had dubbed her: a psychic whose specialities were detecting latent and active psychic abilities in others—and defining specific abilities those psychics might be totally unaware of possessing. She was always present at post-investigation debriefs, another tool Bishop used to regularly monitor the condition of his people.

"What kind of secondary ability?" Tony asked.

"She wasn't sure."

"*Paige* wasn't sure?" With a better than eighty percent accuracy rate, she was one of the strongest psychics on the team.

"No. She said she was, for want of a better definition, getting some kind of interference when she tried to read anyone who was there at the Compound that day. Crackling, like static. And the interference hasn't cleared up in the months since."

"I don't much like the sound of that."

"Neither did Noah. And neither do I."

There was a long silence, and then Jaylene said, "Why do I get the feeling you didn't bring this up just to explain some changes we might have seen in the team?"

"Maybe because neither one of us believes in coincidence. There's been something off about this case from the very beginning, and so far the only thing that keeps turning up, in one way or another, is Samuel."

"But Samuel's dead," Tony said slowly.

"Yes. He is. But how many times have we faced the certainty that, in our world, dead doesn't necessarily mean gone?"

Fourteen

BJ ACTUALLY ENJOYED the cat-and-mouse game, amused by the notion that all those searching the town for him believed he was the mouse.

Idiots.

But by the time the sun was well up and the locals began to cautiously emerge from their homes, he decided he had better things to do with his time than to play with the cops and feds. Especially with the media nosing around and mostly getting in his way.

Killing one of them had not, apparently, discouraged the rest. In fact, there were more of the creatures around now that it was light. Maybe that gave them courage. Or maybe they were just dirt-stupid.

He considered that idly, pausing before abandoning his post to put the crosshairs over first one face and then another, wishing he could take them out. It would be so easy.

Boom.

But this wasn't the time. So he withdrew from the downtown area, smoothly and easily, all according to plan.

I'm out.

Good. Go check on him.

He would have preferred to do almost anything else, but he knew very well what his assigned roles were in the plan. So he merely sent back an affirmative and continued on his way. Once out of the more congested—in a rural sense—downtown area, the houses and businesses were farther and farther apart, and it was easy for him to travel through them unseen.

He used the usual tricks to make certain the dogs they'd finally set on his trail would find no trail to follow, amused yet again as he wondered what those experienced trackers would make of their failures.

Not that he cared.

At last he reached an old but well-kept farmhouse set in the middle of considerable acreage, its white-railed pasture dotted with a few beef cattle and a couple of lazy horses. He slipped up the long, winding dirt drive, taking care even though he knew there was no one around to see him pass.

When he got to the house, he used the key that was always underneath a flowerpot on the wide front porch to let himself in, reasonably sure that the house's occupant would be too preoccupied to hear the doorbell.

He usually was.

Sure enough, BJ could hear sounds coming from the basement. His mouth twisted. He carried his gun and pack to the kitchen and left them on the table, planning to clean the former and replenish supplies in the latter before he went back out.

With the closed basement door so near the kitchen, the sounds coming from down there were even louder, rising and falling like the plaintive cries of some terrified night animal.

Ignoring them, BJ went to the fridge and studied the contents for a moment before deciding he didn't feel like cooking eggs. Instead, he got out the makings of a sandwich. He fixed a generous one, found a beer in the fridge and chips in the pantry, and settled down to eat his meal.

One especially loud shriek from the basement, ending in a wet gurgle, caused him to pause for a moment, but then he resumed eating. When he was finished, he cleaned up after himself meticulously, checked his watch, then got another beer and set about cleaning his rifle.

He needed sack time before the next stage of the plan, but knew only too well he wouldn't be able to sleep with all the noises in the basement. So he kept himself busy for the duration, checking his watch from time to time and more than a little surprised that this one was taking so long.

He'd been in the house nearly two hours before the sounds finally faded into silence. And about damn time too.

Check on him. Clean up.

Dammit.

Ah, shit, I don't want to do that. Place'll look like a slaughterhouse, at least until he has his toy ready for me to take out of here. And, besides, you know he likes to clean up himself. It's part of his fun.

We don't have time for that, BJ, not if you were planning on a nap anytime soon. Don't think you're getting any sleep until you make damn sure he's out too. Give him an injection.

Okay, okay. I'll take care of it.

Just take care of him. You know what'll happen if you don't.

It wasn't so much a threat as it was a promise, and BJ knew better than to argue. Still, he paused long enough to remove his boots and socks, grimacing slightly as he thought about what he would undoubtedly step in during the process of cleaning up. Easier and simpler later to clean his feet rather than his boots, but still not a pleasant thought.

His idea of up close and personal was what he saw through the scope of his rifle.

He opened the door to the basement and started down the stairs, automatically breathing through his mouth.

"Rex?" he called.

"Hey, BJ. When did you get back?" As always, Rex sounded cheerful. And looked it, his eyes bright and the big smile on his pleasant face marred only by the blood smeared across one cheek.

"Couple hours ago. You were busy." BJ reached the bottom step and stood there for a moment, gazing around the brightly lit basement. There were no windows, since it was totally underground, but a combination of big, well-placed lights and a lot of white tile and stainless steel more than made up for the lack of natural light.

Still, BJ was always faintly surprised when he came down here by the modern . . . sleekness . . . of the place. There should, he thought, be iron and old leather and blood-soaked wood, because that was what a torture chamber was supposed to look like.

Not like an operating room.

The thought, as always, was fleeting, especially when BJ saw what had kept Rex occupied for far longer than expected.

On one of the two long stainless-steel tables lay a hunk of bloody meat only vaguely recognizable as a human being. BJ couldn't even tell if it was male or female, not by looking, though he knew it had been a man because he had delivered the guy to Rex early the day before, all trussed up like a Thanksgiving turkey.

His guess was that Rex had been experimenting this time with methods of skinning. That, at least, had been his excited plan.

But the skinned experiment had been left to congeal on the table, abandoned, no doubt hours ago, for a newer toy.

A toy he had apparently left the safety of this house to get for himself.

She lay on the second of the stainless-steel tables, strapped down even though the fight had gone out of her—along with what looked like most of her blood. Numerous small nicks covered her naked body, as did longer and deeper slashes.

It was—almost—artistic.

Blood dripped from the table to join the widening pool on the white tile floor. That didn't look so artistic, it looked messy as hell, especially since Rex had once more forgotten to position the table over one of the big drains in the floor.

Dammit.

The new toy had been pretty once. Probably. She had blond hair, which wasn't surprising since Rex favored blondes. Young. She had plenty of curves. And she was still alive. BJ could see a pulse beating—faintly—beneath the bloody skin of her throat.

"Jesus, Rex, what've you done?"

His cheerful smile fading, Rex said anxiously, "Bubba won't mind this time, BJ, honest. Because Father told me to. And we always do what Father tells us to, right?"

You know you're going to have to kill him one day soon, don't you, BJ? Before he becomes completely unmanageable?

"Right." BJ sighed.

"That wasn't a ghost out there this morning, it was a real sniper," Tony pointed out. "And yesterday. And on Tuesday. Probably the same one, but definitely flesh-and-blood real. With real bullets. And real mad skills with that rifle of his, to say nothing of his apparently magical ability to disappear into thin air while dozens of armed and experienced law-enforcement people hunt for him."

"Yes," Miranda said. "I know."

"So how could any of this have anything to do with Samuel?"

"One thing we knew absolutely about Samuel was that he had gotten better and better in recent years at locating and recruiting psychics; our inside agents told us that."

"Yeah, I remember. And so?"

"Noah believes Samuel didn't bring all those he found into the church, or at least not into the Compound. That he . . . kept some of them in reserve, unknown to the others in his flock, including our own people undercover inside the church. And that those he chose to keep apart were not only the most fanatically loyal but also the more militant, potentially more violent ones. And maybe the strongest psychics."

Jaylene was frowning. "Why?"

"Because he planned ahead."

"Planned beyond his own death?" Tony asked.

"Most of us plan beyond our deaths. We write wills, designate people to handle our property and raise our children, leave our money to the loved ones or charities we wish it to go to."

"Well, yeah, but that's a long way from having armed thugs carry out your bloody revenge fantasies after you're gone. Isn't it?"

"Samuel was a functioning precog, Tony. A seer. He had apocalyptic visions, yes, and those clearly drove him, but there's nothing to say he didn't also have a few visions about his future. His own very personal future. Maybe general, or maybe specific enough that he knew he wouldn't survive that final battle against Noah and the others."

She paused, then added, "Given the cold-blooded ferocity of the murders that led us here, and the equally cold-blooded precision of the sniper still out there, my guess is that Samuel made damn sure he had at least one—and possibly more than one—loyal follower wholly dedicated to avenging the death of their 'Father.' No matter what it takes."

"Oh, man," Tony muttered. Then he frowned. "So why not start killing SCU agents when he had the chance? Because he's had plenty of chances all this week. Even before, if he's been watching longer."

"Toying with us?" Miranda suggested. "Ramping up the danger level to draw more of us in? That certainly worked. Or maybe he was hoping Noah would show up. Because as much as Samuel considered the SCU in general his enemy, he knew very well who built and led the unit."

Jaylene said, "Is that another reason why Bishop isn't here? Because he's more likely to draw fire, possibly endangering the rest of us even more?"

"You know him," Miranda said. "What do you think?"

With no doubt at all in his voice, Tony said, "He'd step in front of a bullet in a heartbeat to save any one of us. I don't believe even Samuel's dark energy could have changed that. So my bet is, he isn't here because he believes it's safer for all of us if he is elsewhere."

Miranda smiled. "I believe the same thing."

"I'm not disagreeing," Jaylene said.

They ate in silence for a few minutes, more because they all knew they needed fuel than because they were hungry or enjoying the food.

"How sure are you about Samuel being behind these tortured vics and the sniper?" Tony asked finally.

"If you're asking whether I've had a premonition of my own, the answer is no. But for months we've known we had an enemy, long before the confrontation at the church. We know Samuel had some SCU members under surveillance more than a year ago, that he studied us and considered us a threat. That before we even knew who he was, he tried to lure us into a trap. We know he had considerable resources. We know he was fanatical and inspired fanatical loyalty among his followers. We know he was a highly functional precog, was able to channel extraordinary energy, was telepathic— and was able to steal energy from people and abilities from other psychics. We know he had a serious God complex, and from that we can safely infer he expected or planned to control at least some events even after death."

Miranda paused, then finished, "Add all that up, and I think it's more than a strong possibility that Samuel has something to do with this killer—or killers. The butcher and the sniper."

"Okay," Diana said, trying to feel as calm as she hoped she sounded, "Samuel wants to live. Do I take it that's him wearing Quentin's face?"

"You'll have to determine the truth of that."

Naturally, Brooke wasn't going to make it easy for her. Or even just less hard.

Diana wished there was a place to sit down in this endless, featureless corridor, because she was tired. And that was terrifying.

"If that is him...what's the point of wearing Quentin's face?" She was trying to work it out aloud, hoping Brooke would offer a tidbit here or there; it seemed to be her preferred way of revealing information. "I know it's not Quentin, he knows I know, so why go on doing it? To keep me rattled? Off balance? Because he thinks it's fun? Why?"

Since those questions elicited from Brooke nothing but an expression of mild interest, Diana tried a different tack.

"He wants to live again. Samuel wants to live again. In the flesh. Has he tried to? No, he can't have. No spirit leaves the gray time without a door. And only mediums make doors. Right?"

"You'd know better than I would, Diana."

She ignored that. "That's the one ability he went out of his way to avoid, the one ability he didn't want. According to Hollis, to the reports, mediums might well have been the only thing he was truly afraid of, and there was no indication he might possess that ability. Or...if it's latent in him, it's something he suppressed his whole life. So it's reasonable to assume he can't make a door for himself. Even with all his power—wait. His power. He's been weakened here, hasn't he? Because power is drained here, energy is drained. He's been here too long. If he couldn't make his own door out of here in all this time, he *really* can't now."

"Not without help," Brooke murmured.

"What, my help? I can't get myself out of here. Which means I can't find the door I made to get here, even assuming it's still there, assuming it's open, or assuming I could open it. What makes him believe I could—or would—help him?"

Brooke merely waited.

"If he could have forced me, he already would have. I think.

Which means he can't force me. Or . . . it means he knows I can't get myself out of here, can't find the door I made." A sudden realization hit Diana. "Wait. If the door I made is still open, even a little bit . . . Hollis will be drawn to it. When she's asleep, when her defenses are down."

She stared at Brooke, a new fear crawling over her. "Is that what he's waiting for? Hollis? Because he could follow her back out the door even if I can't? Jesus."

"Don't you think Hollis can take care of herself?"

"Not in here. Not alone." Diana bit her lip in a moment of inde-cision, then turned and began to retrace her steps. At least, she thought that was what she was doing; the endless corridor pretty much looked the same way no matter which direction she chose.

Brooke followed her. "Where are you going, Diana?"

"Well, I'm not staying here where he thinks he can trap a few psychics, not if Hollis could turn up any minute. This could be a dif-ferent kind of trap now, one to catch her."

"Do you really believe that?"

"I believe this is a bad place and I want to leave it. Now."

The words had barely left her lips before the gleaming sterile corridor sort of shivered around her—and she found herself stand-ing in the silent gray time Main Street of Serenade. There was a bench practically behind her, and she wasted no time in sitting.

"Diana?"

"I just need a minute, that's all." She stared, frowning, up and down the eerily silent and gray street. "And you don't have to tell me there are no minutes here. I know that. But I need to rest awhile. It's getting . . . a little hard to breathe."

Brooke was silent.

"I . . . don't seem to remember getting shot. Shouldn't I remem-ber that if I'm not going back?"

"I don't know. Should you?"

"You're really not going to tell me, are you?"

"Tell you what?"

"If I'm dead. Or if I'm going to die."

"Everything dies. You know that."

"And you know what I mean."

"All I know is that you have truths to discover here. Before you can move on . . . or go back . . . or do whatever it is you're destined to do. First you have to find the truth. All the truths."

"But no pressure," Diana muttered. "Look, whatever happens to me, Hollis doesn't deserve to get sucked into this place. Isn't there any way I can warn her to stay out?"

"Do you think a warning would have any effect?"

Briefly, Diana put her head in her hands. Then she straightened and stared at Brooke. "You know, this answering-a-question-with-another-question shit is getting old."

Brooke smiled.

"So's that," Diana told her. She looked away from the guide to study the street again, something nagging at her. "I was shot. I was shot . . . on purpose. The sniper picked me. All of us were running around in the open, we didn't have our vests on, and if he was watching yesterday—or the day before, whenever—then he probably had all of us marked as cops, maybe as SCU. So why me? I'm not even a full agent yet. This is—was—my very first case as an investigator. Why was I the target?"

"I'm not allowed to reply with a question," Brooke said.

Diana ignored her. "If the sniper saw the SCU as his enemy, why not pick someone who . . . counted? Someone who'd be more of a trophy for him. Miranda was there. Quentin. Hollis and Reese. Why did he pick me? Unless I was a bigger threat somehow. Or . . . I had something he wanted. Something his boss wanted. Like maybe . . . the ability to open a door into—or out of—the gray time. He must have known it was the only sure way to get me here, at least on his timetable."

She turned her head and stared at the silent guide. "He's not just in here trying to get out, he's influencing things out there. Calling the shots—literally. The sniper, the murders: It's all about Samuel."

Serenade

Galen prowled uneasily from window to window, not even aware of what he was doing until Ruby spoke.

"You really want to be out there with them, don't you? With your friends?"

"With my team," he said.

"Sorry you're stuck here watching over me."

"I'm not stuck, Ruby." He made an effort to soften his voice. "Look, Bailey said you didn't sleep on the jet, and you haven't closed your eyes since we got here. Why don't you go try to rest for a while?"

"I'm not sleepy. Bailey said soldiers have to learn to sleep when they can. And I get that. She's sleeping now so you'll sleep later." Ruby studied him with those too-old eyes. "Except I don't think you will sleep later."

"I will. When there's time."

"When this is over, you mean."

"If you like."

Ruby was silent for a long moment, then said almost casually, "Are the voices still talking to you?"

He stopped prowling and stared at her. His immediate instinct was to deny, but somehow instead he found himself asking, "What do you know about that?"

"About your voices? Just that you hear them. Since the church. Since what we did to Father. Since things changed for a lot of us." She paused. "Are they still talking to you?"

"Whispering," he said finally. "I can't understand what they're saying. Can't quite hear them."

"Maybe because you aren't listening hard enough."

"What do you mean?"

Curled up in the big armchair near a dark fireplace, Ruby returned his stare with an odd serenity. "You're . . . shut inside yourself. I expect that's so you can help your team. So you can guard other people, keep them safe. Keep me safe. But it makes a shell around you. A hard shell. Maybe the voices can't get through well enough for you to understand what they're saying."

"Maybe I don't want them to," he found himself replying.

"Are you afraid of what they might tell you?"

Damn.

Galen thought it was ridiculous for him to be confiding in a twelve-year-old girl, but he couldn't seem to stop the conversation.

"I don't know where they're coming from, Ruby. I don't hear voices, it's not my thing."

"It's your thing now."

"Well, yeah, I suppose. But it *wasn't* my thing, so I don't know how to control it."

"Sometimes we can't. Sometimes this stuff controls us."

"That's definitely not my thing," he told her.

"No, I didn't think so. Your thing is . . . not dying. Isn't that right?"

"I heal myself. So far, that means not dying. But everybody dies sooner or later."

"Maybe to really kill you they'd have to cut off your head," she suggested gravely.

Galen was startled, but only for a moment. "You like horror movies," he guessed.

She smiled shyly. "We weren't allowed to watch them inside the Compound. But Maggie says it's good for us sometimes to be pretend-scared. And John likes horror movies. So we watched some."

"I see."

"They didn't scare me, really," she confessed. "Not after the church. Not after Father. But it was nice to pretend bad and scary things aren't real. Nice for a while, at least."

He shook his head and heard himself saying, "Ruby, what are you *doing* here?"

Her face changed just a little, going guarded. And there was a secretive expression in her eyes that he'd never seen before. "John's teaching me how to play chess. You start out with all the pieces on the board. That's why I'm here. Because I'm one of the pieces."

"Ruby—"

"You should try to listen to your voices, Galen. You really should. I think there's something important they need to tell you."

"Do you?"

"Yes."

"How would you know that?" he asked quietly.

"Because I hear voices too. And they always—*always*—tell me things I need to know."

"Like the reason you had to come here? The reason you have to be a chess piece?"

"Yes. Like that." Ruby turned her head, gazed toward one of the windows she was forbidden to approach, and said in the same soft, musing voice, "Right now they're telling me something bad happened again. Something we couldn't stop. Poor thing. She was a chess piece too. She was a pawn. She had to be sacrificed."

We've done a complete sweep of the downtown area," Dean reported to Miranda when she and the others returned to the mobile command center. "Sheriff Duncan pulled in all his people, part-timers included, and even swore in a couple of retired deputies and a few friends he trusts, so we've got enough manpower—barely—to keep a fairly close watch on most of the buildings. But we didn't find the bastard."

"No luck with the dogs?"

"*Nada*. The handlers are as baffled as their dogs seem to be. Do you want to call them off?"

Miranda frowned. "No. No, just ask them to patrol. To crisscross the town independently. Randomly. They can decide among themselves when to take breaks, but I want those dogs visible as much as possible. If nothing else, it should at least make it tougher for the sniper to move around."

"Copy that. I'll go tell them."

"And then you and a few of the other agents go ahead and take your own breaks. Get some breakfast, grab a shower if you like, sleep a couple of hours. Everything's set up for us at the B&B. There are beds and cots enough to go around, though some of us are doubling up in rooms. Not that it much matters, since we'll be on rotating shifts for the duration."

"You guys didn't get much downtime," he noted.

"We got enough. Besides, with more agents on the way and scheduled to arrive by sometime late this afternoon, we should all be able to get a good night's sleep tonight."

Under his breath, Tony muttered, "Damn. Jinx."

Miranda glanced at him, then said to Dean, "Take your time. We're mostly waiting for paperwork—the posts Sharon conducted and ballistics reports. And we'll probably go over the victim files one more time, looking for connections. There isn't much else to do, at least for the next few hours. Unless you've picked up something you haven't mentioned, that is." Dean Ramsey was a fifth-degree clairvoyant.

He shook his head. "Not a whole hell of a lot, I'm sorry to say. At first I thought it was just the general confusion, all the violence, but . . . there's a weird vibe about this place. Can't quite pin it down, but I've never sensed anything like it."

"Join the club," Tony said with a sigh.

Dean offered a wry smile, then said to Miranda, "When I try harder, when I push, it's like I'm picking up some kind of interference, almost like hearing static on a radio."

Tony and Jaylene exchanged quick glances.

Miranda simply nodded. "Don't try to force it. Maybe taking a break will help."

"Yeah, maybe." He didn't sound too convinced but left to follow her orders without argument.

"Interference," Jaylene said. "Why does it make me very uneasy that word keeps cropping up?"

"It's an anomaly," Miranda responded. "And anomalies are signposts. Things to pay attention to."

"Consider me paying attention," Jaylene said. "Because even though the vibes I get are almost always from objects, I'm feeling the weirdness of this place too."

Tony said, "And me. I keep wanting to rub the back of my neck, because it feels like the hair's standing straight out. Not an especially pleasant sensation."

"My question," Miranda said, "is whether this is something natural and specific to the town for some kind of geographic reason or something new. And if it is new, I want to know when it started and whether it's artificial, man-made, or..."

"Or psychic?" Jaylene suggested.

Miranda was frowning now. "Dean can't pick up anything. Neither of you has been able to. I haven't. Reese knew when a gun was being pointed at Hollis and him, but that was well outside town, higher up in the mountains—and before the bomb blast all he was really sure of was that the sniper was watching. Plus, he didn't sense a thing before the sniper shot Diana, and a gun pointed his way virtually always sends up giant red flags. Gabe and Roxanne have a solid internal connection, but otherwise they've been... fuzzy, missing things they should have been able to pick up on easily."

Sighing again, Tony said, "Psychic, then."

"Christ, I hope not. It'd take a hell of a lot of energy to have that sort of dampening effect on so many psychics of different abilities and degrees. And it sounds too much like what was happening in Samuel's Compound on that last day."

"Damn," Jaylene muttered.

"You did jinx us," Tony said to Miranda. "Whenever *anybody* says we'll get a good night's sleep, we never do. Something always happens."

The words had barely left his lips when Sheriff Duncan came in to the command center, his expression grim. "I've got a missing deputy," he said.

"Who?" Miranda asked—and Tony looked at her curiously, because he had the odd notion she knew exactly what the sheriff would reply.

"Bobbie. Bobbie Silvers. As near as I can figure, she hasn't been seen since sometime last night."

Fifteen

WHEN HOLLIS WOKE UP, she had no idea how much time had passed; this was an internal room in the hospital, so no windows allowed any natural light to signal whether it was day or night.

She hoped it was still Thursday; surely she—they—hadn't slept all day, even though she felt as if that could be the case. Hell, she felt as if she'd slept for a week. Her eyes were scratchy, her muscles stiff from apparently remaining in the same position for God only knew how long, and a gnawing emptiness told her she hadn't eaten in too many hours.

She wasn't sure whether DeMarco was awake, until she was able to ease from his loosened embrace and sit on the edge of the narrow bed. Looking at him as she absently finger-combed her hair, she realized she didn't feel the same uncertainty she'd felt earlier about his state of consciousness; he was asleep, and deeply at that.

His face was relaxed in a way she'd never before seen, his breathing deep and even, and the tension she usually sensed in him was absent.

Hollis frowned a little, though she couldn't have said why, exactly, she was bothered. DeMarco had as much right to sleep as she did, after all, and even his seemingly ever-vigilant senses had to rest sometime. None of the team had gotten much rest in the last few days and, besides, she had no idea what he might have been doing before joining them in Serenade or how long he had gone without sleep at that point.

She shook off the thoughts, deciding just to be grateful that there would be no more awkward—on her part, at least—conversation while they lay in bed together.

Move. Don't think, just move.

Given the tininess of the silent, lamplit room, it required only a couple of steps for her to reach the door, and she slipped out without looking back at DeMarco.

They had been offered the use of visitors' restrooms, complete with lockers for their belongings and private showers; it was a kindness provided for the families of patients who spent long days, even weeks, in the various intensive-care units on this floor. Both Hollis and DeMarco had gotten cleaned up and changed not long after Miranda and the sheriff headed back to Serenade, but Hollis felt the need to shower again now, mostly to clear her fuzzy head.

She found herself in a quiet and unfamiliar hallway, and it took a moment or two for her to remember that she hadn't exactly been conscious when DeMarco carried her from the IC unit where Diana lay to this room.

Carried me. Jeez.

Hollis pushed that out of her mind and took a few tentative steps to her left down the hallway, wondering if she was headed in the correct direction. Everything still looked unnatural to her, too faded and colorless to be real life and yet not—quite—the desolate emptiness that was Diana's gray time.

Just creepy enough to make her distinctly uncomfortable.

"Hollis."

Shit.

Hollis turned slowly to find Andrea standing a few feet away. Like the other spirits Hollis had seen earlier, she looked more real than her surroundings did, and her aura was bright shades of blue and green.

It was, Hollis realized, the first time she'd ever seen Andrea's aura.

"You have to help Diana," the spirit said.

"Andrea—"

"You have to help her to heal. If her body isn't healed, she won't be able to come back to it."

"Tell me something I don't know."

Appearing to take the wry comment literally, Andrea said, "She's in great danger. The longer she's in the gray time, the less likely it is she'll be able to get back. Her spirit's being weakened there, and her body is weak here."

"I tried to heal her body. Or help her heal, anyway. I don't think I did her very much good."

"You have to try again."

Since she'd planned to do just that, Hollis nodded but said, "Listen, can't you finally tell me who you are? And why you're apparently attached to me?"

Andrea took a step back, clearly startled. "I—I'm not—you opened a door."

"Months ago I opened a door. I mean, when I first saw you. So why do you keep coming back? Or are you—did I leave you on this side? Can you not go back?"

"Not until it's finished."

"Until what's finished?"

Andrea seemed distracted for a moment, looking around as though she was lost, then she said, "He's trying to protect you, but what he's doing . . . It's keeping you from helping Diana. Can't you feel it?"

"Feel what?"

"He's tried to put a veil between you and the spirit world. Energy. To keep you safe, he thinks."

"Who thinks?"

"Reese."

"Wait. It's because of Reese that everything looks weird and only the spirits seem real?"

Andrea nodded. "He wants to help. To protect. But he can't stand between you and the spirit world. He can't block your natural energies. That's why the real world looks faded to you, because his energy comes from there and only works the way he believes it works there. You have to stop him before he pushes you closer to the spirit world. That's not the way. Especially not now. You have to help heal Diana, and you have to be very much in the living world to do that."

"Last time I had to help Ruby." Hollis wasn't really protesting, just trying to understand what was going on.

"They both have a role to play."

"Andrea, for God's sake—"

The spirit began backing away, fading. "There's a better way to use his energy, his shield. His protection. Tell him that. Help Diana. Everything depends on it, and there's not much time. . . ."

Hollis found herself alone in the corridor once again. She drew a breath, let it out slowly, and then turned back to the room where DeMarco slept. She went in and sat on the side of the narrow bed, put her hand on his shoulder, and attempted to shake him.

"Hey!"

It occurred to Hollis only afterward that rudely awakening a man with DeMarco's background, training, and apparent nature probably wasn't the wisest thing in the world, but at that moment she wasn't thinking about any possible danger from him.

His eyes snapped open, and in the same heartbeat of time his hand moved in a blur and grabbed her wrist. She felt his fingers tighten for just an instant and then relax.

Interestingly, she was never frightened for a second.

"That," he said calmly, "was not very smart. I might have taken your head off."

She pushed that aside with a gesture of her free hand. "Never mind that. You have to stop."

"Stop what?"

"Your shield. Projecting it—I guess. Something like what you did at the church Compound back in January. You've actually got it between me and the real world rather than the spirit world, and you have to stop doing that." Even as she said it, another thought occurred, and she added absently, "I wonder if that's why I couldn't reach the spirit world then. Not the same thing, but maybe your dampening field was doing a lot more than we thought it was."

Without denying anything, DeMarco merely responded, "Who says that's what I'm doing?"

"Andrea."

"Spirit Andrea? The one who warned you about the bomb?"

Hollis nodded. "And she knew what she was talking about then, so I have to listen now. You have to pull it back, Reese; stop trying to stand between me and the spirit world. That's what I *do*, and you can't stop it."

"According to Andrea."

"Yeah, according to her. Also according to her, I have to help heal Diana before it's too late. And I can't do that effectively with your shield wrapped around me. That might even be the reason I went out like a light when I tried earlier to help her heal. Energy pushing against energy is—well, most of it would rebound, don't you think?"

After a moment, he released her wrist and pushed himself up on an elbow, continuing to regard her calmly. "Rebound?"

"Rebound. I push and your energy pushes back." She frowned suddenly. "Why, by the way? I mean, why're you trying to protect me?"

"I wondered when you'd ask that." He hooked one hand around the back of her neck and drew her close enough so that he could kiss her. It was hardly a gentle sort of first kiss, more a kind of claiming

247

just this side of forceful, and by the time it was over Hollis had no doubt at all what it was he wanted.

"Any more questions?" His voice was a little rough.

Very conscious of his fingers moving against her neck and of the hardness of his shoulder beneath her own clutching fingers, Hollis thought, *Wow,* but had sense enough not to say it.

Except he's a telepath and . . . Dammit.

"Um . . . this is very sudden," she heard herself say inanely.

"Not really. We met months ago."

"Yeah, but . . . we haven't . . . I mean . . . You never said anything."

"I'm saying something now."

Casting about for something not inane to say in response, she finally managed, "I think your timing could use a little work."

DeMarco smiled slightly. "Never the time and the place. Hollis, if something happens to either of us, I'm not going to be like Quentin, wishing I'd spoken up when I had the chance. So I'm speaking up now. You don't have to say anything one way or the other, but I wanted you to know that I'm . . . more than interested. In you. In being with you."

She hesitated, conscious of a clock ticking away in her mind with the uneasy urgency Andrea had created. Still, she had to say *something.* He probably already knew, but . . . "Reese, to say I've got a lot of baggage is a huge understatement."

"That's okay. Baggage doesn't bother me. It makes us who we are."

She tried again. "After what happened to me, I don't even know if I can respond *normally* to a man." She hated making that admission but figured once again that he probably knew anyway.

He pulled her toward him again just far enough to kiss her, and this time it lasted awhile.

When she could breathe again, Hollis murmured, "Okay, maybe that isn't going to be such a problem, after all."

DeMarco was still wearing that faint smile, only now there was something sensuous about it. "I'm thinking it probably won't be. But you don't have to worry. I won't pressure you."

"Yeah?" She managed an unsteady laugh. "And when does the not-pressuring me part start?"

"Right now." He kissed her one final time, briefly but not at all lightly, then let her go and got up off the bed. In a perfectly normal voice, he said, "If you mean to try to help Diana, I think we both need time to shower and get something to eat first."

"But—"

"You need energy, Hollis. Fuel. It won't do Diana any good if you collapse because you haven't eaten in more than twenty-four hours. It's well after two."

She resented his normal voice, especially since she couldn't match it; to her own ear she still sounded out of breath and flustered. And full of inane questions. "A.M. or P.M.?"

"P.M. Still Thursday. Come on."

Hollis took his extended hand, conscious of faint panic and a much stronger sense of inevitability.

Some things had to happen just the way they happened.

If she'd learned nothing else with the SCU, she had most certainly learned that.

Washington, D.C.

He was surprised but not astonished when the Director got in touch to arrange another meeting, assuming there had been a change of mind after some considered thought. He was a little annoyed that the venue Micah Hughes chose was a conference room in a small hotel just off the Beltway but guessed it was the Director's attempt to avoid more openly public spots and the risk of recognition.

He found the room without the need to ask a staff member and opened the door fully expecting to see FBI Director Micah Hughes.

Instead, Noah Bishop was seated on the opposite side of the big conference table between them, his hands resting on a plain manila folder. The folder was closed.

"Well, Agent Bishop. Fancy meeting you here." He remained outwardly calm as he came into the room; he had faced too many powerful men across too many boardroom tables to fold at the first sign of trouble. He remained on his feet, resting his own hands on the tall back of one of the chairs but not pulling it out. Once he sat down, he conceded the power position to Bishop and he knew it.

His mind raced, considering the possible ramifications of this, but he had no intention of making it easy for Bishop, no matter what the agent was up to.

"Thank you for coming. We weren't sure you would. I gather you usually choose the meeting spots," Bishop said coolly.

"I'm sure I don't know what you mean."

Bishop shook his head just once. "I didn't intercept the call, if that's what you're thinking. In fact, from all I can gather you seem to have greatly exaggerated the extent of my reach. And my interests. It's never been about power with me. Not your kind of power."

"Of course not. You merely cultivated other powerful people because it amused you."

"No. Because I knew I'd need them one day. When a man like you came after me—for whatever reason." The scar down Bishop's left cheek stood out whitely against his tanned skin, the only visible sign of any tension. "I have to admit, I never expected a reason like yours. Revenge, sure. Retaliation. Even just to remove me before I could become a problem for someone. But I didn't expect to be a kind of rival. This kind, at any rate."

"Agent Bishop—"

"You're so wrong on so many counts it's hardly worth talking about. Except to note that your jealousy and resentment led you down one of the darkest paths I've ever seen."

"So dramatic. Should I ask you to define this 'dark path' for me?"

Again, Bishop shook his head just once. "You do realize that once

I tell him who is really responsible for the murder of his daughter, Senator LeMott will destroy you." It very clearly wasn't a question.

He stiffened but said, "I was in no way connected to that unfortunate girl's tragic death."

"You most certainly were. Oh, I don't have courtroom proof. But I have proof enough for LeMott. Believe me. He had Samuel killed on a lot less. Unlike you, he has complete faith in the abilities of myself and my team. All our abilities."

"So you're going to tell him you saw my face in your crystal ball?" He managed a laugh and knew it sounded convincingly amused.

"I'm going to tell him the truth. That Samuel and his pet monster were fully funded by you in Boston. I don't know whether you were aware going in of exactly what he meant to do—or how he meant to do it. But I do know you continued to fund him even afterward, when you had to know how your money was being used." Bishop's wide shoulders lifted and fell in a shrug. "Not that LeMott will be listening beyond that point. He'll only care that you were the catalyst that got his daughter killed."

"You're out of your mind."

As if he hadn't heard that, Bishop said, "It was an interesting tactic you chose, that attack on three levels. First Samuel's rampage, keeping myself and the team fully occupied, then you dripping poison into the Director's ears about the unit and me, and, finally, making sure I'd know about that poison. And wonder where you got it."

"Maybe you have a traitor on the team, Bishop." Despite his best efforts, the words emerged viciously.

"No. That's what you wanted me to think. Wanted all of us to think. So we'd doubt one another, or at the very least wonder. So the trust painstakingly built up between us for years would begin to break down. And that was really where you overplayed your hand. Because that was . . . very personal, that part of the attack. That was an attempt to gut me—and the SCU. So I had to wonder who could possibly hate me that much. And why."

"I'd be wondering about that traitor if I were you." He couldn't let that go, still believing it was the wedge he needed.

Still hoping.

A very faint smile curved Bishop's hard mouth. "I stopped wondering about that when we faced Samuel at his church. When I felt the power of his mind firsthand. We didn't have a traitor. What we had was an enemy capable of creeping among us—psychically. Unseen. Taking note of what we said and did. And much of what we thought.

"That's the ultimate irony, you know. That you trusted the information Samuel gave you—perfectly accurate information—without questioning where he came by it. Maybe you knew, deep down, what he'd tell you if you asked. Maybe that's why you didn't ask."

"You need help, Bishop. You're a sick man."

"I'm sick and tired of your crusade. And so is the Director, just so you know. He's given me a complete statement of his dealings with you. And he's given me the discretion to use it however I please."

His mouth twisted. "He's a gutless wonder."

"No, he's an honorable man. An ethical man. I knew that. And I knew he would ultimately decide to support the SCU. A decision he undoubtedly would have come to sooner if not for your poison."

He was silent.

"Not that I really needed most of the information Director Hughes was able to give me. I already knew most of it. He was just confirmation."

"How could you know?"

Bishop shook his head slightly. "You're good at a lot of things, but this? This is what I do. Investigate. I had to find a bitter enemy with very deep pockets, and unfortunately there are several. So it took time. Time and far too much of my attention. But one by one, the others were ruled out. It's taken me months, but eventually you were the only one left."

"The Sherlock Holmes maxim? Eliminate the impossible and whatever remains must be truth? I'm surprised at you, Bishop. That's so terribly...old school."

"If old school works, I use it. I use anything that works. Everything. Every tool I can get my hands on—except for one. I never make a deal with the devil."

"If you're implying I did—"

"I'm not implying. I'm stating. You knew what Samuel was, what he was capable of. But you believed he could get you what you wanted, and that was all you cared about. As long as the SCU was destroyed, I was destroyed, then nothing else mattered to you."

"I don't know what you're talking about." The words were almost mechanical.

"I wish I could believe you didn't. I wish I could believe there were lines you wouldn't cross no matter how determined you were to win. To destroy me. But I don't believe that. You knew. You just didn't give a shit about anyone else."

"I'm going to ruin you, Bishop. No matter what you think you have on me, it won't stand up in court. And by the time my attorneys are finished with you, the FBI won't have you. Your own wife won't have you."

"Oh, it won't go to court," Bishop said, ignoring the more personal claim. "You're right. I don't have enough evidence against you for a court case. Not yet, at any rate, though I'm sure there's some to be found when my people know exactly where to dig."

He managed another laugh. "Good luck with that. And since you have no evidence to support these wild accusations, I'll be on my way. You can talk to my attorneys if you have anything further to say to me."

"No, what I have to say to you, I'll say to you now." Bishop picked up the folder lying on the table in front of him and slid it across to the other man. "I want you to take a look at what your money bought you."

"I'm not going to—"

Flatly, Bishop said, "There are two agents waiting outside that door. You'll take a look inside that folder, or I'll have you arrested the instant you step outside. Believe me, I do have enough evidence to detain you. And question you formally. And make a hell of a public mess for your PR people to clean up." He paused, watching the other man seethe, then added, "Or we can avoid all that—at least for now—and you can look inside the folder. Your choice."

After a moment, he reached stiffly for the folder. He opened it, his expression impassive. But then he sucked in a breath, the color drained from his face, and he all but fell as he fumbled for the chair in front of him and sank into it. The manila folder dropped to the floor, leaving him clutching the single photograph it had contained.

Bishop watched him, feeling not a single twinge of compassion for what he knew very well was genuine shock, grief, and guilt. "I could have shown you all the victims of your crusade. But I decided this one was what you needed to see. Money can buy a lot of things. But what it can never buy, what nothing can ever buy, is complete control over events. Whatever you thought your money was buying, *that's* what it bought."

Elliot Brisco stared down at the stark photograph of his only surviving daughter lying in the street in a pool of her own blood. "It isn't true. This is—lie. This is a lie. She isn't dead. She isn't dead?" His voice was shaking, his hands were shaking, and when he met Bishop's gaze his eyes were wide and curiously blank.

"She's fighting for her life. And it doesn't look good, according to the doctors. A sniper's bullet can do terrible things to a human body." His voice was measured, steady. Implacable. "She was collateral damage at best, in the wrong place at the wrong time. At worst, she was a target he intended to hit for reasons of his own. Either way, you've lost whatever control you imagined you had over the situation."

"He . . . Who are you talking about? Who did this?"

"Your pet monster. Samuel."

"He's dead. Samuel's dead."

"Let's just say he left a...legacy behind to survive him. With orders to finish the job you gave him money to start."

"Bastard...bastard..."

Bishop didn't ask whether that referred to himself or the killer—killers—he was after. He merely said, "So you're going to tell me who's been on Samuel's private payroll all this time, on *your* private payroll. Because that's who's doing this. That's who's down in Serenade conducting a war. You're going to tell me who it is, and you're going to tell me everything else you know or believe you know about the situation. Everything. So that maybe, just maybe, I can stop this from getting any worse than it already is."

Serenade

The dogs had had no luck in tracking the sniper, but by four o'clock Thursday afternoon the pair of bloodhounds known in the area as the very best did manage to find Acting Deputy Bobbie Silvers.

Or what was left of her.

They found her just outside the town limits, her naked body tumbled into a shallow ditch off a side road and partially covered over with wet and rotting autumn leaves.

Miranda stood gazing down at the pale face she had carefully uncovered, only distantly aware of Sheriff Duncan's broken curses and the utter stillness and silence of the other deputies and agents gathered around. She looked at that very young face she had barely noticed when it was alive, remembering how Bobbie had worked overtime to find information for them.

Eager. Smart. Ambitious.

Gone.

Finally, Miranda lifted her gaze and found Dean Ramsey nearby. "It's a dump site, but we'll get what we can. Crime-scene protocol," she said quietly.

"Copy that." He moved away, gathering a couple of other

agents with a gesture so they could begin the work of locating, photographing, tagging, and preserving what evidence there was to be found.

"Miranda." Tony was at her side. "I'm feeling a little exposed, even with the trees and our vests."

"We have people covering this area," she pointed out. "Media crawling all over the area outside our perimeter, despite our warnings. And there are no buildings near enough to provide a clear line of sight. I wasn't trained as a sniper, but I can tell you he'd be a fool to be up in one of these trees close enough to see us. So far he hasn't shown a sign of being a fool."

Tony glanced around. "You have a point. Several, in fact. Still, if the plan is to spend any kind of time here, I say we move the mobile command center down here. Otherwise, we should go back into town."

"And what makes you think town is any safer?"

"Nothing solid," he confessed. "But we've done all we can to clear it out and guard the most likely buildings, so it's as safe as it's going to be until we catch this bastard. In the meantime, there's nothing else you can do here—and we still have all those files to go through."

"You're probably right." Miranda knew he was, but she was finding it difficult to turn her back on this poor girl and walk away.

Jaylene said, "When do the reinforcements arrive?"

"Anytime now." She pulled out her cell phone to check for a signal. "I'll get an ETA. Why don't you two get back to the command center and get started on the files? I'll catch a ride with the sheriff."

Without commenting that the sheriff was likely to remain here awhile, Tony merely said, "Watch your back," then turned and followed Jaylene toward the lone remaining SUV.

Watch your back.

She could feel it too, in the very air around them, a skin-prickling sense of danger, of threat. Her training told her at least part of it was psychological; knowing a sniper was still out there, capable of shooting someone in the head from more than a hundred yards away, was hardly something easily forgotten or even pushed aside.

But there was more to it than that. Despite the shield that guarded her mind, her innermost self, Miranda had the uneasy feeling that there was a chink somewhere in her armor and that the enemy knew it.

She shook her head finally, acknowledging to herself that they were—that she was—doing everything possible to protect themselves; there was nothing else to be done except get on with the job. She returned her attention to the cell phone, realizing that she had accidentally brushed a thumb against the wrong touch key—which wasn't so unusual with the sophisticated little unit—and had called up the phone's photo in-box.

She found herself staring down at a brightly colored photo on the cell's screen: a shot of Diana as she had lain bleeding not so many blocks from where Miranda stood.

She looked at it for several heartbeats, then very deliberately deleted the picture, wishing it was as easy to remove it from her memory. She returned to the call screen, only to discover there wasn't even a single bar indicating minimum signal strength.

Sighing, Miranda returned the cell to its specially designed case on her belt, then touched the tiny device hidden in her ear. "Gabe?"

Static.

She estimated she was no more than two miles from the command center, probably less. Far enough, obviously, to have lost the shaky reception they had nearer the center of town. Whether by accident or design, Serenade appeared to be the ultimate communication dead zone.

Now there's a phrase.

Trusting that Gabriel was keeping an eye on this area as per orders, Miranda dismissed the lack of communication as something beyond her control for now and turned her attention to Sheriff Duncan.

"Des?"

"This is gonna kill her mother. I told you about her mother, didn't I?"

"Yes, you did." He had rambled on a great deal during the last frantic hours of searching for his young deputy, so Miranda knew that Bobbie Silvers had lived with her widowed mother in a small house on the opposite side of town, only the two of them left of the family since Bobbie's father had died years before.

"I just...I don't understand. She was a sweet kid. Who'd want to hurt her like this?" He looked years older than he had only days before, deep lines in his face and his eyes red-rimmed and haunted. He gestured toward the body, exposed enough so they could all see some of the numerous cuts and deep slashes that had undoubtedly killed her.

Miranda drew a breath and let it out slowly. "I don't know if it's better or worse to say that to him she wasn't a person. Wasn't a girl who lived with her ailing mother, a girl who worked hard because she wanted to be a cop. To him, she was only...a thing. Maybe just an experiment in how long it might take someone to bleed to death."

"Jesus Christ."

She put a hand on his arm. "Des, let the others take care of her now. You know they'll treat her with respect."

"I don't want to just...leave her."

"I know. But there's something you and I have to do, and it's best done as soon as possible, before the media or helpful neighbors or anyone else beats us to it."

Duncan looked at her, his eyes full of dread.

Miranda nodded. "We have to tell her mother."

Sixteen

DIANA DIDN'T KNOW how much time passed while she sat, frozen, on the bench staring at a gray and lifeless Main Street, but she did know the rest had done her little good. It was still a bit difficult to breathe, and she still felt overwhelmingly exhausted.

Brooke had remained close but said nothing, merely waiting for . . . whatever. Diana had no idea what that might be, until she noticed that Brooke's gaze had focused across the street.

Looking herself, Diana saw the fake Quentin. Going from door to door, trying the handles, opening the doors when he could, only to retreat and continue on down the street.

"What's he doing?" Diana asked.

Brooke looked at her, silent.

Sighing, Diana thought it over for herself, since that was clearly what Brooke expected. She watched the fake Quentin trying door after door, peering into windows—and suddenly she got it.

"He's looking for *the* door. The one out of here." She frowned. "Doesn't he know that it's only a literal door if that's the way it's made, to be something different, something out of place, so it sticks out?"

"He will if you say it any louder," Brooke murmured.

"Oh." Diana watched him for a while longer as he worked his way down the street. "Has he been trying doors in the gray time since he got here?"

"I expect so. He wants out, remember?"

Diana had been trying not to think about that, but knew she couldn't ignore it forever. Holding her voice very steady, she said, "If I...choose to move on...if there's nobody left here to make a door for him to leave, will he remain trapped here?"

"Would you do that?"

Quentin.

"I don't know," Diana said honestly. "I'd like to think I would. That I'd pay whatever price I had to in order to keep a monster like him trapped where he can't hurt anyone else. But..."

Brooke watched her for a moment, then said, "You aren't the only medium who can walk in the gray time, Diana. So your sacrifice would most likely be wasted. Sooner or later, someone will make a door. The only question is whether he's able to last until then."

Diana frowned, her relief passing quickly when she reminded herself that she, too, appeared to be trapped here. "Once before, we managed to...shove something evil through a doorway and beyond. Not back into the living world, but out of the gray time.* To a place where it could never return from."

"Yes. Using spiritual energy. A lot of energy that had been building for a very long time. I don't believe that's an option in this case."

"Then what am I supposed to do?"

"That's your choice, Diana."

She put her head in her hands and counted silently to ten. When she raised her head, Brooke was gone.

Oh, shit.

---

*Chill of Fear

260

Without the guide's presence, frustrating though it often was, Diana felt very, very alone. Except that she wasn't alone. She had to lean forward and stare hard to find the fake Quentin; as she watched, he reached the last building of the downtown area on that side of the street, tried its door, and peered in the front window, and then he crossed the street to Diana's side and began working his way toward her.

She was reasonably sure he wasn't going to find the door he searched for. What she wasn't at all sure of was what she could do to keep him trapped here until all his energy, his very essence, was drained away or pulled apart and he was no longer a threat.

She had the icy feeling that even if she did manage to find a way to hold him here for a while, her own energy would be drained a long time before his was.

She didn't know what to do. What she could do. And she was so tired.

And alone.

The thought had barely surfaced in her mind when she felt the grip of Quentin's hand on hers, so strongly that she looked at her hand fully expecting to see his. It wasn't there. Of course. But, faintly...

Hold on, Diana. Don't leave me.

"I'm trying not to," she whispered.

"They took her off the ventilator a couple of hours ago," Quentin told Hollis and DeMarco. "She's breathing on her own."

"That's a good thing," Hollis said.

"Yeah. But she didn't respond when they tried to make her. Stimulus, they called it. Pain. She didn't respond to pain."

"We'll get her back, Quentin," Hollis told him.

Quentin looked like hell, his face haggard and eyes dark and shadowed with exhaustion, but he was at least clean and shaved due to one very determined nurse.

"She said I couldn't stink up the ICU," he told them with a tinge of his normal humor. "She wouldn't have it on her shift. I said I wasn't letting go of Diana and she said fine, she had experience with sponge baths." He paused, adding, "Damned if she didn't give me one. Which is very disconcerting when you aren't, you know, a patient."

"Or probably when you are," DeMarco murmured.

Hollis had to agree with him, but what she said aloud was, "Did you eat anything?"

"Drank some soup." He paused, added, "That's one very determined nurse. Sophie. I asked and she said to call her Sophie."

"Well, I'm glad she took care of you." Hollis exchanged a glance with DeMarco, then said, "I tried something earlier, when you were asleep. Maybe it helped a little, I don't know, but we think it might work better this time."

Quentin frowned. "What did you try?"

"To help her heal."

"Since when can you do that?"

"I don't know that I can. But I can heal myself. And Bonnie is a medium who can heal others." Bonnie was Miranda's sister. "So I figured it was worth a shot."

DeMarco said, "We think I got in the way before. So Hollis wasn't able to reach Diana, at least not completely."

"But I felt something," Hollis told Quentin. "Even with Reese's shield sort of blocking me, I felt something. I want to try again."

After a moment, Quentin said, "That might not be too smart, Hollis."

She didn't have to be a telepath to know what he meant. "Look, I know Bishop and Miranda have been worried about me. All these shiny new abilities I keep . . . growing."

"It's a legitimate concern," Quentin said slowly. "And if you're trying to heal others now, that's another whole new ability, coming awfully fast on the heels of the last one. Maybe too fast. You can push yourself too hard, demand too much of your senses. Your body. Your brain. It could be dangerous."

"With these extra senses of ours, that's a danger we all face, all the time. But it's no reason not to try, if there's a chance it could help Diana. I want to do this, Quentin."

Quentin looked at DeMarco, who shrugged. "She's determined," he said. "I don't think either one of us is going to talk her out of it."

"You'll anchor her?"

"Definitely." DeMarco lifted one hand, showing Quentin that his and Hollis's fingers were already laced together. "And, like you, I won't let go. I may even be able to help, to . . . boost her signal, so to speak."

Quentin was still frowning. "I'm tired, and I know I'm not thinking clearly. But one thing I do know is that Bonnie can't walk in the gray time, and to my knowledge she's never tried to heal anyone who could. Hollis, this situation . . . It's unique. I mean, you may or may not be able to heal, or help heal, Diana's body. But if her spirit is in the gray time, if she's left that door open only a little, then you could be drawn in there. And with your own energies focused on healing, especially if those energies are intensified by Reese's . . . I don't know what might happen."

"Neither do I." She smiled wryly. "So let's just do the thing and find out, okay?"

He looked at Diana's still face, then returned his gaze to Hollis and said simply, "Thank you."

"Don't thank me yet." She kept it light. "I may do nothing more than short out one of these machines or something."

"Sophie will have a fit," he responded, obviously making an effort.

"I'll worry about that later too." She smiled at him, then looked at DeMarco. "Remember, don't *block* me. It took a while for you to retract that shield of yours so the world looks normal to me again, and I much prefer normal."

Quentin said, "What're you talking about?"

"It's not important right now," Hollis replied. "Listen, I have no idea if it's even possible, but the three of us were all at Samuel's

Compound that last day, exposed to the weird energies there, and we were all sort of...connected. Maybe that can help us now. Maybe we can connect and build on one another's abilities, like we did then."

"I have no idea how that worked," Quentin confessed. "Bishop was sort of the linchpin, maybe because he was the strongest telepath."

"Then I nominate Reese to be our linchpin."

"Thanks a bunch," DeMarco said. "Appreciate the honor, but I don't have a clue how to do it."

Hollis didn't allow that to slow the proceedings, because she was pretty sure that if Reese, at least, knew what she had very carefully *not* been thinking about during the last hour or so, he was liable to throw a protective wrench into the works. "Just everybody close your eyes and concentrate on focusing a bright, healing white light on Diana. I'll do the rest. I hope."

Before either of the men could voice another protest, Hollis closed her own eyes, drew a deep breath, and placed her free hand across Diana's forehead. It wasn't where her injuries were—physically, at least—but Hollis was playing another hunch, this one that she might be able to do two things: help heal Diana's body and help her find her way back to it.

Before Reese or Quentin could stop her.

She concentrated on doing the two very different things, aiming her own energy in a healing blast of white light even as she reached deeper, attempting to find a door she wasn't even sure she would recognize if she fell through it.

She felt the hot pulse of her energy rising, felt it flowing down her arm and through her hand into Diana's body. And she knew, with a sense of excitement and satisfaction, that it was working.

She was healing Diana. She was—

She was falling. And landed with a mental, if not physical, thud. *Ouch?*

"Hollis. Dammit, you shouldn't be here."

Hollis opened her eyes and stared—for a moment dizzily—at Diana, as she sat on a bench in a really cold and creepy gray-time representation of Serenade's Main Street. She had forgotten just how weird and otherworldly the place—time—was, even with her own mini-gray-time experiences of the last twelve hours or so.

Not a place where one wanted to linger, oh, no.

"Hello to you too," she said. And then, cautiously, "Diana, you do know what's happened, right?"

"I was shot. Did I die?"

Hollis was startled by the stark question. "No. No, you're—I'm trying to help heal you now. So we can get you out of here and back to your body."

Diana shook her head slightly. "I don't think that's the way this is going to turn out."

"Of course it is. Quentin's still holding on tight, and soon you'll start to feel better. You'll see." She caught a flicker of distant movement from the corner of her eye and turned her head. "Hey, is that—"

"Shhh. Don't attract his attention. That's the fake Quentin, and he's looking for the door you just opened again."

"Diana—"

"Hollis, it's Samuel. And we can't let him get out of here."

Serenade

"**W**hat I keep coming back to," Dean Ramsey said, "is why here? Why were we . . . led here, herded here, lured here—whatever. Why here?"

"Because it's a perfect shooting gallery?" Tony suggested. He was standing near the open door of the mobile command center, gazing out on a lamplit and mostly deserted Main Street, eerily empty on a cool Thursday evening in April. "Down in a valley, surrounded all the way by mountains that are just close enough for a really good sniper with a really good scope to get off a few really good shots."

"He hasn't shot into the town from the mountains," Miranda reminded him. "Not yet, at least."

"Something to look forward to. Yay."

Jaylene said, "Okay, my question is, once we were here and he ramped up the action with his trusty rifle, why produce another tortured body? What's the point of that? I mean, we're here, we're obviously not going to leave without doing our best to find this bastard, so why kill Deputy Silvers? *Especially* her. That's two Pageant County deputies killed this week, and neither one of them was even a full-time cop. What's the point of that if we're the targets?"

Miranda glanced at Sheriff Duncan, who seemed uninterested, adrift in a pain-filled world of his own, then slid her gaze to his chief deputy, Neil Scanlon. "Am I right in assuming you guys haven't been making enemies of this sort lately?"

He snorted. "Not lately—and not ever. Hell, this has always been a peaceful town. Until this shit started, there hadn't been a murder within fifty miles for years."

"Yeah," she said, "that's what I thought." She tapped a closed laptop on a built-in workstation beside her. "All the torture victims so far—with the exception of Deputy Silvers—connect in some way with past SCU investigations."

Tony turned, leaning a shoulder against the door frame as he looked at her. "So, if it's us, why throw another body at us? A taunt? We're right here and he can torture and kill under our very noses?"

"Maybe. Also a kind of psychological torture. All of us, all the technology and expertise we can bring to bear on an investigation— and he sits out there deciding who lives and who dies. Maybe."

Alerted by something in her tone, Tony said, "You don't think that's it."

"I," Miranda said slowly, "think we have two killers."

Tony glanced quickly at the sheriff and his chief deputy, noting that only the latter was even paying attention to the conversation. "It was always a possibility," he agreed.

"Yeah, well, with every . . . event that occurs, I'm more and more certain. I think there's a cool-headed sniper out there, and I think there's a twisted son of a bitch who enjoys torture. The sniper is the one planning things. The other one just likes to kill. That could explain Bobbie Silvers—if the torturer is somewhere close enough to have found a target of opportunity. All the deputies were moving around last night, trying to secure the town, check on people after the bomb and the shooting. Maybe she simply knocked on the wrong door."

Scanlon said, "Are you saying the son of a bitch *lives* here?"

"I somehow doubt he's camping in the woods. The kind of torture he's been doing requires a quiet, private space. Most likely a cellar or basement. Probably not downtown, but close enough."

Scanlon said something violent under his breath. Mostly.

Sheriff Duncan stirred and said, "I should check on Bobbie's mother. Neighbors were staying with her, but..."

Quietly, Miranda said, "There isn't much more we can do tonight, Des, and most of your people have been up as long as mine have. Now that we have reinforcements from the Bureau and the state police, the rest of us should get some sleep. We'll start fresh in the morning."

The sheriff got to his feet, unobtrusively helped by Scanlon. "Guess you're right. Yeah. I'll see you in the morning, then."

Scanlon followed his sheriff, murmuring as he stepped past Miranda, "I'll see to it he gets home."

When the SCU agents were alone in the command center, Tony said, "Not that I'd ever second-guess you—"

Miranda made a rude noise.

He managed a faint grin. "Okay, so I do that. Why'd you tell them you were sure it's two killers? I thought we were trying to keep that quiet. I'd bet my next paycheck that by dawn everybody in town will know it."

"Including our killers." She nodded. "It's time to shake things up a bit, put the sniper on notice that we know he isn't out there alone. My guess, he has to keep some kind of leash on the other one. And maybe it's slipping."

"Bobbie?"

She nodded. "Bobbie wasn't planned. Bobbie was a mistake. And so, I think, was Taryn Holder, the female victim found up in the mountains by Hollis and Diana. The victim we weren't meant to find."

Jaylene was frowning. "But she has a connection to a past case. She stayed at The Lodge."

"Yeah, I'm wondering about that particular connection. The Lodge is a famous place in the area, drawing visitors from all around. She apparently went on spa trips a couple times a year at least, and that would be the location most well-to-do women in these parts would choose."

"Okay," Jaylene said. "But if she just happened to get herself slaughtered by our twisted torturer, isn't that stretching coincidence a bit too far?"

"Maybe not. Look, I could easily be wrong. But I think we should check a little further into the background of Taryn Holder. She might have another connection we've missed so far. A connection to whoever killed her."

"You're the boss," Tony said.

"Right now the boss needs to rest," Miranda said, getting to her feet. "All of us do."

Dean was also on his feet. "I had a break this morning, so I'm good 'til midnight," he said. "I'll walk you back to the B&B, if you don't mind, and collect a couple of the agents having coffee and sandwiches there." He nodded to Tony and Jaylene. "Your relief will be back here in fifteen."

"Good enough," Jaylene said, and Tony nodded.

Miranda and Dean were mostly silent on the walk back to the

B&B, merely nodding to a few of the agents, deputies, and state cops they passed along the way. There were by now more than two dozen agents on the scene and an equal number of state cops. Added to everyone else already here...

"We're nearly tripping over one another," Miranda murmured. "Patrolling the whole downtown area in pairs means there's a hell of a lot of people wandering around out here tonight. Cable news is still camped just outside the perimeter, despite the warnings; keeping them out of the downtown area because it's a crime scene won't hold for long. Plus, there are a couple of really good reporters here now, and the exposure they can provide will only make him more cocky. If we don't lock this thing down fast, we won't have a hope in hell of stopping the carnage."

"Then that's what we'll do."

They were silent for the remainder of the walk to the B&B. It was nearly dark when they got there. Bright porch lights already burned, and through the screen door they could hear the low hum of conversation as agents and cops took advantage of their hostess's offer to serve coffee and sandwiches to the troops. Instead of entering through the front door, they slipped around to the darkened rear stairs that led up to the second-floor balcony.

Miranda went up, followed by Dean, and knocked lightly on the door to her suite before going in. "We're home," she called quietly.

Dean Ramsey came out of the bathroom, holstering his gun. "Damn, you're quiet as cats. I barely had time to duck into the bathroom." He stared at his double, shaking his head unconsciously. "Could you de-glamour yourself, please?"

"Don't use a magick term. This isn't magick."

"It sure as hell looks like magick."

"Like everything else, it's just energy. And a shift in perspective."

"Well, could you please tell Ruby to cut it out, or shift it the other way, or whatever it is she's doing? Because looking at a mirror image talking back to me is creepy as hell."

"Sorry." *Thanks, Ruby. You can let go now.*

There was a peculiar sort of shimmer in the air—or so it seemed—and Bishop stood there.

Dean shook his head. "That little girl has a scary gift."

Sober, Bishop said, "It's powerful, all right, even more than it was a few months ago. But I don't want to put too much strain on her by having her hold it unnecessarily."

"So I get to be me?"

"If you don't mind. Did you get any sleep?"

"I caught a nap."

"Good. You're on until midnight. Go back down the outer stairs and in the front. You're here to pick up a couple of agents to relieve Tony and Jaylene in the command center."

"Copy that. And tomorrow?"

"I'll let you know in the morning."

"Okay. You two try to get some rest, huh? Even if all goes according to your plan, tomorrow's gonna be a real bitch."

"Good night, Dean," Miranda said.

" 'Night." He slipped out onto the balcony, closing the door behind him.

Miranda locked the door, unfastened her vest and dropped it into a chair with a faint grimace, and went into Bishop's arms. "God, I've missed you," she said.

He held her tightly, nuzzling his face into her neck. "I've missed you too, love. But it's nearly over now."

"You've talked to Gabe and Roxanne?"

"We managed to meet up just after I went out there as Dean."

Miranda nodded. It was normal for her to communicate with him telepathically a great deal when they were alone. But not this time. "What about Galen?"

"I hate not warning him," Bishop admitted quietly. "Hate not telling him what we know now. But it could be the only edge we'll have tomorrow."

"He'll forgive us. I hope. And Bailey?"

"She knows. It goes against the grain for her to leave Ruby unshielded, but there's no other way. Powerful as she is, Ruby won't be able to maintain the illusions we'll need tomorrow if she's behind Bailey's shield."

Miranda drew back just far enough to look up at him. "As much as she's our edge, Ruby is also a potential danger. To us—and to herself. Galen knows what she can do, so they have to be wondering where she fits in."

"Maybe not. Bailey says Galen's locked up tight. Maybe tight enough."

"And if not?"

"The unpredictable variable. There's always at least one."

She nodded. "Brisco?"

"On his way to the hospital. Maybe there by now. I had a slight head start only because my jet was fueled and ready to go."

"Are they okay up there? At the hospital? I haven't been able to sense a damn thing outside our connection."

"Yeah, I felt the effects as soon as we touched down. Samuel had some very apt pupils." He shook his head, then added, "Quentin's holding on. I think Hollis and Reese are trying to help Diana." He shook his head. "I'm still not sure whether alerting her to possible deception in the gray time was a good idea."

"It put her on guard. And she needed to be."

"Yeah. But assuming all that ends well, when she finds out I sent a strange psychic into the gray time with her, she's liable to be...a little upset."

Miranda smiled ruefully but said, "I wish we could see how it turns out, for Diana and Quentin. So we'd know."

"That one's out of our hands, love."

"I know. Still."

He kissed her, and they stood there for a long time just holding each other. Finally Bishop said, "You didn't get any rest at all last night. You need to sleep. Especially now, you need to sleep."

"I'm fine." She smiled up at him. "And I'll sleep. Later."

Hollis wasted no time in grabbing Diana by the hand and pulling her into the nearest alleyway. "We can circle around the back while he's checking the front. He'll never see me."

"Sooner or later he will. And then he'll know you came through a door. He'll know you can get out even if I can't."

"You're going to get out," Hollis told her, keeping her voice low. "I'll be damned if I'll leave you here after all this." She was pulling Diana along.

"You don't understand. That's Samuel. He wants out of the gray time. He wants to live again. And we can't let him do that."

"He wants to live again? You mean in the flesh? Is that possible?"

"Yes," Diana replied simply. "If he gets out. If he can possess a living host."

"Possession is real too?" Hollis shook her head. "Damn, I love my job. Learn something new every day."

"Hollis—"

"Diana, all we have to do *right now* is get out of here without Samuel seeing us use the door. Right?"

"But someone else could—"

"What, come here and let him out? If nobody's come in all this time since he died, I think we can probably feel safe in leaving him here for another week or two. Until you're stronger, until you're healed. And, in the meantime, we'll figure out how to keep his ass here for good."

"Not for good," Diana murmured, thinking. "Only until his energy is . . . pulled apart. Forced out of here. As long as the door to our side is closed until that happens, he'll have to cross over."

"Great. Then we just have to keep our door closed."

"By making sure I don't go to sleep?"

"We'll think of something. The point is that you need to leave here, get back to your body. I didn't pour all my energy into healing you just so you'd look good in a coffin."

As intended, the words shocked Diana out of her lethargy. "Damn, you can be hard-nosed."

"When it comes to saving my friends, you bet I can." She pulled Diana into another alleyway and crept toward the front of the building. Peeking around quickly, she saw the fake Quentin. "Okay, he's more than a block down and still moving away. We should have time to get out of here."

"You can't leave yet."

Hollis started, then stared at Brooke. "Where'd you come from? Never mind, never mind."

"Diana can't leave yet. She has truths to uncover."

"She has a body to get back to," Hollis told her.

"No," Diana said. "Brooke told me when—when I was shot that I came here to uncover truths. If that's the rule, I can't leave until I do it."

Hollis bit back a sigh of impatience. "This is more your world than mine, that's for sure. Okay, so which truths?" She took another quick peek around the corner to make sure Samuel-as-Quentin was still moving away from them.

Diana was staring at the guide. "I know the truth of my relationship with Quentin; I can't deny that, and I don't want to hide from it anymore." She looked down at her free hand, still feeling him holding it.

Brooke said, "That's one truth."

"The truth at the heart of the investigation is Samuel. Not just here but out there as well."

"What?" Hollis demanded.

Diana nodded. "The sniper is his man. Maybe all of it was planned before Samuel died, or maybe he's able to reach out through some kind of connection he formed before he died. That's why I was shot. Samuel realized it was the quickest way to get me back here. To open the door."

"Son of a bitch," Hollis said blankly. "I never even thought about him affecting you or going after you—like that, I mean—because he was always so afraid of mediums."

"Until he needed one to get out of here."

"Irony, I suppose. Or just the twisted humor of the universe. Do Bishop and Miranda know this?"

"I have no idea."

Brooke said, "That's two truths."

"Three," Diana protested. "You said one truth was the truth of why I was shot."

"Three, then. You still have two truths left to uncover. The truth of who is trying to deceive you, and the truth underneath it all."

"Jesus," Hollis muttered. "Diana, we have to hurry. I'm not at all sure I can get us to the door, let alone through it—but I have a hunch Reese will pull me back before much longer. You have to be ready to go too."

Diana leaned a little harder against the cold brick wall behind her, trying not to make it obvious how hard it was to breathe now and how very weak she felt. "Who's trying to deceive me. I don't know who's trying to deceive me. Is it you, Brooke?"

"Why would I want to deceive you, Diana?"

"I don't know. Maybe...maybe to protect this almighty truth underneath it all."

Hollis looked at her with a sudden frown. "The truth underneath it all. Damn, now I know why it sounded so familiar. That's what Andrea kept telling me I had to find."

"Spirit Andrea?"

"Yeah. That's the way she phrased it. The truth underneath it all."

"You mean...the same truth?"

"I guess. She said it was all connected."

Diana looked at Brooke. "You said that too."

Brooke remained silent.

"Huh," Hollis said. "Maybe everything *is* connected. Which means that Andrea isn't attached to me but to this whole thing with Samuel. She didn't show up until that investigation started, until we followed Samuel's pet monster from Boston down to Venture."

Diana shook her head. "So . . . connected to Samuel and somehow connected to me? If it's the same truth, I mean."

"Well—"

"Diana."

The new voice jerked their heads around, but it was Hollis who spoke first. "Andrea. Great, maybe you can—"

"That's not fair," Brooke chided, frowning a little at the seemingly older spirit. "She has to figure it out by herself."

"She's running out of time," Andrea said, her gaze fixed on Diana's face. "And I have to help her."

Hollis had not let go of Diana's wrist since first grabbing it, and now she felt the other woman's tension. "Hey, what is it?"

Diana hadn't taken her eyes off Andrea. "My God. Oh, my God, it's . . . Mama?"

Seventeen

HOLLIS LOOKED BACK and forth between them. "You mean—Andrea is your mother?"

"Andrea wasn't her name." Diana's voice, weirdly hollow in the gray time, sounded numb.

"It was my middle name, the name I went by for most of my life. Until I married. Your father preferred my first name, so I used that."

Diana shook her head slowly. "Missy said . . . you were okay. That you were at peace. Did she lie to me?"

"No, your sister didn't lie. I was at peace. Until . . . they came for me."

"Who?"

"His victims."

"Wait," Hollis said. "You got yanked out of heaven?"

"It was my choice. I could have said no. But they were insistent. All of them, all the victims. His victims, calling me to help them. Poor souls who couldn't move on until he was made to pay for what he'd done."

"Samuel?"

"No." Andrea's eyes were filled with sorrow. "Your father.

Without him, without his money and determination to destroy Bishop, so much of this wouldn't have happened. He believed he could regain control over your life, get you back, if he destroyed the SCU. But even more than that, he hated Bishop. Hated him for allowing you to believe in your gifts, for providing you with a useful life with purpose. Something he could never do."

"Oh, my God," Diana said.

"The truth underneath it all," Hollis said, almost as stunned as her friend was.

Andrea said, "I tried to help, but... I'd been away so long it was difficult for me, just to make myself seen. I was never able to get here, to the gray time, when you were walking here, and it was even harder to make myself seen on the living side. Until Hollis."

"You could have told me who you were," Hollis said. "That might have helped, you know."

"I'm sorry. I was... confused. The bits of knowledge I had when I came back were jumbled. It's taken me a while to sort everything out."

Diana was struggling visibly to come to grips with what she had heard. "But... Dad... He helped Samuel? He helped that monster destroy so many innocent people?"

"You were all he had left. When you tried to break away from him, when you met Quentin and Bishop, he knew he was losing you. He was willing to do anything to stop that. Anything."

Hollis, quite abruptly, felt a tug, and said, "Diana, I think Reese wants to pull me back. We have to leave. Now." She took a quick look around the corner of the building and added urgently, "Samuel's heading back this way. If we're going to leave without him seeing us, it has to be now."

"There's no time," Brooke said to Andrea.

Andrea reached out and caught Diana's hand, holding it for only an instant. "You'll remember," she said. "When you wake up, you'll remember all of it. Have a happy, useful life, Diana. Fight for it. In spite of your father."

"But—wait. No, I want to—"

But Andrea was gone, vanished like a soap bubble.

"There's no time," Brooke repeated.

Hollis made sure she had a firm grip on Diana's arm. "You've found your truths," she said quickly. "Come back with me now, Diana. Come back to Quentin. Reach with me. *Do* it."

Diana looked at her blindly for a heartbeat or two, still obviously stunned, then nodded. "Quentin. I'll reach for Quentin."

Hollis felt a wave of stark relief sweep over her, even as the tugging became stronger. Too strong to resist. She felt herself begin to let go of this place or time or whatever it was and return to her own reality, and in the last seconds as the gray time began to flicker and then fade, she looked at Brooke, maybe to say goodbye.

The guide was smiling. And there was an odd, flat shine in her eyes.

Diana sucked in a breath and opened her eyes, immediately aware of her living, breathing—and very, very sore—body. She saw an unfamiliar ceiling, heard the beeps and clicks of machinery, and realized that she was in the hospital. She felt something leave her forehead and saw that it was Hollis's hand, so she automatically looked to her left.

Hollis was slumped, mostly supported by Reese, but she was very much awake. Pale and with shadows of exhaustion beneath her eyes, but still on her feet. More or less. And grinning. "Hey. Hey, there. We did it."

"You did it," Diana murmured, her voice as scratchy as her throat was. "Thank you."

"Don't mention it. My pleasure. Let's not do it again, okay?"

"Okay."

"Diana . . ."

She looked to her right to see Quentin, feeling something inside

her turn over with a painful lurch: He was haggard and hollow-
eyed, and it hurt her to see him like that. It hurt her and moved her
unbearably to see that he was, still, afraid to hope she was really back.

He was holding her hand against his cheek, and she managed to
move her fingers against his skin.

Scratchy voice and all, she said, "I love you."

His eyes lit up with a warmth she knew she could wrap herself
in to truly begin her happy life. "I love you. So much."

Hollis stopped grinning long enough to look up at DeMarco.
"You think maybe we should leave?"

"That would probably be a good idea."

Diana tore her eyes away from Quentin long enough to say to
Hollis, "You have to tell them. In Serenade. So they know what
they're really up against."

"Oh, yeah. Right. Only—listen, you *are* okay?"

"I'm fine. Tired and sore, but I think the doctors will be surprised when they check under these bandages. Very surprised."

"In that case," Hollis said to Reese, "we need to get to Serenade.
Because it's worse than you know, and they'll need your primal ability to sense a threat and maybe my shiny new ability to heal, and—"

"Yeah, I've got all that," he said, calm. "You're broadcasting."

"Am I? Sorry."

"It's a time-saver." He looked at Quentin, his brows lifting. "I
don't think there's anything else for us to do here, and they'll definitely need us in Serenade. I'm assuming Diana will fill you in."

"I will," she said.

DeMarco nodded. "And we'll tell the others you're okay. Quentin,
you should probably stick close, just in case. I don't think there's a
threat here, but until we get things cleared up in Serenade…"

"Don't worry, I'm not planning to leave her side for the next
fifty or sixty years."

To Diana, Hollis said, "Yours is more romantic than mine. That
might be a problem."

Diana tried hard not to smile as she looked at DeMarco. "She's . . . really tired right now."

"I know. She'll hate herself later. Assuming she remembers. You two watch your backs. Come on, sweetie, let's go."

"Sweetie? You're being sarcastic, aren't you?"

"A little bit."

"Well, I'm not sure I like sarcasm from my—from mine. You might have to fix that."

"Yes, ma'am."

"I mean fix it *now*, not keep doing it. . . ."

As DeMarco took her away and Hollis's rather plaintive voice faded with distance, Diana looked at Quentin and said, "I'm glad he enjoys her."

"Yeah. Reese has a wicked sense of humor; it just doesn't show very often. I think they'll be very good for each other."

"Like you've been good for me."

"I was beginning to wonder," he said.

"I know. For a long time it seemed like there was nothing in my life, and then there was so much I couldn't trust it all. . . . I'm sorry, Quentin."

"Don't be sorry. Some things have to happen just the way they happen, remember? I'd never want to go through the last thirty hours again, but the last year, getting to know you and watching you . . . bloom right in front of me? I wouldn't take anything for that."

"I'm glad. And as soon as I get out of this hospital bed, I'll show you just how much."

"Promises, promises." He saw her fumble with her other hand for the bed's controls and begin to raise the head slowly, and he said, "Hey, are you sure you want to do that?"

"It's okay. I'm just a little . . . stiff. But I won't face him lying down."

"Face who?"

"My father." She stopped raising the bed when she was half sitting up, then took a deep breath and shifted a bit. "Ouch. Quentin, I want you to hear this, okay? Hear it and believe me when I tell you that he is never going to interfere in our lives again. And I'm more than okay with that."

"Diana—"

She turned her head and said, "Dad, you can come out now."

Surprised, Quentin saw Elliot Brisco come around the curtain, apparently from the far corner of the room. His instinct was to rise and greet the man, despite the tension that had existed between them since their first meeting nearly a year before, but what he could feel in Diana kept him still and silent.

"What are you doing here, Dad?"

"I came to see you, of course. As soon as I heard about . . . the accident." His face was pale, and there was an odd stiffness about him, like something brittle in danger of shattering.

"The accident? That's the way you prefer to think about the fact that a sniper shot your daughter in broad daylight on a public street?"

He started to reach a hand out to her, but something in her face, something hard and closed, stopped him. "It—was a terrible thing. Horrible. I'm so sorry that happened to you, Diana."

"I'm assuming you didn't know he was going to shoot me."

His face went even whiter. "Christ, Diana, I swear to you that's the last thing in this world I would have wanted."

She wasn't particularly moved by his obvious anguish. "Yeah, well, the thing is, if you'd understood anything at all about my abilities, if you had just kept an open mind and *tried* to believe what I was telling you was real and not some disease you could cure by throwing money at it, you would have known. You would have known the instant Samuel was killed that he'd have to come after me."

"Do you know how insane that sounds?" His voice was harsh.

"Even now you can't admit it. He had me shot because he

needed my abilities, Dad. He needed what I could do to get out of the place you'd probably call limbo—if you believed in anything not of this world, that is. But you don't. Even now you don't."

"Diana—"

"So much of this was your fault. Because you couldn't bear to give up control over my life, you destroyed so many other lives. Innocent lives. Destroyed them, Dad. Snuffed them out like candles."

"You don't know what you're saying."

"I know exactly what I'm saying. You've been trying to control events since I met Quentin. The same way you always try to control events. Only this time it wasn't business deals or doctors, or just keeping your daughter too medicated to live a normal life. This time it was twisted people with evil agendas of their own. You thought you could control them and use them to destroy the SCU, destroy Bishop."

He hardly seemed to be breathing as he stared at her.

"I wonder what it cost you to hire enough private investigators or pay off enough cops or feds to find the information you wanted—a name. The name of someone who hated Bishop as much as you did and was willing to go to any lengths to destroy him. Whatever it cost, you got that name. Samuel. Adam Deacon Samuel. A man who already had the SCU in his sights, had already begun to test them and test their defenses.

"You didn't much care about the rest, did you? Didn't care how sick and twisted he was. Didn't care about the victims of his evil, their bodies piling up like cordwood. Didn't care about the people in his so-called church, the *children* he was damaging and killing. And of course you didn't believe he had any kind of paranormal ability. All you knew, all you needed to know, was that he wanted to destroy the SCU. So you helped him."

"I made a donation to a church," he said finally, his voice more hoarse than before.

"You made a donation to a monster." She shook her head slightly, her eyes never leaving his. "You'll pay for what you did.

I don't know what Bishop means to do with the evidence he has and will have, but whatever it is, I'll help him."

"Diana—"

"I'll help him. But whatever he does or doesn't do, you're no longer a part of my life. No longer my father. As far as I'm concerned, you're as evil as Samuel was. And the world should be rid of you both."

Serenade

"Told you we wouldn't get a good night's sleep," Tony said to Jaylene, yawning, as they relieved two other agents in the command center shortly after six A.M.

"Hey, I got plenty," she said, sitting down at a console and logging in to the computer. "But then, I went to bed when we got back to the B&B. How long did you stay down in the dining room talking?"

"You make it sound social," Tony complained, logging in at a second work console. "A bunch of us were working things through. Trying to get a handle on the situation. Weren't making much headway until Dean came off duty at midnight and joined us for coffee."

"Coffee at midnight. Yeah, that'll help you sleep."

Tony ignored that. "Plus, that's around the time Reese and Hollis got back. With the great news about Diana being okay. And with more pieces of the puzzle."

"Confirmation," Jaylene said. "We'd already figured out this had Samuel's name written all over it. Or, at least, Miranda had."

"True enough. Nice to have it confirmed, though. And am I the only one who finds it totally creepy that this bastard is still after us from his grave?"

"No."

Tony sighed. "Anyway, when Dean came off duty, he said he'd been pulling up everything he could find on Taryn Holder, looking for a connection to somebody here in town."

"And not finding one, I take it."

"No, but at least he made a solid start. Now we keep looking."

About to start work, Jaylene paused to say, "You know, it hit me last night that we haven't even talked about that poor reporter."

"I hate to be blunt about it, but what's to say? She was warned, they all were."

"Yeah, I know that. And being equally blunt, that's not what I was thinking about. The sniper could have just as easily shot Miranda. So why didn't he? Why choose the reporter?"

"To shake up all the noncombatants around here, maybe." Tony shrugged. "That's what I'd do."

Jaylene stared at him.

"Oh, come on, I mean thinking from the bad guy's point of view. That is what profiling is all about, remember?"

"Yeah, yeah. My point, however, is that maybe Miranda was also right in suggesting that at least some of this could have been designed to draw Bishop out. Offering stark proof that he could have taken Miranda out might be expected to do that."

"So would taking her out," Tony countered.

"That's what a typical enemy might think. But what if the enemy is psychic, Tony? Psychic enough to know that all he'd gain by taking Miranda out would be Bishop paralyzed at best—and dead somewhere far away at worst?"

Tony shook his head slowly. "There aren't half a dozen people outside the SCU who know that the connection between Bishop and Miranda makes them that vulnerable."

"But they are that vulnerable. Kill one, and you'll very likely kill the other as well, or at the very least incapacitate him or her. Because they're connected, and on a level deeper than any we've ever found, even between blood siblings. What if the sniper knows that? Because he's psychic himself, or because Samuel was. And if he knows, what if killing Bishop long distance—as it were—isn't good enough?"

"Then . . . you're right. Taking out the reporter when she was two feet away from Miranda might be expected to bring Bishop here, and in a hurry. Makes sense. Bishop, more than any of the rest of us, is the one Samuel was always after. And the setup here sure as hell has all the earmarks of a trap."

"Which is another indication that the sniper could be local, or at least somehow connected to this place. He's moving around too freely for it to be otherwise. He knows this place like the back of his hand."

After a moment, Tony said, "Tell you what. Why don't you keep digging into Taryn Holder's background?"

"While you do what?"

"While I start checking into the backgrounds of all the Pageant County deputies."

"You seriously think it's a cop?"

"I think that sniper has some serious military training, and if this is home, the only job he might feel comfortable in would be one where he carries a gun."

"It's a leap," Jaylene said after a pause.

"Not a big one. There's been so much confusion since the bomb, even before, that a deputy who knew the terrain could have slipped away long enough to play sniper. And we should rule it out. Hell, we should have ruled it out after the sniper took his first shots."

"True enough. Okay. Let's dig."

Gabriel Wolf studied the old farmhouse, adjusting the binoculars until he had a crystal-clear view. There was no movement, no sign of life.

Maybe he's playing possum, Roxanne suggested.

"Why would he be?" Gabriel kept his voice low. "You kept watch all night, and if Bishop knows what he's talking about, this guy won't pick up on either of us psychically."

Doesn't mean he doesn't know about us.

"Oh, I'm betting he knows about us. I'm betting he spotted us. Bastard has the advantage of knowing this place, and well."

Don't be so disgruntled about it. We couldn't have known.

"Yeah, yeah." Gabriel frowned as the binoculars finally picked up a bit of movement in what he judged to be the kitchen windows. "Hold on. Looks like he's finally up."

About time.

Gabriel watched intently and was rewarded a little more than ten minutes later: A tall, dark man somewhere in his late forties, with a distinctly military bearing despite his casual jeans and a sweatshirt, came out of the house. The rifle Gabriel knew he carried today was concealed in an oversize duffel bag. The man appeared to feel safe, showing no signs of unease or worry as he crossed the small yard and briskly made his way down the long, fence-bordered drive toward the main road. And town.

"Man, I want to take him out," Gabriel muttered.

Not the plan. We have nothing on the other one, you know that. We have to draw him out.

"Yeah. But I don't have to like it." Gabriel touched the almost invisible com device in his ear. "Hey. He's on the move."

"Got him," a voice whispered back. "Our information says the one in the house should give you no trouble. But watch yourself."

"Copy that." He touched the com again, continued to watch the sniper until he was well away from the house, and then left his own place of concealment to begin moving cautiously toward it.

It was just after eight A.M. when Dean Ramsey joined Tony and Jaylene in the command center. He was bearing hot coffee and news. "Check your emails," he advised them. "Word from Bishop."

Tony groaned. "My eyes are already starting to cross from looking at this screen the last couple of hours."

"Find anything?"

"I dunno. Maybe." Tony blew absently on the hot coffee to cool it, staring at the screen. "There's military training here, just not the kind we're looking for. At least—"

Jaylene swore under her breath. She turned her head to stare at Tony. "Check your email. Looks like you were right, Tony. The sniper's connected to this town, all right."

Dean said, "And that's not all he's connected to."

Tony checked his email, opened the file from Bishop, and began to read. Only a couple of paragraphs in, he was swearing as well, and not under his breath. "Jesus. I don't believe it. How did we not know—"

"Because Galen didn't know," Dean interrupted. "The connection went back too far. Finish reading. And then you guys put your coms in. We're moving outside in just a few minutes."

The key was under the flowerpot, as promised. Gabriel unlocked the door and slipped into the old farmhouse, moving with utter silence.

Not as much fun for me, Roxanne noted. *A key, for crying out loud.*

With hardly a breath of sound, Gabriel said, "Keep watch, Rox. Just because he's not supposed to be any trouble doesn't mean he won't be."

Okay, okay. Lemme see. . . . He's in the basement. Door's in the kitchen, Gabe.

Gabriel made his way to the kitchen, still moving without a sound, gun drawn and ready. He found the basement door easily enough, his brows lifting as he noted the bolt locking it from this side.

Keeping something in rather than out, don't you think? Because there's no other exit from the basement. Bishop was right. They must believe the leash has been slipping. Be careful, Gabe.

He unlocked the bolt carefully, then just as carefully eased the door open. As soon as he did, he heard a sound coming from the basement.

Humming.

And a cheery tune, no less. Jesus.

Without responding out loud, Gabriel moved slowly and cautiously down the well-lit stairs and into a very bright basement. There was lots of white tile and stainless steel, and large lights illuminated the space more brightly than daylight.

There were two stainless-steel tables. On one lay a clear-plastic-wrapped body that barely appeared to be human.

The other table was covered with thickly coagulated blood, which was in the process of being washed off and down the big drain in the floor. The man wielding the hose looked very much like the man who had left the house only minutes before, except that he was perhaps a few years younger and there was nothing military in his bearing.

At all.

And there was a definite light of madness in his eyes when he turned his head, saw Gabriel, and smiled.

"Hello. BJ said I could clean up this time. He was too tired last night. Did Bubba send you?"

"Yeah," Gabriel said, holding his voice even with an effort. "Bubba sent me. We need to go to town, Rex."

Ruby crept into Bailey's bedroom early, to double-check, and was satisfied to find one of her guardians still sleeping. Just to make sure, she put her hand on Bailey's shoulder and concentrated for several long moments before stepping away from the bed.

Without much effort at all, she made the bed shimmer and then seemingly transform. Where before there had been tumbled covers and a dark-haired woman sleeping, now there was only a neatly made bed. Good. Bailey would be safe here. Until it was all over.

She went downstairs, finding Galen pouring coffee in the kitchen.

"You're up early," he commented.

"I didn't sleep very well," Ruby confessed. She got cereal for herself from the pantry, then milk from the fridge and a bowl and spoon. "Are you going to rest when Bailey gets up?"

"Probably," he said, joining her at the kitchen table.

She fixed her cereal, took several bites, then said, "You haven't tried to listen to the voices, have you?"

"As a matter of fact, I did," he told her. "Still nothing I can understand. Voices, but not really words."

"I expect they don't want you to hear them now."

He frowned. "Ruby, do you know where the voices are coming from?"

"They were let in when Father died," she told him, her voice matter-of-fact. "Before that, they just listened."

"Listened? To who?"

"To you. To your friends. The team. Father needed a spy. He was pleased when he found them. Because even though they knew about you, you didn't know about them."

Galen began to feel very, very cold. "Ruby, what're you talking about?"

"Your brothers."

"I don't have any brothers."

She looked at him with those too-old eyes. "No, you never knew about them. Your mother never told you the good man who raised you wasn't your father. She made sure nobody knew about him. Changed her name, moved far away from here. Because your biological father was...really mean. He hurt your mother, and your brothers. He would have hurt you if he'd known about you. But your mother kept you secret. Until she was able to run away. She couldn't take your brothers. They were already...wrong. Twisted. Because of him. She knew. She wanted to save you. So she ran away."

"Ruby—"

"I would have told you sooner, but...I didn't know until just after I got here. And even then, it was sort of fuzzy. There were so many chess pieces on the board, you know?"

The coldness Galen felt went all the way to his marrow. He stared at her sweet, innocent face with its too-old eyes and knew without a shadow of a doubt that she was telling him the truth. He had brothers. And, more important to him, they had been inside his head, maybe for a long time, spying on him. And on the unit.

"It wasn't your fault," Ruby told him. "Bishop knows that. The rest will too. Father was awfully powerful. He could do things most people can't even imagine. And he planned ahead."

His training kicked in automatically, and he said, "If they're in me, then they know about you. I have to get you out of here."

Sadly, Ruby said, "I'm sorry. Please don't blame yourself, okay? That's not the way it's supposed to end."

"The little freak's right."

Galen tried, but he was barely able to rise from his chair, barely caught a glimpse of the tall man standing in the doorway, before he heard the muffled sneezes of a silenced automatic and felt bullets slamming into his chest.

Eighteen

HOLLIS CRADLED HER coffee mug between her hands and looked rather blearily at Miranda. "I know I slept. The clock says so. But I feel like I just had a lost weekend or something."

"According to Reese, it took hours and you expended a great deal of energy in healing Diana. That's the way it works when you heal. In a way, you give up part of yourself. Bonnie tells me it's quite an amazing feeling."

Considering, Hollis said, "Right now it's mostly a tired feeling. So you guys already knew about Samuel."

"We worked it out."

"And you've identified the sniper?"

"Yeah, the pieces finally came together, thanks in large part to the information Elliot Brisco provided."

"Glad the son of a bitch did something right. Poor Diana."

"Yeah, despite how well she's handling it now, it's not going to be easy for her."

"Will LeMott destroy him? Brisco?"

"Probably. He's . . . merciless. And we could never have proven anything against Brisco in a courtroom."

"So we let LeMott have his revenge?"

"Let's call it justice," Miranda suggested.

Hollis nodded. "It's fine with me. Jesus. Anyway, what about the sniper?"

"Knowing who he is is one thing. What we have to do now is draw him out."

"And how're you—we—going to do that?"

"Bait." There was a crackle in her ear, and Miranda heard her name. She reached up to activate the tiny com. "Go."

"Got him," Gabriel said.

"He give you any trouble?"

"Nah, came along like a lamb. Smiling yet. But wait'll you get a look at what's in his basement."

"I can hardly wait. You know what to do."

"Copy that."

Miranda tapped the com again, then said to Hollis, "Sure you're up for this?"

"Are you kidding? I wouldn't miss it. I feel like I've been waiting for this final curtain to drop for a long, long time."

"I think we all have. Don't forget your vest."

"Right. Where's Reese?"

"Out there with Dean and the others. And I'm hoping his spider sense is working, because the rest of us are having trouble sensing much of anything." Miranda finished her own coffee and got to her feet. "Stay clear of the command center. I hope I'm wrong, but I've got a feeling it'll be a target."

"So who's manning it?"

"Nobody. See you outside." Miranda left the B&B's dining room, adjusting her vest and the gun on her hip a bit absently and then going out onto the porch. She knew there were agents and cops and deputies all around, but it was peculiarly quiet, and that bothered her.

She touched her com again. "Anything?"

The response whispered back immediately: "No. But Reese is antsy and so am I. Something's not right."

292

"But you're in position?"

"Yeah. Watch yourself."

Miranda strolled along the sidewalk, outwardly casual or preoccupied, wondering if, this time, they had been a bit too clever for
their own good. Hiding Bishop in plain sight had worked once before, but here there was an inside man to contend with and no way
for them to be sure how he would react.

Because he had, so far, played his part to perfection.

She saw Tony and Jaylene standing a few yards from the command center near the front of the sheriff's department and went to
join them. "Gabe should be here any minute," she told them quietly.

Tony, almost idly watching a casual gathering across the street
of deputies and several agents, including Dean Ramsey, said, "Are
we sure the bait will draw him out?"

"It'll draw a reaction," Miranda said. "Beyond that, I don't know
what's going to happen." She watched as DeMarco joined the group
of cops, saying something that made two of them laugh.

"A vision right about now would be nice," Jaylene murmured.

"Tell me about it. Unfortunately, we're flying blind this time."
Whatever else Miranda might have said was pushed aside as she
watched Gabriel Wolf escort a handcuffed man toward the sheriff's
department.

The man was almost shockingly ordinary. Around forty or so,
he was a little above medium height, with a stocky build and an un-
tidy thatch of dark hair. And he was smiling.

"How come serial killers so seldom look the part?" Tony wondered aloud. "Jesus, really the guy next door. That's disturbing."

"He's an animal," Miranda said. "Doesn't matter what he looks
like."

"Oh, yeah, no argument. It's just—"

Miranda saw DeMarco turn suddenly, staring toward a cluster
of trees on a low ridge behind the sheriff's department. In almost
the same instant, the handcuffed prisoner's head jerked, blood and
tissue sprayed out of what had been his face, and as he sort of stum-

bled and then dropped to the pavement there was, finally, the *craa-aack* of a high-powered rifle.

Before the echoes had died, there was a second *craa-aack*.

And then silence.

Many of the cops and agents had hit the deck, but several of them remained on their feet. Miranda caught DeMarco's eye and waited for his nod before walking out slowly to join Gabriel.

With a singular lack of pity, Gabe said, "Well, he saved the state a whole lot of trouble and expense. And deprived the shrinks of another serial killer to study. No great loss, I'm thinking."

As Miranda had expected, other cops and agents were slowly coming to join them, taking their cue from the calm pair standing over the executed prisoner. But her heart skipped a beat when she realized one in particular wasn't among them.

Before she could get her thoughts organized, Chief Deputy Neil Scanlon stepped out of the command center, holding a small, limp body to his chest like a shield. Ruby. She was unconscious at best, possibly already dead.

But there's no sign of a wound, so maybe . . . Goddammit. . . .

"Where's BJ, Miranda?" Scanlon called out, his voice unnaturally calm.

Despite a muttered curse from Gabe, Miranda took a step toward Scanlon. At this distance, she knew she could take him without hitting Ruby. If she could get her gun out and aimed before he fired his. Even without the bulky vest restricting her movements a bit, the odds weren't good.

"He's gone, Neil," she called back, her voice as calm as his. "When he shot Rex, it pinpointed his location for us. And we were ready. Where's Galen?"

"I put a few bullets into him. But we both know that won't keep him down long, right? Long enough, though. Just long enough. Where's Bishop?"

Very deliberately, Miranda said, "He's the one who took out BJ."

Something vicious flashed across that tough face, and Scanlon moved Ruby slightly. "Tit for tat. I'm going to take out your little freak here."

"Why bother? It's over."

"Not quite. If I can't have Bishop—"

His hand was moving in a blur, aiming his gun toward her. Miranda moved as well, instinctively throwing herself sideways.

The *craa-aack* of a rifle sounded almost simultaneously with the duller report of Scanlon's gun. Miranda saw his head virtually explode, saw him tilt and fall toward the pavement, still holding Ruby's limp body. She pushed herself up and ran, reaching the girl only heartbeats later.

"Ruby? *Ruby?*" As far as she could tell, there wasn't a mark on the child.

Time seemed to slow abruptly. Miranda was dimly aware of Hollis racing toward her from the direction of the B&B, aware of other pounding feet and voices, but all she saw was Ruby's pale face.

Then her eyes fluttered open, and she whispered, "He gave me...some kind of...shot. It's okay. I...knew I was...a pawn. Had to...be...sacrificed...to win. I couldn't...hide Bishop...and me too....Tell Galen...not his fault. Don't be sad...." A single long breath escaped her, and her head rolled to the side.

Miranda felt a jolt of pain and thought that it didn't hurt enough, that nothing could hurt enough for the loss of this child.

"Hollis—help her. Help Ruby."

Hollis reached for Ruby, gently removing the girl from Miranda's grasp—and then handing her to someone else. She was speaking, but what she was saying made no sense.

"Miranda, lie back. Easy. Let Gabe help you. Jesus, get her vest off—"

"What're you talking about? I'm not..."

Bishop ran up at that moment, his face ashen. He dropped his rifle and then dropped to his knees, cradling her head. "Miranda—"

She looked up at his face, wanting to reassure him that she was fine, but then she felt another stabbing pain, this one deep in her belly. And she knew what was happening. What had happened.

"No," she whispered. "Oh, God...Noah, I'm sorry...." And then a white curtain fell, and she fell with it into silence.

"Hollis—help her, please." Bishop's voice was hoarse.

As soon as the vest was out of the way, Hollis put both her hands over the bullet wound low on Miranda's rounded abdomen. She went still for an instant, her eyes closed, then looked at Bishop in shock.

"Shit. I can't—Bishop, I can't save him. The baby. He's already gone."

He closed his eyes for an instant, then nodded jerkily. "I know. Just—help Miranda."

She nodded in return, closing her eyes again to concentrate, to pour all the energy she could call up from inside herself to heal....

"Feeling better?" Reese asked, sitting down beside Hollis on the big sofa in the B&B's front parlor.

"The energy's coming back. Slowly. I'm fine. Still worried about Miranda, though. I should be at the clinic—"

"No, you shouldn't. You should be here where you are, getting your strength back. Besides, I think we all know that Bishop and Miranda would rather be alone right now. To grieve."

"Yes. Yes, of course. I heard the medic say she was at least five months along. It didn't show."

"Those loose sweaters of hers. And the vest that was specially made to be a little longer in front."

"She shouldn't have been here."

"Probably not. But they weigh risks all the time, those two. So many people were dying, and they felt responsible. They knew the bodies were bait and this was a trap, for Bishop and for the SCU.

Neither one of them could walk away. It wasn't going to stop until they stopped it."

Hollis nodded slowly. "I know they function best as a team. I know they weigh risks. And it was their risk to take. Still ... I wish I could have done more for them."

"You probably saved Miranda's life, Hollis. You may have even made it possible for her to get pregnant again someday. But there was nothing you could do to save that baby. The bullet did too much damage. He was already gone."

"I know, I know. Just ... I'm sorry for them. To lose their baby and Ruby—I don't know if Bishop will ever forgive himself."

"They did what they could to protect Miranda. The vest should have protected her. And probably would have, if she hadn't dived to the side like that. Her training and instincts betrayed her, for once. As for Ruby ... Well, maybe Bishop shouldn't forgive himself for that."

Hollis looked at him. "You really feel that way?"

DeMarco hesitated, then shook his head. "I don't know. Just like I don't know whether Galen will ever be the same again after finding out the brothers from hell have been using him as a spyglass."

Hollis winced. "Yeah, that's definitely a rough one. I mean, I'm glad we didn't have a traitor on the team, but to find out you have— had—three older brothers with serious mental issues would be traumatic enough without being used like that and then being shot by big brother Neil."

"Yeah. Family."

She looked at him again, not at all sure whether he was making a wry comment or just voicing a wry truth. She cleared her throat. "Um ... listen."

"Yeah?"

"I have a dim memory of saying some ... really weird things at the hospital last night. Because I was so tired. After I healed Diana."

He lifted a brow at her. "I don't recall anything weird."

"No?"

"No."

She began to feel relieved. Suspicious but relieved. *I'll ask Diana later. Or not.* "Okay. Good, then."

He eyed her. "Something else is bugging you. What?"

"You'll laugh."

"Would that be so bad? I could use a laugh about now."

Hollis frowned, then said, "I'm seriously bummed to know you can get yanked out of heaven. I mean...it's *heaven.* Is nothing sacred?"

"What are you talking about?" His voice was patient but amused around the edges.

"Diana's poor mom got yanked out of heaven—apparently— and sent back here to try to stop her father. How crazy is that?"

"Pretty crazy."

It was her turn to eye him. "You don't believe me."

"Sorry. Actually, it's heaven, not you, that I don't believe in."

"Well, I'm not sure I believe in it either. In fact, I'm more sure now that I don't, because if you can get yanked out of *heaven*—"

Hollis glanced toward the doorway and broke off abruptly, her eyes widening. DeMarco watched gooseflesh rise on her bare arm and was aware of a tangle of emotions rather than thoughts.

Astonishment. Wonder. Happiness. A kind of contentment.

And awe.

"Ruby," she murmured.

He waited until she blinked, as though coming out of a dream, and said, "You saw her spirit. Is she all right?"

"She's better than all right. Wow."

Curious, he said, "You see spirits all the time."

"Yeah." Hollis smiled at him. "But this is the first time I've ever seen one...with wings."

Epilogue

IT WAS THE first of June when Sonny Lenox woke up from his coma. The doctors were astonished, though when pressed they tried to make it sound as if they'd known he had at least a chance of actually walking out of the hospital. Still, three months in a coma after a car crash... Well, most patients with that kind of trauma never woke up.

Amazing, the ability of the human body to heal itself.

The nursing staff, a lot more blunt, whispered that he couldn't possibly be *right* after coming out of that. Bound to be messed up.

But he was right enough only five days later to say a few words to the one TV newswoman the hospital allowed to visit him. Right enough to smile, to be able to feed himself almost from the start. To dress himself. And, with more than a little help, to walk.

He dedicated himself to the physical therapy, working hard every single day to regain his mobility and independence. He was quiet, polite, uncomplaining. The nursing staff loved him.

They were saddened, as they had been during his whole stay, by the fact that Sonny Lenox appeared to have no family or even friends; in all that time he never had a single visitor. When he came out of the coma and was able to talk to them, he told them he was alone in the world and hadn't lived in town very long before the accident. He hadn't even found an apartment yet, had been staying in a motel, and didn't doubt that the manager had long ago packed up his meager belongings and given them to some charity. Or sold them, of course.

It was okay, though. He'd get along.

The nursing staff, feeling even sorrier for him, got together some hand-me-down clothing and a used duffel bag and chipped in for new underwear, so at least he'd be able to leave the hospital with *something*.

It required more than six weeks of intense therapy before the doctors were willing to discharge him, but by then the young man was able to smile and thank everyone, and when they wheeled him to the door he was able to get up and walk steadily away, his duffel in hand.

He didn't look back.

In his used clothes, carrying his used bag, he walked slowly but determinedly, with a very specific destination in mind. He had to sit on a handy bench along the way several times to rest, since his stamina wasn't what it should be. What it would eventually be. So it took him more than an hour to walk to a narrow street near downtown, a street that hadn't yet been "revitalized" by money and interest.

There were old apartment buildings not yet condemned but close, an old church with colorful and profane graffiti on one wall, and a ramshackle mission where a small group of dedicated humanitarians did what they could to feed and house the poor.

He stood half a block away and studied the mission for a few minutes, then approached it.

Outside the front door, a young man with leaflets and an intense expression was trying to talk to the few passersby who, very clearly, just wanted to pass by. And the apparent regulars to the mission simply brushed past him, intent only on going inside and getting their meal or cot before the mission ran out of both.

The young man remained determined.

"Sir! Sir, have you accepted Jesus Christ as your personal savior?"

Sonny Lenox looked at him for a long moment, his eyes holding a curiously flat shine, and then he smiled.

"Why, yes, I have. And I'd love to give you my Testimony."

Author's Note

We're now twelve books into the Bishop/Special Crimes Unit series, and because of that we've decided to begin including a bit of additional information for the benefit of both new and longtime readers. We've based these offerings on the type of mail and email I receive, letters and notes asking specific questions.

So here in *Blood Ties* you'll find about a dozen footnotes throughout the book, all titles of earlier books in the series. I've found that many readers want that information, asking in which book a specific character was introduced or specific events took place. I hope the footnotes will provide that information quickly and easily.

Here at the end of the book, I've also provided brief character bios of the SCU team members appearing in *Blood Ties*, bios of the Haven operatives involved in the story, and a list of psychic abilities and their SCU definitions.

This is something of an experiment, so I hope you'll feel free to email me (kay@kayhooper.com) and let me know whether you like or dislike the additional information. If it proves to be popular, we will continue to provide this as the series continues.

And, as always, if you'd like to read more in-depth background facts about the series and its characters, please visit my website at www.kayhooper.com.

Special Crimes Unit Agent Bios

Jaylene Avery

Job: Special Agent.

Adept: Psychometric, is able to pick up impressions from objects. Sees her ability as a tool, pure and simple, and is less interested than most of the others in the scientific aspects of the paranormal.

Appearances: *Hunting Fear, Blood Ties*

Bailey

Job: Special Agent, guardian.

Adept: Open telepath, but her strength is a powerful shield she's able to extend to protect others.

Appearances: *Blood Dreams, Blood Sins, Blood Ties*

Miranda Bishop

Job: Special Agent, investigator, profiler, black belt in karate, and a sharpshooter.

Adept: Touch-telepath, seer, remarkably powerful and possesses unusual control, particularly in a highly developed shield capable of protecting herself psychically, a shield she's able to extend beyond herself to protect others. Shares abilities with her husband, Noah, due to their intense emotional connection, and together they far exceed the scale developed by the FBI to measure psychic talents.

Appearances: *Out of the Shadows, Touching Evil, Whisper of Evil, Sense of Evil, Hunting Fear, Chill of Fear, Blood Dreams, Blood Sins, Blood Ties*

Noah Bishop
Unit leader (Chief, Special Crimes Unit), founder

Job: Special Agent, profiler, top investigator, sharpshooter. Has a few unusual abilities he deliberately cultivated, including lock-picking and computer hacking, and is licensed as a pilot.

Adept: Touch-telepath, exceptionally powerful. Also possesses secondary or "ancillary" ability of enhanced senses (hearing, sight, scent) familiarly known as "spider sense," as well as the shared (with his wife) ability of precognition. Was driven to found the unit out of a strong desire to bring psychic ability into the mainstream as a useful investigative tool. Totally committed to his unit—and extraordinarily committed to his wife.

Appearances: *Stealing Shadows, Hiding in the Shadows, Out of the Shadows, Touching Evil, Whisper of Evil, Sense of Evil, Hunting Fear, Chill of Fear, Sleeping with Fear, Blood Dreams, Blood Sins, Blood Ties*

Diana Brisco

Job: Special Investigator.

Adept: Medium, specializing in the ability to "walk" with spirits in an eerie corridor between life and death she calls the gray time. Like many mediums, also possesses some healing ability, though hers is virtually latent.

Appearances: *Chill of Fear, Blood Ties*

Reese DeMarco

Job: Special Crimes Unit Operative, pilot, sharpshooter. Has specialized in the past primarily in undercover operations. Ex-military.

Adept: Telepath, powerful. Possesses an apparently unique double shield, which sometimes contains the unusually high amount of

sheer energy he produces. Also possesses the primal ability to sense a threat to himself or someone physically near him.
Appearances: *Blood Sins, Blood Ties*

Dr. Sharon Edwards
Job: Special Agent, forensic pathologist.
Adept: Picks up vibes from objects.
Appearances: *Out of the Shadows, Blood Ties**

Galen
Job: Special Investigator, watchdog, guardian, pilot.
Adept: Regenerative self-healer. Also ex-military.
Appearances: *Touching Evil, Whisper of Evil, Hunting Fear, Blood Sins, Blood Ties*

Tony Harte
Job: Special Agent, investigator, profiler.
Adept: Telepath. Not especially strong, but able to pick up vibes from people, particularly emotions.
Appearances: *Out of the Shadows, Touching Evil, Whisper of Evil, Sense of Evil, Hunting Fear, Blood Ties*

Quentin Hayes
Job: Special Agent, investigator, profiler.
Adept: Seer, developing spider sense. His abilities are beginning to change after the events of *Blood Sins*.
Appearances: *Touching Evil, Hunting Fear, Chill of Fear, Blood Sins, Blood Ties*

Dean Ramsey
Job: Special Agent.
Adept: 5th degree clairvoyant. Ex-military.
Appearance: *Blood Ties*

---

*On scene, but active offstage

Hollis Templeton

Job: Special Agent, profiler-in-training.

Adept: Medium. Perhaps because of the extreme trauma of Hollis's psychic awakening (see *Touching Evil*), her abilities evolve and change more rapidly than those of many other agents. Even as she struggles to cope with her mediumistic abilities, each investigation in which she's involved seems to bring about another "fun new toy" for the agent. In *Blood Dreams*, she begins to see auras, the energy fields surrounding individuals. And in *Blood Sins* and *Blood Ties*, other new abilities catch her unaware.

Appearances: *Touching Evil, Sense of Evil, Blood Dreams, Blood Sins, Blood Ties*

Haven Operative Bios

John and Maggie Garrett
Husband and wife co-founders of **Haven,** a civilian organization of psychics who tend to be a bit too offbeat, unusual, or otherwise unsuited for official police work, yet serve well as investigative and undercover operatives in some investigations, most often in conjunction with Special Crimes Unit cases. Maggie is an exceptionally strong empath/healer; John is not psychic.

Gabriel Wolf
Job: Investigator.
Adept: Shares with his twin sister a unique symbiotic relationship; each displays psychic abilities only while sleeping, using his or her twin as a conduit. They are telepathic with each other, as well as clairvoyant and mildly telekinetic.
Appearances: *Blood Dreams, Blood Ties*

Roxanne Wolf
Job: Investigator.
Adept: See Gabriel Wolf info.
Appearances: *Blood Dreams, Blood Ties*

Psychic Abilities

(as classified/defined by Bishop's team)

Adept: the general word used to label any functional psychic; the specific ability is much more specialized.

Clairvoyance: the ability to know things, to pick up bits of information, seemingly out of thin air.

Dream-projecting: the ability to enter another's dreams.

Dream-walking: the ability to invite/draw others into one's own dreams.

Empathy: An empath experiences the emotions of others.

Healing: the ability to heal injuries to self or others, often but not always ancillary to mediumistic abilities.

Healing Empathy: An empath/healer has the ability to not only feel but also heal the pain/injury of another.

Latent: the term used to describe unawakened or inactive abilities, as well as to describe a psychic not yet aware of being psychic.

Mediumistic: A medium has the ability to communicate with the dead.

Precognition: A seer or precog has the ability to correctly predict future events.

Psychometric: the ability to pick up impressions from objects.

Regenerative: the ability to heal one's own injuries/sicknesses (a classification unique to one SCU operative and considered separate from a healer's abilities).

Spider Sense: the ability to enhance one's normal senses (sight, hearing, smell) through concentration and the focusing of one's own mental and physical energy.

Telekinesis: the ability to move objects with the mind.

Telepathic mind control: the ability to influence/control others through mental focus and effort. Extremely rare ability.

Telepathy: (touch and non-touch or open): the ability to pick up thoughts from others. Some telepaths only receive, while others have the ability to send thoughts.

Unnamed abilities include:

The ability to see into time, to view events in the past, present, and future without being or having been there physically while the events transpired.

The ability to see the *aura* of another person's energy field.

The ability to *channel energy* usefully as a defensive/offensive tool/weapon.

About the Author

Kay Hooper, who has more than thirteen million copies of her books in print worldwide, has won numerous awards and high praise for her novels. Kay lives in North Carolina, where she is currently working on her next novel. Visit her website at www.kayhooper.com.